Dreamland

ISBN: 1-4636-0631-1
ISBN-13: 9781463606312

Dreamland

Ron Piana
and
Randi Londer Gould

2011

To Kristine "Kitty" Piana
She knows why…
RP

For my Benj
RLG

All men dream, but not equally. Those who dream by night, wake in the day to find that it was vanity. But the dreamers of the day are dangerous men, for they may act their dream with open eyes, to make it possible.

—*T. E. Lawrence*

I

For the third day in a row—or maybe the fourth, he wasn't sure—Buddy Graves's wife, Dana, left for work without kissing him goodbye. Even when running late, Dana always blew an air kiss, flinging out her hand in a silly wave. But all the fighting about his job, their mortgage trap, and the crumbling neighborhood was coming between them. Now they were finding the smallest of ways to hurt each other, just to defend themselves against this thing they were losing control over.

It was a Monday morning in early June, only a few minutes after nine o'clock, and already, freakishly, blazing hot. Monday was caddy's day at Woodcrest Country Club. The club closed for groundswork and the bosses let the caddies play a round. As a kid, Buddy looped Woodcrest; a year ago, after losing his career, he'd gone back. A caddy again, at 32. He should have felt bad about it, but he didn't. Next to Dana, golf was what he loved most in life. The course was the only place where he felt purely attached to the earth. Give every kid a golf club as soon as he can walk, Buddy always said, and this would be a better world. Or at least more polite.

This morning, when he slipped from bed, he'd lifted the sheet and stared at Dana in her sleep-mussed T-shirt and panties, her smooth flesh, inches away. Hers was a dense beauty, nothing frail. The only thing he'd known in this world that he wouldn't redesign in any way was her body, her hidden parts, the childhood scars of a tree-climbing tomboy.

And after 12 years of marriage, one question still tantalized him: If he gently wedged a knee between her legs, ran his hand down the contour of her back, would she respond with that slight purr that meant yes? But this morning, watching her, he was moved by more than sex. For a crazy moment he felt that if he left the bed, he might never see her again. *It will happen one day*, he thought.

So he hadn't gone to play golf this morning, and for that sacrifice he was left unkissed.

Shaving in the upstairs bathroom, Buddy was still thinking about Dana. Her scent of lavender, a neatly folded washcloth, vapor on the windows, an afterimage of her morning routine.

Then he nicked his chin good, a cut that ran in rivulets—the thin blood of a hard drinker. "*Fuck* me," he said, slamming the razor down on the sink and grabbing a wad of toilet paper to stick on the wound. Dabbing his face in the mirror, Buddy scowled and picked up the razor, skirting the cut where the tissue waved, *like a white flag of surrender*, he thought angrily as he stroked with the blade.

He let out an explosive breath and felt a rushing sensation; a shape had materialized in the corner of the mirror. Jumping in his skin, Buddy made a loud choking noise as the razor clattered to the floor. Crouched on the top stair, so close he could touch her, was the seven-year-old black girl from next door. Their eyes met, she shrank away and blurted, "The bus for camp is gone an' Momma left!"

Buddy's face went hot; a tightness gripped his chest and the thought, *heart attack*, skittered across a synapse. He wore nothing but a pair of tight-fitting boxer jocks and those big eyes of hers looked right where they shouldn't. Like a kid, he covered his crotch with one hand, feeling the awkward weight of his genitals. Ripping his beltless bathrobe off its hook with the other hand, Buddy shouted, "You can't be here!"

Her tiny face crumpled, full of rolling tears and little-girl mouth bubbles. Her teeth looked too big for her mouth and her eyes flashed and flashed again.

"Please, you gotta go home," he said in a panicked whisper.

She flattened against the wall. "Momma's gone. The door's locked!"

"Where'd she go? Can we call her?"

The child wagged her head like a bobble doll.

"Don't cry, *please*. We'll figure this out, but we *have* to go outside," Buddy said, his voice strained and pleading.

Then she was on Buddy, clinging to his arm, an uncomfortable, moist, skin-to-skin sensation. "Mista," she cried, a lost sound, barely audible.

"OK, OK, OK," he said, coaxing her with baby steps down the staircase, fumbling with his free hand to keep the bathrobe closed.

Sunlight pooled at the bottom of the staircase. As he opened the front door, Buddy heard traffic and a lawnmower. The little girl was trembling, making tiny asthmatic coughing noises. "Easy. It's OK," he said in a dry croak.

They stepped out onto the porch; Buddy's head swam in the heat. He bent at the waist, bringing his face close to hers. Wanting to calm her, he took hold of her sleeve, a crinkly yellow crepe material, and said softly, "This is a pretty blouse."

Just then, a car whipped into the driveway next door. Tyrell Walker, the tall, muscular black guy who lived next door with the girl's mother, stepped out of his maroon Honda Accord. He was wearing outsized curved sunglasses and clutching a cell phone.

Tyrell held the phone up at arms length, aiming it at Buddy and the girl, like a gunfighter. The faint mechanical sound of a shutter expanded in the air. He lowered his arm. "Dummy!" he snapped at the child. "Get over here."

Buddy straightened up, squinting into the sun.

"What, didn't you hear, girl?" Tyrell barked.

She tugged with all her weight, but for some reason Buddy held her until she screamed, "Lemme go!" His hand opened and she bolted across the yard, running from him. His legs trembled as he wrapped his bathrobe and called, "What's up, huh? She was locked out."

Tyrell held Buddy's eyes for a moment, then he nodded slightly. As the girl reached him, he swatted at her backside. Propelled by his hand, she ran up to the front door, crying.

After a silence, Buddy said, "Thanks, man," and instantly wondered to himself why he was thanking this guy. He had seen him dozens of times, coming and going at odd hours, but they'd never spoken. Just one of those deals struck in neighborhoods like this—living next to each other, but not really neighbors.

"She was locked out," Buddy called again, throwing up his hands. After a beat, Tyrell nodded, another barely detectable twitch of the head. But it meant something and he wanted Buddy to know. So he did it again, with more emphasis.

They looked at each other. Buddy waited for him to say something, but he didn't. Tyrell just slipped the phone into his pocket and turned slowly toward the house. Buddy felt the hair on the back of his neck prickle and rise.

2

He stood in the glaring sun waiting for the black guy to come out and settle this thing. *Pal, tell me what I did wrong, huh? Your girlfriend fucks up with her kid and you cop an attitude with me?* Swearing to himself, Buddy replayed his favorite angry tirade in his head: *This* fucking *neighborhood, these rude assholes. There's no decency left.*

Air, I need air, he thought to himself, fighting the feeling he was crammed into a suffocating box.

Absently stroking his face, Buddy looked across the street at the elderly black man mowing his lawn. *This old dude saw everything go down,* Buddy thought. *He never misses a trick, slumped over that gassy mower he pushes around the yard.* The old man, Eugene Freyerson, cut his lawn twice a week and constantly puttered around the house. But the place could never kick that rundown look of decay. When Freyerson glanced up, Buddy waved at him, stupidly, like all of a sudden they're friends. Giving Buddy a weary look, the old man disappeared into his house, emerging a few minutes later with his dog. It was a scabby mutt with mismatched parts: a stumpy tail; one flopped ear, the other cocked; a thick chest; a skinny ass. Its hindquarters were paralyzed, and in a daily ritual, Freyerson gripped the dog's back legs as though they were the handles of a wheelbarrow, stutter-stepping behind as the dog pissed on his shoes. *What is it with those two?* Buddy wondered. *Why doesn't the old man just put that dog out of its misery?*

Shading his eyes, Buddy shifted his gaze next door. It finally sank in. The guy wasn't coming out to talk over whatever it was that pissed him off. Buddy sighed, all at once worried. He had that same vague, near-breathless kind of worry he got after being with his first girl, wondering if he'd been safe enough, or if all his careless ways were about to catch up with him. That's when window-shaking rap music throbbed from Tyrell's house, and a hot flash of anger blew Buddy's worry away. *Who could* listen *to that crap?* He stomped into his house, closing the door with force.

Flopping onto the couch, Buddy grabbed the remote and turned on the tube. An ESPN rerun of a John Deere Classic was playing. He watched, sound off, imagining the *ping* of a perfect stroke, the big *ahs* of the gallery, the soft pad of green fairways beneath the feet, the rich chucking sound of Callaway clubs. Ernie Els was leading by two strokes, but Tiger was on his ass, inside his head. Els had a tough second shot, a three wood off the sixteenth fairway. The wind kicked up, flapping his lime green twill slacks. Buddy actually felt the torque sensation in his swing. Nice arm stroke, free as a kid on a swing. Good distance, but the shot lofted a bit high in the wind, hooking just enough to land in the sand, tucked like a big plug of chaw under the bunker's upper lip, a lousy-looking lie. It was all over his face: poor Ernie, he heard Tiger's footsteps.

When Buddy was captain of his high school golf team he was treated like a guy with a future. Coach Thompson used to grab the back of Buddy's neck, pull him close, and whisper, "Buddy, you've got something special, don't let it slip away." There was the golf scholarship to Adelphi. But he blew it off; Buddy wanted to see the world. He saw the world, alright. Eighteen months on a Merchant Marine ship, only to wind up nearly dying in a Guatemalan hospital with a raging infection and fever, his life ebbing away, all because of knife wounds he'd suffered while trying to break up a bar fight between two of his shipmates.

After the ship, there was a string of gigs: laborer, truck driver, short-order cook. Then, just for kicks, he interviewed for a proofreader's job at a medical publishing company in Manhattan. He had no college degree, but Buddy connected with the editor, an old-school Irishman. In a few years, Buddy had worked his way up to a senior editor position. Life was sweet. Buddy loved saying he was an editor; it had class, weight. Shortly after marrying Dana, they bought their house. On spec. It was Buddy's idea. Property values soared. Buddy and Dana were happy. Then the economy imploded. Just like that. Not in slow motion, where you could see it coming and brace for it. All at once America went broke. At least, that's what it had felt like. Buddy's job was eliminated. Somehow, eliminated is worse than being fired. There's no way back.

He still didn't have a degree. Dana had begged him to go back to school, but Buddy was too smart for that. "I've read more books than most college professors," he'd bragged.

A year later, Buddy still couldn't seem to catch his breath.

And right now he couldn't shake the feeling that some final-straw, invisible line had been crossed this morning. On the surface, it was such an innocent thing. So why did he feel such dread blossoming in his chest? *I was trying to help the kid,* Buddy said to himself, hotly. *What did that guy think, anyway?*

He decided not to tell Dana. Keeping secrets from her was another sign that he was not in control of things the way he should be. But fessing up about this awkward incident would just spark another senseless fight. *Better to let it blow over like some natural disturbance that runs its course*, he thought.

Buddy was not used to being home during the day. He turned off the TV and got dressed. He needed to *do* something. He got in his car and drove to Town Hall, flipping on the radio. On NPR, some earnest-sounding academic was explaining why, even though the recession was over, the job numbers would remain troubling for quite a while. *We're running out of money*, that's *why*, Buddy thought as he drove past four closed retail stores on Main Street in Huntington. He nearly sideswiped a mini-van full of screaming kids as he whipped into the parking lot.

This wasn't his first trip to Town Hall. He recognized the woman at the information desk beneath the small rotunda. She was heavy with a round face and short white hair like a man's. She always seemed bored and a bit hostile. "Can I help you?" she asked, distractedly. Buddy explained that he wanted to see the head of code enforcement. She told him to have a seat. Twenty minutes later she announced, "Mr. Sammis will see you now."

Buddy expected Sammis to be older. He was thirty, barely, with the compact, sturdy look of a terrier that put Buddy on edge. Small men, he always found, were forever overcompensating. Still, he put on his game face and smiled.

"Mr. Sammis, Buddy Graves." On the other side of Sammis's desk, Buddy took a seat in a cheaply upholstered chair, its nubby synthetic fabric stained and lumpy.

"So, Buddy, what exactly is the issue," Sammis asked, still working on his computer.

Buddy waited. He wanted Sammis to stop typing and pull his stubborn, clouded gaze away from whatever was fascinating him so on that screen. Buddy wanted to know he had this jackoff's full attention. *Show some common courtesy, damn it. Some respect.*

Finally, Sammis noticed the silence hanging in the air. He looked up expectantly, and faintly annoyed.

"It's my neighbors on *both* sides. I filed a complaint about them three months ago. The yards are unkempt. The grass is this high," Buddy said, his hand hovering, palm down, three feet above the ground.

"Have you spoken to your neighbors about it?" Sammis asked.

"It's not just grass; the houses are falling apart."

"But have you spoken to them?"

"Spoken to them? Didn't you get my original complaint? Some Korean, some character named Cho in Queens bought the houses. The tenants don't give a damn how they look."

Sammis turned back to his computer. "How do you spell your last name?"

"It's Graves. Grave with an S."

"OK, this is an absentee landlord issue. Mr. Cho *has* been notified. His attorney is handling the complaint," Sammis said with an air of satisfaction.

"And?"

"And he still has several months before a summons can be issued. That's the way it works."

"So, when *does* Cho have to cut the grass and fix the gutters and paint the siding and replace the missing pickets in the fence, and all the rest of the shit that's falling apart?"

"It could drag on for a while. You know how it is when lawyers get involved."

Buddy rose slowly, his hands shaking. "Look. Some geniuses on the town board, who I'm sure live in Huntington *Bay*, rezoned *my* neighborhood for absentee landlords like that prick Cho or Blow, or whatever his name is. He dumped a bunch of HUD people next to me and let the places go to shit. But I need to sell my house. And the realtor won't even show it until those places look decent."

Sammis stood abruptly, pulling himself to his full height, which was still a good four inches shorter than Buddy.

"You can't go there, OK?" he said, raising his voice.

"Go *where*, exactly?"

"Where you're going, about the tenants. OK?" he glared.

"Oh, I get it. You thought I might say something inappropriate about my nice neighbors."

"I understand you're frustrated..."

Buddy planted his knuckles on Sammis's desk and leaned forward, his jaw clenching.

"You don't understand just how frustrated I am, *Mr.* Sammis. Get it through your PC head. I'm the victim here, OK? *Not* them."

രൈ⸎

When he heard Dana pull into the driveway, Buddy poured two glasses of wine. He'd already had a few drinks, but he hoped she wouldn't notice. Dana came in wearing her baggy green hospital scrubs and flip-flops.

"Hi, I made some grilled chicken and broccoli. You hungry?" he said, a bit too quickly.

"OK," she said, peering closely at him. "You've been drinking. We had a deal about drinking before I got home, remember?"

"Christ, I had *a* drink, alright?"

Dana walked to the refrigerator, poured a glass of milk and gulped it down. She wiped the milk mustache off with her forearm and said, "Buddy, you never have just *a* drink. But, whatever. I had a bear of a day. I just wanna eat and jump in the bath."

When they sat down at the kitchen table, Buddy chewed slowly and stared at something across the room as Dana talked about a new RN who didn't look or smell clean. Dana—who maintained her maiden name, Burke, since she had started her career before they married—was a head nurse in a trauma unit at Long Island Jewish, and she always spoke her mind. "I told her straight up that she has a big-time hygiene issue, and she better take care of it. She called the union. Can you believe that? I wasted half an hour arguing with the moron rep over that crap."

"Ever wonder why they call you Nurse Ratched?" Buddy teased, trying to jolly her out of her mood.

She shrugged and went on. "I got a call from my mom today. It's my dad's birthday this Saturday. She asked us to come over for dinner. Mom's sort of making a big deal about it." Dana paused a beat and said, "My brother's coming up from Virginia, minus the wife and kids, thank God." She paused again, putting her fork down slowly, waiting. "OK, Buddy, what's going on?"

Buddy wiped his mouth on the napkin, shook his head. "Sorry. Was I drifting?"

"I said, what's wrong?"

"You mean other than everything," he said forcing a grin. "I had a row at Town Hall today about Mr. Cho."

"Who the hell is Mr. Cho?"

"The nice Korean man in Queens who owns the houses all around us."

Dana squinted hard at Buddy. "No, not *that* stuff. Something else is wrong. Christ, I tell you we have to go to my parents' house for a meal and you don't let out a groan? Have we entered some kind of weird parallel universe where my husband doesn't despise family get togethers?"

"Yeah, maybe we have."

"What happened today?"

Buddy closed his eyes for a moment. The morning replayed itself in a flash. For a second he wanted to say *I've got something to tell you*, but some rush of emotion stopped him. He pushed away from the table and let out a breath. "Nothing happened," he said. "Nothing."

3

On Tuesday morning, running late, as usual, Bobbi Holmes swept into the Starbucks where she and Dana liked to meet early in the morning before Dana's shift started and before Bobbi settled in with her laptop to rake muck in *The Holmes Report*. Through sheer doggedness, Bobbi had turned her blog into one of the most widely read—and feared—by people of influence in politics and business. For Bobbi, it was a kind of revenge. Her father, David Holmes, had been a respected journalist. But when he reported information given to him by a source in the district attorney's office—deliberately misleading information that was backed up by the DA's crony—it led to the death of an 18-year-old inner city kid. Nobody seemed to care about that kid except David Holmes, who ended his career a broken man.

Friends since high school, Dana and Bobbi tried to get together for a weekly chat. But it had been harder to find the time since Dana was made head nurse of the hospital's 26-bed trauma unit. Still, Dana looked forward to their morning coffee: she had always found Bobbi's bisexual allure hard to resist. This morning when she spotted Bobbi rushing in, Dana grinned and tipped her head up so Bobbi could kiss her on the lips, their playful greeting. Even if she was having a bad week, Dana was always cheered by seeing her old friend, with her tattoos and body piercings, the *de rigueur* trappings of a cyber chick who rips the mask off hypocrites, frauds, and cheats.

"How's that union thing going?" asked Bobbi.

Dana shrugged and said, "I worry about infection, not insulting a nurse who needs a bath."

Bobbi smiled. "That's what you told the union rep?"

"In so many words. I wasn't polite."

"Glad to see you haven't lost your edge."

"Yeah, caught it from my dad."

"So, aside from that, you doing okay?"

"You know, nothing's really changed," said Dana.

Bobbi leaned closer. "It either gets better or it gets worse, it doesn't usually stay the same."

Dana looked out at the traffic. "Buddy and I are on such thin ice, we're afraid to take a step in any direction. That's the only way I can describe it."

"It's in Buddy's court now," Bobbi said. "He's got to fight his way out of this."

"He won't."

"You've got to talk to him, Dana."

"Goddamn this. I'm trying to figure out life without Buddy and I'm having a tough time doing that."

"Sorry. But if he died, you'd mourn for a while and go on with your life."

"Maybe he thinks he's ruined me for other men."

"Nobody's *that* ruined," Bobbi laughed.

"The golf swing is prepared within the silence of the heart," Dana said dreamily.

"What?"

Dana turned her head. "That's how Buddy talks about golf. It's his true love. You should see how his face changes when he has a club in his hand."

"Well, I can't say it's bad to feel that way about something."

"But that's why he won't move on. Bobbi, he's not on the PGA tour, he's a goddamn caddy and he's OK with that. I hate it. I'd rather he sit at home and stare at the walls. There, I said it. I'm ashamed of him, OK? I *can't* love a caddy."

"But he's still the guy you fell in love with and married."

Dana shook her head. "Not exactly. That's the problem. Losing his job changed him."

"Maybe feeling he doesn't have a way back to a career is what changed him."

Dana sighed. "It's just getting to be too much work, Bobbi."

"The economy sucks. I feel for him."

"It's like he's sick and he can't—or won't—get well," Dana said.

"You still love him? That's the important question."

Dana bit the corner of her lower lip. "Yeah, I do. But I'm afraid that'll change, too. It scares me."

"What made him Mr. Right?"

"I went with a lotta guys before Buddy. He was the only one who surprised me. I never knew what was gonna happen next. He was always impulsive."

"Sounds like you're already talking about this relationship in the past tense."

Dana shrugged, shook her head and pouted. "Maybe I'll try girls."

"You already did," Bobbi laughed.

❧ ❧

Woodcrest Country Club, perched on the wind-blown lip of Long Island Sound, had the feel of a British links course. Once a haven for old-money WASPs, the club was invaded by hoards of arrivistes riding the Reagan wave, mostly Jewish hedge fund guys, real-estate developers, and retail kings—all brash, in-your-face money. Sol Abrams, who owned, among other enterprises, a mail-order company that supplied prescription drugs to every labor union in the tri-state area, was a living distillation of the club's nouveau riche members. When he was hashing out the details of his daughter's bat mitzvah, the caterer assured Sol it would be the *best* affair ever. To which Sol bellowed, "I don't care from *best*. I want every fucking Jew who walks outta there to say, 'That was the most *expensive* bat mitzvah I've ever been to!'"

The prevailing winds of the Sound were a key factor in the original design of the course, as holes that typically play downwind were longer but also open in front to allow the player to bounce the ball onto the green. The holes that usually ran into the wind were shorter with smaller targets. There were only two par fives, with each playing in opposite directions. But more than anything, Woodcrest was the most private of golf courses—a place to make deals, drink, entertain clients, talk shit about sports and money, and cavort with each other's wives and mistresses.

Separated from the starting tee by a thicket of lush poplars and a stockade fence was the caddie yard, the spring-summer home to three distinct groups: the sharp-dressing, smooth-talking, self-possessed black men who barreled up I-95 from the South every summer in a three-car convoy, with their rumbling voices and knowing smiles; the members' college-aged kids on summer vacation who surreptitiously studied these men for clues on how to live the art of cool; and finally, Buddy and a handful of older white guys who were a bit broken down, with weathered faces and wary eyes. A peeling painted sign in the yard remained, the remnant of a kinder, gentler club: *No Profane Language. Clean Up Your Cigarette Butts.* But it may as well have been torn down, so little heed did anyone pay it.

It was a hot and windless day, not a cloud in the sky. With no loops in the offing, the college boys split for the beach, leaving a few caddies playing cards, smoking cigarettes, talking about pussy. Buddy arrived late. It was the slowest day of the week. The caddy master, Jock Macgregor, gave Buddy a look that didn't go unnoticed by one of the black caddies, a guy called Lemon. Over his cards, Lemon called, "Yo, Buddy, Tuesday's with Elaine."

A half hour later, Buddy saw her slow-walking toward the first hole wearing yellow slacks, the same type she was wearing the first time he'd seen her, about 20 years ago. Elaine Weinberg was in her early fifties now. She said a few words to Macgregor who waved his hand. "C'mon Buddy, you're up." Macgregor, a white-haired Scot with a drinker's rosy, blotchy face said, "The other half of Mrs. Weinberg's twosome came down with something. Think you can handle a single?"

"For you, Jock, I'll give it the big try."

Buddy threw her golf bag over his shoulder, walked easily down the fringe of the fairway where Elaine teed up and addressed the ball. The first hole was a straightaway par four. The tee shot should favor the left side of the fairway; fade right and you've got double-trouble sand and long grass. She looked down the fairway, squinting into the sun, and remembered what Buddy had told her time and time again—in the address position, you should only be thinking about the next action: drawing the club smoothly away from the ball.

Buddy watched her swing, following through, finishing in a perfectly balanced position. Her right heel lifted off the ground. Her gold earrings glinted in the sun.

The ball bounced down the fairway, 180 yards from the green, just left of the bunker.

Good girl, Buddy said to himself, walking down the course.

He handed Elaine a mid-fairway rescue club and stepped away. She was a slender woman with nice hips and short reddish hair pushed back behind her slightly large but still delicate ears. She had the shoulders of a young boy, a pretty, sun-freckled face, and small blue eyes that wrinkled at the corners when she smiled.

"I love these new Pings," she said, measuring up her shot.

"Enough to take a stroke off your handicap?" Buddy asked.

"All I want out of golf anymore is to enjoy it, Buddy," she said, exhaling softly with her backswing.

Before playing the back nine, Elaine went into the midway clubhouse to freshen up. Buddy was sitting under an oak tree overlooking the fairway when she walked over to him holding two bottles of cold beer. They clinked bottles. "I like a can of beer better," she said. Her eyes, with their beach-glass blur, gave it away. She'd had a couple of her little friends, the mini bottles of Smirnoff she always carried in her bag. Buddy drained his beer and hoisted the bag. Ten is a tricky par three. The green sits too high to see the pin.

"The cup's on the left of the green today, Mrs. Weinberg," Buddy said, handing her a five iron. "It's bone dry, so you'll need plenty of loft."

"Thanks Buddy. God it's hot," she said, brushing her hair back with her hand.

He walked toward the fairway.

She called, "I still can't believe you're back. And I'm Elaine, remember?"

Her cell phone rang. "Elaine Weinberg," she answered.

Buddy smiled to himself. Hearing her pronounce her name "Weinboig" brought him back to being a fourteen-year-old caddy with the hots for her, then in her thirties, winking at him as she sneaked a quick slug from a mini. Those winks of hers, like airblown kisses, grew sexier, year by year.

Putting out on the eighteenth hole, Buddy said, "Elaine, don't forget, putting is all right hand."

"Sometimes I need to be reminded," she answered coyly. Her clothes were damp with perspiration at the places where the garments hugged her body tightest.

"That's what I'm here for, to remind you," he said, playing along at their flirtatious game that had rekindled when Buddy came back to Woodcrest. They liked each other, in a companionable way. Up until now, it was all innocent, and Buddy wanted to keep it that way, even though he often pictured Elaine in bed, wondering what her body would be like, a softness different from Dana's, what she'd say in his ear, how she would sound.

"You're not going to run off again, are you?" she asked, reaching down to pull her ball from the cup.

Looking at her Buddy said, "No, I've got nowhere to go."

"Good, because I've got something I want to talk…"

Just then, a car horn blared. Buddy and Elaine turned. Spraying gravel, the car pulled up by the cart path. The dark-tinted driver's window rolled down, revealing a beefy red face with eyes that turned snakish. "Get in, now!"

The Mercedes CL-600 smelled of thirty-dollar Cohibas and Ralph Lauren cologne, scents that pinched Elaine's nostrils. Her husband, Isidore Weinberg, whom everyone called Izzy, pulled away before her door closed. At 60, with his thick-necked body and rough manner, Izzy was still the robust cattle baron from Modesto she'd met 25 years ago. Elaine could never get over the novelty of a Jewish cowboy. She fell hard for him, this bad boy, with his dark hair raked back, his love of booze and broads and Vegas, his ostrich leather cowboy boots, and that Broderick Crawford voice roughened by Scotch and tobacco.

Twisting around to look out the rear window, Elaine watched Buddy walking with her bag toward the clubhouse.

"I thought you were playing with Judy Fried. Lemme guess. She got 'sick' again, right?" said Izzy.

"Yeah, Judy's delicate that way."

"I'll give you delicate!"

"Sure you will. Stop yelling, it makes my head hurt," Elaine said, giving Buddy's fading image one last glance.

"Did I not tell you to get another fucking caddy? Did I not?" Izzy barked.

Elaine closed her eyes and breathed in slowly. "He helps my game," she said flatly.

Izzy mashed the gas, hurtling past startled grounds workers and down a long winding road that skirted the edge of the course. Coming to a meticulous, Tudor-style house he stopped and turned to Elaine.

"See that nice fucking house? Our pro lives there," Izzy said, stabbing the air. "We pay that goy asshole Brad Mueller a hundred and fifty K. Plus the house. *He* can make your game better. And word has it he's got a schlong that hangs halfway to his knees. Just like his old man Mike. You oughta remember that dick. You can have *both* of them. Just *do not* embarrass me with that motherfuckin' caddy, that *Buddy*," he spat.

Elaine turned her face to the window. "My God, you're a pig."

With thumb and forefinger, Izzy gently pinched the small wattle of flesh hanging from Elaine's neck. "Yes, but you're my darling little piglet. Now, get another fucking caddy, Mrs. Weinberg, or I'll run his ass outta here."

4

Buddy was in the shower scrubbing down, his afternoon loop at Wood-crest cut short by a thunderstorm that swept off the Sound on wild threads of lightning. The storm sent his foursome off in a let's-get-the-fuck-outta-here stampede. They were at the same hole where, six years earlier, Fred Baum and his caddy were torched by a bolt of lightning. "Fuck the storm, I'm workin' an eagle," were Baum's last words as the rest of his party hightailed. It was a sweet three-footer he could make with his eyes closed. Baum's caddy handed him his putter, then *kafuckinboom*! Fred Baum, wholesale furniture king of the East Coast, and his caddy, a black ladies' man called Cool, were both blown out of their shoes.

Stepping out of the shower and toweling off, Buddy pulled on a pair of running shorts and started thinking about dinner. Padding to the kitchen, he peered into the fridge, making a mental inventory of the ingredients there. Dana liked a good meal after her 10-hour shift at the hospital. Like her father, she had a quicksilver metabolism; she could eat like a horse and never show it. He'd love two more pounds on her, one on each ass cheek.

Because of the heat, Buddy was thinking frittata and salad as the door-bell rang, twice in quick succession. He prayed it wasn't the Jehovah's Witnesses. Buddy could be polite to a fault, a weakness in himself he hated. He had let these sad-sack proselytizers, always a pathetically young plain-Jane among them, prattle on about how divine love meets every human need until—

Opening his front door, Buddy felt a hot rush on his neck. Two feet away was the black guy from next door. Buddy's eyes swept him, taking in the Marine tat on his right bicep. The guy was built solid, with closely shaved hair and wide set eyes. They started hard at one another, each waiting for the other to speak.

"We gotta talk, man," said Tyrell.

Feeling his heart suddenly bound up and hammer against his ribs, Buddy said, "Talk about what, exactly?"

Tyrell turned his head side to side, stretching his neck, like a buzzard huffing. "C'mon, you know about *what*. We got us a problem here, man. We gotta talk," he said, motioning for Buddy to let him in.

"Whoa, wait a minute. What's the problem?" Buddy said, anger rising in his voice. "Yesterday with the girl? She came to me because she was locked out. Now if *anyone* should—"

But Tyrell pushed past him, leaving Buddy standing at the door, open-mouthed.

"Get the fuck out of my house!" Buddy shouted, flinging the door open, motioning wildly.

Tyrell waited a beat and said, "You gotta chill. We got a bad situation here."

"Situation? There *is* no situation. Get the fuck out!" Buddy felt breathless and cursed himself for trembling.

"My name's Tyrell. What's yours?"

Buddy pinched the bridge of his nose, closed his eyes, then lunged, grabbing Tyrell's left arm. Tyrell spun loose, yelling, "Don't fuckin' touch me!" Buddy heard himself make a guttural noise in his throat as he launched himself at Tyrell again. But Tyrell was quicker, stepping back and ripping a piece of paper from his pocket. "You better cool your shit and look at this!" he said, widening his eyes.

Buddy's hands shook as he took a deep gulp of air and stared at the paper. His face went slack and he shook his head as if trying to clear away the confusion. "I don't understand," he said. "I don't understand," he repeated, looking now at Tyrell.

"What's your name, man?" Tyrell said, a sly confidence in his voice.

"I'm going to call the cops if you don't get the fuck out of my house *now.*"

Tyrell shrugged as he stepped into the dining room and sat down. "Go ahead, call the police," he said, carefully flattening the piece of paper on the table. "Go ahead man, I'll be here waitin' for 'em."

Buddy studied Tyrell for a moment. He blinked hard, and said, "What do you want?"

"I said I wanna know your name. When I do business with a man, I wanna know his name."

"Business? We don't have any *business,*" Buddy said, looking away, then back to Tyrell in a quick jerk.

"What's your mothafuckin' name? You gotta know that much."

The question hung in the air. It seemed to confuse Buddy. After a moment, he said, "Buddy. People call me Buddy."

"That your real name? Or a nickname?"

"My real name is Harmon," Buddy said, sitting down, staring at Tyrell. "What the fuck do you want?" The anger had drained from his face. Suddenly he looked very tired.

"I don't like Harmon. Sounds like a fuckin' redneck. Buddy's better. Buddy's cool," Tyrell said with a soft snort. Then his face turned serious and he slid the paper toward Buddy. "We gotta figure this shit out, man."

Buddy looked down. It was a grainy picture of him on his porch holding the little black girl's hand. In the photo, she's crying, struggling to break away. Buddy's bathrobe is open, showing his boxer jocks...too small, too tight, showing too much of him. Buddy is staring at her, half shaved, and his eyes don't look right. He felt his chest tighten again, same as the morning when he first saw her. "Figure *what* shit out?!"

Tyrell cocked his head, then looked away, as though he was deep in thought. When he turned back to Buddy, his face was blasted with a grimace of hate. "She tole me what you did to her. That's my girl's girl. I gotta take care of my blood. Now, there's a couple a ways we can go."

Buddy sat bolt upright. "What the fuck! I don't know what you're talking about. She, she, came into my house." Buddy stopped as though he'd run out of oxygen. He looked at Tyrell, bewildered.

"I call her Dummy," said Tyrell. "She a dummy alright. She had a hard life an I gotta take care of her."

"I never touched that girl! Jesus, I can't believe I'm even *having* this conversation."

"I got her on videotape, man, tellin' the whole story. And I got this picture. Man, it's hard to get away with any shit today. All this 'I gotcha' shit started with Rodney King, some shit."

"Get the girl over here. I want to hear what she said I did."

"You ain't givin' the orders. I'm the fuckin' boss of this show!"

"You fucking nig—" Buddy said, slamming his hand on the table.

"There you go. N-word almost popped out, huh?" said Tyrell, smiling. Then he leaned forward. "Gimme me twenty dollars."

"What?"

"Think of this as your first test. You gimme twenty, or I'm gonna put this mothafuckin' picture all over the Internet. Gonna send it to the hospital your wife works at. All the fuck over the place. Mr. Buddy, child molester. There've been little girls kidnapped and raped. You probably read about it in the paper, that one down in Florida. Shit, you know what happens to a child molester. What's that nice wife of yours gonna say? Now gimme twenty."

Buddy sleepwalked to the entry table where his wallet sat. His face was drained of color and his skin felt clammy. Thumbing through the few bills in his wallet, he pulled out a twenty and handed it to Tyrell. "I don't have a lot of money, you bastard," he whispered. "I'm a fucking caddy."

"You a what?"

"I'm a caddy. At the golf course."

"A caddy?"

Buddy nodded slowly.

"A caddy who drives a nice BMW."

It was humiliating having to explain himself to this prick. Buddy's eyes stung with angry tears as he sank into a chair opposite Tyrell. "I bought that car before I lost my job. It was stupid. I never even liked it," he said, his voice faltering.

"Your wife—"

Buddy leapt up, shaking. "You so much as *mention* her again and I will fucking *end* you! You hear me, you cocksucker?"

Tyrell stood and reared his head back. He stepped away from the table, ready to move. "Now we killin,' huh? You're killin' me, I'm killin' you. Wait till Dummy's momma starts killin' too. That bitch can do some killin' for sure."

Barely able to breathe, Buddy started to speak, but Tyrell raised his hand. "No, we ain't killin.' We gonna handle this without killin,' *Buddy*."

"Just please get the hell out. I told you. I don't have any money."

Tyrell tapped the picture on the table. "Maybe not, but you got a house, my nigger," he said, smiling. "You think this shit is over. I'll be back. Then we'll talk business."

On the way out, just before the door slapped shut, Tyrell laughed. "A mothafuckin' caddy."

5

Over the sound of traffic moving past the open window, tires grated on gravel. A car door slammed. Buddy was slouched on the living room sofa with the TV on and the sound off. He stiffened as Dana came in and walked past, blowing a kiss, apologizing for missing dinner, saying she's *starved*. He noticed an extra bounce in her step.

"Wow, you smell like bleach," he said.

"Infection control. Tell ya about it after I eat."

"Huh?"

"I said, after I eat."

All the sounds seemed intensified, ringing in Buddy's ears. He could hear, acutely, the rustle of Tyrell's picture, folded in the pocket of his shorts. Dana bustled about the kitchen, banging cupboard doors and pouring herself a glass of wine. But just below the surface of her noise, Buddy heard her sense of purpose, like she was here on Earth on some sort of assignment. It was what he loved about her—and envied, to the point of crushing sadness.

"Let's get a puppy, Buddy. Just for the hell of it!" she called out. "You wanted one. It could sleep with us," she said giddily, sounding like a happy kid.

"Christ, you want a puppy?"

"I'm just being...*God*, is this frittata good...I'm just being silly, that's all," she said.

In a dry-run of the horror show he'd been holding at bay, Buddy said, in what he thought was a whisper, "I need to tell you something." His heart squeezed.

"What'd you say?" Dana asked, walking from the kitchen in her nurse scrubs, a huge wedge of frittata in one hand, a plastic spray bottle in the other.

"I said you smell like bleach."

Wolfing her food, she said, "No, after that...you need to *what?*"

"The puppy, is that what you mean?"

"No, something about *something*, was that it? Christ, I don't know."

Buddy leaned forward, staring intently at Dana. He noticed a tiny bloodstain on the sleeve of her green scrubs. She was bobbing her head as she chewed, hearing some inner music. "You're in some mood," he said. You had a drink?"

Smiling, Dana waggled her hips. "Yup, just one, *maybe* two. With Bobbi. I stopped by her place on the way home. She always has a bottle of Jack. God, I love that woman."

"You should watch out. Bobbi gets you drunk, she'll take advantage of you," Buddy said morosely, only half joking.

"She's my friend," Dana said, laughing. She pointed the spray bottle at Buddy and yelled, "Bang!"

"What's that all about?" he asked suddenly annoyed.

She scrunched her face at him. "You're no fun. Stop being such a downer, OK? I can't take that."

Buddy had never heard her use that term before, downer. He bristled and let out a huff. "Well, you haven't been that much fun yourself, lately. Christ, you don't even kiss me goodbye anymore," he said softly, but with force.

"Honey, no offense, but listen to me now. Let's not get started, OK? I had a good day, and I just want to have some fun for a change."

"Get started with what exactly, Dana? With me? That I'm a fucking downer, is that it?" Buddy sat back hard on the sofa and slammed his hand on the arm rest.

"Sometimes I could scream," she said, "All of a sudden we're here, once again!"

"And I'm always the one who brings us here, *right?*"

Dana held up the spray bottle, pointing it at him. "Remember that infection-control protocol I got published? Well, a researcher at Health and Human Services saw it, and he's coming up from DC to talk with me about writing a set of guidelines. That's what I wanted to tell you, Buddy. I was happy, and I'd had a drink, and I wanted to share my news with you. That's all. I don't want to fight. Christ on a *bike!*" she said, flinging the plastic bottle across the room.

Buddy glared at her. She glared back, her lips drawn into a tight line. Dana walked to where Buddy sat and bent down, bringing her face within inches of his. Looking directly into his eyes she said, "Listen, Buddy. I really think that most everything bad that *can* happen between us has *already* happened, and from here on things will get better, OK? I've *got* to think that." Dana's voice softened. "It's important for us both to think that." She grabbed his hands and pulled him toward her. When she kissed him, Buddy could feel his heart slow. "C'mon," she said, leading him to the bedroom.

"Congratulations," he said.

"Huh?"

"On the HHS thing. It's exciting."

&

Climbing the stairs to their room, Buddy thought about their first night in the house. They were making love to the sound of a rainstorm, when a metallic boom of a car crash suddenly shook the windows. They ran out into the night: one moment, handfuls of warm flesh, the next moment, cold rain and that eerie post-crash quiet. At the intersection, an SUV had buried into a bread van. The van's driver was sprawled on the road moaning, a gleaming white section of his femur bone sticking through his pants. Dana went right to work. Buddy stood there, fighting the urge to vomit. After it was over, they showered together. As Buddy apologized for being such a wimp, Dana turned and kissed him, saying into his mouth, "C'mon, let's finish." At that moment he knew he could never be as brave as Dana. But in the final breaths of their lovemaking, Buddy also knew that Dana was unquestionably his, that moment and forever.

Now his legs shook as they walked into the bedroom. Dana was out of her clothes in two quick, balletic movements. She pulled at his shirt, urging him to hurry.

"I need you," she breathed. "Lie on your back." Dana tossed the covers aside and took Buddy in her strong able nurse hands, breathing harder now. She stroked him for several moments, hushing him every time he started to speak. Mounting him, Dana moaned softly as he entered her. Her back arched as her buttocks rose and fell. Leaning down, she kissed him with quick fluttering kisses that grazed his lips. "Don't worry," Dana whispered. "Please, for God's sake, don't worry." The sound of her voice astonished and soothed him.

"I love you," Buddy said. "I love—"

"Just fuck me," she said, "just fuck me slow."

Her rhythm began to quicken, and Buddy could sense she was close to orgasm. All the signs he'd learned over the years: the flush of her skin, the small whimpers caught in her throat. His hands grasped her hips as she moved, and he held on, held on until she cried out. With a strangled shout, Buddy let himself release.

Afterward, Buddy went into the bathroom first. "Just bring me a washcloth," Dana said, sleepily. "I want to lie here for a while. Or is it lay?" He stood with his arms braced against the vanity, eyes closed, listening to the water splashing in the sink.

Tyrell, he thought, the name coming unbidden. *I'm in a spot, Dana, a real tight spot. Something I don't fully understand is happening to me and I want you to know that it is not my fault.* Buddy moved his lips in silent mime, desperate to say the words out loud.

"Hey," Dana called, "I met the guy who lives next door."

Buddy froze. He turned off the water and for a long moment he felt faint. His heart was drumming so hard he could actually see the air throb with each beat. Finally he took a breath. "What, honey?"

"I said I met the guy next door. Funny, huh? After how many years we've been living next to him?"

Buddy cleared his throat, trying to calm himself.

"He was getting out of his car same time as me," she continued. "Seems like a good guy."

Buddy came out of the bathroom naked.

"What the hell did he say to you, Dana?"

She sat up, puzzled at his tone. "He just said hello. What else would he say?"

6

"I'm talking about chutzpah. We lost it somewhere. Look at Ground Zero. For ten years it was a fucking hole," boomed Izzy Weinberg, bobbing his head in a cloud of cigar smoke. "And don't the ragheads just love that? We shoulda started construction the next fucking day." Izzy headed toward the green on the eighth hole, a heavy-footed, locomotive shuffle that said hop aboard or get the fuck out of my way. The rest of the foursome, all men who shot in the low eighties, followed in his wake.

At the ninth hole Izzy pulled out his cellphone, hit the clubhouse number on speed dial and barked, "We're dying of fucking thirst out here!" In minutes, a dazzling blonde came zipping down the fairway, her golf cart a mobile bar. Pulling up, she smiled at Izzy.

"How ya doin' doll," he said, flashing four banana-thick fingers. "Four IBMs, Courtney." Izzy's golf partner—Sy Roth, a first-time guest at Woodcrest—looked puzzled, so Izzy explained. "IBMs are Izzy Bloody Marys. You use vodka instead of tomato juice. My girl Courtney here knows just how I like 'em. Fellas, this beauty went to Duke University's Fuck You School of Business."

"Izzy, I think you mean Fuqua," Sy said, rolling his eyes.

"Yeah, that's what I said. Anyway, she's a tough, very smart girl. But the economy tanked. That's why she's here for now, serving drinks to you schmucks instead of kicking your asses on Wall Street."

The men laughed with Courtney, watching her dimples deepen, taking in her body, wondering whether Izzy had gotten her in the sack yet.

"First day on the job I asked Courtney if she'd ever made love to a nice Jewish boy," Izzy said as he knocked the ash off his cigar. "Never got an answer, so I take that as a yes."

Courtney colored slightly, bit her lower lip in amusement, and chirped a laugh.

"Courtney," Izzy said, "you know Barry Blum and Stink Feet—I mean Sammy—Cohen." Izzy could never resist calling Sammy by the nickname he earned in the locker room where the fumes rising from Sammy's socks could knock over a bull at twenty paces. Tilting his glass at his playing partner, Izzy said, "this is my guest, Sy Roth, a big shot insurance guy. Maybe Mr. Roth can get you a position, huh, Sy?"

Roth nodded, studied his drink, and said, "Jesus, Izzy, I never saw a transparent Bloody Mary before."

Izzy raised his glass. "Here's to Harry Feld. The schmuck made room for the living. That's what the dead do best."

Sammy Cohen's head jerked. "Jesus, Izzy, Harry was good people."

Courtney busied herself making another round, as Izzy's head turned like a gun turret. "Sammy, you putz. Harry was a greedy fuck who shoveled his wife's inheritance into Bernie Madoff's pockets and ended up with Madoff's balls in his mouth. I'm supposed to cry over that?" Slapping his hip, Izzy said, "A man takes care of his own money."

Sammy drained his drink. "So far we've lost about twelve members to the Madoff scandal. Mostly older. They lost their shirts and moved on. But Harry was younger. He still had something to prove. He took it personal. *Very* personal."

"You know it was his wife who found him in the garage with the car running," Blum said.

"A fucking shame," said Roth. "That prick Madoff should rot in Hell."

Izzy made a fist, showing his horseshoe-shaped diamond pinky ring. "I bought a few racehorses. Just for fun. They run two minutes a month. The rest of the time all they do is eat, shit, and sleep."

"Sounds like my son," Roth said, to hoots.

"Moral of this story, take care of your own money," said Izzy.

Glasses lifted in the midday sun. A toast to money, never enough.

"Next week I leave for Scotland. Two weeks, mostly business, but I'm gonna play the Old Course. Thank God for golf, 'cause the food in Scotland sucks and they got the homeliest women in the world there."

Courtney passed another round, looked over to the caddies, Buddy and LT, and shared a private laugh.

"But you always bring your own split-tail, right, Izzy?" said Blum.

Izzy shot him a look and handed Courtney a hundred-dollar bill, whispering in her ear.

Cohen chimed, "Yeah, but he makes her fly coach, don'tcha, Izzy?"

Izzy shook his head, reflecting. "On her fiftieth birthday Elaine asked me how she looks. I tell her fine, with her fancy clothes and jewelry on, but naked, her ass looks like an accordion. She calls me a bastard and starts bawling. So I say, stop crying and get it taken care of like the rest of the girls your age do."

"You *are* a bastard," said Blum, sucking air in a loud whistle. "Christ, how do you drink this stuff?'

"I'm honest to a fault, period. I drink enough to stun a fucking mule, and still run my businesses, all of 'em."

Roth sighed. "I'm lost. What's your wife's ass have to do with this guy Feld killing himself or your fucking race horses?"

Izzy waved his hand. "This is too deep for you, Roth. Drink up, let's play golf."

"Christ, Weinberg, you are hard fuckin' company," Roth said, handing his empty glass to Courtney, blowing her a kiss.

ᔐᗕ

LT was one of the black caddies Buddy had befriended. A fifty-year-old self-anointed philosopher, LT was nicknamed for his obsessive use of "lemme tellya" in each of his utterances. As Izzy and the rest of the foursome ate lunch in the clubhouse, Buddy and LT lounged in the shade on the back nine, waiting for them to return to the course. Buddy's mind drifted back to Tyrell and that picture. He felt like he was falling backward, cartwheeling his arms, kicking against the air with his legs, helpless. It was a deranging sensation. Buddy tried to focus on what LT was saying, just to feel grounded in something. LT was rambling on about his favorite subject: pussy. "Lemme tellya, Buddy. That mothafucka Weinberg is a pussy hound. All young cooze, too. Fat an ugly as he is, shit. See, Buddy, it's all about money and pussy. Lemme tellya, an ugly mothafucka like Weinberg gets more pussy than me an you can dream of. An I am a muh-tha-fuckin' booty-call *master*. Them bitches crawl all over me. Lemme tellya, Buddy, everything boils down ta money an pussy. That's the long an short a that shit. An there ain't more trouble on this earth than white pussy, lemme tellya. See, I'm preferential to independent black bitches with bubble butts an attitude to match. Ask Tiger Woods about white pussy. He married the whitest bitch in the world, gave her all the shit she wants, man goes an gets a little pussy on the side, an what's that bitch do? Attacks him with a golf club. Never satisfied. I coulda tole Tiger. White pussy ain't nothin' but trouble."

In the sun's glint, Izzy Weinberg emerged from the clubhouse. Both caddies stood. He motioned them back down.

"Here ya go," he said, offering two ham and cheese sandwiches and two cold bottles of beer. "I know it's against club rules for caddies to drink on the course, but what the fuck, right fellas?"

LT took the beers and said, "Well, there are rules and then there are rules."

Izzy nodded at LT, waited a beat. "That's absolutely right. Couldn't have said it better myself." Then with a phony crocodile smile he turned to Buddy. "You don't break the rules, do ya Buddy? Never had a beer under this tree before?"

Buddy checked himself, not taking the bait. He shrugged, lifted his sandwich and said, "Thanks for lunch, Mr. Weinberg."

Izzy turned and snorted. Then he unleashed a vicious fart that ventilated the seat of his Kelly green slacks, curling LT's nostrils. "Oooeee, that a nasty mothafucka. I took a direct hit on that shit," LT said, a beer in each hand. "What's up with Weinberg? Lemme tellya, he's playin' you, man, you do know that. But I ain't sayin' shit no more. Lemme tellya, that dude is playin' you."

Buddy shrugged and stood, but LT's words had hit home and the effect of Izzy's parting shot was still blasted on his face.

7

The house next to Buddy's had a split personality. A castaway on the outside, with foot-long grass, weeds sprouting in the gutters, the paint grayed and peeling like dead flesh. But inside, the rooms with their shopworn furniture were kept neat and clean. The cloying sweetness of musk incense and the bitter tang of Lysol clung to the walls.

Sinking lower into the couch they bought from the thrift shop at St. Vincent DePaul's, Latreece Williams waited for Tyrell to look up from his laptop. Lord, could that man talk. She just wanted to chill and watch *The Biggest Loser.* After a day of sponging old white ladies' wrinkled asses, bitching on their aches and dead husbands, Latreece just wanted to be left to her simple pleasures—cooking, watching TV, getting high. She'd just smoked some Mexican weed, righteous shit she'd bought from Leo, her Hispanic dude who lived off Route 110. Leo was someone she could trust. When he wasn't working at his brother-in-law's landscaping business, Leo tended to his own crop under the grow lights.

Staring at Tyrell, Latreece became conscious of herself in a dreamy way that made her uncomfortable. She was here now, again, caught up in another man's drama. Tyrell didn't waste any time, she gave him that. He'd developed a theme, a special alertness, one that flashed between burning malice and burning love. Tyrell was a man with plans, with ambition, and right or wrong, it impressed her; she'd never seen it in any of her other men. He'd told her a thousand times that of the seven deadly sins, sloth ranks at the top of his hit list. But his patience was being tried; turning thirty flipped a switch in his head and lately he'd been getting strange, going off on hour-long rants, all this *blackness* shit, this new movement. Latreece knew one thing: there ain't nothin' new under the fuckin' sun. Another thing she knew: Tyrell hated white folks like nobody she'd ever seen.

"You be wastin' your life sittin' on that couch watchin' TV, jus like you doin," said Tyrell, raising his head, still tapping away at the keyboard.

"That what you goin' ta school for? Ruinin' other folks' good times?" asked Latreece.

Tyrell pursed his lips. "I'm goin' ta college ta better myself, so I can take care a you an Dummy, get ya nice things. Ya know, live the mothafuckin' dream. I got me my GI bill. I got me my vet's benefits. I'm plannin' ahead. You gotta have a five-year plan," he said sharply.

Latreece ran her fingers through her hair. "I seen five-year plans before. I seen *twenty-five to life* plans, too." Dropping her voice to a whisper, she hissed, "That's the kind a plan her daddy's got." Latreece jerked her head toward Tashanda, who sat like a little brown moth, wide-eyed, two feet from the TV.

Tyrell stood up with his laptop and walked past Latreece, motioning for her to follow.

He sat at the kitchen table. Latreece stirred the pot of chicken stew simmering on the stove, took a whiff of the fragrance wafting from the pot, nodded to herself, and sat across from him.

"What up with that negative bullshit, huh?" said Tyrell. "You *like* cleanin' old white bitches' backsides? I am tryin'—no, I am *gonna*—change things. Ain't that the big word, now? Change? Ain't that how that half-white bitch got hisself elected? Change and suckin' up to white mothafuckers. Well girl, we gonna change."

"You can't change nothin' if you upstate," she said with a head-waggle that vibrated down her long sturdy body. "I am so scared you gonna get in trouble with the law, that you're doin' something wrong. Baby, I can't lose you."

He lifted her hands, kissed them one at a time, lowered them onto the table, stroked her fingers.

"Look," he said, "First thing you gotta know is the difference between what's legal and what's right. There is things doin' out there in our community that might be against the mothafuckin' law, but they right as shit to the dudes doin' it, OK? In Bed Stuy there was liquor stores on every corner. Lotto, check cashin', there it is. I watched my uncle come out of a store with a fifth a Gordon's every mothafuckin' day. One day, drunk on that shit, he got inta a fight, killed a brotha an ended up getting shot by the cops."

Latreece drew her hands away. "That fool dead because he fucked up. My daddy's dead the same way. So, you gonna be a fool, too, Tyrell?"

"My point is, they peddle that shit, and it's legal but it ain't no righter than the brotha sellin' his shit on the corner. One a my classes at Nassau Community, we analyzed that shit. Alcohol's the baddest drug out there, but it legal. Now, what I'm doin' is right. Right for us, right for her," he said, motioning in the direction of the TV.

"Right? You sure 'bout that?"

"That mothafucka perved your daughter. You heard her, what he did. You don't think that what I'm doin is *right?*"

Latreece looked out the window. "She all messed up. It's my fault. I was wrong when I had her. God, how sorry I am for that. I tried to blame it on being young an stupid, but it don't work no more."

So sweet, so solid, even after what she's been through, Tyrell thought.

"That day she went into that white dude's house, I had an early client, that ol' bitch Mrs. Landry. She throw a fit if I'm one minute late. I tore off that morning, didn't realize the damn bus for camp had already come," said Latreece, her voice shaky with guilt.

"Forget that shit, OK? We rollin' now. We gonna own this damn house." he said. Tyrell turned to the laptop, excited. "Look here. This brotha came to my school. He a smart mothafucka, an he don't take no shit. Look," he said, pointing to the screen. "*Home ownership grew among white, middle-class families after World War II when access to credit and government programs made buying houses affordable. Black families were largely left out because of discrimination, and the effects are still being felt today,*" says Lance Freeman, assistant professor of urban planning at Columbia University and author of There Goes the 'Hood."

Latreece read slowly, stopping midway to say, "I'm so proud you goin' to college. This cool, but ain't it blackmail, what you're doin' with that dude next door? Ain't that illegal?"

Nah, it's a kind a reparations."

"Say what?"

"Look, we gonna make a bad white dude pay for what he did. See, now we playin' like the law. That's all."

"But how you know this shit ain't gonna blow up, Tyrell? Huh?"

He paused, and gave a big wink. "Cause I got the goods on him. An I mean the *goods.* See, there's a thing called *Webtribution.* You use the power of the Internet to, what you call, uh, *leverage* yourself in a deal like this. How you think white people operate?"

"I ain't worried 'bout white people, I'm just worried about you."

"He a mouse in a corner and I'm the big black cat," said Tyrell, running his tongue across his lips. Pointing at the laptop he repeated, "Webtribution."

Latreece edged her chair back, stood and leaned across the table toward Tyrell, her breasts swaying. She took his lower lip in her mouth and sucked gently. "You gettin' too damn smart, college boy. I don't know half the shit you talkin' about," she whispered as Tyrell cupped her breasts.

"Turn off that stew," he said. "I need some a *this*." She smiled, and turned toward the stairway. On the way up to their bedroom, stumbling once, Latreece said, "Promise you won't get in trouble."

"I promise, baby," Tyrell said, yanking his shirt off. I *own* that mothafucka. He got nowhere to go. Now I squeeze him. We rollin.'"

Kicking the bedroom door shut, Tyrell turned toward Latreece as she shed her dress and panties. He reached down to grasp and knead her bare buttocks, lifting and parting the flesh. "Damn this ass, damn this ass a yours."

8

From the elevated green on the sixteenth hole, the gated community of Windermere looked like an extension of Woodcrest Country Club. In a way it was. The sprawling, perfectly manicured four-acre plots and the $3 million-plus mansions were home to the crème-de-la-crème of Woodcrest's membership; you had to wait for someone to die, or kill your way to get in.

It wasn't the money or prestige that drew people here. It was being part of a big story, one written by men like Izzy Weinberg, the guy other men secretly hated, the guy they wanted to be. They envied his sense of purpose, relentless drive, and willingness to take big risks to amass money and power, the most potent of aphrodisiacs. Izzy had bedded their wives—short harmless dalliances, boozy sex for fun—and the husbands had knowingly turned a blind eye. In a perverse way, they wore the mark of a cuckold as a badge of honor; somehow it bound them to Izzy and allowed a little bit of his luster to rub off on them.

Izzy and Elaine were at their dining room table, separated by an expanse of polished wood and flickering candles. The room was airy; its peaked, eighteen-foot ceiling gave it a cathedral-like feel. Izzy was dressed in a business suit, his big square gold cufflinks reflecting a bit of flame. A young, light-skinned black woman in a prim maid's uniform came in and stood just to the right of Elaine, meeting Izzy's eyes with hers.

"Jasmine, you can remove Mrs. Weinberg's plate. She doesn't have much of an appetite, but I'm sure she'd like another drink," said Izzy.

He lit his cigar and puffed luxuriously as Jasmine cleared the plates and brought Elaine a cocktail, served on a silver tray. Then she waited. Izzy blew a huge smoke ring that sailed across the table, making a bluish halo over Elaine's head. "My angel," he laughed, then turned to Jasmine and said, "When my driver gets here, show him where the bags are. Put the leather case with my laptop in the back seat. When it's time to go, tell him to have a drink ready for me. He knows what I like."

Elaine took a long sip from her drink and swirled the glass. Her eyes were fixed on the ice cubes as she said, "So, Izzy, what's in Scotland, exactly? You might have told me…"

"…but I forgot," Izzy said, finishing her sentence, leaving the words in the air.

"Yes, that's right."

"Three Chinks. I coulda met them in China, but it's better doing business on a golf course in Scotland than in *that* puke hole. The Chinks are nuts for golf."

"So now China's a puke hole, is it?" said Elaine, bobbing her head, very slowly.

Izzy smiled. "*Every* place, darling, but the *U...S...of...A...*is a puke hole; some holes just have more puke than others."

"God I love you, Izzy," Elaine said, not bothering to hide the sarcasm in her voice. "But really," she said, lifting her drink in mock toast to the surrounding opulence, "Don't you have enough money?"

"There's *never* enough money," Izzy said, "and besides, this deal is bigger than money. With this deal, I can make my mark, leave my footprint."

"Your footprint," she repeated numbly.

"*Our* footprint, baby. It's always for you *and* me, Elaine, my doll."

"Then why aren't you taking me with you?"

Izzy was brought up short. They looked at each other.

"Would you have come if I'd asked?"

"No," Elaine said, shaking her head. "But it would have been nice for you to ask."

"I'm sorry, baby. I just didn't think Scotland would be any fun for you. Where could you go shopping? And their food is godawful. Who the fuck eats sheep lungs boiled in intestines?"

"So, what's the big deal you're working on...with your Chinks?"

Izzy ground out his cigar on a hand-painted Limoges cake plate. He hadn't minded indulging Elaine's desire for a set of 16 of these things, each one of which cost $1,350 at Tiffany's. But he would have preferred that they weren't painted with birds of the Nile. Fucking Arabs. Walking to Elaine's chair, he stood behind her, bent down, and gently massaged the meat of her upper arms. "It's too early to talk about it," Izzy said, his Hungarian superstition flaring. "I don't want to jinx things up." Slipping his left hand into her camisole, Izzy cupped and lifted her breast, exposing it with a flick of his finger. She tilted her head, sighing.

"Christ, you're still a hot piece of ass, you know that?"

Elaine made a harrumphing sound.

"You can go see our pro while I'm gone. He can give you a few pointers with his eight iron."

Suppressing a laugh Elaine said, "Jesus, Izzy, you turn women into pigs. But I'm not one of your skanks."

Izzy rolled the nipple of her breast between his thumb and forefinger and whispered, "Honey, all I'm saying is, have some fun while I'm gone. But just remember: Izzy's got little birdies that watch his back."

With his other hand he pulled a business card from his pocket, flicking it like a card dealer. "Doll, I want you to go see Joel Friedman. He's the best cosmetic doc on the East Coast. I already spoke to him. He can tighten your ass, lift your tits, tuck the chin. Bingo, there goes fifteen years. That's how much I love you," he said, slipping the card into her cleavage and kissing the top of her head.

Elaine pulled it from between her breasts and leaned forward, stretching her hand out until the card caught fire in the candle flame. "*That's* how much I love *you*," she said, in that breathy voice Izzy remembered so well. He felt a pulse in his groin, suddenly thinking of Elaine when she was young and wild, ready to do it anytime, anywhere. Then anger. He snatched her hand back just as Jasmine stepped into the room and announced, "Your car is ready, Mr. Weinberg."

9

The phone rang, but Buddy just stared at it until it stopped. A minute later, his cell phone rang. The caller ID said "Dana" so he flipped it open. Why hadn't he answered their home phone, she wanted to know. Could he please go over to Bottles & Cases and pick up some Johnny Walker Black Label for her dad's birthday tomorrow? She was running late and talking breathlessly into the phone. He could see her scurrying down the hospital corridor, the phone jammed up against her ear as she wrestled with files clasped tightly under her arm.

Holding his hand over the receiver, Buddy took a good sip of Scotch, felt it burn, and said, "*oooh, man*" aloud.

"Hey, are you OK?" Dana asked. "You sound funny."

"I'm a funny guy," he said, reflexively.

"Don't ridicule yourself," she huffed.

"Was I?"

"C'mon…I love you, Buddy," she said, her voice so softly pitched he could barely make out the words.

"Do you?"

"You know I do. Sorry for being late on a Friday. I have to wrap up a few things. I'm a little nervous about my meeting on Monday with the CDC guy, that's all," Dana said.

But Buddy detected something else and said, "Nervous? More like happy."

Dana hesitated, unable to find the right words. Her stomach lurched. This was the oncoming collision she was trying to avoid.

"I *am* happy, Buddy," she blurted, her voice high-pitched, trembling with emotion. "I want you to be happy, too." All she heard in response was Buddy breathing and then, in the background, a loud rapping sound. "What's that? Is somebody at the door?"

"No, it's nothing. I mean, I don't know. Let me go, OK? I'll see ya in a bit."

Another *rap, rap, rap,* made Buddy's heart leap.

"Buddy," Dana persisted. "Who's there?"

"I don't know, I gotta go," he said, snapping his cell phone shut and storming to the door. Through the glass, Buddy saw the silhouette, tall and lean, head cocked to the side. He grabbed the knob with a violent twist, and pulled. Tyrell stood there, holding a laptop. A sweet stench of pot wafted in.

"What do you want, huh?" said Buddy moistening his lips. A truck roared by, and he imagined pushing this guy under the wheels. "What do you *want?*"

"You know," Tyrell said, "I'm here to settle up this shit." He stepped in, brushing Buddy's shoulder.

Buddy jumped in front of Tyrell, raising his hands and said, "You get the fuck outta my house, *now!*" He reached out to shove Tyrell back onto the porch, but Tyrell spun away, gripping the computer like a football as Buddy came at him again, taking huge ragged breaths, as though he was drowning. "You can't come into a man's home like this," he rasped.

Standing a few feet apart they looked at each other. Buddy lowered his hands, more stunned than angry as he pointed to the door, waving his finger.

"*Man?*" said Tyrell, turning toward the dining room, "If you was a man, I wouldn't be in your mothafuckin' house in the first place." He put the laptop on the dining room table, flipped it open and said, "Let's do this shit."

Buddy's eyes darted from the computer screen to Tyrell. "Never talk to my wife, again. *Ever.*"

"Just being neighborly, *Buddy.*"

"I don't want you near my wife," Buddy said. "And you're not my neighbor."

"Yeah, Buddy, I know all about that. We fucked up your neighborhood," Tyrell said sarcastically. He moved the cursor on his laptop and clicked. "But here's what I wanna show ya. This is my Web page. See this? That's the picture of you an Dummy. This here is a video I took; it's short but it makes a point."

It was hard for Buddy to keep looking. "What's wrong with you?" he said.

Ignoring Buddy, Tyrell picked up a paper napkin and blew his nose in it.

"*Look,*" said Tyrell, clicking open a YouTube-type video.

The little girl, Tashanda, was on the screen, squirming, stifling the urge to cry. Off camera, Tyrell asks her what happened with the white man. "He made me touch him," she says, her face twisting.

"Where?"

"On his pee pee," she says, barely audible. "Then he put his hand on me."

"Where?"

"Here," she whimpers, touching her crouch.

"Then what'd he do, darlin'?"

As he watched Tashanda talk, Buddy's knees buckled slightly. He walked to the kitchen and poured a glass of Scotch. Taking a quick sip, he shouted, "You made her say that, you sick fuck! Now get out!"

When Buddy turned around, Tyrell was standing there, almost in his face. Buddy stepped back, glaring at him. "I'm not giving you *anything*. I will not be blackmailed."

Tyrell nodded to himself, as if gathering his thoughts. Then, speaking in quick, clipped tones he said, "Listen, Buddy. You molested a little black girl. People gotta pay for what they do. You can pay two ways. First," he said, pointing at the laptop, "I can put this shit out all over the place. Have you arrested. Oooweee. You go upstate. Know what happens to nice lookin' white boy bitches that molest little black girls? Huh?"

Buddy moistened his lip. "*No*," he said. "This is bullshit!"

Tyrell shrugged. "Or you can pay us. Sell your house, give me a certain amount. Done. To me, it ain't no choice, white boy."

"A certain amount?"

"We'll get around to that soon, I gotta think it over. I ain't fuckin' greedy," Tyrell said with a wicked smirk.

"I can't sell my house. Not on this shithole of a block." Buddy said, sounding almost gleeful. If he's trapped here, so is Tyrell. This genius's plan won't work, Buddy thought.

Tyrell walked back to the dining room. He knew he was in control and could take his time making his next move. Smiling, Tyrell closed the laptop and picked it up. He walked to the kitchen, where Buddy was bracing himself on the counter, his arms locked, his head hanging to his chest.

"Lower the fuckin' price!" Tyrell shouted. He rambled on about the nuances of the housing market, spinning off into a diatribe about the racial inequities of the GI Bill. It left Buddy's head numb.

"What the fuck are you talking about? Get the fuck out of my house you sick bastard!"

"Sick! You callin' *me* sick, you white mothafucka!" Tyrell bellowed. "You the one who's sick. You and all your fuckin' white ass friends, thinkin' you so fuckin' superior. You *owe* me. You owe *me* and every black man, woman, and child in this fuckin' country. We'll see who the man and who the piece a shit is now!"

Tyrell turned to leave, saying with mock politeness, "Don't bother, I know my way out." He closed the front door behind him so carefully, Buddy wasn't even sure he was gone.

Pouring another long glass of Scotch, he walked to the living room, sinking into a chair. His lips moved, but he doesn't say anything. Sliding off the chair to his knees, Buddy clutched his head and moaned. "Good Christ, how did this happen to me?"

10

After a night of tossing from one bad dream to another, Buddy got to the course on Saturday morning just as the sun was rising over the Sound. Breaking caddy protocol, he walked from the yard and asked the starter, Jock Macgregor, if he could get an early loop. "I've got something I need to do," Buddy said. A look passed between them, some shared understanding as Macgregor said, "Sure Buddy, I'll give you the Steins, senior and junior. They play so fast you'd think they don't even like the game. You'll be in before noon."

"Thanks Jock," said Buddy.

In his heavy Scot's brogue, Macgregor said, "OK, Buddy, but you can do me a favor now. Come down with something on Tuesday, eh? Elaine Weinberg's assistant called me before my first fuckin' cup of coffee, asked that I make sure you're her caddy. I don't want to get involved, OK?"

Buddy stepped forward, and bent toward Jock's ear. "There's nothing to get involved *in*, Jock."

Macgregor turned to his clipboard. "Just the same, Buddy, make sure you have a case of the flu on Tuesday."

On the back nine, when the Steins went into the midway clubhouse for a quick bite, Buddy made a call from his cell phone. "Hey, Russ. Listen, I got jammed up and I need some legal advice. I know you're not a lawyer anymore, but you used to be. So can you help me out?"

❧ ❧

When Buddy stepped through the door of Finnegan's Taproom, Tommy the bartender called out, "Hey stranger," and pointed to a table in the back where Russ sat hunched over a pint of dark ale. Buddy braced for the inevitable turning-back-the-pages-of-time. Russ Dunn lived alone, in the worst of all places—his own past. Buddy had already heard the same story dozens of times, but he and Russ went way back and listening was the least Buddy could do.

Russ looked up as if surprised to see Buddy. "Mr. Graves, man, you look like shit. Who's cutting your hair these days?"

Buddy smiled and sat. "Hey, yourself, Mr. Dunn," he said, ruffling Russ's red hair. "How are you?"

Russ drained his pint, held up two fingers to signal Ginny, the waitress, and said through a repressed belch, "For someone who hasn't taken a solid shit in three years, OK I guess."

"The price you pay for drinking yourself to death," said Buddy.

Ginny delivered two pints. Buddy raised his glass and nodded, like a friend waiting to take a familiar journey. As if on cue, Russ's eyes teared up as he shook his head. "Jesus Christ, Buddy, I had it all: partner in a big law firm, knocking down six figures, beautiful wife, kid on the way. I'd made a life. And it all went to shit. How could it happen? All that effort reduced to this," he says pointing to his ale. "It still amazes me," he continued, a look of beleaguered wonderment growing on his booze-bloated face as he recounted how his pregnant wife, Claire, was killed three years ago on a rain-slicked road a half mile from their home, just about the same time he was being lap-danced at a bachelor party in the VIP lounge of the Paradise Club in Manhattan. "I didn't want to do it," he said morosely. "I got no fucking pleasure from it, that's for sure. The fucking groom started it and I followed. My wife and baby dying in a heap of twisted steel while I'm drunk and coked up, rubbing numb genitals with a twenty-two-year-old tramp. What does that make me?"

Buddy looked at him, offered a half smile, a smile that was supposed to convey an answer to an un-answerable question.

"Buddy, what does that make me?"

"A guy who made a mistake. An innocent fucking mistake, Russ."

"Have you ever had a lap dance?"

"No."

"There is nothing fucking innocent about it. Assholes like me think that doing shit like that, just because we could, made us freer, somehow more in love with the world. But that lap dance got me. Now I'll never love the world again. You fucking call that innocent? Jesus, Buddy!"

When Russ finally trailed off, Buddy murmured the requisite regrets, practiced over the years. After two more pints he described to Russ his Tyrell problem. Then he pulled the picture from his pocket and placed it on the table, unconsciously holding his breath as Russ stared at it, transfixed. It was a minute before he looked up.

"My God, Buddy, this looks…bad," he said, picking up a swizzle stick left by a previous customer and tapping the picture. Buddy recoiled reflexively as the end of the swizzle stick jabbed the image of his threadbare boxer jocks.

"Jesus, it looks like you got a boner," Russ said solemnly.

Buddy sighed noisily and shot Russ a what-the-fuck look. He described the video, that trumped up, coached performance. "Russ, what can this bastard Tyrell do, legally?"

"Cases like this, with a challenged kid, and their trying to keep their stories straight, any half-assed defense attorney would tear this shit apart. But this isn't about the law, it's about this picture. And that video. Christ, Buddy, I mean, if I didn't know you, seeing this stuff…whew, it's fucking bad."

"OK, I know all that," Buddy said.

"Jesus, I mean, you didn't have a boner, did you?"

"Can we get off that, please."

"Sorry."

"Any suggestions, Russ?" Buddy asked, his face suddenly drained of color.

Russ leaned forward. "I don't know, man. My advice is to play along for now. This Tyrell sounds like a funny guy, like he's convinced himself that what he's doing isn't really wrong. It also sounds like he's making it up as he goes along."

"There's nothing funny about him," Buddy said, looking away. "Not one fucking thing."

Russ reached out, grasped Buddy's forearm, and squeezed. "You've got to tell Dana, Buddy. Get her on your side before any bad shit goes down."

Buddy closed his eyes and let his head fall back.

"Life can turn on a dime," said Russ. "Mine did, and I don't want to see this ruin you, man."

Buddy braced his hands on the table, pushing himself up, slowly.

Russ pulled a printout from his pocket and held it up, his eyes glazing over. It was a picture of a trailer in the middle of a vast plain. "I put a down payment on this," he said wistfully. "It's a little parcel in west Texas, in the middle of nowhere, and it's dirt cheap. One day soon, I'm gonna go to the pound, adopt an old dog, one that no one wants, move out there, sit under an awning, and drink. And when my old dog dies, I'm gonna shoot myself."

Buddy studied his friend for a long moment. "Do you know how crazy that sounds?" he said, his voice cracking.

"Tell Dana, Buddy. You've got a good woman there. She'll understand. Let me know if I can help. I'm easy to find, at least for now."

II

In the Presidential Suite of the Old Course Hotel in St Andrews, Scotland, Izzy Weinberg peered out the window at the fairway on the seventh hole, a brutal par five that was quickly vanishing from sight under the long shadow of night. In one hand he gripped a tumbler of single malt Scotch—his third nightcap. In his other hand he held the telephone receiver. When Elaine answered, Izzy smiled and said, "Hello, beautiful."

"You're drunk," said Elaine.

"I'm lonely,"

"You don't sound lonely."

"What's lonely sound like?"

After a long pause, Elaine said, "How are your nice Chinese men doing?"

"Nice? Those dog-eating yellow fucks. We met for drinks. Tomorrow we play golf and talk business. How are the kids?"

"They're here in bed with me."

"Sounds lovely. You being a good girl?"

"Of course. By the way, I took your suggestion."

"Huh?"

"I screwed the pants off our golf pro today. You weren't kidding about his schlong. He has to strap that thing to his leg," Elaine cooed. "It brought tears to my eyes."

"In your dreams, kiddo. But I love it when you talk dirty," Izzy said. Then, pressing the receiver to his lips he added, "Did you call Friedman, my cosmetic doc?"

"Your doc. God I love you Izzy. Everything's yours."

"What I pay for is mine. So did you?"

"No more games, Izzy. I'm *tired* of it."

"Games? Grow up, Elaine, OK?"

"That's what you call it? Growing up?"

"Stiffen your spine to the reality of the world we live in. Women your age and your wealth do not have saggy tits. If they do, shame on them. That better?"

"I'll say goodnight if there's nothing else, sweetheart," breathed Elaine, blowing an elaborate air kiss into the receiver.

After hanging up, Izzy padded into the bedroom. Gazing over the rim of his tumbler, he appraised the single bare leg protruding from the emerald duvet, like a pale lily in a green vase. A moment passed before the bed's occupant stirred, rustling the covers and revealing the top of a very blonde head. Izzy let loose a long breath, like a man surfacing from the deep, as he approached the bed and placed his empty glass on the night table. The bed sagged under his bulk as he sat and drew back the covers. The blonde smiled sheepishly and crossed her arms over her breasts. "Guess I drank a little too much Chateau Latour, Mr. Weinberg."

"I told you, doll, unless its business, you call me Izzy."

"OK, Izzy," she said, and then she made a blowing sound. "I feel like such a bitch. I overheard you on the phone. *Sorry.*"

Izzy looked at her and gently placed his hand on her hip. "Don't be. My wife and I have an understanding. I told you that too, remember?"

She furrowed her brow. "I heard you ask about the kids?"

Izzy laughed, "My dogs, three Pomeranians. Moe, Larry, and Curly. I call 'em the kids. My two daughters married nice mannered squares. One's in Manhattan, the other in Connecticut. We don't see them much."

"Izzy Weinberg, a dog lover. Who would have thought?" she mused, leaning on an elbow.

"Dogs are loyal and they don't talk. What's not to love about that? Now turn over, doll."

His eyes widened as they swept her backside. "Oh, God that tuchus is so perfect," he whispered. "Only schmucks paint pictures of flowers and mountains. If I were an artist, I'd paint nothing but the female ass."

"That's nice," she said.

"Nice?"

"Yeah Izzy, it was nice," she said.

He nodded to himself and said, "So, what did you tell your dad?"

"That I was hired as an account executive for Weinberg Associates, sixty-five K to start and full bennies. He Googled you and was very impressed," she said.

"He Googled me, huh?" Izzy said with a shrug.

"Yes," she said, lifting her hand to tuck back her hair. "Thanks again... for this opportunity."

"Don't thank me. I saw talent and chutzpah the first time we met. But talent is only ten percent of the game. Hunger, desire, that's what makes success. You hungry?"

"I'm starved," she said, as Izzy smiled.

"You handled yourself well tonight, with class," he said. "The Chinks were drooling all over you, especially that goofy-looking character, Qian Qichen. He's the big guy. They don't see women like you. Those Chink broads look like goldfish on legs."

She muffled an explosive laugh with her pillow, then cocked her face at Izzy, "My God, I've never known a guy like you."

They fell silent, analyzing the calculus of this shared intimacy. She was still dizzied by it; that tidal-wave urgency that radiated from Izzy had drawn her here. It came as a job offer. Being naked in bed wasn't part of it. It just happened. People, even big important people, bent to Izzy Weinberg's wishes, so why not her?

"Who are your associates, anyway?" she asked.

Izzy snorted, "*I'm* my associates. When you're sleeping, that's when associates fuck you over. Remember that kiddo, now that you work for me."

She gave a funny little salute as if working for Izzy were a form of active duty.

"You act like you come from money, but you don't, do ya?" Izzy said.

"I want good things, lots of them," she said dismissing the question without a hint of irony.

"Don't ever stop wanting. *Ever*," Izzy said with authority.

"But, what about…"

"Shhhh," Izzy hushed her. Stroking her pale, up-turned ass, Izzy said, "This beats the shit out of serving drinks at the golf course, doesn't it Courtney?"

"God, yes," she said. "Oh, God yes."

With an odd lilt to his voice he said, "Now go to sleep, have pretty dreams and get ready for tomorrow."

అ✑

Late that same night in New York, Buddy and Dana were returning from her father's birthday celebration in the Hicksville neighborhood where she grew up. It was a tree-lined place of neat conformity populated during the 1960s by cops and firemen who'd fled New York City to rear families. As they drove, a light rain began to fall, giving the air in the car a moist, cottony quiet. Dana rolled up her window and rambled on about the party: her mother's usual overdone pot roast and string beans, the uneasy rift between her father and brother, her brother's whining about money, her mother's expanding ass, her father's teary-eyed, right-wing diatribes—the commonness of her working-class roots.

"I love my family, but God do I hate that place," Dana said forcefully. "All the Budweiser and American flags. I know what they're gonna say two minutes before they open their mouths." Buddy pretended to listen, but his mind was elsewhere. He vaguely heard her switch gears, talking about her upcoming meeting with that researcher from the CDC. The nervous trill in her voice drilled into Buddy's thoughts. He hesitated, but when she paused, he caught her eye and said, "There's something I need to tell you."

12

"What is it? What is it you need to tell me?"

For a moment, Buddy felt paralyzed, as if the desperate urgency in Dana's voice had severed his spine. Dana asked him again, her voice ringing with fear and mounting anger.

"Let's just wait until we get home," he said.

The air in the car grew close and tense. "It's about last Monday when you didn't play golf, isn't it? I *knew* something was wrong, but you lied and said it was nothing."

"I didn't lie," he rasped, choking on a surge of emotion as the car pulled into the driveway.

The rain had picked up, blowing down from the night sky in howling gusts. Next door, the house was lit up like a cruise ship, the glare of lights in every room. *As if they care about electricity bills*, Buddy thought angrily.

Dana was out of the car before it came to a full stop, slamming the door and bolting toward the house. She was waiting for him in the living room, arms crossed over her chest, her face blank.

"Well," she said, "What is it?"

He tried to talk, but he couldn't get the words out.

"*Well?*" she said again, clenching her jaw.

"I love you. I'm sorry," he said, walking to the living room. He sat on the sofa in a falling motion.

Three long strides and Dana was standing over him. "Sorry? Christ, Buddy, sorry for what?"

He sucked a huge breath that made him lightheaded.

"Did you hear me? I love you," he said again.

Dana sat on the coffee table across from him. Their knees touched and she pulled back, stiffening.

Buddy swallowed hard. "Last Monday, after you left for work I was upstairs shaving. All of a sudden, the little black girl from next door is at the top of the stairs watching me."

Dana threw her head forward. "*What?* I don't understand. What was she doing in our house?"

"She missed her bus, you know, for camp or something. Anyway, she was locked out of her house and she was scared. Our door was open, so she just fucking came in. Walked up the fucking stairs. Jesus, it happened so fast. I got blindsided, Dana."

"Christ, I'm afraid to ask. Did something happen with her?"

Buddy nodded very slowly, almost as though he was drifting to sleep. "I told her she couldn't be here. I must have yelled at her. But see, she was scared out of her head. So I took her downstairs. When we got out on the porch," Buddy said, turning toward the window, "he was there. All of a sudden he was there."

"*Who* was there?"

"The black guy from next door."

"Tell me what happened with that kid. Tell me now!"

Slowly, painfully, he described that morning, everything down to the feel of the little girl's hand in his, trembling, clutching with incredible strength, as though she never wanted to let go. When Buddy told her that Tyrell used a cell phone to photograph him and the girl, Dana reared back and shook her head *no*, closed her eyes, and turned away. Then she shouted, "Oh fuck!" and slapped the table, letting out a burst of crazy laughter. "I can't believe this! Why didn't you tell me?"

Buddy pulled the picture from his pocket and spread it on the coffee table. "I know it *looks* bad, but there's an explanation."

Dana cocked her head to the side. "Oh my God," she said, bending at the waist. Her eyes sharpened as she studied the picture. Then she looked up abruptly and said, "Jesus, it looks like you have an erection."

"I was in the bathroom, shaving, smelling your soap, thinking of you, and..." Before he could say another word, Dana launched a balled fist into his face, snapping his head back. He yelped as Dana lunged forward, slapping wildly and screaming, "How could you do this to me? *How could you do this?!*"

Buddy wrestled himself away and grabbed her wrists. He bolted upright, twisting her arms as he screamed, "How could I do this to *you*? You fucking cunt! What did I do to *you*?" Dana stamped on his toes and together they fell over the coffee table. She kicked at him and slid away sobbing. Then they were both sitting on the floor, breathing heavily. Buddy's lip was bloodied. He wiped it with the back of his hand and let his head fall to his chest.

Sobbing, Dana said, "You can't look me in the eye, can you?"

Buddy lifted his head. "OK, I'm looking you in the eye, so what?" he shot back.

"You hurt me, my hands, you hurt me," Dana said, choking on a new surge of tears. "I don't cry. Buddy, look what you've done, you've made me cry."

"Dana, Jesus, I'm sorry, but you..." Buddy began, but Dana waved her hands for him to stop.

In a bitter, soft strangled voice she said, "When I was a girl there was a man in the neighborhood, Mr. Summers, a nice man, quiet. He commuted to the city every day. He had a cabin cruiser and he'd take kids out for rides on the bay with his son, Will. There was this one kid, Pete Reardon, a friend of Will's. One day Pete came back from a boat ride and told his parents something had happened. We never found out what, but there was talk about dirty magazines. That's all there was, neighbors whispering to each other. But it was enough. Mr. Summers was ostracized and he slowly disappeared. I mean he lived in the same house, walked to the train every morning, but it was like he wasn't there anymore. We never saw his wife. His son, Will, started getting into trouble, bad trouble. Mr. Summers turned gray, not just his hair, all of him, this fading gray man. We called him the gray man. He ended up hanging himself in his garage."

Buddy slid toward Dana and reached out as if to console her. Her face twisted and she pushed him away, saying "No!" Then she continued. "Years later, a friend of mine ran into Pete Reardon in a bar. Pete was on leave from the Air Force. After a few drinks, my friend asked Pete what really happened on Mr. Summer's boat that day. Pete just looked at him and said, 'Nothing, nothing at all. I was pissed off at Will. I liked this girl, Carol Lang, but she liked Will. It was a way to get even with him.' Pete just shrugged and said, 'Girls do funny things to your head.' That's what he said. A life ruined with just whispers, people talking over fences and at cocktail parties. There wasn't any real evidence, just rumors."

"I'll get us out of this, I promise," said Buddy. "Please believe me."

"How?" she asked. "Jesus, he could put that picture on the Internet. This is so fucking sick."

"That fucking nigger bastard!" Buddy said, spitting the words out.

Dana sighed, a quivering sound. "There ya go. I was waiting for that. You call me a cunt, call him a nigger. I come home from my father's birthday party and end up in the gutter."

Dana rested her head on her arms, her shoulders sagged, defeated. "God, I feel sick," she said. Then she looked at Buddy. "I know nothing happened with the girl, but somehow you brought this to our doorstep. I have a career, a family…"

"More to lose than me, is that it?" Buddy said, bitterly. His breath caught in his throat. How could he possibly tell Dana about the video with that pitiable little girl?

"You've been sliding away for the past year," Dana said. "Now you've finally dragged me down. *Happy?*"

"Don't say that!"

"I've already said it, and you can't take words back," she said, wearily, standing slowly.

"It'll be alright. You'll see," Buddy said, running his fingers through his hair, not realizing that Dana had already left the room.

13

Buddy rose slowly and sleepwalked his way to the kitchen, with only the thought to have a drink. The ice cubes clinked in the rock glass. As he reached for the bottle of Smirnoff, Dana yelled from upstairs, "Atta boy, that's right. Have one for me!" Ears like a bat, Buddy thought sourly. He felt hollow inside and the liquor didn't help any. He listened to Dana pad around upstairs. The toilet flushed, then nothing but silence. He sat numbly in the kitchen. An hour passed. He was an early riser, not used to being up so late. On top of everything, even his schedule was being dicked with. Then he said, "fuck it," loud enough for Dana to hear, walked quickly from the kitchen, and began making his way upstairs to bed. *His* bed in *his* house. He was halfway up the steps when Dana shouted, "No! Don't even *think* of coming up here."

Her voice was brittle and harsh. It stopped Buddy in his tracks. He hesitated, trying to make up his mind before he called out, "Don't give up on me, Dana. This isn't my fault. I don't know how you can blame me. Jesus, I truly do not!"

He waited. The low hum of traffic. His breathing. Nothing else.

"I love you. Do you hear me, I *love* you. *Please* Dana."

Dead quiet. He could feel his heart beating, a sensation so uncomfortable he pressed his hand to his chest. "Don't lose faith in me," he said, not knowing or caring whether she heard.

Buddy stayed on the couch, not sleeping, just dozing off and on, only to wake with dread settling heavily in his gut. At sunup he went into the kitchen and made a pot of coffee. As the room filled with light he sat, trying to find a way out of this trap. *Maybe Russ was right*, he thought, bleakly. *I have to play along with Tyrell, wait until he makes a mistake or maybe just realizes what a fucked up thing he's doing, although that's not likely.* Buddy touched his lip. It was swollen and tender. The coppery taste of blood was still in his mouth. *Dana and I fighting like white trash. It's come to that.* "Christ," he said aloud, wondering whether this was the thing that would finally push Dana away. If he lost her, none of this crap would matter. He'd just pick up and leave. Tyrell didn't know that, yet. It was the coward's way out. But he'd do it if he had to.

The morning floated by, an unhinged limbo. At about noon, the upstairs toilet flushed. Buddy prayed he'd hear Dana come downstairs to talk this out, but his prayers yielded nothing. He was debating having a cold beer when he heard rap music and loud laughter from next door, an explosion of noise on a quiet Sunday afternoon. "Look at this, that fuck's having a party," Buddy whispered, feeling the sudden heat of anger flash up his spine as he walked to the front door and stepped out onto the porch. The driveway next door was zigzagged with cars. Most of them had dark smoked windows. A spiral of grill smoke rose over the fence. It smelled good. Then he heard Tyrell's voice, that high-pitched, forced cool that went through him like a bone saw.

Buddy went back inside, feeling trapped, like a bug in a jar. His hands were trembling. "You're losing control, Buddy boy," he said, kicking off his loafers and climbing the stairs, one cautious step at a time, like a burglar.

He paused before entering the bedroom. Dana was on her side, wrapped in sheets like the victim of a crash he'd set in motion. One half of the room, the side he slept on, was carpeted in green Astroturf. A cup, approximating a golf hole was recessed in the middle. The noise from next door barely seeped in, muffled by the humming air conditioner. Buddy shut the AC and cracked a window, filling the room with party noise, loud laughter, and rap lyrics…"*For the nigga that be talkin' loud an holdin' his dick, talkin' shit, he better lay low; for the bitch that say I shot some shit outta my dick, got her sick, she better lay low.*"

"Nice neighbors we have," said Buddy.

Dana let out a soft moan and pulled a pillow over her head. Buddy closed the window and clicked the air conditioner back on. When he pressed the iPod play button, a jazzy singer drawled laconic lyrics. Then he grabbed six golf balls off his dresser, dropped them on the turf and took up a putter that was leaning against the wall. He lined the balls up and said, "It was my big idea buying this place. I know I talked you into it. Hell, the market was exploding and everybody was flipping houses, so why couldn't we do it? Turn a quick profit, then upgrade. But I waited too long and we got caught in the bubble. *That's* what I'm guilty of."

He set up and stroked the first ball into the cup. "You do not focus your eyes on the ball when you putt. Pick a spot one inch in front of the ball that you want the ball to roll over, and that's where you look," he said, stroking the next ball into the cup. "From six feet, I'm money."

"From beneath the pillow Dana said, "*Money, ha, ha.*"

"Well, that got a rise outta you. It was at my expense, but I'll take anything today," Buddy said, stroking in the third and fourth ball. "I'll give it to your father, Big Frank. He was right." Then, in a deep, throaty voice mocking Dana's father, he said, "'Buddy, a house on a main road in an area called The Junction will eventually end up going colored. Not that I got anything against coloreds, but you might get yourself in trouble before you're finished in that place.' Boy, if ol' Frank only knew."

Dana rose on an elbow and sat up shakily. She looked feverish, as though she'd lost weight. Sweeping her arm in the air, Dana rasped, "Do not mention my father. This, *this* would never happen to him."

Buddy stroked the fifth ball into the cup, straightened and pointed the club at the window. "That's what that son of a bitch wants. *Us* to crumble. Why are you turning on me? I fucking told you what happened!"

"That picture," she screamed, bursting into hot tears. "That picture. Jesus, I can't get it out of my mind, and I'm your *wife*. Who will believe you?"

"You, right now. I need you to stand by me!"

But her expression suddenly went blank and she sobbed into her hands, crying, "How could you do this to me?"

Buddy studied her for a long, strained moment, started to speak, but choked on his words. He took a deep breath and stroked the last ball. It stopped an inch from the cup. He closed his eyes and shook his head. Then, in hurried, angry motions he clicked off the iPod, turned off the AC, opened a window, and walked from the bedroom to the tunes of the party...*Bust on bitches belly, rub it they tummy, lick it, say yummy, then fuck yo' man.*

14

Buddy was on the couch sipping coffee Monday morning when Dana came down the stairs carrying the large briefcase from her years at nursing school. Her hair was pulled back in a ponytail. As she reached the front door, Buddy called, "Running away from home?"

Dana paused and turned her head, unable to conceal a restrained smile. "Not yet," she said.

"Are there plans in the future?" he said, without a hint of sarcasm.

She looked him straight in the eyes. "I'm sorry for last night. But I don't know what else to say, because if I start thinking about that picture I might just go back upstairs to bed. And I can't let that happen because I have sick people to take care of."

"Good luck with your meeting today," he said.

As Dana's car pulled out of the driveway, Buddy did a double take, hearing her stereo blaring as she headed down the road, a Doppler effect, like a fading scream. *So unlike her*, he thought. His next thought was golf; it was caddy's day at the course. Why not? It beats staying home, brooding, he thought. On the fairway he could clear his head. Buddy was throwing his clubs in the trunk of his BMW when the scrape of sneakers on gravel spun him around with a start. Tyrell was an arm's length away, wearing a T-shirt emblazoned with Spike Lee's face. "Check this, my man Buddy. Boy cries poverty and he goin' golfing. Only a white boy's got the mothafuckin' brass for that shit," Tyrell said, dragging the words out syllable by syllable. Buddy slammed the trunk and glared at him.

Tyrell stepped forward reaching out. "Gimme twenty."

"Fuck you," Buddy said, red-faced, twirling his car keys angrily.

Without missing a beat, Tyrell pulled a digital recorder from his pocket and clicked. The little girl's voice and sobs pierced the hot morning air. Tyrell raised it over his head, volume up, doing an inane soft shoe dance in the gravel.

"You're a piece of shit," said Buddy.

"An you're my bitch. An you're beginning to piss me off, child mo...les...*ter*," Tyrell bellowed.

The words had a shocking affect on Buddy. His face lost color, as if everything leached out of him. He took a twenty from his wallet, crumpled it and flung it on the ground.

"Pick that up, mothafucka. Hand it to me like a man," Tyrell said in a low firm voice.

Buddy stormed past him, slipped into his car and blew out of the driveway, spraying gravel and sending Tyrell jumping back and yelling, "Be ready to settle up, mothafucka!"

Two hours later, Tyrell was at Nassau Community College, sitting, as usual, front and center, listening raptly to Professor Jerome Brown's lecture. The course—The Politics of Race and Poverty—had become Tyrell's intellectual Petri dish, each session a cathartic experience. More than once, he'd chided a classmate, usually a younger brother, for not paying attention— texting or even sleeping—during a lecture. It amazed Tyrell. What brother *wouldn't* be charmed, politicized, radicalized, by Dr. Jerome Brown, author, talk show guest, visionary, a brother with street cred who, as a youth, had done an 18-month bid upstate on a pimped-up drug charge. Tyrell was more than charmed. Brown's searing critique of American racism and his "I ain't nobody's bitch" attitude had bored into Tyrell's marrow, given birth to his dreams.

As Professor Brown wound up his lecture, pacing back and forth, speaking in a hard, controlled cadence, Tyrell manically typed notes on his laptop. "Even a cursory examination of history makes it perfectly clear that the pillars of America's white-dominated society are based on a profound hatred of African people. But beware, because American racism has been purposely domesticated and made hygienic for contemporary taste. Therefore, it is incumbent on people of color to understand that property ownership is the difference between lofty aspiration and accomplishment, between poverty and sustained wealth. Moving forward, we must establish a new social contract," Professor Brown said, as the class ended.

As the lecture hall was emptying, Professor Brown called, "Tyrell, got a minute?"

Tyrell walked over, playing it cool but beaming as he gushed, "As always, great lecture, Professor Brown."

"Thanks. Listen brother, call me JB, friends do. Man, I am very impressed with your project outline," he said, staring a bit inquisitively at Tyrell. "Where'd you come up with the idea? It's radical, that's for sure."

Tyrell said, "When you assigned the project, to write an essay creating a justification for reparations, I thought about you comparing white imperialists to a huge mob of looters who felt entitled to our labor, our lives, and our women. Reparations by the American government just seemed like asking the mob for a handout. Jus didn't seem right."

Brown nodded, studied Tyrell, and raised his eyebrows. "The *man* would say you're portraying yourself through this project as a heroic victim of white supremacy, when in reality, you just a whining nigga who needs to get a job and take personal responsibility."

Tyrell said, "Right. So my project took a different approach, creating a brother who takes matters into his own hands, using whatever means necessary to obtain land ownership and establish a new social contract. Jus' like you said."

"Yeah but this wild brother using this young sister in an Internet blackmail scheme, using the white guy as an indentured servant..."

Tyrell broke in excitedly, "No, it ain't really a blackmail scheme, it's Webtribution, all for the cause, like you said, about white slave masters routinely brutalizing black girls and women, justifying their dehumanizing treatment by labeling them sexual savages. I'm turning the tables."

Brown held up his hands. "No man, right, Webtribution, I mean it's cool, I'm looking forward to seeing your paper come together. "Maybe I can get Spike Lee interested in turning it into a script for a movie," Brown added, half-seriously.

"You know the brother, don't you?" said Tyrell.

"Yeah, I know Spike, he cool," said Professor Brown. Then, as an afterthought he added, "You know Tyrell, yours was the last outline to come in and by the way it was written, it looked like the idea for the project just, well, like something happened to inspire it."

"Yeah, something did. I got lucky I guess, JB," said Tyrell with a sly, confidential smile.

"Look, I'm really interested where you're going with this. Gotta tell ya man, I haven't seen passion about a course like this since, well, never. It's very cool to see a brother so engaged."

"This course changed my life," said Tyrell.

15

That afternoon Dana was at Bobbi Holmes' place telling her haltingly about Tyrell and the blackmail scheme. Bobbi listened without saying anything, as if a cold wind had taken her breath away. Dana finally stopped, her body slouched in a soft convulsion of relief like a spring uncoiling. "Some shit, huh Bobbi? It still feels like a waking dream," Dana said quietly.

"My God, Dana, how could this happen?" Bobbi said in a pained voice, placing her hand on Dana's knee.

Dana lifted her head; let it drop like a weight. "Buddy, that's how."

Bobbi paused, weighed her words. "I know what you're saying, but this could happen to anyone today…"

Dana shook her head, cutting her off. "No, Bobbi. I don't believe that. His father had a lot of bad luck. Buddy grew up watching it, one disappointment after the other. Could that be it?" Dana said, a sudden frantic edge in her voice.

"No. No way. Rotten luck isn't inherited. It just happens. But what are you going to do?"

"Right now I just have to work at not falling apart."

"You won't, you're too damn strong," said Bobbi.

"Really? We fought like animals when he showed me that picture."

"Who wouldn't?"

Dana leaned forward, her eyes widened. "I mean physically, Bobbi. I punched him so hard his lip broke open. It was like some sick reality show…" Dana pulled up, a look of disgust on her face. "You know, I hit him once before and it made me sick, the violence made me sick…Did I ever tell you I got pregnant when we were dating? There was alcohol involved, of course. But me, a nurse. Christ, how goddamn stupid."

"It happens," said Bobbi with a knowing grimace.

Dana continued, "I had an abortion. Then, after we'd been married a few years, we wanted a family. Two miscarriages later I found out we were a chromosomal mismatch. One night, after too many Scotches, Buddy made a crass remark about the abortion and the miscarriages, something about his three sons. I lost it and punched him, damn near broke his nose."

"Look Dana, my advice: Go to the police, *now*."

"Police? I don't know," Dana said, her eyes darting about as if looking for an escape route.

"You can't let this warped bastard do this."

"Jesus, the picture, Bobbi. If I didn't know Buddy…"

Bobbi continued evenly, "I'd like to shoot that low-life sonofabitch. I'm the first one to champion the use of the Internet, but this Tyrell is just a common thug with a bigger platform."

"He's not common, and that makes it all sicker," said Dana.

"I'm afraid to ask."

"From what Buddy said, Tyrell is self-righteous about it like he's channeling some weird black revolutionary stuff. It figures. Buddy couldn't even get a regular blackmailer. Another nail in the coffin, *my* coffin," Dana said.

"Don't say that. This is Buddy's load, not yours," Bobbi said.

Dana looked away, thought to herself, then said. "I know, and that makes me sad. I still like watching the way he moves, like he's always on the golf course approaching his next shot. He's the easiest man to talk to, never judging, so easy."

"That's a nice thing to think about. But what about your career? It's about to take off and you have got to make that your focal point," Bobbi said. Then, glancing at her watch she added, "You meet with Roy Hickman from HHS later this afternoon, right? Dana, this is such a terrific opportunity, you can't blow it."

"I know, I know. This thing with Buddy could not come at a worse time. Right now it's tough to focus."

"Look Dana, I know it's easy for me to say, but push the other shit aside for the next hour, please, for *you*," Bobbi said firmly.

Dana was in her office waiting for Roy Hickman, doing Lamaze-like breathing to settle her nerves. She'd freshened up and changed into a cotton dress, trying her best to ride the energy wave of Bobbi's pep talk. Bobbi was right—the one thing in her life that she still had control over was her job, taking care of sick people. If Buddy's karmic place in the world was the golf course, hers was the hospital ward.

Dana glanced at Hickman's CV. Not only was this guy a PhD, he had a law degree from the University of Virginia. Hickman joined the World Health Organization in 1985 as a field supervisor in western Africa, right at the onset of the HIV epidemic. In 1989 he was appointed Chief of the Inter-Country Strategic Support Team in Harare, Zimbabwe, where he oversaw technical and clinical support to strengthen health systems in the southern

African countries. He'd been with Health and Human Services since the new administration took office and appointed him as some sort of infection czar, for lack of a better term. *So, what's this globe-trotting big shot gonna be like*, she was wondering when the door opened and Hickman stepped in, wearing a linen suit that badly needed the attention of an iron. "Roy Hickman," he said, crossing the room and extending his hand.

Nice handshake, syrupy Southern accent, hard blue eyes, about forty or so, no bullshit attitude, Dana assessed as she shook hands and sat across from him.

"May I call you Dana?" he said.

"Yes, please," she said, all at once at ease.

"Great. I'm Roy. Why can't everything work easy like that?" he said, smiling.

"That'd be nice," Dana said. "Boring, but nice," she smiled mischievously.

Hickman caught Dana's eyes with his. "So, let's talk about St. Mary's."

Dana flinched reflexively. "St. Mary's? Sorry, I thought you were interested in my guidelines on nosocomial infection?"

"I am. But St. Mary's is part of it. You headed their neonatal unit, just out of nursing school. That's impressive."

"Mr....I mean, *Roy*, I fell into that position. The head nurse was killed in a crash, so it just happened. It wasn't an easy time. I was young, a bit strong-willed," Dana said, then stopped, realizing Hickman was studying her, waiting for her to finish.

"There'd been a long upward curve of infections in that ward," he said. "Babies were getting sick, dying. When you took over, the babies stopped dying. How?"

Hospital talk. Dana was in her element now and it showed on her face. She waggled her fingernails in the air, a girlish gesture. "I instituted a fingernail policy, cut short, daily inspections. The housekeeping staff was another part of the problem. They just pushed bacteria around and watched the clock. My educational intervention didn't work, so I fired their butts off the ward. Made my nurses do all the cleaning. I led the way, showed them how to treat infectious hazard points that are hard to sterilize. That's when I started using the 10% bleach solution on *everything*. I ran my ward like a military base," Dana said.

Hickman nodded, made a mental note.

"Then you know I was fired," Dana said.

"Yeah. I also know that babies started dying again," Hickman said, promptly.

"The union didn't appreciate my style," Dana said.

"So I heard."

"I have problems here, too," Dana said with an indifferent shrug.

"Unions," Hickman said with a head shake, signaling he was on the same page. Then he sat back, paused for a moment and said, "The new administration has put me in charge of developing a task force on hospital-acquired infections. HAIs are going to be the next mesothelioma and the personal injury lawyers are gonna descend on this like a swarm of locusts. They smell green, billions in class action suits."

"Well certainly most HAIs are preventable. But you gotta kick some ass," Dana said.

"We're fully funded for one year. Well funded. And I've got the leverage to *persuade* institutions to adopt HAI-prevention methodology. I've plotted out the strategy, state-by-state on a worst case basis. It's going to be challenging, to say the least."

Dana leaned forward, touching her face, and asked, "And you want my guidelines?"

"No, I want you," Hickman said.

16

That afternoon, Tyrell was in the small upstairs room he'd staked out as his office. His laptop was open. There were stacks of books and journals everywhere; small tottering edifices to his growing awareness of the history of black struggle. Wearing a Kangol cap turned backwards, checking himself out in the mirror, he did a little foot-shuffle to the rhythmic syncopation of headnodic beats. Tyrell sucked hard on a blunt, held his breath, and exhaled a huge cloud of smoke, smiling at his image.

His spell was broken by a peal of laughter. He spun around. Latreece was behind him, propped in the doorway, watching him pose. She was laughing hard, that saucy laugh of hers he'd come to see as more mean than happy. "Look at my cool-ass nigga!" she said. "Shit, for a second I thought it was Mr. Samuel L. Jackson hisself!"

"What the fuck you doin' home?"

"My afternoon client died," she said, stepping forward and grabbing the blunt. "Mrs. Loretta Longstreet. Her bitch-ass daughter called me when I'm dressing my morning client. Said her mother had stroked out. Didn't sound too upset. White people funny that way," Latreece said. She took a long, satisfying hit, exhaled, took another, started moving to the music, shimmying her hips. Then she stopped and plucked a vial of pills from Tyrell's desk. "What the fuck is this?"

Tyrell snatched it from her hand in a languid motion like a striking snake. "That's my shit, my business."

Latreece folded her arms across her chest, leaned back. "*Really*," she said, bobbing her head forward.

"Yeah, *really*," Tyrell said. "For your information, this shit is Adderall, they give to kids with ADD. But if you ain't got ADD it acts opposite, helps you think. Lots of dudes at college take it during exams. It helps me think."

"Think?" she asked. "About what?"

"All the shit I need to think about, that's what," Tyrell said, his voice thick with anger. He tried to dazzle her, rattling off scattershot sound bites of Dr. Brown's lectures, new social contracts, white privilege, how the brothers today have gone soft, his dark eyes flaring in the afternoon light bouncing off the walls and floor.

Latreece didn't try to follow, she just let him rant and said, "I don't know what the fuck you talkin' about. But we gotta talk. This shit is getting' way outta hand."

"I ain't got time for this shit, Latreece, so get it out girl," Tyrell said.

She frowned. "OK, *Tyrell*. For starters, what up with my baby, huh? I come home, she says 'Daddy's upstairs.' Daddy? You ain't her daddy. She used to call you Ty, now it's Daddy?"

"You should be glad I'm here, and not her *real* daddy. We close, that's all."

"Since this," she said, pointing towards Buddy's house, "that's when you got close."

Tyrell stepped toward her, flaring his nostrils. "That it? That's what we gotta talk about?"

She held her ground. "You gettin' crazy on me. Is it the pills? Or is all this shit what that professor been fillin' your head with? What up with that shit? What about me?"

"This is about you! Don't you get it?"

"I guess I don't."

"It's about makin' our own place in the world. Gettin' respect. Building a community for black folks," Tyrell said, with a preacher's sing-song intonation. He grabbed her wrist and towed her over to the laptop, jabbing his finger at the screen. "See that? That was a black revolutionary movement called MOVE."

"Those some funky-ass lookin' niggas," Latreece said. "What that brother holdin'? A *live* chicken?"

"That's John Africa," said Tyrell, "he founded MOVE, a bunch a revolutionary naturalists in the ghetto. See that shit. They were makin' their own place. No mothafuckin' whites."

"Hmmm," Latreece grunted.

"They were fire-bombed by racist police. America," Tyrell said solemnly.

Still fixated on the chicken, Latreece said, "Shit. That dumbass never hear of Kentucky Fried?"

Letting the remark slide, Tyrell said, "We gotta token black president but the same shit's been happenin' for two hunert and thirty mothafuckin' years. We got no movement, nothin' goin' on."

Latreece squinted at the screen, then she flashed her eyes at Tyrell and blinked, as if trying to get a better focus. "What the fuck those niggas got to do with us?"

Tyrell looked stunned. He touched the screen, the image of John Africa under his finger.

"What do you want, Latreece, huh? What the fuck do you want?"

She put her hands on her hips. "Tyrell, I am a hard workin' woman. I bitch about it. But I'm good at what I do. Now, I don't know where all this stuff is goin'…"

"What the fuck you want, bitch!?"

"*Bitch?*" she screamed, coming at him.

"Momma, *momma*," Tashanda called from downstairs. "I'm hungry."

The tiny voice stopped Latreece in her tracks.

Calling, "OK Baby, Momma's comin.'"

Latreece moved to within an inch of Tyrell's face, her ghetto gold hoop earrings glinting. "I wanna big-ass flat-screen TV an a new couch to park my ass on after work so I can watch *American Idol*, in my own house, like you promised, *Tyrell*. That's what the fuck I want."

Latreece turned on her heel. The only movement in the room was the rise and fall of Tyrell's ribs as he took deep, angry breaths.

17

Buddy looked skyward and squinted at a huge billowing cloud, dreaming. *If I could only settle all my scores, all my worldly problems here.* Even with his world turned upside down, his wife wearing the look of a woman on the verge of leaving him, all that and two holy tons of shit more, he still played scratch golf. He was looping the course with LT, who shot a pretty nice game himself. But Buddy's cool mastery, his effortless swing, that monk-like concentration, left LT shaking his head as Buddy putted out on the eighteenth hole.

"My man Buddy, the only time I don't think of pussy is watching you play. Man, you should be on the tour. Lemme tellya, it ain't too late, my brother," said LT, pulling a can of Miller from his bag and cracking it. Buddy just smiled. "Yes it is."

As Buddy walked to his car behind the caddy yard, Brad Mueller, the club's pro scooted up in a cart, one foot on the dash, his Nike cap, cocked backwards on his head, chewing gum with aggressive energy. He was a few years younger than Buddy, well-built, good-looking in a bland sort of way.

"Hey Graves, how'd you hit 'em today?"

Buddy popped his trunk and stowed his clubs before turning.

"Not bad."

"So, you lined up for the club tournament?"

"Nope, Macgregor hasn't posted the list yet," Buddy said, closing the trunk.

"I'm playing with Weinberg's foursome. Izzy loves to win," Mueller said.

"Who doesn't," said Buddy, with a tight smile. *That fuck really thinks he's cock of the walk.*

"I asked Macgregor for LT. That nigger's funny as shit."

"Remember to call him nigger to his face, he loves that."

Mueller snorted, "Well I sure as shit can't have *you* carrying our bags."

"And why's that, Brad?"

"C'mon Graves. Izzy Weinberg doesn't want you dogging his wife," said Mueller. "You best leave that kosher gash to me."

Ron Piana, Randi Londer Gould

Buddy put his hand on the door handle, telling himself to open it and slide into the car. He started, then paused and said, "How's your old man hittin' 'em these days, Brad?"

Mueller glared at Buddy. He started the cart and popped the brake.

"Him being an ex-golf pro and all," Buddy said, smiling innocently.

The remark stopped Mueller cold. "You just can't stop congratulating yourself for beating him," Brad snapped. "That one time. In that one tournament."

"Yeah, but I think it really got into his head, a teenager showing him how it's done. He really wasn't the same after that, was he? I guess some guys get mind-fucked and just can't seem to shake it loose," Buddy said with mock sadness, opening the car door.

Mueller's face flushed red. "You're a fuckin' loser Graves," he snarled. "A fuckin' asshole, dirtbag, piece a shit, fuckin' loser," he said, squirting away in the cart.

❧ ❧

Buddy drove to Finnegan's Pub to meet Russ Dunn. Russ had left a message on his cell, saying he wanted to see him and that he had a plan for Buddy's problem. Buddy had little to no faith in Russ's plan, whatever it was, but considering all his other terrific options, he figured he'd show the courtesy of listening. Besides, he could use a few pints before going home to Dana.

Russ was at the same table as the last time they'd met, and Buddy wondered aloud if Russ was renting office space at the bar. Russ hoisted a pint and smiled just before it touched his lips, "Well, we all pay rent for every space on this earth, in some way or another."

A pint was waiting for Buddy. He sat and drained half. Dispensing with the usual handshake and the "hello Mr. Dunn" greeting, Buddy said, "So?"

"Man, aren't we in a bear of a mood. Tough day at the office?"

Buddy tilted the rest of the pint down his throat, smacked his lips. "Nah. Some guys just can't let the past go."

"Wanna elaborate?"

"Nope. So, you called me."

"I did," said Russ, nodding thoughtfully.

Buddy signaled for a round, saw the familiar look on Russ's face, braced himself.

"Did you ever have a lap dance, Buddy?"

70

Buddy smiled sadly. "Russ, *Russ*. Christ, I'm in the southbound lane driving north, and you're asking me about a fucking lap dance."

Russ drifted. "It's the most intimate of experiences, especially with a stranger looking directly into your eyes. It's the lack of penetration that drives the intimacy. I've had insomnia for three years. There's a taste in my mouth that won't wash away."

Buddy looked at his friend, thought seriously about getting up and leaving.

The pints arrived.

"You were the only one who'd listen," Russ said, lifting his glass. "The others listened at first, but you know how it is in America. You're supposed to buck up and move on. After a while, I was the dark cloud no one wanted around. Except you, Buddy. You always listened. You're the easiest man in the world to talk to."

"Yeah, that looks good on the resume: easy guy to talk to," Buddy said, distractedly.

"Well it should, because it means something, it gives value to people," Russ said, his eyes beginning to well up as he continued. "Here's the enduring mystery of how I drowned in self-made oblivion…"

Buddy's mind settled somewhere between Russ's words. He felt himself being dragged away by an undertow. Then Russ tossed a business card on the table and said, "Plan A. We need time, Buddy, time to think, time to let this maniac screw up."

Buddy picked the card up and looked at Russ, "What the hell is this?"

"Me," said Russ.

"You're now a real estate developer?"

"Yes, for the immediate future."

Buddy shook his head. "Why do I feel like this is gonna be an epic fuckup?"

Russ shrugged off the remark and explained his plan over three more pints of ale. Except for the slight shaking of his hands, Russ seemed in control of himself, more so than usual.

Buddy considered what he'd said for a long moment. "And what exactly is this gonna do for me?"

"Time, buys you time."

"Time, that's it?"

"For now, that's all we have."

"Jesus, I don't know, I just don't know any more if I'm even fucking capable of making a rational decision," Buddy said to himself, letting out a huge breath.

Russ rubbed his ears, scratched his nose. "Buddy, there's more to it than that," he said.

"More? I must have missed something."

"The nuances, Buddy, the nuances will throw this guy off his game."

"Nuances? Game? This is not a fucking game, Russ!"

Russ looked around, made a *shhhh* sound and said, "So when's the best time to catch this bird?"

"In the morning. That way he might not be stoned off his gourd and you've got an even chance of being sober," Buddy said without a hint of humor. "Please do not set off this crazy fuck. He's like friggin' Magua."

Russ winked and gave a thumbs up. "Buddy, this is Russ you're talking to."

18

Buddy pulled into his driveway shortly after three. *Time*, that's what Russ was offering Buddy; a silly scheme that just didn't make sense. He knew Russ would do anything for him, but trusting a man who was committing slow-motion suicide by alcohol was simply trading desperation for an illusion of control.

Getting out of the car, Buddy saw the old black guy across the street mowing his lawn. It was sunless, humid, and pushing ninety degrees. A bead of sweat trickled down Buddy's face as he watched the old man stop every few feet to pick up the trash thrown from passing cars. McDonald's wrappers, cigarette packs, empty beer cans. Thin as a rake, bent and huffing, Eugene Freyerson moved slowly, painfully, like someone thawing from a deep freeze. *Jesus, that ancient fucker cares enough about his little sun-scorched piece of the planet to risk heat stroke*, Buddy thought.

He glanced down the road. Unkempt houses, for-sale signs everywhere. Ground Zero for the bomb of despair. Buddy shook his head and went inside.

He was half drunk on ale, so calibrating his consumption-to-Dana's-arrival-time, Buddy figured he'd finish the job, have two shots of Jack, leaving just enough time to shower, gargle with Listerine, and prepare dinner. He'd do a pasta alla puttanesca: fistfuls of garlic, capers, anchovies, all booze-breath killers. As he was running down the list in his head, Buddy noticed the voice-mail light flashing on the answering machine.

"Hi Buddy, it's me, just wanted to let you know I won't be home for dinner. Sorry, but the interview went well. Dr. Hickman wanted to carry on the discussion over dinner. I'll fill you in when I get home...Love you."

Buddy played the message three times, analyzing Dana's voice, her inflections, crazily trying to gauge any the loss of intimacy. The words, "love you," sounded like an afterthought. Who was this Dr. Hickman? A guy or a girl? There was a quivering intimacy in Dana's voice. Waves of sadness rolled over Buddy. "Where are you?" he said aloud. He opened a can of anchovies, pricked a salty filet with the tine of his fork and dangled it in the air. "Fuck pasta alla puttanesca."

෩෨

That night, at nine-thirty in Scotland, a cold sea-spray pelted the floor-to-ceiling windows of the Presidential Suite in the Old Course Hotel. Birch logs crackled in the outsized fireplace. Izzy was in the main sitting room, watching the fire. He was wearing a burgundy paisley silk robe, an unlit cigar in his hand. The butler had just finished laying out a platter of smoked salmon and was twirling the bottle of Dom in the ice bucket. A large Charles Rennie MacKintosh-inspired table dominated the room on which an open laptop and several piles of bound leather folders were neatly arranged.

"Shall I pour the wine, sir?" said the butler.

Izzy looked over. "No, thank you. That's all."

As the butler closed the door, Courtney appeared wearing a lush white terrycloth robe. Her hair was damp. She clicked off her mobile phone and slipped it into the pocket.

Izzy watched her. "Everything OK?"

"Yup, just checked in at home. Big sisters can be overbearing," she said with a shrug and a wry smile, combing her hair back with her fingers.

"Sure she means well," said Izzy. "On the other hand, overbearing's usually a ruse for jealousy."

Courtney gave a little nod, acknowledging Izzy's ability to always see between the lines.

"So, is big sis jealous?" asked Izzy, motioning for Courtney to sit as he got up to open the champagne.

She sat, crossed her legs, and cinched her robe. "She's married to a teacher. Nice guy. They have a three-year-old and a five-year-old. She loves the guy I dated at Duke. His name was Derek Quigley, an All American lacrosse player. Derek's big dream was to be a lacrosse coach. Sis thinks I should be part of his dream," said Courtney.

"It'd make *her* comfortable," Izzy said, uncorking the champagne with a soft pop.

Courtney gave an exaggerated nod. "So, about tomorrow."

Izzy filled the flutes, looked at the fire, the windows, Courtney. He kept looking at her and seeing new things. "You've been studying your tush off. Tomorrow, you go shopping, spend the afternoon in the spa. I need you relaxed."

Courtney stood and strode to the table. As she tapped the keyboard on her MacBook, a stylish PowerPoint presentation popped up on the screen. A rotating globe of the Earth appeared, zigzagged with connecting lines, like the veins of an immense circulatory system.

She sipped her champagne and said, "Our presentation is double-checked, the AV guy has been prepped and re-prepped until he's about to scream 'leave me the hell alone, bitch,' and I've reserved the Macallister Room from six until whenever we feel like leaving. Presentation, cocktails, dinner, then I suppose you men will smoke your heads off."

Good," said Izzy. "Come on, let's have a little nosh."

Courtney made small *mmm* sounds eating the smoked salmon, which Izzy found charmingly young and intimate. After they finished, she held out her flute and said, "So Izzy, how did you get here? Knowing that would help me."

Izzy filled her glass, watching the bubbles as they fizzed up into a cloud that threatened to overflow the rim, but settled back down at the last moment.

"How'd I get here?" he said, picking up a shard of leftover salmon with his fingers.

"Yes."

He squinted slightly as if making a mental calculation. "You're bold. People don't usually ask me questions like that," he said, with a just enough sternness to bring color to Courtney's face.

After a moment he said, "Cows."

"Cows?" Courtney repeated softly.

"Beef cattle. My uncle Louie was a rancher out in California. He took me on. I liked the hard work. And I saw opportunity. Fast-food burger joints were starting to explode. I had a knack for deals and engineering. I invented a system to process the cattle a lot quicker. There used to be hundreds of slaughter houses, in the US. But I made some deals, and now there are about six. You can thank me for that. But I'd advise you to stay away from ground beef. It's loaded with shit," Izzy laughed.

Courtney folded her legs up, shaking her head and laughing to herself.

"Business is about filling needs. Deals are about human nature, which is all based on varying degrees of dominance and submission. *That* will come in handy tomorrow. Anyway, after fucking up the country's meat supply, I got out of the cattle business. I saw a better opportunity. Old people. You know how many pills old people take? I broke into pharma. Again, perfect timing. My stock options blew off the charts. I sat on the boards of four major companies and parlayed those positions into nursing homes. All the time I'm doing the lobbyist schmooze in DC, wining and dining and greasing those phony fucks. Now I have senators on my speed dial, and Medicare and Medicaid are my piggy banks. Weinstein Associates owns and operates a hundred and thirty-eight nursing homes from Maine to Florida, from low-income to luxury. They're cash-fucking-cows," Izzy said.

He leaned over, refilled Courtney's flute, then his, clipped the end of his cigar and lit it.

"I've been working this deal with the Chinks for five years now. They tend to extend negotiations to gain advantage and they won't deal until they see a strong relationship. They want this project for several reasons. Due to many kinds of mercantilist policies, China runs by far the world's largest balance of payments surpluses. These cannot be spent at home and are too large to put anywhere other than the United States. For now. Their world is shaped by the interaction of *yin,* which is passive, and *yang,* which is tough, active. Right now they consider the US very *yin.* They laugh about us becoming the France of the twenty-first century. That interpreter, Lo? He's our guy. He gives me all the dirt."

"I'm surprised they *let* him be our guy," said Courtney.

"William Lo comes from a very influential family in China. Surnames are important as is patriarchy," Izzy said. "It's a sexist society, so including you in this is an oddity to them. But your part of the presentation is the DC connection. Just make them feel like you know every important schmuck on the Hill *very* well."

"*Very* well," Courtney said.

Izzy winked. "See Courtney, like everyone else in the world, the Chinks want to be like us. They won't say it, but they do. And they want my game-changing project—as long as we convince them we're not France." Then, looking her in the eyes, he said, "OK, my turn. What brings *you* here?"

Without a second's hesitation, Courtney replied, "A father with a 154 IQ who speaks four languages and ended up as a waiter in a German restaurant, and he hates Germans."

Izzy nodded, a big slow movement, made an O with his lips, and pursed out a perfect smoke ring that drifted over Courtney's head. "And you sure you don't want to be part of Derek's big dream?"

Courtney lifted her hand as if catching the expanding ring of smoke and said with a teasing iridescence in her eyes, "Does it look like I do?"

19

The front door opened, then clicked shut. Buddy lifted his head and glanced at the clock; it was just past three a.m. He heard Dana kick her shoes off at the bottom of the staircase. On the way up she tripped, said "fuck," under her breath, then tripped once more near the top. Buddy reached toward the night table, grabbed a sip of water, and popped a mint into his mouth. Her silhouette appeared in the doorway. She stopped as if thinking something over. By the time her knees touched the bed, all she had on was a pair of bright white panties. She slipped under the covers.

"You're not asleep," she said.

Buddy turned over to face her.

"You've been drinking," he said.

"You too. That mint gave it away, Einstein," she replied, a bit thick-tongued.

"But *I* wasn't driving."

"Me either, I took a car. Dr. Hickman expensed it for me."

"Wow. Well?"

She reached under the covers, said, "*Wow,*" with a throaty laugh, sliding over, leaning in so their eyes got close. He smelled drink on her. She moved his hand onto her hip. Even though she was still slender, her curves had more flesh than when they'd first met.

"So what about the interview with this Hickman, a he or she?" Buddy asked, an unexpected tear pooling in his eye.

She sighed vodka-tonic breath into his mouth. "Hickman's a he and he offered me a job. Christ, I didn't expect that."

"Congratulations. Did you take it?"

"We have to talk."

"You talked all night with him."

"I meant us, *we* have to talk."

"So talk."

"Not now," she said, breathing harder. "He asked if I had any skeletons in my closet, joked about whether I was married to the mob."

Buddy didn't say anything. He felt he should, but his mind had drifted, touching Dana, smelling her. Even knowing that she'd been out drinking with another man, he felt detached from all the dirt of the here and now. He was a thousand miles away, thinking about Dana before all this had happened, wondering how much it had already changed her.

"Oh, Buddy," Dana said, letting a few long seconds tick away. Then she held his head tightly and kissed him and almost instantly her panties were off. Buddy heard himself gasping. Dana whispered his name in his ear as she grabbed his hands, pinned his wrists, climbed over him and spread her legs, telling him to fuck her, saying she needed it, that sometimes girls just need to get laid. As they joined and fell into a steady rhythm she whispered into his shoulder, "*I'm scared.*"

At ten o'clock on Tuesday morning, Buddy and Dana were still in their love-rumpled bed. Groaning, she slipped out of bed, shuffled to the bathroom and snatched the aspirin bottle from the medicine cabinet. Scooping water from the faucet in her cupped hand, Dana swallowed two pills and mumbled she was going in late. "Hey," she said coming back into the bedroom, standing next to his side of the bed, "why aren't you at the course?"

"I've come down with something," Buddy said, stretching.

"What? You're not a malingering…"

"*Shhhh…*" Buddy said, cupping her warm breasts in his hands. She went slack, then stiffened just a bit, a reflex that stirred him.

"You got lucky last night with a boozed up girl."

Her unwashed scent made him restless with desire. He pulled her toward him, kissed her neck, and moved a hand down across her belly. She clamped her legs shut, held him at bay for a few moments, and then relented. As they found that perfect fit, a car swung into the driveway next door. Russ Dunn stepped out wearing a $2,900 Canali suit that'd been mothballed for three years. He cleared his throat, a moist guttural sound. Then he stiffened his spine and marched up to Tyrell's front door.

Rap music throbbed from inside. Russ mentally gauged the decibel level and banged three times with appropriate force. Standing there in the heat, he visualized a frosty pint of Bass Ale, that first-of-the-day beer buzz. Then the door popped open and there was Tyrell, wild-eyed, reeking of dope.

Russ smiled. Just as he said hello Tyrell snapped, "Don't want nothin.'"

"Mr. Walker," Russ started.

"An what up with bangin' a man's door like that?"

"Sorry sir, I didn't see a..."

Tyrell lurched out, reaching up to a nearly invisible button on the door jam, triggering an anemic *ding-dong*. "You gotta look, man."

As Tyrell reeled himself back in, Russ snapped his business card out. "I'm Russell Dunn, real estate developer and independent contractor with HUD, Mr. Walker. Can we talk?"

Tyrell glared, rasping away at Russ's booze-starved nerves. He snatched the card irritably. "OK, what?"

"Well, I'd like to discuss a housing opportunity..."

"I don't own this place," Tyrell said, closing the door.

Russ shouted through the door, "But your neighbor, Mr. Graves, said you were informally negotiating to buy it. We've made an offer on *his* house."

The door swung open. "Say what?" said Tyrell, raising one eyebrow. Before Russ got a word out, Tyrell explained that talking business required a trip up to his office.

Russ followed Tyrell upstairs into the small room where an arctic blast of refrigerated air made him shiver. "You could hang meat in here," Russ joked, as Tyrell motioned to a chair. Russ sat on the edge of his seat, transfixed by the stacks of books and magazines; a laptop open to a video of the burning of LA, the Rodney King beatdown-inspired uprising; posters of Malcolm X, Eldridge Cleaver, Stokely Carmichael, Mumia Abu-Jamal; an audiotape of Huey Newton railing against the prison-industrial complex. He had the feeling that this eclectic mass of propaganda had been assembled almost overnight, like a shark frenzy of black radicalism. And another peculiar thing: cotton balls and empty pill bottles littered the desktop and floor. *This dude is definitely overmedicated,* Russ thought.

Tyrell flipped on some Bob Marley, lit a huge blunt that filled the room with sweet ganja smoke. He took a rib-cage expanding hit and jet-streamed the smoke into Russ's face. Inhaling reflexively, Russ felt a definite buzz. "Mr. Walker, I *do* work with the government," he said with a goofy smile.

Tyrell grinned, showing lots of teeth. "You gonna bust me, mista government man?"

A nervous chuckle. "Don't get me wrong, Mr. Walker, I'm not connected with law enforcement, I'm simply saying..."

"Cut out that 'Mr. Walker' bullshit. My name's Tyrell!"

Russ cleared his throat, looked into Tyrell's bloodshot eyes. "Well Tyrell, as I said, I'm a real estate developer, working with housing and urban development..."

Tyrell flung his left hand in the air, sucked the blunt with his right, and blew another direct hit into Russ's face. "I know all that, but please inform me precisely about your dealings with Buddy Graves as they pertain to me. In other words, what up with that mothafucka?"

"For the sake of background, please bear with me," Russ said. Then, as the Thai-stick high intensified, he paused with his mouth hanging open. Marley wailed on about revolution. Angela Davis's eyes popped off a poster, all whites, big as half dollars. Huey Newton's crazed Black-Marxist rhetoric looped in Russ's head, his mouth still agape.

"What the fuck you doin?" snapped Tyrell. "Talk!"

"Oooheee, I'm high as a mothafucka," said Russ.

Tyrell snorted, grinning wickedly. Their eyes stayed locked as Russ continued, "So, I'm in charge of a regional initiative that the administration has launched. It's actually a more radical form of the old empowerment zone model, which I'm sure you're familiar with."

Tyrell gave an affirmative nod. "So, you wanna put a bunch a niggers in these houses, that right?"

"Well, I don't use the N word, but yes, that's part of the grander scheme. We've targeted this area as a possible model for the project called the BOSP, which is an acronym for Black Opportunity and Solidarity Project," said Russ.

"What about that mothafucka Cho?"

Russ's mind froze. Tyrell pinned him with a hard stare. "Yes, ah, Cho, well we'll get to Cho in a few..."

"That Korean mothafucka owns all these houses, so what you gonna do with him?"

Russ, was flooded with relief. *I can pull this off,* he said firmly to himself. "Well, like all the rest of the predatory speculators that got caught in the housing bubble, Mr. Cho's investments have gone underwater, and he'll be amenable to unloading his assets at a market-adjusted price. The housing crash has, in effect, helped create this opportunity for us."

"So, that mothafucka Cho is takin' it in the ass."

"In a manner of speaking, yes."

"So what's your point?"

Russ explained the project, Tyrell's putative position as a project leader, the monthly stipend he would earn, the added dividends and perks as the project demonstrated growth and development assets, and how, once and for all, they could address the inequalities within the system that generations of institutional racism had produced. Tyrell was mesmerized by Russ's meandering, ass-kissing discourse. "And what about that mothafucka next door?" he asked.

Russ hesitated thoughtfully. "Seeing that Mr. Graves's house is on the market, we made an offer; however, he said he was engaged in some kind of preliminary talks with you and was reluctant to entertain our bid."

"Don't worry about that shit, I'll *un*-entertain his ass if it means gettin' more brothers and sisters in here," Tyrell said.

"So, you have a history with Mr. Graves that might serve the project's interest?"

Tyrell's eyes burned straight through Russ. "You could say that. But our man Buddy, he got a bad attitude."

"Well, from our brief meeting I did get the feeling that Mr. Graves is a nattering nabob of negativism," Russ blurted.

"What the fuck? Nattering *who* bob?"

Russ scrambled for an improv, then pointed to a poster on the wall. "Yes, you know, the term that Brother Cleaver coined to describe the white power structure during the period of the silent majority, which was code for the underlying racist cult in mainstream America."

Tyrell tripped over his tongue for a moment, then snapped, "Yeah, right, that mothafucka is one nattering nabob of negativity, but his ass is mine an I'll keep the punk short-leashed."

"Your first obligation is to demonstrate that as a project leader, you'll take initiative to begin the area renovation," Russ said.

Tyrell swept his hand around the room. "You know, it's white-bread mothafuckas like you who made all this shit necessary. I hope there's a special Hell, just for white fools like you."

"Well, believe it or not, Tyrell, I'm on your side," Russ grinned.

20

Dana did a double-take when she answered the front door and found Russ Dunn standing there in an outsized suit, smiling at her, moon-faced and sweaty, an apparition from the past.

"Hello Dana. Long time," he said, squeezing the words through pursed lips.

"Well, hello Russ," she said. "You practicing law again? I mean…the suit."

"No, not exactly, just doing a little day trading of sorts," he said, his voice dying in this throat.

Dana sniffed the air. "Have you been smoking pot?"

"No, but unfortunately Mr. Walker was, and I got caught downwind," he said, squeezing his lips around each word.

"Jesus, Russ, why are you talking like that?"

"I don't want him to read my lips," he said, his eyes bulging as he motioned toward Tyrell's house with his head.

Dana stepped back, folded her arms, started to respond, and then stopped, letting out an exasperated sigh. She opened the door with a snappish jerk. "Buddy's in the shower. You wanna wait?"

"Just give him this, please," he said, pulling out a business card.

As she took the card, their hands touched. "You look good, Dana," Russ said, turning quickly and walking to his car.

☙❧

They were at the kitchen table. Buddy was fresh from the shower, hair wet, the towel wrapped around his waist. He'd hurried down without dressing when Dana called up to him in that stern head-nurse tone he'd come to dread.

She read the note scrawled on the back of the business card: *Spoke with Walker about Plan A—meet me at Finnegan's one pm*. She made a blowing sound and said, "OK, what's this about Russ being a real estate developer?"

"It's a way to hold off that madman we've got living next door; I've already told you that."

"I know you have, but it's making my head hurt thinking that after all we've been through—all we're *still* going through—you'd get involved with that washed out drunk, Russ. *Jesus,* Buddy."

"Russ was a top-notch lawyer. He's had a hard life."

"Getting a lap-dance wearing a cocaine mustache while his pregnant wife is dying in a car wreck, *hmmm*. Somehow my sympathy runs short with your friend Russ Dunn," she said.

Buddy looked at her, then turned to the window. "That's how you sum him up, like that. He suffers every day of his life. I can't even imagine it."

Dana glanced at the clock. It was very quiet. "We have our own problem, Buddy. What are you going to do about Tyrell?"

"I don't know. Right now I just want to stall that bastard," he said without conviction.

Dana considered something for a long moment. "I was offered a job. I wanted to talk to you about it. But now I don't. This nightmare of yours is sucking the life out of me," she said.

Buddy saw her bottom lip quiver. He reached over and clasped her hand. She pulled away.

"Tell me about the job, Dana, please."

"There's nothing to tell. Drop it."

"I'm trying my best to stay on an even keel here, OK?" he said.

She laughed out loud, a cruel, forced laugh.

"Tell me about the fucking job, *please*," he said, slapping the table.

"Do you think you can predict what this guy next door will do?" she asked.

Buddy pictured Tyrell walking into the house and suddenly felt panicked.

"No, of course you can't," she said. "I was offered a position on a government infection control pilot program, a hundred and sixty thousand a year. But I can't take it Buddy. They do extensive background checks. That wouldn't be a problem if it weren't for…" Suddenly there were tears in her eyes.

"Dana, please, c'mon. My God, I'm so proud of you. Take it, please," Buddy said, leaning forward.

She wiped at her eyes with her hand. "Take it? What happens when that picture of you and the girl goes viral on the Internet, when you get arrested, or when we lose our house? My husband's a child molester. How do I explain that to Hickman? Should I tell him to speak to Russ Dunn, huh Buddy?" she said, rising from the table.

"Child molester. Child molester. Don't ever say that again, and Christ I mean *never!*" Buddy shouted. Then, as Dana walked from the kitchen, he held his head in his hands and called, "Dana, *Dana*, what the hell is happening here?"

She stopped. "We're falling apart Buddy. That's what's happening here."

"No, no we're not. I won't let that happen."

She took a step, then stopped. "You don't have control over this Buddy."

"Take the job."

"Mind the time, you don't want to be late to Finnegan's," she said sarcastically.

Buddy felt the veins on his forehead expand. "Take the job Dana."

Her mouth twisted. "You damn right I will," she said.

21

In the din of Finnegan's lunch crowd, Russ's voice was just part of the background buzz in Buddy's drifting thoughts.

Russ shifted his weight in the chair. "Buddy, you're not paying the slightest attention to what I'm telling you."

Buddy looked at Russ, lifted his pint, took a long sip and replied, "Yes I am. But I got a bad feeling about this."

"If you don't watch out," Russ said, framing his words carefully, "that attitude will make this one sorry self-fulfilling fuck of a prophecy."

Buddy smiled sadly, "Listen man, I really appreciate what you're trying to do, but it just doesn't seem like it will work. Nothing does. It's like Dana said this morning: I don't have control over this."

"We can slow the pace. This guy is a train wreck in the making, believe me."

"Yeah, and I'm a passenger on that train," Buddy said, kneading his forehead.

Ignoring the comment, Russ signaled for another round, and said, "And by the way, your wife is still a fine piece of ass, if you don't mind my saying so."

Buddy looked into his empty pint. "This shit is like the last straw. I'm gonna lose her, Russ, I just know it."

For an instant the background chatter paused, as if everyone in the bar was taking a deep breath. And in that quiet pocket Russ's voice boomed. "No you're not; don't even consider that! My God, three years ago…"

Buddy couldn't handle another sobbing, lap-dance replay so he quickly intervened. "OK, Russ, so go on, Plan A, what do you have?"

"You've led something of a charmed life up until about a year ago, haven't you?" Russ asked, out of nowhere. Buddy noticed a sudden cold, sobriety to his tone.

"I really don't know how charmed it's been, except for Dana. I've made my share of mistakes."

"You know, Buddy, in my dreams—which occur *nightly* my friend—everything is so dark, I can't even see my hands. I stumble around trying to find my way to a voice that's calling for help. I know the voice, and I know that I'll never be able to reach it."

"I'm sorry, Russ. Christ I'm sorry about everything. That's what I am. Fucking sorry."

"Me too, that's why I'm going to pack up and head to my trailer in Texas soon."

"That's where you're gonna shoot yourself, out on the porch, after your old dog dies?"

Russ nodded.

"When?"

"Soon as this mess you're in gets settled."

The beers arrived. Russ made a blessing sign with his hand over the pint glasses.

"Christ, this just keeps getting better," Buddy said with a heavy sigh. "OK, about Plan A."

Buddy listened with a kind of perverse curiosity as Russ told him the spiel he gave Tyrell about HUD and the development plan. "I promised him money, if he could deliver as project leader. I put him in charge of alleviating you of your house."

Buddy jerked his head up. "You did *what*?"

"Don't worry. It's all bullshit. I told you: we need to stall him."

"You told this fuck to take my house from me?" Buddy turned his head and said, as if talking to an invisible person next to him, "What the fuck did I do? I thought it couldn't get worse. I get involved with Russ Dunn. Now it's worse. Good job Buddy, you fucking asshole."

"Hey, hey, it's all bogus," Russ said. "Means nothing. It just gives this wingnut what he needs. Self worth, a mission."

"A mission?" Buddy said, turning his head and blinking hard several times as if to regain focus.

"Don't worry, Buddy boy. We'll keep him engaged in his lunacy until he fucks up."

"I'm *part* of his lunacy, you fucking maniac! Jesus *Christ*."

"Well, one thing I told him he has to do as project leader is to start cleaning up the neighborhood, and that's a good thing for you, right?" Russ said. Then with a half-hearted smile, he added sheepishly, "Don't be surprised if he presses you into service, so to speak."

Buddy's face went red. He began to stand but Russ grabbed his wrist.

"Buddy, I know it sounds strange, convoluted, but…"

"Con-fucking-voluted? It's *stupid*," Buddy snapped, ripping his hand away. "Dana was right. I can fuck up my life all by myself; I don't need any help from you."

Russ's face crumpled, and for a second Buddy thought he was going to cry. He sat back down, shaking his head. "Russ, I'm sorry, OK? I know you're trying to help, but this plan, it's just fucking weird, man. It doesn't do anything except…" Buddy stopped, shrugged, and chuckled to himself in resignation. "I'm circling the drain, here."

Russ pursed his lips, thought for a second, then said, "Buddy, it does one thing. It keeps that picture and that video off the Internet. As long as this guy thinks you are still under his thumb and he needs you to help him realize his fucking grand dream, he won't destroy your life." Russ leaned closer and said in a hushed tone, "Right now that's the only thing preventing you from being publicly accused as a child molester."

Buddy exchanged a charged glance with Russ. The girl's face, the feel of her damp skin, her quivering voice, flashed in his head, and for a moment he thought he was going to vomit.

22

Later that afternoon when Buddy got home from Finnegan's, Dana was gone. He looked at the notepad by the refrigerator—their little message space. It was blank. He stared at it, a deep stinging sensation in his chest. He thought about their morning love-making session: Dana's passion for sex, that rushing physical release, undiminished, even by all the crazy shit that was going down. Afterwards, as their bodies were laced together, Buddy had asked if she still loved him. She leaned into him for a heartbeat, hesitated, and said yes. *She's pulling away, inch by inch and there's nothing I can do*, he thought miserably.

He checked the answering machine. One message. *It's gotta be from Dana*, he thought, pushing the button, his heart pounding.

"Hi Buddy, this is Elaine. I missed you today at the course. Anyway, I hope you're feeling better. I need to talk to you about something. When you have a free minute, if you could give me a call on my mobile it would be great. 555-6898."

Buddy replayed the message again. Then he made himself a drink and called Elaine.

"This is Elaine," she answered on the first ring.

"Hey, it's Buddy."

"One sec," she said. Buddy heard a door close.

"Hi Buddy. Feeling better?" she said, slightly out of breath.

"Oh yeah. Quick recovery."

There was a pause. He heard her walking, breathing.

"Sorry about that. Uh, Jasmine's in the next room," she said in a partially muffled voice.

"It's OK."

"Anyway, there's something I'd like to talk about with you. For obvious reasons it's gotta be before Izzy gets back from his business trip this Thursday."

Buddy hesitated. "I really don't think that's a good idea, Elaine."

"Please, I need to run something by you," she said.

The word "need" spoken by a woman tripped Buddy's switch.

"Alright," he relented.

"Good. Can you meet me tomorrow night in the Harbor Club bar, say seven? Does that work?" she asked quickly.

"Sure, I'll see you then," said Buddy. There was a noise in the background, a voice, and Elaine hastily said goodbye.

Buddy refilled his drink and went into the living room wondering what in the world Elaine could need to talk about. *This is trouble*, he thought, letting out a barking laugh.

"Here's to you, Buddy," he said aloud, raising his drink in a mock toast to himself. "You're being blackmailed by some crazy motherfucker next door. You've got yourself tangled up in some half-assed Russ Dunn scheme. You're about to have cocktails with the wife of Izzy Weinberg who, if he found out, would bash your head in with a nine iron and then skull fuck you. What other shit can you possibly pile on top of this shit storm?"

He flicked on the tube to ESPN. With the sound off, Buddy watched Rickie Fowler tee off on the fourteenth, a 465-yard hole with a dogleg that squeezed the landing area between the fairway bunkers and a stand of trees. His flattish, lashing swing with its tremendous power caught the ball pure, sending it rocketing into the pale blue sky, like it had wings.

Talking to Buddy had taken Elaine's breath away. Her chest was pounding, her underarms damp with perspiration. She bent over the sink and splashed water on her face. Then the bathroom door swung open. Without looking up, Elaine said, "Don't you know how to knock?"

"Oh I know how to knock. Stay bent over like that. I'm gonna knock on your back door," the man said, grabbing Elaine's hips roughly.

"Don't," Elaine groaned, catching his image in the mirror above the sink.

"Is that what you came for, to talk on your cell phone?"

"Maybe," she said.

"Maybe *not*. You came to get fucked. I know how you like it," he said, bending over her back, whispering harshly in her ear. "You want me to pump you so hard you'll forget where you are."

Elaine grunted as he lifted her skirt and shoved her thong aside, probing her ass.

"Let me hear you say it."

"Please," she whimpered, breathing hard.

"You just love to play this game, don'tcha," he said, running his hand between her legs. "Bet you were some hot tramp back when."

"Fuck you."

In a quick motion he took Elaine by the upper arms, squeezing the soft flesh.

"Don't, I'll bruise," she shouted as he spun her around and swept his arm under her legs, kissing her mouth and lifting her.

"Yes you will," he said, carrying her to the bedroom.

23

Latreece was parked deep into the couch, sipping a tall rum and Coke, and watching *Dancing with the Stars* when Tyrell came through the front door like he was being chased. He plopped down on the couch and grabbed the remote. As he pointed it at the TV, Latreece snatched it away. "Yo, excuse *me*."

"Look, I need to see *The Factor*. Five minutes, then it's yours, OK?"

Latreece tossed the remote into his lap, narrowing her eyes. "That's all you had to say. What's up anyway?"

He shrugged, switched channels.

Latreece paused, studying him. "*Tyrell*, there's a damn commercial on, talk to me!"

"Professor Brown's on Bill O'Reilly. I wanna watch the brother tear that cracker up," he said. "That's my man there on TV, Latreece."

"Your man? What about your woman, huh?"

He looked at her. "We ain't fucked in two weeks, an you actin' weirder every day," she said wagging her head for emphasis. "You still takin' them pills?"

"I got business an school an a whole lotta other shit I'm takin' care of," Tyrell said.

"Business? Now you got business," she said. "Man, you better let me into this world a yours cause I'm gettin' very jealous."

He drew Russ's card from his pocket and handed it to her. She glanced at it and flicked it back to him. "OK, who is Russell Dunn?"

"He's a real estate developer, works with the government. Wants me to head up the Black Opportunity and Solidarity Project. Make this a black community."

Latreece gave him a queer look and sucked her cheeks. "No shit?" she said through an explosive laugh.

Tyrell ripped out of his pocket a contract Russ had him sign. "This funny, huh?" he yelled. "You know who the fuck that white mothafucka John Adams was, huh, Latreece?"

She glared at him and pulled away. "I know a brotha that better cool his nasty- assed attitude and stop gettin' all up in my face. That's what I know."

"John Adams said power always followed property. OK, we been shut outta that club too long. I'm working with the administration now, we gonna pull together property for the community, start some real shit again, like we had in the sixties."

Latreece did a double-take. "Where were you, jus' now?"

"Over at that ole fool's place cross the street. He got the cancer," Tyrell said with a smile.

"Why's he a fool? An what does he have to do with us?"

"He's *my* fool. An he got the cancer," Tyrell said, widening his smile to a cartoonish proportion.

Latreece grimaced. She opened her mouth to speak but Tyrell made a hushing motion and cranked up the volume. "Look, there's my man, Professor Jerome Brown. You gonna see me on this show one day," he said as the music died and Bill O'Reilly began:

"With me tonight is controversial black studies professor Dr. Jerome Brown, author of the upcoming book *Rage Without End: Why Black and White America Will Always be at War*. OK, professor, controversial title. No surprise there…"

"Why is it when a black man speaks truth to power he is always marginalized as controversial?"

"Isn't it irresponsible to lay down that gauntlet when things have improved so much in this country? I read the galleys that were sent to the studio, and, so you're basically saying that black rage is, for lack of a better term, more or less a disease that's infected black America, but frankly, I just don't buy the premise. It sounds like an excuse for…"

"Generational failure."

"No, I didn't say that…"

"You were thinking that, thinking that all this talk of black rage is just another excuse for lack of personal responsibility…"

"Now you're a mind reader, now you can read minds, that's it…"

"The white mind has been hard-wired to respond to the black man, much like the immune system rejects 'the other' as foreign, something to be destroyed. So, yes; I can read your mind as it pertains to racialism!"

"Whoa, OK, let's get back to the book. OK, here you say rage is a disabling mental condition that can be lethal. It is the end product of repeated and subliminal insults and humiliations…I thought Obama had ushered the country into a post-racial era, so…"

"That's a myth, post-racial. What does that even mean, man, define that term, tell me what the hell it means, Mr. O'Reilly, tell me, because I find it offensive!"

"Oh c'mon now. You know as well as I do what it means. Electing an African-American as president by a large majority of Americans shows we've moved closer to a color-blind society. Is there still racism? Sure, but certainly not in the harsh terms that prevented people from opportunity."

"If that statement weren't so filled with pathological white-man's code I'd laugh in your face."

"You know I've had other black activists..."

"Activist? Hold on, don't put me in that crowd, OK, I am a scholar, not some activist dancing in the street, putting on a orchestrated minstrel show.

"OK, fine, but my point is that Al Sharpton, for instance, and although we have our disagreements, at least there's a message of hope there, you seem like a defeatist, like there's no hope for..."

"For some Disneyland melding of black and white America? There is no hope for that. You drove a stake into the heart of hope two hundred years ago!"

"Wow, listen, I've done this a long time and I don't think I've encountered an anger level like yours...no wait, we're running out of time and I want to get to something else you said in the book about drugs, which I think is important..."

"The systematic importing of drugs into the black community, which I documented in the chapter on crack in LA, right. Substance abuse produces its own pathology in our community, driving the rage deeper down under layers of neurasthenia. We see that chronic condition festering in the inner cities of this country. Sullen, displaced people, the walking dead..."

"So that's how you characterize the state of the American black community, the walking dead?"

"When rage percolates to the surface, it roars out like lava."

"Ok, we'll have to leave it at that, at the exploding volcano. Thanks Professor Brown and good luck with the book..."

Tyrell eased back into the couch and handed Latreece the remote. "My man told it straight," he said.

Latreece put her hand on his leg, squeezed and said, "Tyrell, what's goin' on? I mean, first it was this Webtribution thing. I was scared, but I'm down with that, after what he did to my girl, but now you goin' off with all this crazy radical stuff…"

He knocked her hand away. *"Crazy?* You seen my man on TV. You sayin' he crazy?"

"I just wanna know what the fuck is goin' on!"

Tyrell relaxed. He smiled to himself, nodded. Then he stroked Latreece's cheek, brought his hand down and squeezed her thigh. "Ya know, when I was growin' up in Brooklyn, all I wanted to do was play football, be a runnin' back for the Boys and Girls Club. That's it. No one worked harder than me. I tried out, did real good, was flyin' high. The night before the cuts were posted, I couldn't sleep. I'll never forget comin' down the hall to the gym. There, on this big white sheet, posted on the wall, was the list…" Tyrell stopped, tightened his grip on Latreece and shook his head.

"C'mon baby," Latreece said

"I was on the cut list. I couldn't believe it. I just stood there, feelin' humiliated. After the season started, I used to go to the games, hopin' our team would lose. Prayin' our team would lose, prayin' someone would get hurt, paralyzed…"

Latreece leaned against Tyrell and said, "Hey baby, that was a long time ago. We all get hurt."

Tyrell wet his lips and took a breath. "That ain't what this is about. I learned then about not being part of a team. Latreece, we ain't now and never will be part of this team. White America, the big mothafuckin' team. We been cut from the time we in our momma's belly. That's why we gotta make our own team. That's what I'm gonna do."

"Baby, baby, c'mon, please."

Tashanda came into the room eating from a box of Cheerios. She sat down at Tyrell's feet. Latreece flicked the channel back to *Dancing with the Stars.* "Look at Queen Latifah dance, sugar. Momma wants her to win," said Latreece.

Cheerios spilling from her mouth, Tashanda said, "She a real queen, momma?"

Tyrell leaned forward until his face was at the little girl's. "She ain't no queen, Dummy. She just pimpin' for the white man."

Screaming with delight, Tashanda giggled and threw handfuls of Cheerios into the air like confetti.

24

Later that night, Jerome Brown was having drinks at the Monkey Bar on East 54th Street with Mark Neal, professor of Black Popular Culture at Rutgers University, *Vanity Fair* editor Graydon Carter, and a tall blonde woman dressed in black named Fay. Critics had already panned the food, but no matter: Monkey Bar was the Elaine's of the 21st century, the place for celebrities, media moguls, and their hangers-on to congregate—and Graydon's own little clubhouse.

The group was seated at Graydon Carter's table, strategically placed to see the whole room, and in turn be seen by everyone who came in the door. Brown sipped his drink, opened a manila folder before him and said, "O'Reilly and I actually had a glass of wine together in the green room after the show."

"I never met the man, personally," said Graydon, lifting his drink, "but I'm sure he's a roaring *arse*hole. But you more than held your own, Jerome. In fact, you made him look like a *complete* arsehole."

"Why do you say *arse*hole instead on *ass*hole, Graydon?" Fay asked.

"Because I'm half potted, that's why. And when I'm half potted I say *arse*hole and I pronounce bastard, *bosstud*, like Ted Kennedy would. Does that clear up this pesky little pronunciation matter for you, Fay? Christ, that *bosstud* Teddy could be a world-class *arse*hole, but I miss him. Warts and all, I miss him."

"Actually he wasn't a bad guy," Brown said, raising his voice slightly.

"Wasn't a bad guy?" Graydon said, arching his eyebrow. "Christ, that wonderful *bosstud* was the Lion of the Senate."

Brown forced a smile. "I was talking about Bill O'Reilly, Graydon."

"Oh, *that* arsehole."

"Yeah, he's just a ratings whore, putting on a show, like the rest of them. But as I was saying about my idea for a cover story featuring…" Jerome began, but Mark Neal interrupted, jutting out his chin, "Graydon, I am still so moved by that stunning portrait of Tiger on your cover, wearing the black wool skull cap, his bare chest, holding those barbells with a look of resignation. I completely agree with what that blogger said: those barbells might just as well have been slave manacles! Man, that was genius."

"Tiger," said Graydon, pursing his lips. "Tiger Woods, you mean."

Mark looked at Jerome, then back to Graydon. "Course I mean Tiger Woods. Is there another brotha named Tiger who we'd give a fuck about?"

Graydon let go with a world-weary sigh. "That's not the point, Mark."

Mark scratched his head and chortled. "What *is* the point? I mean we all know who I was talking about, don't we?"

"We've truncated his persona, sliced his gravitas in half, that's the point. All these people who go by one name, like Sting and Bono and Pink and Cher and Jewel—Christ, they're all a bunch of self-involved *arse*holes. Sting! What an *arse*hole. What if he were stung by a bee? Would I say that Sting got stung? Christ, then *I'd* sound like a complete *arse*hole."

"Why don't you say, 'oh, horse pucky,' Graydon?" Fay asked.

"Horse pucky? Why the fuck would I say that?" he shouted.

"Because I think people who say '*arse*hole' also say 'horse pucky,'" you prig!"

"People who say 'horse pucky' are *arse*holes, period," Graydon said standing up a bit shakily. "I've gotta drain the dragon."

"Me too," said Fay.

"You don't have a dragon," said Graydon. "Christ, at least I hope not."

After they tottered off, Jerome whispered fiercely, "Yo, Mark, what the fuck was that bullshit about? Tiger, blogger, manacles. What the fuck was up with that?"

"Easy brother, I was free associating with Graydon, man."

"Free associating! I'm trying to get some ink with that mothafucka. That's *Vanity Fair* my brotha."

"Yeah, I know. But did you hear that honky-assed bullshit about *arse*-holes and Sting and stung and all that other bullshit? My man, I think your boy here is a mothafuckin' bone smoker."

"I do not give a fuck what he is or who he fucks. That is *Vanity Fair*. No more mothafuckin' free associating, OK brotha?"

When Graydon and Fay returned, Jerome ordered another round of drinks and spread the contents of the folder on the table. Graydon lifted his drink and said huffily, "Christ, there I am pissing like a rhino and this ridiculous little prick at the next urinal asks if I'm that guy Christo. You know, the one who swaddled the Grand Canyon in polyester and made those hideous fucking 'gates' in Central Park. Christo, another *arse*hole with one name. So I made this jerk's day and said 'yes I am Christo. Now go home and tell all your lovely friends that you pissed with Christo and that he was a fucking *arse*hole to you.'"

Jerome laughed politely and said, "Anyway, Graydon, this student of mine I was talking about. Did a stint in Afghanistan. Picked up a Purple Heart. But there's not a patriotic bone in his body. He just enlisted to beat doing a bid upstate. Check out these e-mails he's sent me. Man, it's like doing a psychological autopsy on this dude. I mean he's a reinforcement of my thesis on race, but I feel like Dr. Frankenstein, like I've created him."

Carter was reading the e-mails, one after the other. Licking his fingers, brushing back his silver mane, sipping his drink, wrinkling his nose, mumbling to himself. "This is some shit. You've really lit this guy's fuse, Jerome. Fascinating."

"It's part of an excerpt from my book that Simon & Schuster is publishing next month. I've changed some of the details so no one can identify him. So you like it for the cover, Graydon?"

Carter furrowed his brow, an affect he'd practiced for moments like this. "Well we don't publish scholarly work. Our readers want compelling stories."

"I realize that," said Jerome, "and this was written as a popular book. It explores, like only I can, the latent, just-below-the-surface black anger. It debunks any bullshit about post-racial America. I've threaded these e-mails throughout the text, embedded Tyrell's psyche on the pages. I demonstrate how easy it is to radicalize angry black males. It'll scare the shit out of people."

Graydon paused in thought long enough for Brown's ass to pucker. Then he said, "Let me look it over. It's certainly timely, running an excerpt of your book. We can post it online if you give us a Web exclusive."

Brown could feel the heat rise in his face.

"So JB, what's the title of your book?"

"*Rage Without End.*"

Graydon sipped his drink, smiled, and said, "I love it."

25

On Tuesday evening, Courtney was standing in a stall in the ladies room in the Old Course Hotel, wearing a black Donna Karan suit with Manolo Blahniks and a string of pearls. From head to toes, she was still tingling from her day at the spa. In twenty minutes she'd walk down the plush hallway to the conference room where Izzy's five years of networking in China was on the line, where her think-on-your-feet moxie would be tested. A bead of sweat trickled from her armpit and rolled down her inner arm. She crossed her legs, an angry impatient gesture as she silently mouthed "fuck you" into the cell phone, cursing herself for returning her sister Kate's call. Of all fucking times.

"Kate, they washed my hair with cherry bark extract shampoo, then they smeared sweet almond oil on my scalp. You'd love it!" she said with manufactured excitement.

"Why aren't you registered in a room?"

"You called the hotel? Why didn't you just call my cell first?"

"You're not registered."

"So? I'm registered with my company. Kate, c'mon, *stop*. For once, be happy for me."

"Christ, Courtney, do you know what you're doing?"

"I'm working, building a career," Courtney said softly.

"Is that what they call it now?"

"You know what? I don't give a fuck if you *are* my sister. You have got to stop this *now!*"

"Just fucking tell me that you are not sleeping with that old Jew. Jesus, just tell me that."

"Hey. I am working, right now."

"Well, while you're 'working,'" she said sarcastically, "Derek's out of his mind. What do I tell him?"

"Tell him I'm on a business trip, that's what you tell him."

"He's been offered the head coach position at Manhasset. He wants you to know that."

"Look. Derek and I, we were a thing in college, OK? Leave it alone. I have."

"Well, he hasn't. You were playing him."

"Derek was a boy then and he's a boy now. He'll be one when he's eighty."

"I don't understand you. You've got this perfectly great guy, who's crazy about you. And you want to throw it all away just so you can sleep with that fat old bastard. What would Dad think?"

"Alright, I *really* have to go, Kate. I'll talk to you when I get back."

"You're in over your head. You know that."

"And loving it," Courtney said in a sing-song voice.

"Just *please* tell me you're not sleeping with that Jew, please."

"Do not fucking say that again. Mr. Weinberg is my *boss*."

"My God, you *are* doing him…"

"Gotta go."

"Oh Jesus I think I'm gonna be sick."

"Then stick your finger down your throat and make yourself puke. You'll feel better," Courtney snapped, disconnecting the call.

Qian Qichen, the Chinese official who held the destiny of Izzy's project in his hands, stood outside the conference room smoking an unfiltered Camel, his favorite cigarette. How Americans could vilify such a fine product was beyond him. *Political correctness will be the stake in America's heart*, he thought as he gazed across the hall at the door of the ladies room. His mind turned toward Courtney. This odd young woman had gone in there fifteen minutes ago. What could she be doing? The possibilities stirred him…

Fifteen stories above, in the master bathroom of the Presidential Suite, Izzy lifted his dripping face from the ice-water bath the butler had set out for him, the pores of his face tightened by the frigid water. Freshly shaved, massaged, and manicured, he stared at his image in the mirror. His hair was neatly swept back, falling to his collar, a bit long in the back. It gave him that little edge of bravado, he thought, *just for the Chinks*.

Izzy slipped two fingers under his ribcage on the right side of his barrel-shaped chest, checking to see if his liver was distended. It was the one bit of neurotic behavior he allowed himself. Satisfied, he lifted his tumbler, took a modest drink of single malt Scotch. Then he gargled ferociously with mouthwash. His custom-tailored Brooks Brothers suit and cigars were laid out on the bed. "I'm a Brooks Brothers man; I do not wear Euro-trash designers," he'd once explained when asked why he didn't favor the more stylish garments tailored on Savile Row. As he dressed, Izzy rehearsed his presentation in a deep, sonorous voice, one that could lash or soothe.

Inside the conference room, the video input screens glowed, casting an aqueous light on the ceiling. The head AV tech, a tall, rake-thin thirty-year-old named Sean, wearing huge black-framed glasses, was doing a last minute sound and visual check. "OK, twenty bloody minutes to show time and I'm still hearing too bloody much treble and my bloody blue spots are not screen center," he barked at his two assistants. Earlier that afternoon, he'd met with Courtney. She'd come out of the spa in her terrycloth robe. Her hair was wet and gleaming. The scent of chamomile wafted off her. Knowing she was naked under the robe made it hard for him to concentrate until she said, "Sean, if this presentation goes off without *one* technical glitch, I'm going to hand you an envelope that is going to make you very happy."

William Lo, the interpreter, had arrived and was talking with Qian Qichen when the other Chinese delegates, Wei Jianxing and Li Lanqing, came down the hall languidly smoking cigarettes. The four men chatted for a minute, and then Qian Qichen looked at his watch. An attendant opened the door and they stepped into the conference room.

The semi-circular table was set with ashtrays, laptops, and bottles of iced Perrier. A moment after the men sat, the room went so dark they couldn't see each other. Soft rhythmic music pulsed. A blue spotlight illuminated the area before the video screen, and then there was Izzy. The lights brightened, the music faded. On the screen an image of a globe appeared with multi-colored lines of circumnavigating light. Then the words, TRANS-FORMING THE WORLD, appeared in striking bold letters for two seconds. Blank screen. William Lo's jaws tensed, like a batter waiting for a hundred-mile-an-hour fastball.

"We are fortunate," Izzy began, "because we have the power to re-shape the way the world communicates—the way we do business, the way we share, the way we touch each other. How many men can say that?

"Tonight, we'll define four essential elements to success: the purpose, the engineering, the security, and the politics. We'll have a Q&A during each part of the presentation, so, don't be polite," Izzy said, smiling to himself, clearing his throat, inaudibly. "First, let's look back to May 10th 1869, when an illustrious group of bankers, railroad tycoons, politicians, and railroad men gathered to be honored as the golden spike was driven into the final length of track that spanned this continent, uniting a nation. But there was one large group wholly invisible: the Chinese, the thirteen thousand railroad men from China who had dug the tunnels, built the roadbeds, and laid the track for the second half of the transcontinental railroad across the most precipitous mountains and most inhospitable deserts in the West. These Chinese men had become faceless, they had disappeared." Izzy paused for dramatic tension, looking right into Qian Qichen's eyes. "Think of the irony of this moment," he said as the screen flashed a startling image of a sleek, futuristic train jetting through a subterranean tunnel. "Gentlemen, The Isidore Vac-Train, New York to LA, spanning the continent in *one* hour."

26

Waking, Buddy blinked in the dark. He reached across the bed, touched rumpled sheets and pillows, and in his sodden state thought for a moment that Dana was next to him. When he raised his head the nausea struck, then a sharp pain behind the eyes. He rolled on his side and looked at the clock. It wasn't yet nine p.m. *Good God*, he thought to himself, *I thought it was morning*. He rolled out of bed and went into the bathroom. "Fucking Russ," he said aloud. He was still half drunk. Closing his eyes, Buddy gripped the sink. With his right hand he turned the faucet handle, bent and slurped the cold rushing water. He drew himself erect and stared into the mirror. His eyes were swollen. His hands began to shake. He said "fuck" and ran his fingers through his hair and thought of his father. *Maybe the old man really did know the score*. When Buddy was still a pimply kid, his dad looked him square in the eyes and said, "Sonny boy, most of what a man becomes in life is determined when he's still crawling around screaming at the world."

It wasn't fatherly advice, it was a warning: some of us are done for from the get-go.

Thanks Pop.

There was his father, a tall immaculate man swirling a tumbler of cheap Scotch for all it was worth, wishing it was three fingers of Blue Label, dreaming his faded dreams would still come true. Staring at the TV, saying, "This guy Cronkite's a no-good louse. I think he's a Communist." Rearing his head back and bellowing, "Take a good look around you, Buddy. By the time you're old enough to shave, this country will be in the toilet."

Thanks Pop.

Buddy walked to the bedroom window and gazed at the traffic flowing by on Pulaski Road. He pulled out his cell phone and called Russ. Five rings, then, "Russ Dunn here, how may I help you?"

"Hello Russ. Never heard you answer your phone like that."

He laughed in answer, then mumbled something Buddy couldn't make out.

"I'm not sure how we left off. I'm a bit confused," said Buddy.

Silence.

"Russ, you there?"

"Right here, Mr. Graves. A little noisy downstairs. I think a softball team just walked in—assholes attached to bats and beer," Russ said, sitting by the window in his two-room apartment over Finnegan's Taproom.

"So Russ, I think we need to talk about this, maybe rethink things."

Silence.

"Russ, you there, man?"

"Yep, just me and my own self looking out at these people on Greene Street," Russ said. Behind him a TV was on without the sound, a soft ghostly eye casting the only light in the otherwise dark room. "My fucking room with a view."

"Me fucking too," said Buddy, noticing a figure across the street coming out of the old man's house. It was a moonlit night, and as the figure came to the edge of the road it was illuminated by the glow of headlights from the traffic. Tyrell, it was Tyrell. Buddy felt a pain in his chest, a clawing, visceral reaction as he watched Tyrell dart between cars in a bouncy slow-mo, a careless disregard for his own safety. Buddy wished some teenager, texting while driving her daddy's Escalade, would run over him and crush him. But that won't happen, Buddy knew. Tyrell was a survivor. He may be as unstable as quicksilver, but that bastard would never die. His cocky self-assuredness came off Tyrell like a choking cologne, and it stuck in Buddy's nostrils, making him feel wooden.

"You know Buddy," Russ said, "sometimes I find myself daydreaming, like I'm on autopilot. It's like I'll be driving on the Sprain Parkway and I keep missing my exit. I'm supposed to get off at Exit 23, but I can't seem to concentrate, so all of a sudden I'm at 24, then 25, then 26...has that ever happened to you, man?"

"Yeah, it's happening right now," Buddy said distractedly, watching Tyrell weave across the road toward his house. Then, as though he'd just veered off the highway, Buddy imagined Russ sitting in front of a double-wide in the middle of Texas, drinking bourbon with an old dog lying next to him. He could see Russ's face clearly, its peaceful faraway look. He could hear the dog let out a long groan, roll to its side and die. Russ strokes the dead dog's head, drains his drink, and then picks up his pistol and shoots himself in the head. All that Russ is—love, success, lap dance, loss, guilt—gone in a burst of light, his human essence surging upward into a towering Texas sky.

A loud rapping at his front door snatched Buddy from his fog. It sounded like a taunt, one he promised himself he would not rise to.

"Russ, I gotta go."

27

When Buddy opened the door he noticed that Tyrell had lost weight. On his already lean frame, it was striking. He looked gaunt, as though he had AIDS, and he stank of sweat and pot. Buddy turned his eyes to the side and said wearily through the screen. "Go away."

"You supposed to look a man in the eyes when you talk to him," said Tyrell.

Buddy paused. "We have nothing to talk about."

Tyrell studied Buddy through the screen. His lips parted, showing his teeth. "I'm not feelin' the love, bitch."

"Did you not hear me...?" Buddy started, but Tyrell's fist shot like a striking cobra, punching through the screen, glancing hard off Buddy's chin. Buddy's eyes flashed white spots. Tyrell was mashed up against the door and when Buddy lunged forward, Tyrell threw a short punch that caught him solidly on the nose. Buddy staggered back, more from the shock of what was happening than the blow itself. He tasted blood, felt dizzy, and then Tyrell was through the door, bursting in like a one-man SWAT team. Buddy rushed at him, went down to tackle him but Tyrell caught him on the forehead with his knee. It sent Buddy to the floor, semi-conscious.

Tyrell was breathing hard but was otherwise calm. He walked past Buddy's supine form. Buddy heard water running. Then Tyrell appeared with a damp dish towel. He dropped it onto Buddy's lap. Buddy picked it up, a slow hesitant motion, and cleaned his face. "You broke my fucking screen," Buddy said.

"Jus' like a white boy. Man beats you down, and all you worried about is a *screen*," Tyrell said.

"Fuck you."

"How many fights you been in? Two?" Tyrell asked, waving two fingers in the air, walking from the foyer into the living room. He planted himself on the couch.

Buddy staggered to his feet and looked at the pink stain on the dish-cloth, wondering how he'd explain the door to Dana. He went into the living room.

Without looking up, Tyrell spread a document on the coffee table. "Ever watch the O'Reilly Factor, Buddy?"

"No, I hate that motherfucker," Buddy said.

Tyrell chuckled. "Bet you do," he said, shaking his head in mock disgust. Then, eyeing Buddy, he said, "Happy, huh? See what you made me do? Sayin' we got nothing to talk about…OK, sit down an look at this."

Buddy felt his face, looked over at the hole in his screen door and said, "Fuck."

"Fuck the mothafuckin' screen," Tyrell barked, tapping the document with his finger.

Buddy shifted his weight from one foot to the other. He thought about the kitchen drawer, the big butcher knife. "You know how this is going to turn out, don't you?" Buddy said coldly.

The two men glared at each other.

"It's going to end up bad all the way around," said Buddy. He sat across from Tyrell. Outside, the traffic rolled by.

"This is gonna turn out *my* way. You just haven't accepted it yet, bitch," Tyrell said, pushing the paper toward Buddy.

Buddy leaned in closer. He read. Then without looking up, he said, "You expect me to mow your lawn and paint that man's house across the street?"

"You got to spread the love to my people, starting tomorrow after you get back from caddying. Shit, you a mess man. How that girl a yours put up with it?"

Buddy rose shakily and told him to leave, pointing at the door.

Tyrell ignored him.

"*Five shots couldn't drop me, now I'm back to set the record straight with my AK, I'm still the thug you love to hate, mothafucka, I'll hit 'em up,*" Tyrell chanted, closing his eyes for a long second.

Buddy started to the door. Tyrell got up and called, "You ain't the only mothafucka in this jackpot."

Buddy stopped in his tracks. The implication was clear: Dana. He took a deep breath to tamp down his rising anger. He stepped into the foyer and opened the front door. Looking at the fist hole, Buddy shook his head.

Tyrell stopped at the door and looked across the street. "Ol' Uncle Gene, mowing those mothafuckin weeds. Old fool."

"He's your uncle?" said Buddy.

"Naw, I call him that, make him feel good. He ain't got no family," Tyrell said. Moving to the door, he stopped. "He ain't my uncle but he is my brotha. This don't rub off, bitch," he said, stroking the dark skin on his arm.

28

From a seat in the AV room, Courtney watched...

"Purpose," said Izzy, letting the word hang in the air, widening his stance a bit, as if to get greater purchase on the earth itself. "Some forty odd years ago, I had my fist up a cow's ass, checking to see if she was pregnant," he said, placing a rigid index finger at the crook of his elbow, showing just how deeply he'd buried his arm in the animal. "A young man holding a dream in a balled fist, up a cow's ass, feeling the world was his for the taking. That same cow sneezed in my face and gave me encephalitis. Damn near killed me, but never, not once, did I hold anything against the cow. That was my business, the one I chose. So when you shake Izzy Weinberg's hand, you know where it's been." Izzy paused, raised his right hand. A journey of four decades, deal after deal, to arrive here.

"No man can speak for another. So I'll tell you *my* purpose. I've spent nearly five years going back and forth to your country discussing a groundbreaking business deal on a mode of transportation that first made headlines in the 1970s when a scientist from the RAND Corporation, Robert Salter, published a series of elaborate engineering papers about VacTrains. These trains are designed to travel in evacuated tubes built deep underground—deep enough to pass beneath entire continents or oceans, enabling rapid travel. VacTrains can make runs between New York and LA or New York and London *in one hour.* Think of it, gentleman. I have, every single day since I first read Salter's papers. Now think of something else: For forty years we've had the capability to build these VacTrains, but we have not done so.

"Our last great scientific and engineering achievement, for all of mankind, was putting men on the moon and returning them safely to Earth. Yes, it was a fantastic accomplishment. But since then, where has that drive, that can-do enthusiasm gone? Where is our forward motion? When President Kennedy, in the spirit of Cold War competition, challenged us to make the moonshot, the worry over cost was quickly brushed away. But with Vac-Trains, ah...toes will have to be stepped on."

William Lo froze, momentarily stuck on the American idiom about stepping on toes. When he finally translated it, Qian Qichen smiled; he nodded and motioned for Izzy to continue.

"Big toes that generation after generation of progressively weaker men were afraid to step on. My purpose is not driven by money. In fact, I'll probably lose a great deal of my personal fortune in this venture. My purpose is to set in motion an engineering project that will change the world. I want my footprints at the head of that project, leading the way. I want to be at the head of this great beast of change that will connect the planet's major cities."

Qian Qichen turned and whispered animatedly to his countrymen.

Izzy cleared his throat. "We've recently seen that an erupting volcano in Iceland can paralyze air travel for weeks. Every day, hundreds of flights around the world are delayed or canceled because of weather conditions. Our major airports have become the dysfunctional playgrounds of international terrorists. Storms and accidents bring our highways to a standstill. Human lives, goods and services, business deals, our economies and social networks—all can be held hostage by acts of nature *over which we have no control.*"

As Izzy spoke, he moved his hand across the interactive screen. A wild network appeared—of storm systems, power failures, and clogged traffic in major cities around the world. Then, beneath his moving hand the chaos faded, replaced by simulated VacTrains moving like mercury through tubes connecting throughout the world. "VacTrains are not weather sensitive, nor, as you'll hear later, are they vulnerable to the threat of terrorism that has added to the nightmare of air travel."

Izzy continued, giving a taut, explicit summary of the international consortiums and government subsidies needed to move the project forward, emphasizing that demonstrating success on the initial New York-Los Angeles line would pave the way for an international system. At that, Qian Qichen held up his hands, signaling Izzy to stop as he conferred with William Lo, who said, "Secretary Qian wishes to know: What American toes will need to be stepped on?"

Without hesitation, Izzy said, "The airline, trucking, and train industries. Major labor unions, the Teamsters in particular. Several Native American tribes, the governors of about ten states, and an assortment of powerful political interest groups on the left and right."

Lo took a deep breath. Qian Qichen thought for a beat, then said something. Lo translated. "Secretary Qian asks if that is *all* the toes that will be stepped on."

"All the big ones," Izzy said, without a hint of irony, then added, "An international VacTrain system is an Everest on which no man has dared to make an assault."

Izzy guided the meeting like a maestro. "Our next two speakers will appear via videoconference," he said, introducing first the German engineer Carl Becker, speaking from Frankfurt. Becker had designed a cost-effective and technologically proficient way to dig the massive tunnels that would be required. It blunted the critics who harped about the costs and logistics of the project. Becker spoke English flawlessly, but his harsh German accent was confounding Lo, so much so that Izzy asked the engineer to slow down his presentation. Becker, an imperious, wild-haired genius in his late seventies, glared for a moment, irate at the interruption, but he continued more deliberately.

"Our patented method allows for excavation below an area, without opening the area above the dig. We construct at least one pair of diaphragm walls at opposite ends of the site. These walls extend from the surface area to beneath the lowest level of the excavation. Either before or after constructing the walls, a plurality of tunnels are bored under the surface area, extending from one diaphragm wall to another, with a diameter that will allow them to accommodate one or more VacTrains..."

At the close of Becker's presentation, the Chinese delegation peppered him with questions on the details of the engineering problems. It was a brutal grilling, and Izzy strained to keep his poker face intact. But Becker was prepared; he expertly fielded each query, his intellectual prowess on full display. When it was over, Izzy smiled as he thanked Becker, the image of the massive tunnel-boring machine fading on the screen.

Next, he introduced the head of project security, an ex-CIA operative named John Styron, who beamed onto the screen, standing in front of a large interactive electronic board that simulated various scenarios. "To begin," Styron said, "let's look at the major flaws in the current way we screen luggage and passengers at airports.

"Each VacTrain passenger is part of our individualized security system, which takes advantage of the unique characteristics of DNA, and combines biotechnology and micro-electronic technology. This is a proprietary process, in which we encapsulate and protect DNA on a non-silicon-based chip. In essence, we are creating a DNA security access microchip that is virtually impossible to replicate, and can be authenticated by an electronic digital signal. In effect, every passenger is prescreened for life, prior to their first trip. This proprietary technology will permit the DNA-embedded marker to remain within the microchip for many decades..."

After Stryron summed up, Izzy addressed the men in the conference room.

"Gentleman, we'll conclude with the final presentation. We've discussed the purpose, as well as the economic, engineering, and security challenges. Now we come to American politics, the one thing that, unless handled with incredible deftness, can bring our project to a crushing halt."

The lights dimmed once again and brightened as Courtney took her place at the podium. Izzy couldn't help notice Qian Qichen lean forward in his chair, his eyes widening as Courtney began her presentation. "Our government says we must innovate, we must reduce dependency on oil, reduce greenhouse gasses, protect the environment, create jobs, and repair our infrastructure. But as with so much of political posturing, this has amounted to posturing wrapped in rhetoric. So, how do we get the US government to embrace this very controversial undertaking? Let's look at our strongest link in this political puzzle. President Obama is enthusiastic about this project, but he doesn't operate in a vacuum. He must negotiate a complicated maze of political operatives and agendas…"

The interactive map responded to Courtney's light but firm touch as she spoke about the various committees and sub-committees and their respective congressional heads. She gave hints about each of the politician's personal quirks as a cast of Washington's powerbrokers moved across the screen. The Chinese delegates stared intently at Courtney as she analyzed the machinations of the nation's capitol. When she finished, the screen's image faded and soft music filled the room. With perfect poise she asked, "Are there any questions, gentlemen?"

Qian Qichen, never taking his eyes off Courtney, asked a question that Lo interpreted, "What gives you confidence that these men will take the political risks needed for this project?

Izzy held his breath.

"American men, even the powerful politicians whom I've just described, are different from you, Mr. Secretary. They don't bring centuries of culture and patience to the table. Instead, they tend to be capricious. Their decision making is driven by short-term gains and flirtations with high concepts from which they can make political hay." Here, she glanced at Lo, who smiled at her reference to hay, understanding the idiom, and motioned for her to continue. "Therefore if you can get one or two of the key players, the rest will follow."

"And how does such a young woman know so much about these powerful men?"Qian Qichen asked through Lo.

"Well, when I was an even younger woman, I spent four years in Washington as an intern for several of the men we've discussed here. Although DC is an immensely complicated mix of power and desire, it is also very much a small and intimate club. If you're part of that club, people around you let their guard down."

Silence hung in the air as Qian Qichen thought for a moment. Izzy felt a vein in his head throb like a pump, as he waited. Then Qian spoke, and for a moment Lo looked flustered. He cleared his throat and said, "The Secretary wants to know if letting one's guard down with an intern is like what President Clinton did?"

Courtney let the question hang in the air for a moment. "Thank you for your attention, gentlemen," she said, smiling benignly.

29

On Wednesday, Roy Hickman came to Long Island Jewish to meet with Dana again before returning to Washington. He left the door of her conference room ajar as he stepped out for a moment. Looking into the hallway, Dana could see her nurses walking by. Amidst the high drama of sickness and bedpans and wails of pain, these nurses passed their down-time with idle chit-chat about their kids or their sex lives, or hospital gossip about who was *doing* whom. Dana could finish their sentences; she was in a familiar place and it felt good. But there was a part of her that hated settling into the comfort zone of Dana the head nurse. Would she stop there, looking into a mirror one day when it was too late, asking herself if that's all there is? Dana's parents had helped her through nursing school. She remembered flirting out loud with the idea of going to med school, which elicited her father's innocent, but chiding laugh, and her mother's breathy aside that "all of a sudden being a nurse isn't good enough for my daughter." Dana's parents were from a generation of hard-working dream crushers whose religion was scrimp-and-save; her mother could squeeze four sandwiches out of one can of store-brand chunk light tuna.

She thought about Buddy, reluctantly. The other day, she'd screamed at him that she was sick of sparing him the truth about things. That over the past year she'd watched the beautiful talented guy she'd married die a little bit, day by day. But then, sex with him was so good, it had left her angry and bewildered. Buddy hated to argue, hated to hurt her in any way. She knew that. Buddy loved life, he really did, and he loved it in the way only a gifted person can. Watch him on the course, as she had, and you knew he had the gift. It wasn't just the way he played or the energy he radiated; it was as though he carried his own private sun. Soon after they'd fallen in love, he told her, "Most people are confused until the day they die. But all I need is an eight iron in one hand and your ass in the other. My two loves! With that, I can fly."

Then why, she thought, were you so reckless with both?

"The turkey wraps looked best," Roy said, coming back into the conference room holding a tray. "Hope that's OK."

"That's my caf go-to dish, thanks," Dana said, looking at him as he set the tray down and mouthed "sorry" as his BlackBerry buzzed again. From the purple dents beneath his eyes, Dana knew he was a workaholic who rarely slept. Otherwise, he had a surprisingly boyish face for a guy who'd been, among other things, on the frontlines of the AIDS epidemic in Africa. *That sort of life aged a person,* she thought, *but it hasn't seemed to affect him.* She wondered what his secret was. During their business dinner, she added to her mental dossier of him: He was divorced long ago, no kids. He liked bourbon and steak, so he wasn't a health nut. *What keeps him looking so young?* she wondered. He was an enigma to her, a Southern man with a rakish masculinity. In her imagination, he came from a storied past of horses, guns, gambling. She'd Googled Hickman, but didn't find much of anything about the man himself.

As he ate and talked, Roy pointed to his laptop's glowing screen. "Medicare is hemorrhaging red ink, and the administration wants to put a tourniquet on it. You remember I told you when we first met that they're focused on clusters of HAIs, how and why they seem to aggregate."

"Right," said Dana. "One of my favorite authors, Joyce Carol Oates, lost her husband to a hospital-acquired infection in 2008—at Princeton Medical Center, no less. He went in with pneumonia and came out dead a week later."

"Well, it turns out that nursing homes are a particular problem," Roy said. "They're hot beds of infection. We've put together a color-coded chart, five levels from beige to red."

"Like the terror-threat stuff," Dana said, taking a big bite of her wrap, suddenly famished.

"Right, the government's big on coded stuff, colors. Sort of childlike," Roy said, opening a manila folder, one of several he had piled next to him.

"Poor red, always the bad-guy color," said Dana, looking at the map on the screen.

Roy looked up. "Who was it, James Dean maybe, said 'red isn't a color, it's a warning?'"

Dana felt her face grow warm as she glanced down at her cardinal red top.

Roy paused, looking at Dana's empty plate. "Lord, you have an appetite. I should have ordered in lots of Chinese. You Yankees love that stuff, right?" he asked, grinning.

"No, please, I usually don't eat so fast. I guess I forgot to have anything today. Been sort of crazy," Dana said, stopping herself.

"So, do you?"

"Pardon?"

"Like Chinese food?"

Dana smiled and stared at him boldly. "I like everything," she said.

Roy slid a folder across to her. "Anyway, these are yours. It's all explained in there. Wish I could spare you the fine print, but you need to read it all. Your letter of commitment is dated September 6th, right after Labor Day. That's when we kick off with the week-long workshop in DC. All the major players will be there—HHS, CDC, DoD, and Homeland Security. Maybe even POTUS."

"POTUS?"

"President of the United States."

Dana said, "*Wow, wow,*" in a reedy, girlish tone she regretted. She took a deep inward breath, all at once feeling that it was too quiet in the room.

"I know it seems crazy, but after 9/11, things got weird. Everybody's worried about biological weapons, and resistant bacteria are high on the list of national security concerns. So anyone working on projects like this is vetted pretty carefully," Roy said.

Dana nodded solemnly, trying not to let her expression betray her. "Well, it'll be exciting to work with all those big agencies," she said.

"Hope you feel that way after a month in DC. So moving forward, I'll need your finalized guidelines by the end of August. That gives you a couple of months. Doable?"

Dana snapped an affirmative nod. "You bet."

Roy fingered some papers and looked at her, his face reddening slightly. "Your husband is good with this, the traveling and all?"

Dana nodded.

"It can take a toll on you. I know."

"Yes, he's fine with it, excited for me, actually."

"I read about him on the Internet," Roy said.

Dana felt a panicky rush. The picture of Tashanda and Buddy flashed in her head. *Could he know about that?*

"You didn't tell me he'd won the Junior Nationals in golf. That's quite an accomplishment," said Roy. Sensing her unease he added, "Stuff comes out during any background check. I wasn't prying. In this business it's hard to separate your personal life. We work so closely and so many goddamn hours, But we do keep things separate. *I* do, OK?"

Dana nodded again.

"What happened to his game? He sort of went off the radar after the Nationals."

Dana sagged in her chair, feeling elated and depleted all at once. She knew men: Hickman wanted to find out more about Buddy so he'd know more about her without having to ask any direct questions.

"Roy," she said, "Buddy was special. But he thought he could leave the thing he loved for a while, come back, and have it be the same as before he left. It wasn't."

"Oh…"

"Anyway," she said, "I'm really looking forward to working with you."

"Good, me too," Roy said, reaching his hand out. "I'm glad to have you on board."

As they briskly shook hands, Dana turned to the laptop. "Roy, what's the long red 'Priority' line from Maine to Florida?"

Hickman pursed his lips. "Clusters of HAIs in a hundred-and-thirty-eight nursing homes, owned and operated by Weinberg Associates."

"They own them all?"

"It's not 'they,' it's 'he'—one guy, Izzy Weinberg. And he's a wheel horse."

Seeing the question on Dana's face, Roy said, "Wheel horse, a Southern term."

"Is it good or bad?"

"Can be both. A wheel horse like Weinberg makes his own set of rules. But when his rules are at cross-purposes with our rules…well, it causes problems. Izzy Weinberg is on our radar," Roy said, adding with a smile, "now *your* radar."

30

Standing up to leave, Roy Hickman said, "Once your security clearance is complete, I'll be in touch. In a couple of weeks, you'll get a BlackBerry and a laptop, loaded with the programs we'll be using."

As they shook hands goodbye, it finally sunk in: her life was undergoing a dramatic change, maybe too fast. Dana's chest fluttered with insecurity and a sudden dread. It showed on her face. As Hickman was going out the door, he turned and smiled. "I know the feeling. You've got my number, don't hesitate to call."

Dana nodded, returning the smile. But listening to Hickman's footsteps fade away down the hall, she bristled a bit, wondering what feeling he knew, exactly. *No, Roy Hickman, you do not know what I'm feeling.*

Dana gathered her folders and went back to her small office off the nurses' station. A heavy-set nurse pushing a crash cart paused. They traded a few words as Dana slowed, just enough to be polite. But she kept walking, not in the mood for small talk. As Dana passed, the nurses at the desk stiffened imperceptibly. *They won't miss me,* she thought to herself.

Her office was not much bigger than a broom closet. Dana sat at her desk. For several minutes, she did nothing but listen to the sounds of the hospital—electronic hums and beeps, the hypnotic lilt of rasping lungs, and narcotic-softened moans. She opened her laptop and looked at the calendar. September, after Labor Day, when the country gets back to normal, Hickman had said. She liked that; "normal" had never sounded so good. Dana looked at a framed picture on her desk; she and Buddy on a ferry crossing from Montauk to Block Island, a quick getaway shortly after they married. They'd stayed in a small cottage on the northern side of the island that reminded Dana of photos she'd seen of Ireland, green and wet. It stormed the whole time they were there. Perfect weather for lovers who don't want sunshine, Buddy had said. They'd sipped sparkling wine in the mornings and had long sessions of luxurious sex, after which they would lay in each other's arms listening to the wind-whipped rain on the windows, Buddy telling stories about his adventures as a Merchant Marine. I can't get enough of you, Dana had told her young husband, over and over again.

She opened the folders on her desk and read through the pages for about an hour, poring over the dry government text with all its acronyms and statistics. For some, it might have been boring. But Dana found it fascinating. On the cover of the pilot program document, Roy Hickman, PhD, was listed as Executive Operations Director. Just below his name was the title, Executive Field Specialist. That was where her name would go: Dana Burke, RN, Executive Field Specialist. She said it aloud, three times. Then she said, "POTUS," and imagined herself talking to the President. She swallowed, closed her eyes. *Is this really happening, or am I dreaming?*

She remembered something she wanted to do before calling it a day. The hospital administrator, William Jenkins, had composed a letter to the staff, explaining what Dana would be doing during her year-long sabbatical, her September departure date, and the nurse who would assume Dana's duties. She wanted to read the letter, which had been e-mailed to everyone. Jenkins was not happy about losing one of his stars to the government, but having someone from his hospital take a lead position in such an important initiative was certainly a feather in his cap. Dana assured him that she'd be back in a year, but Jenkins smiled wryly and said, "No you won't."

She checked her messages. That's when she saw the red-flagged e-mail with an attachment and the subject line, **OPEN THIS NOW, OR ELSE.** A childish taunt, but she stopped breathing as she moved the cursor and clicked.

As Dana read aloud softly, she felt her body go numb. *I have made a deal with your husband, Buddy Graves, that will TEMPORARILY keep me from taking drastic action like sending the above attachments to everyone of importance who works in this hospital, starting with the head man, William Jenkins! If I were you, I would make sure that your husband complies with my course of action as I have spelled it out to him, because if he tries anything funny, everyone you work with will know that you are married to and, in that manner, an accessory to a child molester. The aforementioned attachments are only the tip of the iceberg.*

With shaking hands, Dana clicked on the first attachment. It was the same ugly picture Buddy had shown her, but she saw that it had been doctored, Photoshopped maybe. The little girl's face was twisted with fear, streaked with tears. And Buddy's crotch had an ominous bulge, as though some surreal mollusk was lurking beneath the surface of his boxer jocks. She clicked on the other attachment. A video appeared, a scratchy peep-show, the girl talking. Dana watched for a few seconds through a gauze of shock, then she abruptly deleted the message, closed the laptop, grabbed the telephone receiver and dialed. An aching pain moved up from her shins, through her groin, into her belly. When Buddy answered, she hissed, "Did you know about this?"

"Dana? What's wrong?"

A hard-edged chuckle, then, "You fuck."

"Dana, tell me what's happened, please."

Dana sucked air, felt her eyes well up.

"Dana, please, Jesus Christ…"

"That thing you got involved in just came into *my* life!"

"What happened? Did that fuck do anything to you? I will *kill* him…"

"Shut up with your macho shit. It's too late for that. He e-mailed me that picture of you and the girl—and a video. A video! Did you know about that? You never mentioned anything about a fucking video! He said that if you don't play along with him, he'll send that photo and that hideous video to everyone at the hospital."

"How'd he get your e-mail?"

"Oh Christ, Buddy, you are a fucking idiot sometimes. He could have seen the parking sticker on my car, or the name of the hospital on my scrubs. All the department heads' e-mails are listed on our site. What's the difference how he found out? He's now threatening *me*."

"Jesus, I'm sorry Dana. He won't do anything, I promise."

"He already has!"

"I promise I'll…"

"Fuck you and your promises, OK? You do whatever he tells you to do. I do not give a fuck anymore."

"Dana."

"I want out of this mess, do you hear me? There, I've said it!"

"Dana, please just come home. We need to talk…"

She slammed down the phone.

Buddy held the receiver, as if expecting Dana's voice to return. She'd never hung up on him before. Dana was a hard, plainspoken woman, but never harsh or rude. He'd pushed her to that nasty corner of her psyche. The silence around him, like the pang in his chest, was leaden with regrets. *I've aged my wife*, he thought. *One of the worst things a man can do is make his woman careworn.* She had seen him when he was good, floating inches above the ground, golf clubs magic wands in his hands. Now she watched him becoming nothing, a lean man blown away like dust. Dana had once told him that she could have sex and not fall in love. *But you can't do that Buddy*, she'd said, *that's where we're different: you love too much.* It was a warning: your weakness will bring you to the edge of a cliff.

Buddy went to the bedroom and stared out at the small globe of light from an upstairs window next door. The room Russ had sat in with Tyrell. Over pints of Bass ale, Russ had described the room in minute detail, with a kind of fascination that unnerved Buddy. The light in the window seemed to pulse, a heartbeat of radioactive energy. Buddy pictured Tyrell, a man who didn't quite fit any stereotype he could come up with. Buddy wanted to pigeonhole him, make him a cardboard figure he could cut up and dispose of. But he couldn't do it.

Tyrell had reached out to his wife. Next time he would touch her.

"Tyrell, I will kill your black ass, graveyard dead," Buddy said aloud. "Do you hear me, you vile sack of shit? If you ever come near my wife in any way, I will stab your fucking black heart and watch your blood spurt like a fountain. I'll…" Buddy stopped abruptly and shook his head violently, trying to wrest something clawing his brain. His rant was nothing more than a drowning man's fantasy, and he knew it. Buddy Graves was not going to kill anyone. *No blood on your hands, you coward.* He went to Dana's dresser and began leafing through her clothes, panties, sweaters, T-shirts, touching each folded garment. His wife, her scent. He pictured Dana's sharply etched profile, the childhood scar under her left nostril. How could he protect her? Was it too late?

31

Buddy stayed up all night, praying to hear the crunch of Dana's car tires on the gravel drive. She didn't answer her mobile or return his text messages.

Thursday morning at eight o'clock he was sitting on the caddy's bench under a huge weeping willow, waiting for his foursome to get up to the first tee. The Cohens and the Golds—combined, nearly three hundred years of kvetching. A nightmare. This was Jock Macgregor's idea of a joke. So slow was this group of sun-leathered *alter kockers*, the Scotsman told Buddy to cancel his plans for the evening.

That's right, everybody's getting a piece of Buddy, he thought. *Just keep chipping away at me.* But he didn't care about everybody, just Dana. The last time in bed with her, even though it had been wonderful, she was dazed afterward. Not from the afterglow of sex; there was a disconnectedness, pushing him away. He could feel it coming off her body like shark repellent.

"I love you Dana," he said aloud, wanting to hear the words hang in the air. Buddy watched Milly Cohen stepping up to the tee, her ankles, shins, and arms thin as dried twigs. All that was left of her in this life was packed into the space that her ass, gut, and enormous tits occupied. Her shot was not more than seventy yards, but she hit a straight ball, dead center fairway. Just as Lori Gold set to address her tee shot, the sun came roaring out from behind the clouds, throwing a spotlight of glaring heat on the foursome and touching off a scramble for caps, sunglasses, and sunscreen.

By the eighth hole, the Cohens and Golds were starting to melt. Sammy Cohen went off the fairway to take a leak behind a stand of pines. The two women were up ahead sipping diet Cokes and talking. That's when Bob Gold said, "Take my shot for me, will ya Buddy?" and flipped a silver flask in the air.

Buddy caught the flask in his left hand. "I really can't, Mr. Gold."
"Can't what?"
"Drink on the course."

"But you'll take the shot for me before Cohen gets back, won't you?" he pleaded, holding out his three iron hybrid.

It was a tricky fade shot, about 210 yards, with bunkers on three sides. The green was bone dry, and the pin was sitting high on the right-side slope. Gold would need a howitzer to make it halfway. Buddy took a quick shot from the flask and tossed it back to Gold. "That's too much club," he said, taking a five iron from the bag. He settled his feet, inhaled and exhaled, looked once at the flag, then addressed the ball and swung, an easy controlled backswing, moving fluidly through his downstroke. The ping of perfect contact. Buddy stepped back, watched the ball sail into the air, a slight fade, then it plopped near the top lip of the green and rolled back, coming to a rest seven feet from the pin. He heard Gold gasp.

"Easy two-putt for your bird, Mr. Gold," Buddy said calmly, handing the club to the old man who was shading his eyes, mouth agape, shaking his head slowly in dazed wonderment.

Just then, Stink Feet Cohen stepped from behind the pines and headed back to the fairway, adjusting his zipper with a dainty squatting motion as he walked and squinted at Bob Gold. "What the fuck are you grinning at?" he called. "I got a prostate as big as a casaba melon and I gotta piss every time I even *think* about having a drink."

"Fuck your prostate. Do you see where my ball is?" called Gold.

Cohen stopped midway across. He shaded his eyes and looked toward the green. Then he turned and looked at Bob Gold. Then he turned and looked at the green. Then he turned and looked at Bob Gold.

"What's the matter, Cohen, you look like you're ready to plotz," Gold called.

Cohen went down the fairway. "That's not your ball," he barked. "That is *not* your fucking ball, Gold. No one in this club, especially an old fart like you, hits that kinda shot."

"Whose ball do you think it is? I hit the shot of my life and you're in the bushes jiggling your Johnson."

Cohen stared again at the green. Then he turned to Gold and said, "It's a fucking stunner, Bobby. I'm sorry as hell I missed seeing that. It's like God hit the ball for you!"

After nine holes the foursome threw in the towel. "Jesus," said Milly, "I feel like a liver spot on legs." Bob Gold took Buddy aside and paid him for a full 18-hole loop, then slipped him a tip—five crisp C-notes.

"Mr. Gold…" Buddy said.

126

Gold made a *shhhhh* noise and waved his hand. "Buddy, you know who I am, right?"

"Bob Gold of Solid Gold Electronics & More," said Buddy, reciting the jingle.

"Right, the biggest fish in the fucking pond. But you know what? I've got a son about your age. You know what he sees when he looks at me?"

"The biggest fish in the fucking pond?"

Bob Gold shook his head. "He sees me dead. He's already sitting shiva. My son, the social worker, that's what he went to college for. He wanted no part of my business. Too embarrassed by the schmaltzy commercials, and being the son of Solid Gold Bob. He was too busy smoking dope, chasing co-eds, with hair down to his ass, saving the world from guys like me. Now he's got a wife, two kids, and a mortgage, and all he does is bitch about money."

Gold paused, running his tongue across his lips. "I don't know why I told you all this. Getting old makes a guy funny. But you're just an easy fella to talk to," he said softly.

"So they say," said Buddy.

He looked at Buddy. The rims of his eyes were red. "You know, at first I wanted it to be a joke on Cohen. But then it felt too good for a joke, you know what I mean?"

Buddy nodded.

"Thanks for taking that shot for me. *Really.*"

"What shot?" Buddy said innocently.

32

The waiters cleared the dishes and refreshed the drinks, placed a bottle of Camus XO on the table near Qian Qichen. They moved about the plush room like mimes, and then they were gone. Led by Secretary Qian, the Chinese delegation lifted their snifters of cognac, and drank happily. Izzy had chosen traditional Chinese music to be played throughout the post-presentation dinner: the *pipa*, a four-stringed lute played by Lui Fang, known in China as the Empress of the instrument.

"If the audience is not moved by the music, particularly if it is a master-piece from the guqin core repertoire, it is usually the player's fault and not the listener's," Qian said through Lo the interpreter. "Do you agree...Izzy?" Qian added in English, forcing out the foreign sounds. He fixed his eyes on Izzy, then, sipping his cognac, on Courtney.

"It's always the player's fault," Izzy said, somewhat absently as his knee met Courtney's under the table, a slight but meaningful bump.

A glossy-covered prospectus sat next to each of the Chinese dele-gates. It contained the final numbers, the torrent of red ink it would take to push the project forward with all the players in the band—a dizzying array of international power brokers. But Izzy knew money wasn't the deal-breaker. The Chinks were flush. Qian finished his cognac and put his snifter down, sliding it forward. He lit a cigarette and looked at Izzy. It appeared he might smile. But he didn't. His associate sitting directly to his left lifted the Camus XO bottle and refilled the Secretary's snifter.

Through a stream of cigarette smoke, Qian began to speak. Lo, as if reciting from memory, translated. "When the world was still young, there were ten suns. Each took a turn being pulled through the sky in the chariot of their mother, goddess of the sun. One day, however, the ten suns decided to travel across the sky together. They greatly enjoyed their journey..."

Just then, as the Secretary's voice went aloft with the emotion of his fable, a fly as big as a Concord grape buzzed over his head, distracting him. To the consternation of the Chinese delegates, the fly strafed Qian, a miniature attack helicopter, circling the Secretary's head as if to gain momentum for another assault. Then, like a grizzly grabbing a salmon leaping from a stream, Izzy's big paw swept into the air, snatched the fly and threw it to the table, where it lay stunned and helpless. Izzy leaned forward, picked it up by the wings, dropped it into his crystal clear martini, and lifted the glass, draining the eight ounces of gin, fly and all. Izzy turned, made a formal gesture with his hand for the Secretary to continue, now unmolested by the fly.

As they were bidding each other goodnight and farewell, Izzy offered his hand to Qian. He studied Izzy's hand for a moment. Before extending his own hand, he placed a rigid forefinger halfway up across his forearm, indicating how far Izzy had pushed his own hand up the cow's ass. Izzy reached out with deference and shifted Qian's finger three inches up to his elbow. The Secretary smiled.

‡ﾐﾓ

Izzy and Coutney stopped in the hallway, just outside their room. As Izzy was opening the door, Courtney reached up and pinched the rim of his ear. He flinched, just perceptibly, not from the pinch, but from the look on her face. She moved closer. He pulled back, the better to see her. "That was so unfuckingbelievable with the fly, Izzy. *Christ!*"

He nodded and said, "We just took a huge step toward closing the deal of the century."

"Kiss me," she said, leaning into him.

Izzy squinted at her. "You gonna kiss a guy who just swallowed a fly?"

"I'm gonna do more than kiss," she said.

‡ﾐﾓ

Afterward, lying in bed sipping flutes of Dom, Courtney, resting on Izzy's chest, listening to the drumbeat of his heart, said, "What was up with that ten suns stuff that Qian was talking about?"

"His dick, that's what was up. He couldn't take his eyes off you even when he tried. That parable shit—his stab at a pick-up line," Izzy said.

"It's original, I'll give him that," said Courtney.

"Would it have worked? If the project were on the line I mean?" Izzy asked, running his knuckle down her spine.

"You mean, would I have slept with him to save the project?"

"Yes, that's what I mean, hypothetically. Deals might be opened with sex, but never closed," said Izzy. "Self aggrandizement is the machine that drives the world, and sex oils the machine. So?"

"I'd have screwed his eyes round," she grinned.

Izzy laughed so hard, Courtney's head bounced like a ball on his chest.

When his laughing subsided, she sat up, sitting pertly cross-legged next to him.

"Fucking gorgeous," he whispered dreamily, reaching out like a blind man, feeling the nipple of her left breast.

"May I ask you something?" she said.

"Don't ask if you can ask. Just ask."

"What's going on with you and that caddy, the tall guy, Buddy?"

Izzy did a double take. "You're asking me about some caddy, now?"

"He's not just *some* caddy."

"Your point?"

"You don't take things personally, Izzy, but with him…" Courtney said, with a little shrug. "Just wondered, strictly as a business matter."

"Business matter, huh?"

"I want to know why you do things. It'll make me better."

Izzy shifted, propping his bulk against the headboard. Finishing his champagne, he gazed into the empty glass and said, "Every American baby is told a fucking lie: *'You can be President,'* meaning of course, you can be anything. But I never bought it. Not a Jew boy. Someday, maybe. But fuck being President, I knew I could be *something*."

"*Everyone* can be *something*," Courtney said, slightly defensive.

"Yes, unless they throw it away with both hands. Mr. Buddy Graves *was* something. When he held a golf club it wasn't steel and graphite, it was poetry. Effortless fucking poetry. That kid had something guys would kill for. He was rated number one high school player in the *country*. Buddy could have made millions on the pro tour. I've known him since he first came to work at the club as a teenager. He was a horny little *pisher* with the hots for my wife and, I'm sure, punchin' his dummy nightly over her. She's still a tomato, but back then, wow, so fucking sexy. So Buddy's carrying for me and Elaine in the summer tourney. Our pro—as was, and still is the custom—played with one of the guests. Back then, the pro was Mike Mueller, father of the current pro, Brad. Elaine was having a thing with Mike. I knew about it, but I told her, 'I don't mind if you have some fun on the side, I sure as fuck do. Just don't bring anything home.' Anyway, I started drinking too early that day, and like the roaring, scheming asshole I can be…"

Courtney laughed with pleasure, a dazzling show of white teeth, jiggling breasts, undulating belly—a completely uninhibited motion of body parts.

"Do you want to hear this?" said Izzy, eyes widening.

"Yes!"

He paused, thoughtfully, then said, "Christ, am I having fun," as he reached out to stroke her thigh.

"Me too," she said, brushing his hand away playfully, motioning for him to continue.

"So, knowing that Buddy was hip to Elaine and Mueller's *schtupping*, and knowing how much it burned him, I say, 'I'm too fucking drunk to play golf. Buddy's gonna play for me. Up for a little sport, Mueller? Sure ya are!' Buddy and Mueller go head-to-head and I'm dropping five large on the kid just to make it interesting. At that point, we'd finished the front nine and we took a quick drink at the clubhouse. Word of my little game spread like *that*," Izzy said, snapping his finger with such force it sounded like the crack of a gunshot. "Anyway, by the time we hit the tenth tee, we had a small gallery that grew with each hole, guys dropping big bucks, making crazy side bets. It was a wild three-ring circus and I was the fucking ringmaster."

"Oh God, you must have been cracking up," said Courtney, imagining the scene.

Izzy shook his head soberly. "I turned Buddy Graves loose on Mueller. Courtney, it was an execution—of a man's confidence, his self worth. Stroke by stroke, that kid broke our pro down. He was a cocky little prick back then. And of course, for him it was all about revenge for Mueller having been in the sack with Elaine. Anyway, Graves starts murmuring shit, talking to Mueller in these little asides out of the corner of his mouth. He sliced the man's balls off.

"Buddy threw all convention out the window and made his own rules. Hitting a fucking nine iron when anyone in their right mind would hit a five, just to fuck with Mueller's head. There must have been about fifty members, all drunk, all filthy rich, following him, oohing an aahing at the shit he was pulling. By the seventeenth hole, Mueller, a tall strapping guy of forty, looked like he'd shrunk three inches and aged ten years. He hit a piss-poor approach shot into the sand by the side of the green. Horrible lie too. Graves looks at him and says, "Hit that a bit thin, Mikey. You'll need a shovel to get it out. But hey, at least you're pin high."

Izzy paused a moment to refill their flutes. In a softer, but more intense voice he said, "Then from about 90 yards out, Graves drops his ball four feet from the cup. A little backspin holds the ball in place like Velcro. Walking to the green, he starts talking privately to Mueller. Christ, it took Mueller three fuckin' strokes to get out of the trap. It was *painful* to watch. He was broken, in front of all of the club's biggest members. But that wasn't enough

132

for Graves. He takes the rake from the sand trap, walks up to his ball, and using the rake as a putter, he drains it. Mueller did not play the eighteenth. *He did not play.* Said he was suddenly sick. That man was never the same. The bounce was gone from his step. So, after the smoke cleared, I told our board that we should shit-can Mueller, bring Graves in as the pro, and groom him for a PGA career—our golden boy. So what does Mr. Buddy Graves do? He says no, he wants to go see the world. What an asshole. He spit in my face, turned his back on his own talent, and pissed away a golden opportunity. And now he's a fucking caddy. So there it is."

"And that's a sin in your book, isn't it? Turning your back on an opportunity."

"Absolutely."

Courtney held up her flute and looked at Izzy through the rising bubbles. "And we pay for our sins."

"One way or another," Izzy said firmly, his voice tinged with sadness.

33

An obscenely loud cigarette boat spewing fumes was docking when Buddy pulled up to the Harbor Club, an upscale waterside steakhouse. Elaine was in a corner booth in the lounge. She waved and smiled when she saw Buddy following the maître d' to the table. She was wearing a low-cut dress with a chunky blue topaz necklace and matching earrings.

"Hiya Buddy, you're a love for coming," she said, standing and giving him a peck on the cheek.

Buddy ordered a Scotch. She took a cocktail napkin and reached across the table to rub off her lipstick, saying she didn't want to get him in trouble. The waiter brought his drink and another vodka martini for Elaine, even though she hadn't ordered one. They touched glasses. "It's freezing in here," she said. Buddy slipped off his blazer in a quick motion and put it over her shoulders.

"Thanks Buddy," she said. "I always seem to underdress." Elaine sipped her drink and smiled.

They fell silent. Buddy looked at her and said, "So, here we are."

"Yep, here we are. I've been sculling my irons a bit," she said.

Buddy swirled his drink and said, "Chances are your club-head is whipping ahead of your hands as you try to scoop the ball into the air. That puts the leading edge of the club into contact with the ball. At impact, the back of your left hand should face the target and your right wrist should bend slightly away from the target. But you know all that."

Elaine said, "So, have we broken the ice?"

"I fell through as soon as I walked in here."

Elaine took a breath and said, "I'm sorry about how things have turned out for you, Buddy."

"Don't be."

"You've had rotten luck."

Buddy looked at her.

"Oh hell," Elaine said, "I shouldn't talk like that, as though I know your life. It's presumptuous, sorry."

"It's OK, Elaine. I don't mind."

"You wouldn't," she said.

Another awkward silence hung between them. Then there was an explosion of voices as the gang from the cigarette boat piled in. They'd been drinking. Elaine frowned. "I like the view here, but lately they've been getting a lousy crowd." She took Buddy's hand and stood. The maitre d' rushed over to carry their drinks as Elaine pulled Buddy through the crowd of muscled guidos and big-haired women. They came to a small, quiet private room with a view. "I should have started here, but I love barrooms," Elaine said. Turning to the maitre d' she said, "John, would you please freshen our drinks and bring a bottle of that champagne I like."

"Right away, Mrs. Weinberg."

They sat looking at the sun setting over the sailboat-dotted bay. A waiter came in with the drinks and John appeared a moment later with a bucket of iced champagne and two flutes.

Elaine lifted her drink. "So, where were we?"

"We were talking about my taking over the operation of Lehman Brothers," said Buddy.

"You're funny, you know that?" she said.

"Oh, yeah, I'm known for my financial acumen," Buddy said.

Elaine laughed, and in the same breath said, "At the end of the summer I'm pulling up stakes and leaving my husband."

"Oh," said Buddy, caught off guard. "Gee, I'm so sorry, Elaine."

"Don't be. I'm not. It's not like that. I mean, I've got my reasons for splitting up with Izzy and none of them are sad."

"He doesn't seem like he'd be an easy guy to leave."

"*Nothing's* easy about that man," Elaine sighed, exasperated. "He doesn't know yet," she added hastily, shivering. "But that's not really why I asked you here, to tell you I'm leaving Izzy." Elaine reached down and pulled a manila envelope from her large Coach bag. She withdrew a creased and yellowed piece of paper. "Remember this?" she asked.

Buddy stared at the paper. "You kept it."

"I keep everything," she said, taking a big gulp from her drink, working up her courage. "My father told me to make good friends, lots of them. I have a friend, a fella named Arty Wagner."

Buddy said, "The Arty Wagner who worked with Jack Nicklaus?"

"Yes, *that* Arty Wagner. I told him about you."

"About *me*."

Elaine put her hand on his wrist. "Remember when you were seventeen and I asked you to draw your dream golf course. You didn't say anything for two weeks, so I thought you'd just blown it off. Then you showed up with this."

Buddy turned in his chair and stared through the window. "That was a long time ago."

"Well, I dug this out and showed it to Arty two weeks ago," she said, pointing to his annotations in the margins.

"The first hole, 435 yards: Creating contours that appear to be based in nature is one of the hardest challenges that architects face in the field...the oblique angle of the green to the fairway combined with a deep bunker along the right of the green creates maddening angles of play..."

"He wants to talk to you," Elaine said.

"About what?"

"A job."

"Doing what?"

"Designing courses. He's my partner in a golf course design firm, among other things, all golf related. We already have several contracts lined up."

Buddy looked at her. He blinked hard and shook his head. "My God, Elaine," he said, giving a short laugh to disguise his emotion. "I mean, I'm flattered, but I'm not a designer. I just..."

Elaine squeezed his wrist. "You *are* a designer, you just don't know it," she said.

In a rush of excitement she explained the plan she'd been working on with Arty Wagner for the past two years. They had the contacts and the contracts, and a state-of-the-art facility in Scottsdale, Arizona. They had capital—hers, Arty's, and investors.' Buddy's commitment would initially require a month or so in Arizona, then travel on an as-needed basis.

"Come with me, Buddy," she said. "You're too good."

"Too good for what?" he said, a slight irritation in his voice.

"For *this*," she said sweeping her arm, her meaning clear.

Buddy turned in his seat. "Jesus, Elaine, I think you're exaggerating my capabilities."

"Arty knows talent when he sees it. You're a natural." Then Elaine smiled and said, "Open the champagne, OK?"

Buddy popped the cork and said, "Celebrating something?"

Elaine waited until both flutes were filled. "You bet. *So?*"

Buddy noticed the small pulse in the vein of her neck. It made his heart flutter.

Before lifting his flute he said, "I've got some issues I'm dealing with right now, Elaine."

It had already occurred to Elaine that Buddy's life had become more difficult of late. The stress showed on his face. She said softly, "With your wife?"

Buddy said, "Yes. But it's more complicated than that."

"Can I help?"

Buddy shook his head.

"Buddy," she said, gripping his forearm, "if you worked with me, it might help *uncomplicate* things. Money has a way of doing that."

He looked at Elaine and for a second thought about kissing her. "Did it uncomplicate things for you?"

"For a while," she said. "I want you to do this with me. This is a game-changer for you Buddy."

He swallowed, pictured Tyrell, and blew air through his lips in a whooshing sound. "I have to talk to my wife."

"I'm going to be tied up with some things for the next couple of weeks. Talk to your wife. Then talk to me, OK?" Elaine said. Her deeply set eyes, rimmed in blue eyeshadow, gave her a haunted look. She leaned forward a bit. Their knees touched under the table. The group in the bar from the cigarette boat exploded with whoops. Elaine shook her head and said, "I really want you to take this opportunity, Buddy. It won't come again, for either of us."

Their knees touched again, prickling the nape of his neck. Elaine pressed the sketch into his hand.

"Hang onto this. Talk to your wife, then give me a call. Don't leave me hanging," she said with a sudden insistence that excited him.

"I'd be a damn fool if I did," he said.

34

Later that night, Elaine's car pulled up to the Tudor house on a hill that was surrounded by hundred-year-old oak trees. She parked in the back behind a large shed, dabbed on some lip gloss, rubbed perfume on her wrists and neck, and then reached under her dress to perfume her thighs. She stepped out of the car and walked quickly to the back door. Taking a key from her purse, Elaine let herself in. She tossed an envelope onto the kitchen table— payment for her Rubirosa. By the time she walked into the living room he was on her, ripping the straps of her dress down to her hips. He yanked her bra off, popping the clasps, and moved her across the floor in an urgent, vulgar dance. Reaching under her dress, he slid his hand beneath her panties and his fingers into her.

He kissed her mouth, clashing teeth. He kissed her neck and ran his tongue upward, licking her face like a dog, grabbing and squeezing her ass cheeks. "You came back for more?" he said.

Elaine moaned.

He tore her dress off and mashed her onto the leather couch. He put his hand on her neck.

"You're hurting me," she gasped.

"But that's the way you like it," he said.

He turned her over roughly and slapped her ass. She screamed like she'd been scalded. He told her to shut her mouth. He slapped her ass until it was red, then he entered her from behind, gripping her hair for leverage. It was a sweltering night. Outside, there was a loud bang, an electric hiss from an exploding transformer. The lights flickered. The air conditioning sighed and died. Almost instantly, the air in the room was heavy with humidity. Sirens sounded in the distance. The heat and the wail of sirens intensified his angry thrusting. Their bodies shimmered with sweat.

When he was finished, Elaine looked like the victim of a gang rape: hair disheveled, makeup smeared, clothes torn and in disarray. She lay panting—and satisfied. He watched her get dressed. Cracking his knuckles, he smiled, inhaled deeply and told her about the young bitch he'd had sex with earlier that day. "She had a bangin' body, taut and sexy. Her tits didn't sag like yours."

Elaine walked to the drink cart, poured herself some of his best brandy, then threw it in his face and walked out.

ॐॐ

It was just past one a.m. when Elaine got home. She made herself a drink, walked upstairs, and turned on the light in her bedroom. As she caught sight of herself in the mirror, her hand fell away from the switch, slowly. "Christ, Elaine, you look like an old slut."

She took her drink into the bathroom for comfort and had a long cool shower, scrubbing her body with a heavily soaped loofah. She thought about the upcoming appointment she'd made with Izzy's plastic surgeon. Leaning against the marble tile, she laughed out loud, bitterly. Vodka and tears mixed with the sputtering shower water rushing over her bruised body.

Elaine dried herself with a plush towel, then smoothed lotion on her arms and legs, buttocks and belly. She slipped into a nightgown and went downstairs to the study to make a nightcap. The answering machine light was blinking. She pressed the "play" button. Izzy's voice filled the room: *"Hello sweets. We'll be in tomorrow afternoon. But I've got a few things to tighten up before I get home, so don't expect me before Saturday. Give me a buzz. Things went swimmingly in Scotland, whatever the fuck that means. Got my Chinks lined up like ducks in a row. I'll fill you in over dinner. I've already made reservations at Mirabelle. Lots of kisses, my love. Have you been a good girl while Daddy's been away?"*

Izzy's message ended with his deep rumbling laugh, sounding as though he and no one else knew the score.

"Good girl," she repeated aloud, rolling the words around in her boozy head. "Oh yeah, Izzy, a good girl who pays for rough sex. The kind of fucking that leaves her sick and cleansed all at once."

Elaine stood there for a while, as if waiting for the room to clear of an unpleasant odor. Izzy sounded half in the bag. Knowing how much it took for him to get that drunk, she wondered what he'd been celebrating and with whom. Then she said aloud, *"We'll* be in tomorrow? Who is we?"

35

"If the weather was like San Diego and we could get rid of about a million or so useless souls taking up room on this island, it would be a *grand* place to live," Izzy said to Jack Herzog, his chauffeur of more than 20 years. "Jack, did you hear me say *grand*? Do I not sound like a goy WASP fuck? See what spending time in the UK does to an old Jew?"

"Ditto on the useless souls, and negatory on you ever sounding like a goy WASP fuck, Mr. Weinberg. Pardon my French, Miss Mears," Jack said, raising the glass partition between him and his passengers.

They were driving on the Long Island Expressway, and even though the mercury was splurting past 90 degrees, Izzy had kept the windows rolled down until they'd cleared the airport, just so he could smell the jet fuel. He loved it, the perfume of movement and commerce. Nestled in the sprawl of the stretch limo sipping champagne, Izzy and Courtney were still on a high from the Scotland trip. Courtney finished her flute, then lolled her head back, dozing off next to Izzy. He stroked her hair and whispered, "You drop to sleep like a stone. That's the sign of a clear conscience."

Courtney purred.

Scrolling through his iPhone contacts list, Izzy tapped the screen to place a call to a power broker on the Congressional Black Caucus. As he gave his Cliff Notes roundup of the trip, the Chink victory, the road ahead, *blah, blah, blah,* Izzy mimed jerking off. Courtney propped open one eye and laughed silently as Izzy mouthed, "he's an invaluable ally."

"I *know* the issues, but we gotta swing your people on board with this," Izzy was saying into the phone. "It's all good," he said as the long black car pulled up in front of Courtney's parent's split level in Levittown.

As Courtney gathered her purse and briefcase Izzy wrapped up his call. Turning to Courtney he said, "Everything's in motion for your new digs. Buzz me if anything goes out of whack. I'll be in and out of DC in the next few weeks for more meetings. For right now, take a little downtime."

"I hate downtime," said Courtney.

"Me too, but take it anyway. You're gonna have a huge workload coming up."

The next door neighbor, a paunchy guy drinking a Coors Light on the porch, gave an anemic wave as Jack followed Courtney up to the house with her bags. Her father's silhouette moved across the living room as she thanked Jack and opened the door.

William Mears was stiff as a tailor's dummy as his daughter came into the house. He was dressed in a waiter's tux, his jacket off, smoking a cigarette.

"Hiya, Dad," Courtney said, spreading her arms as she walked through the living room.

He intercepted her hug by reaching up and taking her hands. He squeezed them and looked at her disapprovingly.

She pulled away and crossed her arm across her chest. "*Hi,* Dad."

"Courtney, how've you been?"

She looked at him. "I *was* fine, but I'm starting to detect some weird shit here."

His face reddened. "That's the kind of language you use."

"Oh, Dad, please."

"What happened to you?" he snapped.

Courtney spun around and walked into the living room to her bags.

"Listen, young lady," he shouted.

She looked at him. "I'm listening."

Walking toward her he said, "You were making fifteen dollars an hour plus tips serving drinks on a golf course. Now all of a sudden you come home dressed like this, in a limousine. What are we supposed to think?"

"We?"

"Right, your sister's as concerned as I am."

"You are supposed to think that I got a good—no, a *great* job. A career, OK? That is what you're supposed to think!"

"That's what they call it?"

Courtney's eyes narrowed. She sat on the couch and crossed her legs and said, "That was right out of Kate's mouth. What has she been telling you?"

"We're family, Courtney, family."

"Answer me."

"Answer *you?*"

Courtney leaned forward nodding emphatically, "Yeah, Dad, answer me!"

He stubbed out his cigarette and whispered violently, "She told me that you were off with some Jew in Scotland. Now you tell me," he said, backing away. "What am I supposed to think? I did not raise you like this!"

"I was *working*. Jesus!"

He looked away.

"Look at me, Dad. I make more money now than Kate and her husband combined. And I am just starting!"

"At...what...cost?"

Courtney laughed, a high-pitched jolt in the air. "From where I'm sitting, there *is* no downside."

"What about Derek?"

"What about him?"

"For Christ's sake, your relationship, Courtney."

"Dad. Listen to me. I had a college romance with Derek. If I led him on in any way, I'm sorry about that. But that's all it was. He has to come to grips with that, and so does Kate."

Courtney lifted her cell phone in the air and played a manic voice message from Derek, begging her to call him. "This is the latest one to come in. I've deleted nearly a dozen of these messages. What does this sound like to you?"

"Like a man in love. Christ, a man in love."

"He sounds crazy."

Her father sighed heavily, his shoulder sagging.

"Your sister is concerned. She's built a life for herself and she wants..."

Courtney stood upright and cut him off. "I do not want her life. It is just not me."

"Is there something wrong with being happily married, having children, living a clean life?"

"I'm really not sure I like where this is going," Courtney said warily.

He looked at her. "You will not live under this roof, the home your mother and I built—may she rest in peace—like *this*."

"What does that mean?"

"You're a smart girl, figure it out."

"I don't have to. I'm moving out in September. I have an apartment."

He lit another cigarette, coughed, a raspy moist sound. "Did *he* get it for you?"

Courtney said, "You bet your ass he did."

36

On Tuesday, Latreece had just finished her shift and was standing by the road waiting for Tashanda's camp bus when Buddy pulled into his driveway next door. As he got out of the car, he caught the full heat of her glare. She wet her lips and shouted, "I oughta kill you for what you did to my baby."

Buddy slammed the car door and turned up to his house.

Latreece mumbled to herself, tapping her foot in angry rhythm, until she couldn't contain it any more. Hands on hips, she came across the strip of overgrown lawn dividing the two houses screaming, "You just walk away. You ain't even man enough to say nothin.'"

Buddy whipped around. "Your boyfriend's a sick fuck! That's what I have to say."

"You callin' *him* sick?!"

Buddy, red-faced with hate, his neck bulging, said, "Bring the girl here. Let *her* say what happened. You'll see it in her face. She's part of his lie and you're part of it too!"

The door exploded open and Tyrell bolted out, shirtless. "Latreece! Get your ass over here. Stop talkin' to that mothafucka!"

He bounded into the yard, coming nose-to-nose with Latreece as they shouted at each other, circling back toward the house in a temper-heated dervish. Then the bus pulled up and Tashanda bounded out and joined the fray, laughing first then crying for them to *stop*. Buddy stood with his door half open, transfixed, watching until they were back in the house. He looked across the street at the old man's house, thought for a second, sighed and slowly head-butted the door, whispering, "Jesus H. motherfucking *Christ*, this is insane!"

Wearing a demented half smile, he walked in, pulled a cold can of beer from the fridge and fell onto the couch with the phone. He rubbed the back of his neck; it was kinked and knotted.

He paged Dana. Something he never did, but he hadn't seen or heard from her in several days; he'd reached fuck-it-all mode. Then he dialed Russ's cell. After three rings, Russ answered, "This is Russell Dunn."

"Russ, did you not see the caller ID saying it was your old pal Buddy?"

"A reflexive response, Bud. Your boy Tyrell has a habit of calling me at odd hours. Dude, this guy is fucking spinning out of orbit. It's taking all my brilliant savoir faire to keep him under wraps. So, how are you doing?"

Buddy sat for a moment, staring at the floor with his mouth agape.

"Well, I haven't seen or talked to my wife in I don't know how many days. For all I know, she's shacked up with her new boss, this government hotshot. I just got home from caddying for a couple of twenty-five-year-old assholes, and now I've got to go across the street and paint a ninety-year-old black guy's house, for which I will receive not one fucking dime. On top of all that, Tyrell e-mailed Dana the picture. And the video. Did I mention there's 'videotape?' That fuck threatened to send the photo and film to all the hospital brass if I crossed him. Nice, huh? So, in answer to your question, I've had better fucking days, Russ."

"Well, so far, I think Plan A is working," Russ said.

"When are you going to Texas to shoot yourself? Maybe I'll join you. We could call it Plan B."

"C'mon, man, don't give up so fast."

"This whole sorry mess is absolutely crazy. How did we get here?"

As soon as he heard ice cubes swirling in Russ's drink, and that long sigh signaling lap dance time, Buddy knew it was a mistake to ask that. He interrupted and told Russ about Elaine's offer. "If I take her up on that, maybe we should just play Tyrell until I leave—walk away from the house. Into which I've sunk most of our net worth."

Russ gushed with emotion, "Christ, Buddy, sounds like you and Dana *both* struck gold. I'm happy for you. But please think this through. You love Dana, and I know she loves you. There are ways to navigate the rough waters ahead and I urge..."

"Save the marriage counseling, Russ. What about the house?"

"Walking away isn't as easy as it sounds. Tyrell could still..."

"Fuck Tyrell!"

Russ said, "You could quit-claims-deed the house to me. I could deal with Tyrell and..."

The call-waiting tone beeped. It was Dana. "Russ, I gotta go."

Buddy hit the flash button, and took a second to compose himself before saying, "Where have you been?"

"Don't conversations usually start with hello?"

"I guess there's nothing usual about us anymore."

"I won't argue that. I've been crazy busy, just crashed here at the hospital. Lots of shit going on."

"We have to talk, something's come up," Buddy said.

"Oh Christ, tell me now. If it's bad news, just tell me now."

"It's not bad. For once, it's not bad."

He heard her exhale before she said, "I'll be home tonight, but late, so don't wait up."

"Don't tell me not to wait up."

"OK."

"When I met you," said Buddy, "sleeping was the furthest thing from my mind."

"Mine too," she said.

37

Tyrell bear-hugged Latreece onto the couch, a slow-motion thump; not a violent action, just one meant to calm her, bring the situation under control. The TV was on—Oprah and Dr. Phil were chatting it up; upstairs a rap tune thumped behind a closed door: "*Yeah, clear enough for ya, why niggaz look mad? Picture me rollin' in my 500 Benz, I got no luv for these niggaz, no need to be friends...*"

Tashanda splayed on the floor like a rag doll, crying in fits, kicking her feet, babbling incoherently. Latreece squirmed forcefully. "Get your mothafuckin' hands off me!" Tashanda took up the refrain: "*Mothafucka, mothafucka,*" she screamed over and over.

"Look at this shit. Ah c'mon now, we goin' crazy here," Tyrell said softly into Latreece's mouth.

Latreece was wild-eyed. "Not *we*. *You* goin' crazy, an takin' us with you...Now lemme go!"

Tyrell eased his grip. Losing patience, he barked, "Dummy, shut the fuck up!"

"Mothafuckyou, mothafuckyou," Tashanda yelped.

Tyrell and Latreece laughed, the tension draining out of them.

Giggling, Tashanda jumped up and started dancing to a tune in her head.

And just like that, the emotional storm blew over. Latreece settled on Tyrell's shoulder. Tashanda lept onto the couch wriggling between them. Latreece sighed and said, "I wanna make dinner for us. You all skin an bones. I wanna have dinner, tell you about my day, hear about yours, then go upstairs and..." Latreece paused, putting her hands over Tashanda's ears, "*Fuck* like we used to before all this crazy shit started, OK?"

Tyrell's left eyelid twitched, his lashes undulating like a millipede.

"Baby, baby," Latreece cooed, struggling to coax him. *Bring this crazy mothafucker under control*, she thought to herself. She stroked his crotch, squeezed, breathed into his ear, saying she wanted to suck him dry.

"Tyrell said, "Ok, baby, but first let's look, watch him go to work for me."

"Say what?"

Tyrell jerked a thumb toward Buddy's house.

Latreece scowled. "Can we not talk about him? For one night, can you please get that mothafucka off your mind? Baby, I want to make it special for you."

Tyrell got up without answering. He walked to the window and stared out across the street. Latreece sighed and picked up the remote to change channels. "There ya go, honey-bunny, watch your show while Momma makes dinner," she said to Tashanda. Latreece paused, looked at Tyrell and thought about when they'd first met. How he looked so cool in his clean baggy jeans and shirt, sunglasses, chains, like a rap star.

She said softly, but loud enough so he could hear, "I'm gonna start up smokin' dope again, this shit don't stop. I want my man back."

Tyrell was too absorbed in his own thoughts to hear Latreece. She got up and went into the kitchen, clattering about as she cleaned and cut up a whole chicken she'd bought at Armelino's Market. It was twice the price of Stop & Shop, but she liked the sign in Armelino's window: *Are chickens don' do drugs.* She fired up half a blunt, inhaled deeply and felt an almost-instant buzz. Swaying her hips, she seasoned the pieces with Old Bay, salt, pepper, and powdered garlic. Then she heated her cast iron skillet, put in two heaping tablespoons of Crisco, and dredged the chicken in flour, waiting for the grease to heat. Latreece laid in the first few pieces, heard the pop, watched the skin sizzle, sniffed the sweet greasy air. She was turning a drumstick when Tyrell called from the living room, "OK."

"You say something?" she called, her voice tinged with anger.

"I said, *OK*."

Latreece came out of the kitchen, a pair of tongs in her hand. "An what does that mean, OK? OK *what*?"

He waved her over and pointed to the window. Tyrell snatched a small pair of binoculars from the windowsill, the kind handicappers use, and peered through them. Buddy was making his way across Pulaski Road, toward the old man's house. "That boy is white-bread white," he whispered, passing the binoculars to Latreece. She watched Buddy disappear behind the bushes that shielded Eugene Freyerson's front door.

"OK, what's this got to do with us, the *house*?"

Tyrell smiled toothily, "I'm makin' my Buddy boy hop to."

She shot him a look, passed the binoculars. "You're one crazy ass nigga."

Licking his lips, he said, "This crazy ass nigga's ready for some sweet black pussy."

He roped his arms around her waist.

"And where does this brotha think he's gonna get that sweet black pussy, huh?"

As Tyrell's hands dropped to her ass, she said, "*Sheeeeiit*, my chicken," and sprinted for the kitchen.

38

Buddy raised his hand and then paused, suspending the moment as long as he could. He thought about Dana, Elaine, Russ...Tyrell. He looked back across the road at his little starter house, the one they'd bought on spec to ride the market, turn a big profit, move on to bigger and better things. Buddy let out a soft snort. Turning back to the door, he knocked, banging his knuckles on the wooden frame in anger.

He waited, knocked again. Waited. Put his ear to the door. Waited. He turned away just as the door opened.

His face flushed seeing the old man. He cleared his throat. "Mr. Freyerson, I'm Buddy Graves. I'm here to paint your house."

"Then why were you walkin' away?"

Buddy fumbled his hands. "Well I...I thought you might be asleep, or something."

The old man grinned. "Or dead, huh?" he said, with a sly wink.

Buddy opened his mouth to protest, but the old man waved his hand and opened the screen. "You young folks got no patience. Anyways, come on in; let's see what we're doin' here," he said, extending his hand. The power of his grip took Buddy by surprise.

The house was dark and airless, like a monk's cell. It smelled of dog, Aqua Velva, and old age. The mutt was lying in the corner on a tattered dog bed covered with hair. He raised his head and perked his ears when Buddy walked in.

The old man led Buddy to the kitchen that adjoined the small living room where, hanging on the wall in white plastic frames, were pictures of President Kennedy, Martin Luther King, Jr., a grainy photo of a boxer, and a small picture of a wedding couple just beneath a paint-by-numbers picture of a black Jesus.

Freyerson pulled a chair out and said to the dog, "We got company, Old Sam."

They sat. The old man appraised Buddy with dark eyes that were at once bemused, aloof, and slightly suspicious. "I was movin' Old Sam's bowels when you knocked, that's why I took a minute. He's paralyzed in his hindquarters, so I got to help him. The vet said he should be put down. That was three years ago."

"I'm sorry," said Buddy.

"I ain't," said the old man. "He's work, but he's worth it."

Buddy looked over at the dog and smiled.

The old man said, "So, he payin' you for this, right?

Buddy's eyes were suddenly wary. "Who?"

"You OK?"

"Pardon?"

The old man scratched his head. "I'm old but I ain't dumb."

Buddy waited.

"There's funny business goin' on around here, an you got caught up in it."

"I'm not sure I know what you mean."

The old man picked at a callous on his palm. "That boy Tyrell's mouth waggles like a duck's ass, all this nonsense about his big project. Black ownership, all that jive, like black ownership is some kinda new idea he come up with. Callin' me Uncle Gene, shoot. I gave him what for over that. I been around too long to get hustled."

"I'm just here to paint your house, Mr. Freyerson," Buddy said, softly.

To get a better look at Buddy, the old man leaned back. "Right, that's what you're here for." He thought for a few seconds before stating firmly, "I got the cancer, or I'd be paintin' it myself. I told that boy Tyrell as much."

"I'm sorry."

The old man winced. "Stop sayin' you're sorry. There ain't nothin' 'round here to be sorry about."

Buddy nodded to himself. "What kind of cancer do you have, if you don't mind my asking?"

"If I minded, I wouldn't a told you. I got the prostate cancer," he said. "Prostate, same as my daddy died from."

"Pro*state*," Buddy said reflexively.

The old man jerked his head. "That's what I said, *prostate*."

"Sorry. Most people say 'prostrate.' I shouldn't have assumed."

They looked at each other as a faint farting sound filled the room. Buddy struggled not to grimace from the smell. The old man paused, and said, "Old Sam's gassy. Comes from not bein' able to move his bowels his own self. I'm used to it, but I know it's nasty."

"What's nasty?"

Freyerson cocked his head toward the dog and mouthed the word *gas*.

"I didn't notice anything," Buddy said, matter-of-factly.

The old man studied Buddy for a moment. Then he smiled. "Well, I'll give ya an 'A' for politeness. So let's get this old house painted."

Buddy stood. "Where's the paint, Mr. Freyerson?"

The old man stood. "I imagine it's at the Home Depot."

"You don't have the paint?"

"The boss-man, Tyrell, said he was supplyin' paint an labor."

Buddy shook his head in exasperation. "*Right*…OK, what color do you want, sir?"

Freyerson dropped back in the chair. "It just figures, that big-talkin' Tyrell sends me a greenhorn."

Buddy pinched the bridge of his nose. "What's wrong?"

The old man sighed. "You can't just run out there an slop paint on a house. It's gotta be prepped. At least the front where that southern sun hits it."

"Prepped?"

"Of course," Freyerson said.

He stood up and shuffled back behind the kitchen. Buddy heard him rooting around. "I can tell I got my work cut out for me on this project," he mumbled, as he reappeared with several putty knives and a steel brush. "There's a ladder back yonder," he said. "We still have a few hours 'fore dark."

"Yeah, *we*," Buddy muttered under his breath.

૱૱

Buddy climbed the ladder and began scrapping just below a tiny screened window that was probably there for a defunct attic fan. It was early evening, but still so hot he felt like a melting candle, sweat dripping down his face, under his arms. He could faintly hear the old man singing to himself, or maybe to the dog. *What the hell that old guy has to be singing about, I don't know*, he thought. A horn blared, brakes screeched, distracting him. Buddy swore as a sliver of wood buried itself in his forefinger. That's when the first one got him on the earlobe, fiery hot. Then the air around his head filled with buzzing. He yelled, dropped the putty knife and half slid, half fell down the ladder. Jumping around in a mad tarantella, he tore off his shirt and swatted the air, screaming. Freyerson's door slapped open. The old man grabbed the garden hose and doused Buddy with shockingly cold water, hitting his chest and face with a hard chilling spray.

Back in the house, Buddy pulled still-writhing wasps from his hair. There were so many welts on his face, it felt like acne. The old man came from the back room with a squeeze tube of ointment. "Ooh eee, good thing you ain't 'lergic to them SOBs. Here now, daub this on," he said.

Buddy's whole body fluttered every time he touched his face.

"Least we know exactly where they been hidin.' I was wonderin.'"

Buddy looked at him, stunned. "You knew there were wasps up there?"

"Well, I knew there was a nest. Didn't know exactly where. Hard to tell less ya stand there watchin' 'em, and I ain't got time for that."

"Jesus Christ!" Buddy said.

"OK, let's leave Jesus outta this. We gonna get revenge."

"What do you mean, we?"

The old man just chuckled, "Boy, you shoulda seen yourself, dancin' around like one of them fools on Soul Train. Anyway, we'll go to the Home Depot, get some wasp spray. That stuff kills from 20 feet, so you won't have to go but halfway up the ladder."

"Man, I'm calling it a day. I need a shower," Buddy said.

"If we don't kill them things, you won't be able to paint."

Those watery yellowed eyes, that face as dark as cast iron, the scar running down the cheek, knuckles all busted and arthritic, the scent of Aqua Velva, old dog farts. It got to Buddy. *What a sentimental sucker you are*, he thought.

"OK, I'll run up to Home Depot and get some bug spray," Buddy said, standing and fighting to keep his cool.

"I better go with you. That way we can get a color chart, plan things out."

Buddy started to the door.

"Please pick me up after you go change. I gotta feed Old Sam an take him out back. Won't be but an hour or so," the old man said.

Buddy stopped. "An hour? I'd like to get this done before dark, Mr. Freyerson."

"That ain't possible."

"Why not? All we're doing is picking up some insecticide and spraying those bastards."

"Cause we can't hit 'em 'til dark. That's when they nest up." Crouching with a comic lunge, Freyerson said, "A sneak attack, pow! Man, you *are* a greenhorn."

Old Sam farted. Buddy shivered, sneezed, touched his face. "Oh, for fuck's sake," he said under his breath as the old man rambled on about wasps and nests and paint colors for the house.

"I'll see you in an hour, Mr. Freyerson," Buddy said, slightly huffy, pulling open the screen door.

"I never rode in a BMW," the old man said. "That's a class ride."

Buddy smiled to himself and said, "Well you haven't missed much, Mr. Freyerson."

39

Later that night, a storm blew in across the Sound. Latreece said *"wow"* and stopped making love to Tyrell. She jumped up from the bed to switch off the air conditioner and fling open the windows, filling the room with rain-whipped air, thunder-booms and the back-glow of lightning flashes. "I love the sound of the rain," she said turning. But when she came back to bed, she'd already lost him. "C'mon baby, let's keep fucking."

They went through an hour-long animated session of grinding and groping, desperately trying to rekindle the lost spark. Frustrated, Latreece rolled off him with a heavy sigh. "You shouldn't a got outta bed," he fumed.

"For *five* seconds. I wanted to hear the rain. It's romantic."

They lay for a long time without talking. Tyrell rolled toward her, smelled the sweat-sheen on her face, kissed her mouth, stroked her breasts, her arms, her legs. "Baby, let's stop," Latreece said.

He sat up and swung his feet onto the floor. Placing his elbows on his knees, Tyrell dropped his head and said, "What the fuck is wrong *now?*"

Latreece sat up, covering herself with the sheet. "Tyrell, we just spent an hour trying to get back into it...you never had a problem like this, not before you..."

He grimaced. "Before what?"

"You just seem all distracted."

"What are you talkin' about, bitch?"

Latreece narrowed her eyes. "That gonna get you real far, callin' me a bitch."

He stormed out of the room.

She called, "And where you going?"

"I gotta pee. That OK?"

Tyrell slipped past the hallway bathroom and tiptoed into his office. He slid open his desk drawer, grabbed a bottle, and popped four amphetamine tablets. Then he stole into the bathroom, flushed the toilet, ran water in the sink, and came back into the bedroom. Latreece was standing next to the bed, arms crossed over her chest.

"Drop the attitude," he said.

"Somewhere along here you made a choice," she said.

Tyrell threw up his hands. "What the fuck does that mean?"

"Him, next door," she said, pointing toward Buddy's house.

The pills hit. He heard ringing in his ears. He came right up to her.

Without backing down, Latreece said, "He didn't look like he was lying."

"That mothafucka's a born lie, you got that, huh?"

Lightning flashed and cracked *caaaaboooomb*, just outside the window. They both jumped. Laughing nervously, Latreece shook her head. She felt tears well up in her eyes. "I can't go on like this no more," she said, suddenly sobbing. Tyrell moved toward her, woodenly. She put her hands up to stop him and said with her shoulders shaking, "I need my Momma."

"She can't hear you," he said gently. "I'm here now."

"Right," she said, stiffening. "I wanna show you something."

He followed her into his office. She opened his laptop.

"You been goin' into my shit?" he said, leaning over her.

Latreece ignored him. She pulled up a website—the Holmes Report—and clicked on the lead story:

Black Separatist Prof Canoodling White Hottie

So much for hip-hop-quoting professor, Jerome Brown's street cred with the black radical set. Our urban guerilla photog nailed the race-baiting prof—just off a scream-fest on the O'Reilly Factor—buttering his white-bread lover while in Detroit promoting his provocative book "Rage Without End," due out soon. In a telephone interview, Celia Dupree, Brown's ex who divorced him last year, told *The Holmes Report*, "It doesn't surprise me an iota to see Jerome with a white girl. She might not have as big expectations as a sister, if you get my drift." Ms. Dupree joked that the only thing big about Jerome Brown is his ego. She went on to say that his love for one color, green...

Tyrell swept the article. He studied the pictures of Professor Brown smiling, touching, kissing, the white bitch. Latreece put her hand on Tyrell's shoulder, whispered his name. He reared his head back.

"What you lookin' at this trash for?" he asked, jumpy and nervous.

"Tyrell," she said.

"Why you lookin' at me like that? OK, so JB's with this bitch. So what? Pussy makes a man stupid. I can testify to that!"

Latreece did a bobble-head waggle, said, "So, they ain't enough sistas out there, that big-talkin' brotha gotta get stupid over *white* pussy?"

Tyrell closed the laptop, a slow deliberate motion.

"White pussy," he said, letting the words hang in the air like stink.

"He's playin' you," she said softly, reaching out, touching his face.

Tyrell's jaw clenched. "No he ain't. But me an Jerome got some business to settle."

40

That same night in Detroit, just past eleven o'clock, Jerome Brown was walking down Brush Street toward the Atheneum Suite Hotel, dictating into a Sony digital recorder, "Malik Shabazz, the Black Nationalist despised and vilified by the white establishment press, the righteous brother who single-handedly energized the new Black Panther Nation told me he has exceptional solutions for the racism that plagues the city of Detroit. But Shabazz is a mild-mannered spokesperson for the plight of black America compared with Reverend Leroy Hannah, a terror-eyed underground proselytizer, filling the holes in the hearts of dispossessed inner city black men with new-found purpose. Not the brand of purpose that gives white America a warm fuzzy feeling, no Protestant work ethic that keeps them niggas outta trouble, away from white women. Fuck no, Rev Hannah's ecclesiastical canon is rooted in the supremacy of black maleness, an ideology of hatred for prettified racist white society more potent than a million cobras. You actually feel it radiating off his prison-hardened body, and, even for a brother like me who's worked the mean streets of the ghetto, it is fucking intimidating. He hisses, "How did we end up here, an isolated island against the white darkness. They have been our stalkers!" Like Islam, his message is purposely simple, and therein lays its power to radicalize young black males searching for a place, a brotherhood, a gang, seeking an enemy, a fatwa…"

Brown was still dictating as he keyed the suite's door.

"I'm home, darling," he sang playfully.

"Jerome, do you ever answer your cell phone?" Mindy Banks called as Brown came down the hall to the sitting room. Mindy was at the desk working at her laptop. Brown cast his gaze over her shower-damp hair, pink velour shorts and a tight black T-shirt. She wasn't wearing a bra, and the outline of her breasts and nipples was visible.

He clicked the recorder off and picked up the room service menu. "I'm starved and thirsty. Let's order in."

She kept typing. He opened the menu, waited a beat, and then said, "Mindy. *Hello.* It's nearly eleven-thirty, what are you doing?"

She spun around. "I'm working. I got an urgent call from my assistant. We're putting out some fires. Graydon Carter called. *Twice.*"

Looking startled, Brown tossed the menu on the bed. "What fires?"

"I called, but you never answered," she said curtly.

"I was working, interviewing a fuckin' crazy brother for the next *Vanity Fair* piece I'm gonna propose. He's not the kind of guy you interrupt for a phone call. He gave great copy, but the dude is serious as cancer. Did a nine-year bid for manslaughter. We were in his 'undisclosed' location. Think 'black KKK' on steroids. So what the fuck did Carter call about? We hit the stands tomorrow."

Mindy turned to the laptop and pulled up a webpage. "Obviously you haven't seen this," she said, opening the screen. "Have a seat, check this out," she said.

Brown sat down, reading carefully, a silent anger building. He sat back, balled his fist and slammed the desk. "Who the fuck is behind *The Holmes Report?*"

Mindy was behind him. "Bobbi Holmes. She started blogging a few years ago, sort of a faux Page Six, covering mostly local stuff in Manhattan. Low-grade tabloid fare. But she gets around, has a lot of contacts. And over the past year she's upped the ante, going for the jugular on high-profile targets, like you."

"How in the hell did they get those pictures? We weren't together, except for..."

Mindy completed the sentence, "Except for that one time, Jerome. We were careful, but she's got some juice, and she's a really good writer. She's got to..."

"You call this good?" Brown shouted, shutting the laptop and bolting upright in one motion.

"Yeah Jerome, she's good."

"Who the fuck *is* she?"

"She's a journalist, graduated from Columbia, then..."

Brown jerked his hand in the air in a "that's enough" motion.

"My bitch of an ex-wife talked to her, this Holmes bitch. Jesus Christ," Brown said, rubbing his eyes. "How many people read this shit? How'd you hear about it? And what did that bastard Graydon Carter want?"

She crossed her arms. "*The Holmes Report* gets about 20,000 hits a day. At Banks Marketing, we make it our *business* to hear about everything. Carter saw the article and went bat-shit. He thinks it makes you *and* him look foolish."

Jerome spoke slowly, processing his thoughts, word by word. "OK, so this Bobbi Holmes put a piece on her trashy blog, some punk-bitch paparazzi snapped a shot of us kissing. It's just free ink, right? I mean, any publicity's better than none."

"This stuff hurts your brand, Jerome."

"My brand? I'm a professor, a writer!"

"Right, baby, but your black radical cred is your brand. Having a white lover undercuts that."

Brown walked to the phone by the bed and called room service. He ordered a bottle of Absolut vodka with set-ups, and two double shrimp cocktails. "Maybe this will just go away, fade into the ether," he said.

"I guarantee that she has got more dirt on you—on *us*."

"Carter went bat-shit, huh? he said. *"Bat-shit,"* he repeated, a sour look on his face.

"But we're gonna turn a negative into a positive. I spoke to Karen Wyckoff over at Stern & Casey. O'Reilly's foaming at the mouth. He can't wait to interview you again. You're doing *The Factor*. They're working on it as we speak."

Jerome's head jerked up. "Girl, you're crazy! That fucking Mick cock-sucker will fry me alive, paint me as a fraud, just another phony race-baiting nigga riding the gravy train of hate. Tell Wyckoff I just came down with terminal sickle cell anemia, tell her I had a stroke, got hit by a bus. Tell her anything, because I am *not* doin' *The Factor*!"

"Jerome, you gotta set this right."

"By getting my black ass phonied-up on national TV by Bill O'Reilly?"

"No, you control the interview...by going out of control. Have a throw-down, laugh in his face. Tell him you picked up your white bitch, *me*, like you do periodically, just to use and abuse her. Bring up Eldridge Cleaver and what he said—that his rapes of white women were a political statement. Go off on Bill, on white bitch America. Send O'Reilly over the edge. He's got this Irish Catholic prudishness about women, so push his fucking button!"

There was a knock on the door. Room service.

Brown poured two drinks. He took a long sip and said in a low voice, "This thing that's happening now, maybe it wouldn't have if we'd—no, if *I'd* been more careful. I was so sure of myself..."

"Jerome, people like Bobbi Holmes live by planting themselves in other people's business. Don't let her."

"It's not just that."

"Then what is it?"

Brown said "*ennh*," and stared into space. "I was there at Lenox Hill, at the end, when the breast cancer had taken over my mother's body. She was a strong woman, she held on and on. One night, her breathing slowed, then her eyes opened and she let out a long breath and looked at me. You could see the sadness in her eyes—not about dying, sadness for *me*."

"Jerome," Mindy said, grabbing his knee and squeezing. "I know it's tough on you. She didn't live to see your success."

"No, no, it's not that. The truth is, I don't give a fuck about going on O'Reilly. It would make me sad, *very* sad, to play that game. Even if it's for the fuckin' greater cause," he said, with a wave of his hand.

Mindy took a breath. "Look, I'm not gonna lie. This whole thing with you has been exciting, it's given me life, even this shit. We're gaming the system just like everybody else, only better. Why shouldn't we cash in too?"

"We, huh?" he said with a sarcastic edge to his voice. Then his shoulders slumped. "Sometimes, like now, I feel that what I'm doing—it's almost like I'm fighting with myself. I believe some of this shit, I do. But sometimes when I hear myself…maybe I think my mother would be ashamed."

Mindy sighed, kissed his forehead. "Let's just get through this. Graydon thinks it's brilliant, he's down with going on O'Reilly, K? The publicist at Random is cool with it too. She's confident it will help book sales. But it's up to you."

Jerome closed his eyes, laughing softly. "You didn't listen to me."

"Sure I did!"

"'Down with this, *K?*' Girl, when'd you start taking like that? It makes me feel like I'm…" Jerome stopped, shook his head.

"Fucking a kid?" she said, cozying up to him.

Jerome dipped his index finger into his drink, ran it down her nose, and said, "Yeah." Then he put their drinks on the night table and kissed her. She sighed but pulled away, moving to the laptop.

"Baby, I don't want to break the mood, but there's something else you should see."

"What now?" Brown said wearily, getting up to stand behind her and look over her shoulder.

Mindy pulled up his Gmail. A thread of "High Importance!" e-mails from Tyrell. "I started to read them, then my head began to throb," Mindy said, clicking on the first message.

Subject: A dream deferred?

*Professor Brown, Jerome, my brother in arms, our world, our **black** world, has a dome over it, and whites are not allowed in. We are smart, powerful, energetic, confident brothers in the struggle, have I been so astoundingly naïve to think, to believe that you…*

Subject: A trial run at black celebrity?

*Jerome, I have seen the **white** demon up close…you, better than anyone I have ever known has articulated the emotional weaknesses of our adversaries, we are not equally matched belligerents, we have the power, so, how could you be* *played as a pawn by that white cunt(s)...you do know how tenacious and committed I am...*

Brown read half of the dozen or so e-mails, each one more bizarre and angry than the last. He closed the laptop, took a drink, and fell back on the bed, depleted.

Mindy sank next to him and wriggled out of her pink shorts. "I think your boy Tyrell has gone over the edge."

Moving his hand between Mindy's legs, Brown said, "I know Tyrell. I can handle him. Trick with a dude like that, you gotta be in control without letting him know it."

"Like O'Reilly," she said.

"Right, like that mothafucka O'Reilly."

41

At three-thirty in the morning Buddy was in the living room watching re-runs of the WGC Bridgestone Invitational. Tiger Woods, wearing a weird-looking goatee, had just missed a six-foot putt.

He didn't hear the front door open. Dana closed it with the delicacy of a cat burglar. She stepped into the living room and put her briefcase on the floor.

"Tiger is mind-fucked," Buddy said to himself, "he is toast."

"Should I care?" she said.

Buddy lurched forward. It was muggy and oppressive outside and Dana had brought a bit of the air in with her. Her tall silhouette in the dim light soothed his tired eyes.

"Not really, just an observation," Buddy said, trying to sound casual. He didn't want to make her feel uneasy that he was still awake in the middle of the night.

"Things caught up with him," Dana said quietly, a catch in her voice. Stepping to the couch, she squinted and said, "Jesus, Buddy, what happened to your face?"

"Yellow jackets, lots of them," he said.

She shook her head. "Yellow jackets? Where, at the golf course?"

"No, Mr. Freyerson's house. Nest was under a shingle, but we got 'em. Gassed the bastards."

She thudded her forehead with the heel of her hand. "Who the hell is Mr. Freyerson?"

"The old black guy across the street."

Dana sat across from him, picked up the remote and flicked off the TV. "So what were you doing there?"

Buddy told her about the conversation with Russ, the old man, his connection to Tyrell. Dana leaned on the armrest as she listened.

"You all right?" she asked suddenly.

Buddy flinched. "What do you mean?"

Dana looked at him. "I don't know. This whole thing. It's still a hell of a shock, but I'm over blaming you."

"Are you?"

She hunched her shoulders. "Maybe." Pointing with her chin toward the house next door, she added, "But I'm not over being scared."

"I know."

"I'm exhausted. Let's go to bed," she said wearily.

Laying next to one another in bed, clad in their underwear, felt like an uneasy truce.

"There is something else I wanted to tell you," Buddy said. "Some good news." Haltingly, he told Dana about Elaine's offer. The story came out in puffs of sound, as though Buddy was trying to blow out a flame. Dana listened quietly, staring at the overhead fan, her jaw sagging. She turned and edged closer to him.

"That's the Elaine you had the hots for when you were a kid, right? I used to like hearing about her, but it always made me jealous."

"I can't imagine you jealous."

"Well, I'm happy for you Buddy. *Wow*. She kept that drawing all these years. Like she was waiting for you."

He shrugged, touched her neck, and stared intently at her. "It still might not happen," Buddy said. "You don't know her husband."

"She sounds like one determined lady. About you."

"Don't say that. This is business."

"I know all about business," she said with a sharp, jaded edge to her voice that made Buddy wince. He wondered what had prompted her to say that. Something from her past? Or something from the present, this new venture of hers?

Their conversation faltered. It was quiet, just the soft buckle of moist wind gusting off the Sound. Buddy listened to his wife breathe, swallow, the delicate music of the body he knew so well. His eyes closed as he thought of what to say. Then the pulse of rap music broke their uncomfortable silence as a car pulled into the driveway next door. Buddy flinched. When the music stopped, they heard the car door slam. It was so hushed in the post-rain morning they could hear footsteps. Then nothing, a full minute of nothing. Finally, the door next door opened and closed.

Letting out a breath she'd been holding, Dana said, "God, it sounded like he was coming into our house. That's next, I guess."

"No," Buddy said firmly. "He will not fucking come in here. Right now that cocksucker imagines he's on some kind of black power trip and that he controls me. Let the motherfucker think that. He is spiraling out of control and that works in our favor. It gives us time."

"Time for what?" said Dana.

"To get out of here."

"Just leave our home?"

"It doesn't feel like our home anymore, at least not to me."

"Oh fuck, Buddy!"

"Well does it?"

"No, it fucking does not," she said bitterly.

Buddy told her about Russ's idea of signing the house over to him.

"That sounds like it might just set off this guy Tyrell. Then what? He posts that video on YouTube and plasters that picture all over the Web?"

Buddy turned toward her, groping for the right words. He had so many unaskable questions. "Once this bastard's phony accusation gets out, he loses power. He's shot his load. He wants to keep this going as long as he can. I'll just play along," Buddy said. "Then, when the time is right, we just leave in the middle of the night."

"What, like a couple of thieves? I leave for DC, and you go to Arizona?"

"For now."

"'For now' usually ends up 'forever,'" she said.

"Christ, Dana, don't say that."

Dana gripped her hair in both hands. "How did this happen?" she moaned.

"I left the front door unlocked," he said, feeling suddenly drained. *And I was careless with things*, he thought bleakly.

"My family keeps asking what's going on and I don't know what to tell them," Dana said. "But I know that something has happened, and it's changed us. First me, now this freaky thing with you and Elaine."

"Freaky?"

"Wrong word, but you know what I mean." She put her hand on his leg. Her palm was warm. "I'm happy and scared shitless at the same time. We have this time bomb ticking next door. It's like we're trying to escape before the explosion, but we don't know when it'll detonate. Tell me everything's gonna be alright."

"Everything's gonna be alright," he said touching her shoulder. Then he slid his hand across her belly and between her legs, which parted instantly, a mechanical reaction. His head was between her legs then, as he pulled her panties off. Through ragged breaths he heard her say to herself, "Jesus, no matter what, we still fuck."

42

The sun was just rising when they went down to the kitchen. Dana leaned against the counter in her panties and a T-shirt Buddy had bought her online from Cry Baby Ranch, a funky Western clothing store he'd heard about in Denver. In sepia letters on a white background, the shirt said "Cowgirl Justice: Get a Rope" and was studded with six small Swarovski crystals. Watching the coffee drip, Dana said her schedule for the next couple of weeks would be "all over the place."

"Does that mean you won't be coming home some nights?" Buddy asked, trying to soften the worried edge in his voice.

"I'll have to play it by ear."

"What's that mean?

"C'mon Buddy."

She poured the coffee and sat across from him. "Want some eggs and toast?"

"You know I don't eat in the morning."

"You look like a sunny-side *up* kinda guy," she said, with a coy smile.

"Christ, you're making me feel like a bachelor."

"If you *were* a bachelor, what would that make me?" Dana said.

"My sexy babe," he grinned.

❧ ❧

Buddy settled into a rhythm. He caddied, returned home, had a beer, walked across the street, and painted Eugene Freyerson's house. The old man had chosen a slate blue that reminded him of clean-looking, sturdy houses he'd seen in pictures of Cape Cod. Each successive night, Freyerson would step from the house a little bit earlier for his inspection, giving a hard-won nod of approval. And despite Buddy's insistence that he wanted to keep working, the old man would say, "Well son, that's a fair day's work. Rushin' just gets you to Sloppy Town."

Buddy had finally finished the prep and made a good dent on the first coat. He wanted this over, but Freyerson was a hard man to press. He had his routines. From the first day, he had been feeling Buddy out. Now Freyerson was inviting him in for a drink. They'd sit down in the kitchen and the old man would produce a Mason jar filled with whiskey and a peach, explaining that this was how his daddy kept his home brew when Freyerson was a boy down South. The whiskey he poured for Buddy was just plain store-bought, but he kept it in the Mason jar with a peach to preserve the memories.

"Old men are justa box of bones and memories, some they'd like to forget," Freyerson said, sipping the whiskey, closing his eyes and sighing.

"And some you'd like to keep," said Buddy.

Freyerson smiled and nodded, "They just there, gettin' fuzzy 'round the edges."

The two men talked. Freyerson had a sly way of prying into Buddy's life. But most of all, he wanted to know about Tyrell and his monkey business. Buddy deflected the questions as best he could, but he revealed enough for the old man to draw his own conclusions.

≈∽

On a night in early July, the old man confided that the thing he feared most was "All heimer disease."

"Wouldn't know where I was, who I was—worst, who Old Sam was. Nah, that's a thing that I don't want. Instead, I got the cancer. Some trade-off."

Buddy, three whiskeys in, said, "What did the oncologist say about your cancer, the stage?"

"Say what? Look, I went to the clinic, because I was wakin' up all hours of the night, had to pee. Then it started hurtin'," he said, sitting back, waving his hand in the air. "Anyway, no need to get into all that. The doc there did a bunch of tests."

"DRE, digital rectal exam."

The old man made a face. "Stuck his finger in my behind, if that's what you mean. Damn, can't see how them sissies like gettin' a willy up there."

"So what were the results?"

The old man got up, went to the cupboard, pulled out the report, and handed it to Buddy. He took the paper, studied it for a few moments, and said, "Mr. Freyerson, you don't have prostate cancer."

The old man sat, paused, looked at Buddy. "I guess I ain't sure what you just said."

"You have BPH, benign prostatic hyperplasia, not cancer."

"You wanna run that by me in English?"

"It's a condition that makes your prostate gland enlarge, get bigger. It squeezes the urethra, the pee tube that runs from your bladder. That's why you feel like you have to urinate. It's a bit uncomfortable, but it won't kill you. There's a procedure they can do to reduce the size of your prostate."

The old man stood, walked in a funny little circle, scratching his head and mumbling. He turned, leaned on the table, and stretched his head out. "You mean to tell me I don't got the cancer?"

Buddy nodded. "No sir, you do not have cancer."

"You a caddy, not a doctor!"

"I was a medical editor before I was a caddy. I am telling you. You don't have cancer, Mr. Freyerson."

The old man let out such a forceful whoop it threatened to blow Buddy back in his chair. Old Sam jerked his head up and whined.

"You hear that, Old Sam? Daddy don't have the cancer!" He grabbed Buddy's hand, tears welling in his eyes. "Bless you son. Damn, I'm eighty-five years old. I thought I was a goner. I'd lie in bed worryin' about who'd take care of Old Sam. You took a heavy weight off my shoulders. Bless you, boy. Bless you!"

Eugene poured a celebratory drink and asked Buddy how it was that he went from a fancy job like an editor to a caddy. Buddy told him it was a long story better suited for another night. Freyerson, high on whiskey and the commutation of his death sentence, peppered Buddy with questions about his life, his wife the nurse, all the funny business next door, preempting each query with a "I don't mean to go where I ain't been invited, but..."

Some of the questions touched a raw nerve. But like most men who had knocked around, Freyerson knew the ways of the world. When he sensed that Buddy had had enough, but was too polite to say so, the old man stopped, and poured out some more whisky.

Buddy said, "My turn," and pointed to the shelf in the living room, right beneath the portrait of Martin Luther King where a small pearl-handled pistol sat. "I've wanted to ask why you have that pistol sitting there in plain sight."

"So I can get to it if I need to," Freyerson said.

Buddy looked at him.

"How else do you expect an old man to protect hisself?" he asked.

"I'm just not used to seeing a gun out in the open, I guess."

"You a Yankee, that's why. I'm a colored man from the South."

"Right," said Buddy.

"There's a story behind that gun. A memory."

"Are you going to tell me?"

The old man smiled. "Yeah, but not tonight, son. I just wanna enjoy this new lease on life." He raised his glass. "You made an old man happy tonight, son. You know, you an easy fella to talk to."

"So they say," said Buddy, lifting his glass.

43

Izzy returned home from Washington in the early evening, tired, exalted, his head spinning with the details of his trip. His driver, Jack Herzog, put Izzy's bags in the sitting room and asked if there was anything else. Izzy said distractedly, "No, Jack." But Herzog, waiting for more, put his fist to his mouth and coughed. Izzy turned and smiled, "Shit, Jack, take tomorrow and the next day off. In fact, if ya want, take the missus out to the place in the Hamptons. I'll ring that hump at the East Hampton Point, get you my table. Live it large, Jack."

"Thanks, Mr. Weinberg."

"Thanks yourself, Jack," Izzy said. As Herzog turned to the door, Izzy called, "Jack, how long you been driving me?"

"Not sure, exactly."

"Me either. How old are you?"

A look passed between them.

"A bit younger than you, Mr. Weinberg."

Izzy half grinned. "Good answer. Listen Jack, I got some stuff percolating. Can you commit to a few more years, at a heavier schedule?"

"This is what I do, I drive," Jack said.

Izzy nodded. "We'll talk."

"I'm all ears."

"But listen, let's fix it so that, except when I'm doin' business I'm Izzy, OK?"

Jack cocked his head, studied Izzy. "Sure," he said, opening the door. "Goodnight Izzy. My best to Mrs. Weinberg," he said with a theatrical lilt.

Izzy was pouring himself a Scotch when Elaine called from the hall, "All of a sudden you're a mush? After all these years, you're now pals with your driver?"

Izzy said, "Mush I'm not. You know me, doll, I do everything for a reason."

He turned to see Elaine in the doorway wearing a peach-colored silk peignoir and five-inch Jimmy Choos. He took a sip and studied her, a quick smile. Pointing to her shoes he said, "Better watch out kiddo. You might get a nosebleed in those."

Elaine shimmied like a showgirl, unbelted the dressing gown and let it slip to the floor. Naked, she placed one hand on her breast, the other on her ass, over the small surgical scars that were like angry slashes. "Well, you like? The tits are a benelli mastopexy and my ass is the Brazilian butt lift. Does J-Lo have anything on that?"

Izzy waved his hand. "*Vavavooom!* Jesus, I got a hard-on you could cut glass with."

"You can look, but don't touch. I'm off limits for a few weeks."

"You can't get laid for a few weeks?"

"All for you, darling," she said, slipping back into her wrap.

Izzy walked to her. They looked at each other. He fingered the little wattle under her chin.

"You forgot something."

She knocked his hand away. "No I didn't. That comes later."

"When?"

"Hey, I want you to lay off Buddy Graves for me, OK?"

"Fuck Buddy Graves."

"I'd love to," she said, staring at Izzy.

"You're a pistol, Elaine. So aside from the crush on him, what gives?"

"Nothing. I like him. And he's having a hard time."

"Of his own fucking making!"

"What*ever*, OK? Just give it a rest with him."

Izzy shrugged. "Sure, I'll tell Macgregor we want Graves caddying for us in the club's tourney in September." He took her hand and guided it to his crotch. "But right now, what are we gonna do about *this*?" he said.

"Save it for that shiksa slut of yours."

He pulled back. "That's a nasty word."

"Shiksa or slut?"

"Courtney Mears works for me. She's my assistant."

"Your last assistant was a guy named Mort. Were you fucking him too?"

"No, but he did try to screw *me*. That's why Mort is no longer employed—anywhere."

She narrowed her eyes with playful malice. "*Oooh*, don't fuck with Izzy."

He grunted a laugh.

"So she went from drink girl to Izzy's assistant. Let me guess: that meteoric rise was because of her brains, right?"

"For your information, yes, she's a fucking barracuda with brains."

"Your never-ending talent search, huh?"

Before he could answer she said, "Get me a pillow, will ya hon? A nice soft one. My tuchus feels like a piñata."

Izzy left the room, and for a few seconds her mind drifted to Buddy, wondering where he was, what he was doing. She pictured his hands, fingers of a musician, long and sensitive. Then the room filled up again with Izzy. He tossed her the pillow and said, "Lucky pillow, having all that nice ass."

A look of pain crossed Elaine's face as she sat, made an *oooh-ah* sound and said, "Fix me a drink?"

Izzy made a vodka-rocks-twist, delivered it and looked at Elaine appraisingly as he stood in front of her.

"What's up with you, kiddo?"

Taken by surprise, she didn't answer. It's hard to hide anything from Izzy. What could she say without revealing too much?

He pressed. "Don't bullshit Izzy. You know it can't be done."

"I got a tits and ass job so I'll look fancy on your arm. It's good for business, that's what's up," she said.

"Good for whose business?"

"Your business. Is there any other?"

Izzy cupped her face in his hand, a face still so pretty that it made him sad, for a fleeting instant. "So," he said, "If I were Buddy Graves, standing here, what would you do, my love, despite your delicate condition?"

"You'll never know, darling," she said, giving his genitals a playful squeeze.

44

Jerome Brown was in high spirits, back in New York, in his room at the Algonquin, basking in self-approbation as he worked the phones. The online *Vanity Fair* piece, "Rage Without End," hit the news like a cruise missile, exploding a firestorm of controversy. It was sliced and diced on talk shows, blogs, editorials in the *New York Times* and *Wall Street Journal*. The cable news crazies on the right and the left feasted on the red meat, courtesy of Professor Jerome Brown. He took calls from the heavyweights in the black community—Sharpton, Belafonte, Jackson...

After six champagne cocktails at the Ritz, Graydon Carter—still obsessing about *The Holmes Report* expose—called and bleated his pleasure over the rave reviews: "I'm coming all over myself, Jerome!" Brown thanked him for installing that image in his brain. But Brown's celebration was missing one thing: Mindy Banks. In the aftermath of *The Holmes Report* blog post, she was laying low, working from her apartment. He missed her shifts from cool detachment to super-heated energy.

Jerome hesitated before making his next call. He considered *not* making it. Thought about it until his head hurt. But Tyrell's manic e-mails were now bordering on stalking. The monster that Jerome had switched on needed to be unplugged.

First he rang Mindy. "What are you wearing girl?" he asked, his voice rumbling in a passably good Barry White imitation.

"*Nothing.* Jumping into the shower. Wish you were here to scrub my back."

"Jesus, Mindy, this is driving me crazy."

"Then stop calling and asking what I'm wearing. It's driving me crazy too."

"OK, listen, I gotta call Tyrell. The cat sounds like his cork's ready to pop."

She hesitated before saying, "Jerome, I tried..."

"I know, I *know*, but the copy was just too good, and he was feeding the beast. Anyway, I'm gonna conference you in, maybe you'll hear something I don't. Just remember to mute your phone."

"Doh," she said. "Anything else?"

"Yeah, rub your pussy and whisper my name."

"In your dreams," said Mindy.

Eerily, Tyrell answered on the first ring and launched into the conversation as if it was already in progress. Jerome found it impossible to follow: Buddy, reparations, land ownership, old Uncle Tom with cancer, Spike Lee film, Rodney King, prison industrial complex…

He pulled the phone away from his ear and gazed down at 44th Street. Tyrell's race rant became a distant buzz. Every minute or so, Jerome said the requisite, "I feel ya brotha," as he flipped through a sheaf of Tyrell's e-mails, fascinated and repelled at the same time by the erratic and frantic pace of Tyrell's self-indoctrinated rationalized hatred. One e-mail, with the subject line **Amerika Rwanda** read: "My brother Jerome, I seen the pictures of Rwanda, those places—churches are the most graphic and symbolic—filled with bodies shot with Kalashnikovs or hacked to death with machetes. Skulls and spines, brown blood stains, missing feet, hands, dogs scavenging, licking the floors. Know what I think lookin' at the pictures? The oppressor, WHITES…an me with my machete, my panga, slaughtering the cockroaches, the brother of one's enemy is also an enemy…"

After ten minutes, Tyrell paused long enough for Jerome to say, "Oh, my brotha. You know, things aren't what they seem. You've read too much of this stuff without having the proper historical and social context. That creates a false reality. Can you dig that? I mean the struggle has changed, Tyrell, we gotta change with it. You get that, brotha?"

An uncomfortable silence reverberated.

"Tyrell, you there?"

Silence.

"Tyrell, did I lose you, brotha?"

"Yeah, you lost me, *brotha*," Tyrell said, his voice cracking with barely suppressed anger and sarcasm. "That shit about false reality…there ain't *nothin'* false about black peoples' reality. An' that shit on the Web, you with that white whore, that *really* lost me."

Jerome took a breath, steeled himself. "*Listen*, Tyrell, like I said, things aren't always what they seem. That white whore was, well, like brother Cleaver said about raping white bitches, it's a political statement. The mothafuckin' bitch-ass white boy who snapped that photo doctored the actual scene for political purposes. They're out to destroy me, discredit my work, silence my voice. And about false reality, all I meant was, even the most impassioned revolutionary like you—and my brotha, I have seen your work, your maturation into a primal force, one that is needed to revitalize the struggle—you lead it in a new direction. The other brothers out there been cutting whitey too much slack. You keepin' a tight leash on him."

Slience. Jerome waited. He heard Tyrell's breaths, panting.

"I didn't mean to question you JB. I lost my head man. Been workin' on crazy shit."

"Hey, I know it man, but that picture of me and the white bitch, wow. Pictures can really distort the truth."

Tyrell snickered. "Let me tell ya 'bout a picture. Remember the project you assigned on reparations?"

"Sure do. You got the only A in the class, one of the most creative projects I ever saw."

Tyrell snickered again. "Well, I did it. It wasn't just theoretical, ya know." In a confidential whisper, he told Jerome about Dummy and Buddy, about the picture, the blackmail scheme. Jerome squinted, as if in pain. As he listened, he silently mouthed, *you crazy mothafucka,* over and over. *Just wait until he finds out about the Vanity Fair piece,* he thought. *He's gonna recognize those e-mails and pull* me *into this shit.* Jerome waited for Tyrell to finish, and said, "My brotha, blackmail is a mothafuckin' felony. That's hard jail time. Maybe you should rethink this shit. I mean, you can't help the struggle if you're doing a bid upstate, know what I mean?"

"Oh my brotha, believe me, I do know what you mean. Lemme aks you somethin.' Do you know that Langston Hughes poem about dreams? I memorized that motherfuckin' poem because my man Hughes was talkin' about me."

Tyrell began to recite:
"What happens to a dream deferred?
Does it dry up
like a raisin in the sun?
Or fester like a sore—
And then run?
Does it stink like rotten meat?
Or crust and sugar over—
like a syrupy sweet?
Maybe it just sags
like a heavy load.
Or does it explode?"

Tyrell slammed down the phone, breaking the connection with Mindy, who had been listening in. Jerome rang her back.

"So, what do you think?"

Mindy paused. "That dude is flying one crazy-nigger freak flag."

"Watch it," Jerome said heatedly.

"What, you don't agree that he's fucking insane?"

"He's a brotha. And he's got a point."

"And I suppose you think, because I'm white, I don't understand that."

"You *can't* understand it."

Mindy opened her mouth to speak but just shook her head. She felt a tiny seam starting to rupture.

45

Izzy reached over and ran his fingertips along Elaine's spine, slaloming down the silky camisole she wore, stopping on the soft rise of her backside, smiling to himself. "You sleeping?" he asked, in an inpatient whisper. She shimmied her shoulders. When his hand continued down, gently cupping her left buttock, she turned, body first, then her head, a heart-shaped shadow appearing on the puffy down pillow.

"I *was*," she said, lifting her head to look at the clock. "Christ Izzy, It's four o'clock in the morning."

"I'm leaving in an hour, remember?"

"No, should I?"

Izzy slid closer, wrapping an arm around Elaine, kissing her neck, his hand lingering on her puppy belly-soft flesh. "I told you I was going to DC to schmooze up some assholes. Lately, you're not listening."

"Oh."

"What's on your mind?"

"Right now, *sleep*."

I'm taking the car."

"*Why?*"

"So I can work on the way down. Just makes more sense."

He felt, more than saw, her expression change, as if she'd come fully awake and was suddenly lost in thought.

"Elaine, my love, do not take your car out if you're drinking. The last thing I need now is a tragedy, you paralyzing some schmuck, OK? You need to get out for a drink, you call the service, cause Jack's with me."

"The last thing *you* need, huh?"

"The project, Elaine, not me. I'll need you on my arm," he said, fondling the wattle under her chin. "So finish the job."

"Fuck you," she said.

That's my girl," he said, rolling from bed like a slap-happy walrus.

"Is *she* going with you?"

"No. Do not drink and drive."

∽∾

As Jack stowed the bags in the trunk, Izzy sipped his coffee and said, "This DC thing is gonna get pretty regular. You OK with that?"

"Piece of cake, I-95, cruise-control, done," said Jack.

"I meant with the missus. OK on that end?"

"Sure, she'll take the bus to Atlantic City with her twin sister. Those two," he said, shaking his head and laughing to himself.

As they barreled down I-95, Izzy worked the phones and studied government sub-committees, union contacts, and geographical surveys. Jack was listening to a book on tape. Izzy paused to gaze out the window at the passing scene. He rolled down the partition. "Jack, what's the book?"

"Seabiscuit," he said. "The gal who wrote it has some kinda syndrome where she can barely sit up. Wrote most of it lying on her back. Took her ten years."

"I like her already," Izzy said as Jack turned the CD player back on and closed the partition window.

For 260 miles, that was the extent of the conversation until Jack eased the long black sedan up to the Hay-Adams Hotel in downtown Washington.

Izzy had a Tanqueray and tonic in the lounge while Jack checked them in. He tried calling Elaine, but her cell phone went right to voicemail. Her mobile was never off unless she was screwing somebody else or trying to punish Izzy and make a point. Considering her post-op condition, Izzy figured she was making a point. He called Courtney. She answered on the first ring, and asked him to hold on a second. Izzy heard voices, then the phone muted. A moment later Courtney said, "Sorry, Izzy, my sister and her kids are here." She sounded like she'd been running.

"You OK?"

"Yep, just need some space."

"Just as soon as they finishing remodeling your condo you can move in September. Just about six weeks."

She started say something, but stopped.

"Courtney, if you need space now, go to the Westmoreland Plaza. I'll call ahead, get you a suite."

"No, it's OK. So bring me up to speed."

Izzy filled her in on his agenda, said he'd e-mail notes from the meetings. He told her to rest, because soon they'd be working 24/7.

"Sounds like a slice of heaven," she said, breathy again, as though she was running. But Courtney wasn't running, just powerwalking down the sidewalk ahead of her sister. As soon as she clicked off, Courtney stopped, turned, and closed the distance between them. Kate backed away.

"Kate, what is wrong with you?" Courtney said, her voice shaking.

A neighbor, Bill Huckabee, stole a sideways look as he yanked the starter cord of his new Toro lawnmower. Courtney glared and mumbled something about "these people and their precious little lawns" as she marched back to the house with Kate tagging behind. Once inside, Courtney started for the bathroom.

"Do *not* pretend I'm not here," Kate snapped. "And what was that shit about *these* people? *We're* these people, Courtney."

Without turning, Courtney said, "Speak for yourself." Then she snatched her bathrobe from the closet and said, "Look Kate, I just want to shower. I had a huge blow with Dad this morning. I will be out of here, in just a few more weeks."

"Dad's worried sick about you!"

"Oh please."

"He hates what you're doing."

She spun around. "What, building a career? Something *he* never did."

"You know, that was mean," said Kate. "You've always been tough, but never mean."

"Mean? You should have heard what he's been saying to *me*."

"He thinks this guy is using you."

"And where do you suppose he got that idea?"

"*Please*," Kate said. "Just think this through. We're on your side."

"Funny, you go away and you think people will change, but they don't."

"What's that supposed to mean?" Kate said, feeling her face go red.

"Forget it."

"Derek's home from lacrosse camp soon," Kate said quickly.

For a moment it was if Courtney had forgotten how to breathe. "Leave it, Kate."

"He wants to see if you guys can fix this."

Courtney grabbed her iPhone from the side table and started reading aloud text messages from Derek, each one progressively more vicious: "'C, let's get together.' 'Hey, bitch, why don't you return any of my phone calls?' 'You conceited cunt, do you think you're too good for me?'"

Kate backed off, her eyes welling. "Stop, stop! He's desperately in love with you and you ignore him. Just shut the fuck up and stop being so selfish!"

Then the doorbell rang. Kate wiped her eyes on her sleeve and went to answer it.

Courtney was in the bathroom naked, waiting for the shower water to get hot when the door opened without a knock. She jumped in her skin, grabbing a towel.

Kate stepped in holding a white box with a dozen long stem roses. She held it out. Through tears she said, "It's from Derek."

46

It was two o'clock in the afternoon. Izzy's dinner meeting was at seven-thirty. He had an appointment for a massage and steam at four. Time to kill. He had Jack drive him to the Pentagon 9/11 Memorial in Arlington. Standing at the spot where those fucking jihadists crashed American Airlines Flight 77, his chest tightened and a quick hammering queasiness clawed at him.

It turned Izzy's stomach the way they reported that 64 people were killed on Flight 77. No, it was fifty-nine American souls who were lost on the plane, one-hundred-and-twenty-five in the Pentagon. Don't include five fuck-ing Muslim terrorists in with the dead Americans. He closed his eyes, imag-ined a single whining, lowering engine in the pale blue sky overhead, a leaden sadness in the air, screams, an explosion. Then he imagined huge wooden gallows, with hundreds of nooses, and his hand on the lever. Izzy opened his eyes, made a blowing sound and said, "Let's go Jack. I need a drink."

☜☞

From the table in the private room at the Capital Grille, you could see the glistening dome of the Capitol. As soon as Izzy walked in, the manager was all over him, rechecking the laptop, desk, lighting, music, all the details that Courtney had gone over and over with him on the phone. Picturing the manager holding the phone up and mouthing "bitch" brought a smile to Izzy's face. She was some girl.

They were all smiles and handshakes over the first round of drinks. Senator Ted Winslow, ranking member on the Science, Commerce & Trans-portation Committee and Congressman Mike D'Amico, Chair of the Trans-portation and Infrastructure Committee. Winslow brought his aide, Kathy Werner, along. She was a hotshot lawyer who traded a big-bucks partnership at a top firm for the power corridors of Capitol Hill and all the perks that came along with it.

Winslow's wife, Debra, had lupus, a debilitating, erratic disease that cost Winslow a fortune in medical bills, and killed their sex life. Accord-ing to Winslow, Debra was becoming his sickly, despairing saint, plunging herself into work for one charity after another. Izzy found it easy to ply his quarry with booze and shake loose such intimate details. One thing he always drummed into Courtney: You never know what piece of information will save your life.

Izzy didn't like Winslow; the senator always wore that phony, game show-host smile. And that fucking pompadour: how did he get it to stand up like that? It was ludicrous, him trying to look like Jack Kennedy. But women threw themselves at him. He was a ranking Senator, a player, and it got him laid regularly. Winslow was one of the big swinging dicks in the Senate, and like him or not, Izzy needed him.

Over the first course, the talk was light-hearted DC gossip. The main dish came, the maître 'd served the wine and vanished, and Izzy turned on his raconteur's charm.

"So, I'm in Scotland playing the Old Course with my Chinese investors, and the head guy, Qian Qichen, pulls out a flask of XO. These schmucks smoke like Turks and drink like fish. Anyway, we throw a couple back and through the translator, who is *my* guy, Qian starts talking. He's got this kiss-and-tell grin thing going, breaking open the hairless yellow chest of China, and giving me a peek at its beating heart..."

Kathy Werner, glowing from two Cosmos, gave Izzy a little bitten-in grin and said, "Izzy Weinberg, the poet," which elicited a snort and sarcastic laugh from Winslow.

Izzy, nodded at Winslow, smiled at Kathy Werner.

The senator hoisted a blood-rare chunk of seared Kobe beef on his fork. "I've been to the mainland enough times to know that China has its share of problems," Winslow said. "Sure, they've got cash to burn, but their infrastructure's a house of cards."

Congressman D'Amico chimed in, "You're spot on Ted. It's one disaster after the other over there. They keep a lid on it, but it's coming to a boil."

"With all due respect," said Izzy "this is a country that *knows* from public works projects. They built the friggin' Great Wall, for Christ's sake. And now they're spending ten billion dollars on a highway from Hong Kong to Macau that'll connect thirty-five ports in the Pearl River Delta, the center of their economic boom. In the end, gentlemen—and ladies," Izzy said nodding at Kathy Werner, "it's all about cash and attitude."

Kathy gave Izzy a penetrating look over the balloon of Petrus she was sipping with pleasure. Izzy was aware of her interest in him. *She's not beautiful, but she has a good figure*, he thought as he sized her up: devilish glint in her eyes; beautiful skin; a slightly potty mouth—he liked that; an explosive, fun laugh; enough brains to be a challenge. *But she might be having a thing with Winslow. Careful.*

"Now it's true," said Izzy, "that part of the reason they're kicking our ass is, what the Chinese government wants, it gets. Qian went to great pains to let me know that it's their ace in the hole. Hell, in China they line up hundreds of people who are only *suspected* of being drug dealers, line 'em up in a stadium full of families, with kids cheering like they're at a football game, and to the roar of the crowd, they shoot them in the head, *bang, bang, bang*, one after the other. Then they cut out their livers and kidneys and sell them on the European market." Qian gave me a big ol' wink and said, 'You Americans are worried about McDonald's Happy Meals.'" Izzy knocked back the rest his drink in one gulp as the others laughed sardonically and nodded.

The rest of the dinner went as Izzy planned. He gave a trimmed-down version of the Scottish presentation, dazzled them with all the technical bells and whistles, and ended with a ringing patriotic "this-is-our-Sputnik-moment" closer.

"God, I feel like standing up and saluting!" said Kathy Werner.

Twirling his wine glass in the air for emphasis, Winslow said, "You've got my attention Izzy, but the costs are staggering."

"Costs are relative to value," Izzy said firmly.

D'Amico, looking to Winslow for support, said, "Costs are also relative to the times. Technically, we might be out of the recession, but we're still broke."

Izzy leaned forward, shot them looks, then said, "We'll put a million Americans to work. How's that for a stimulus?" Then he rattled off a series of investment instruments, how they would be leveraged with government union pension plans and interest rate derivatives. When he saw Winslow begin to glaze over, Izzy smiled and said, "C'mon, I'm boring you. Let's go to the bar for a nightcap!"

Standing, Winslow smiled and said, "Well, POTUS *does* like trains."

Izzy raised his hand, made a double pulling gesture and went, *whooo, whooo!*

On the way to the bar, Izzy took Senator Winslow's elbow by thumb and forefinger and, as he watched Kathy Werner's ass nestle onto the bar stool, whispered, "By the way, Ted, did you know of an intern from Duke a few years back, a blonde gal named Courtney Mears?"

Winslow's head jerked, a barely perceptible motion. He paused, looked around, then said warily, "Yes, I believe I do remember her. A blonde from Duke."

191

Izzy pursed his lips, nodded.

"Why do you ask, Izzy?"

"Oh, no reason. She was a drink girl at my club. She mentioned once that she'd worked on the Hill for some senators."

Winslow nodded, trying to calculate what Izzy was driving at, what things he might know that Winslow would rather keep under wraps. Just as they stepped toward the bar, Izzy said, "So, Ted, what was she like, anything you remember?"

Winslow snaked his tongue across his upper lip. "In a word…" His voice dropped and he said, almost apologetically, "In a word, she was ambitious, *very* ambitious."

47

Izzy had just sent his last e-mail when the telephone in his hotel room rang. He checked the clock on his laptop; it was 12:15 a.m. Elaine, Courtney, Jack, or anyone else on his personal list would ring his mobile. "Who the fuck is bothering me at this hour," he said aloud, lifting the receiver.

"Yes!"

"Yes, before I *ask*?"

Izzy cleared his throat. "Who is this?" he said, immediately recognizing the voice.

"It's too late to be so polite. You know who it is."

"Good morning, Kathy," said Izzy. "Trouble sleeping?"

"I'm a night owl. Anyway, I figured you for one too. That was fun tonight, Izzy. Exciting might be a better word."

"It's an exciting project. I'm looking forward to bringing your office into the mix."

"Anything I can do toward that end, let me know."

"Isn't it a bit late to still be talking business?" Izzy said.

"You're a reductionist, Izzy. I like that," she said laughing. "In this town of bullshit, it's refreshing."

He could hear the booze in her voice. "My wife says I'm the kinda of guy you wanna kiss and kill."

"Smart lady. So, what are you doing, now?"

"I'm looking at an unlit Arturo Fuente Opus X and deciding whether or not to keep it unlit."

"Big decision?"

"No, not really. The size of a decision is relative to its consequences."

There was a pause during which Izzy heard the clink of ice cubes twirling in a glass. "So Izzy," said Kathy Werner, "want some company? I'll bring a match."

❧❧

A half-hour later on Moore Street in Levittown, all the sleepy little houses were buttoned up for the night. It was a typical middle-class neighborhood in America's first suburb, tree-lined and neat as a pin. Slumped behind the steering wheel of his red Dodge Charger, Derek Quigley watched Mr. Mears standing in the driveway, slowly finishing his cigarette, as if he were putting off going inside to bed. The end of another day as a waiter…He finally took his last drag, stubbed out the butt on his shoe, threw his waiter's tux jacket over his shoulder, and went inside. The kitchen light flicked on. A few moments later the house went dark except for the faint glow from Courtney's window.

Courtney was cross-legged on her bed working on her laptop. The only other glow in the room was the nightlight near the dresser. Hearing the front door open and close, she cringed. She could hear her father moving about heavily, tired from hauling trays of sauerbraten and two-pound lobsters, serving Beefeater martinis to nasty, alcoholic WASPs. The fridge door opened. Courtney could hear the faint *psss* of a cracked beer, and then his heavy footfall as her father made his way upstairs to his room.

Derek watched the wan glow from Courtney's window. It was the same small room she'd grown up in, shared with her sister, Kate. Those two always fought for the top bunk bed. And Courtney always beat out her older sister. On top, that was how Courtney liked it. Riding on top…Derek felt himself getting hard. He checked his BlackBerry, scrolling down to look for new messages. He wondered if she put the roses in a vase next to her bed.

The lacrosse camp owner's whiny voice still rang in his ears. "Derek, it was great having a guy of your brand value here. Duke lacrosse champ. That's what gives my camp its cache. But let me tell you something for future reference, something you need to understand now that you're gonna be head coach at Manhasset. You've got to ratchet it down a bit. These are high school kids, man. Yeah, they play at a high level, looking for scholarships, but a kid can't get a scholarship in a wheelchair. You scared me a few times out there. You gotta keep that Irish temper of yours in check."

Derek pinned down the camp owner with his eyes, felt him squirming in his skin and said, "Not my style, Barry. I push 'em hard and leave everything on the field." He collected his check and drove the 234 miles from Ithaca, stopping once to piss on the shoulder of I-87.

Derek slipped from the Charger and loped toward her window.

Courtney had just finished her last e-mail to Izzy, relieved that his meeting in DC had gone well. She looked over a few documents she needed to study. Then she updated her calendar and to-do list, adding her car lease appointment and the punchlist for the contractor at her duplex in Manhasset. Clicking on her favorites list, she opened up the floor plan of her new apartment…the view of Manhasset bay, the roof terrace, the dual fireplace, a stainless steel island in the kitchen. Playing with the interactive floor plan,

Courtney envisioned herself in her new place, her new life. *Soon, very soon,* she reassured herself. *I wish it were tomorrow.*

Derek pressed his forehead to her window. Courtney's back was to him. He craned his neck, searching the room for the roses. She closed the laptop and got out of bed. Derek felt his whole body tense, then the adrenaline rush. All those dreams of her were like cut-up photos he'd scattered and rearranged in his head. He put his ear to the screen, trying to hear her movements over the hum of the air conditioner in the window. Then she got into bed, lights off, show over.

Derek turned to the house next door and saw a manicured flowerbed. He stepped over and ripped out a pink flower. With his pocketknife, Derek made a small slit in Courtney's screen and inserted the stalks. Taking a breath, he pulled himself away from his delicious dream, remembering Courtney's naked body, her dirty mouth, her hunger for more and more... then he rapped on the window, a hard punctuating noise in the soft summer silence. Running toward his car, he heard a muffled scream.

48

It was early August. The sun had just peeked over the Sound, buffing the tops of the 100-foot poplars behind the clubhouse with a coppery patina. Buddy was in the caddy yard sipping a Starbuck's and listening to a haggard-looking LT recount the carnal pleasures from which he'd just separated himself an hour ago.

"Jesus LT, you smell like you've been dipped in a vat of aftershave. What is that shit?"

"Aftershave? Man, this shit is Unforgivable by Sean Jean. It is some classy mothafuckin' cologne," LT said, deeply affronted.

"In lieu of a shower?"

"In lieu of mothafuckin' nothin'. I got so much pussy, booze, dice-rollin,' James Brown hot pants dancing,' Jamaican weed smokin' shit on me, no mothafuckin' shower gonna wash it away," LT said, firing up a Kool.

"Congratulations," Buddy said, with an offhanded sarcasm he regretted at once.

LT gave him a look and snorted, "Lemme tell ya, you gotta get out more, man. I am seriously worried about you, Buddy."

Buddy glanced at LT, then looked away. "Sorry man, didn't mean to sound like an asshole."

"Hey, forget it. You jus' can't help yourself."

"Fuck you."

"Anyway, don't change the mothafuckin' subject."

"Which was?"

"Pussy. Money an pussy, the forbidden candy. An it's money gets you to the candy store."

"You're a regular philosopher, LT."

"You bet your mothafuckin' ass I am. So, while we're on the subject of money an pussy, how *is* Mrs. E-laine Weinberg gettin' along these days?"

Buddy felt a twinge of anger, then shrugged nonchalantly. "How would I know? She hasn't played in a few weeks."

"OK. Be that way."

Buddy looked at him. "Here we go. What way?"

"No mothafucka is an island," LT said with a look so somber, Buddy found it hilarious. A short, hard laugh spritzed coffee from Buddy's mouth.

"Laugh, OK? But them mothafuckas up in the pro shop talkin' all kinds a shit," said LT.

Buddy studied LT, realizing that their affinity for one another had stirred a protective instinct in LT. "Brad Mueller?"

LT gave a slow affirmative nod.

"Did he say anything about Mrs..." Buddy began, then said, "Aw, fuck him."

"Course he did, man."

Buddy looked around the yard. The caddy called Lemon was tossing barbeque-flavored potato chips to a pigeon. With a mirthless smile and a vacant look, Lemon shook the crumbs from the bag, dropped it to the ground, and lit a cigarette. Buddy could taste LT's cologne in his mouth. He thought about leaving this place and sighed inwardly, wondering how much separated his life was from Lemon's.

"You gotta take this shit seriously," said LT. "Mueller's got the inside line on lots a shit goes on around here."

Buddy flung the rest of his coffee on the ground, crushed the cup, and tossed it into the trashcan. "Can't do anything about people talking."

"Them mothafuckas talk like I was invisible. That's the way white folks be around a brotha."

Buddy was lost in his thoughts for a moment until Macgregor, the caddy master called, "Graves, LT! Roth foursome!"

With thumb and forefinger, LT flicked the butt into the air and said with an oversized wink, "You in that mothafucka Mueller's head. He's been at the range, been chippin,' puttin,' all keyed up for the tournament. He wants to tear the course up, beat your record."

"Let him try. So, what'd he say about Mrs. Weinberg?"

Walking up to the first tee where four multimillionaires in garish golf outfits were waiting, LT snapped his fingers to a beat buzzing in his head, long fingers the color of tobacco, waving in the hot air, his hand flapping loosely on his wrist. Turning his head to the side as he walked, LT said, "Talks like he knows her. An that boy gotta *nasty* mouth."

Buddy felt a heat in his ear and a numbness inside, like he'd just been slapped across the face.

☙ ❧

Elaine sipped her drink and took deep breaths until the air went in and out of her chest without catching in her throat. She was lunching at the Harbor Mist with her golf course venture partner, Arty Wagner. For the second time, Arty told her she looked like a million bucks. Elaine gazed out across the bay as Wagner talked about blueprints, course layout, the pro center, the special branding their venture needed to stand out in a competitive international market. But in that moment, she was thinking about leaving Izzy. She was afraid—not so much of him, although that was certainly part of it. Elaine felt such an impossibly strong inner tug for a different life, she thought it might carry her away, as if on a rip tide.

"Elaine, you're here, but you're not," Arty said, spreading a pile of documents across the table. The waiter came to take their order, but Arty waved him off. Raising two fingers, he signaled for another round. "These are the partnership agreements and the employment contract for Buddy Graves."

Elaine ran her hand over the papers, nodded, nibbled her lower lip. She saw it clearer now, the size of her decision. *Being scared comes with the territory*, she thought pensively.

The waiter delivered their fresh drinks. Arty ordered two chopped salads with grilled wild salmon. "So, while we're on the subject of Buddy Graves, what's up with him?"

"I haven't spoken to him since our initial conversation about this. I've been busy getting my ass lifted for Izzy. Well, really more for me. Hey, I *do* look great, don't I? But, anyway, I'm sure everything's set with Buddy. I'll call him."

Arty Wagner took a deep, thoughtful breath. "He shoulda been here today."

"He had to work. I'll fill him in."

"No personal days in *his* career, huh?"

"*Arty*," Elaine said, peering at him over her drink, her right eyebrow arched.

Wagner leaned back as if to get a better look at her. "I have to be honest with you, Elaine. Your friend gives me pause. I mean, yeah, he has a special interpretation of the game, but still, he seems to have frittered away a lot of talent. He's not exactly the poster boy for diligence."

Elaine bristled. "You're not in this alone, Arty. We're partners. And I am putting up a lot of my personal wealth to kick off this venture. I do not intend to wind up with just my dick in my hand."

"Charmingly said, my dear, but you can make an error in judgment too. I'll give you this: he's a very nice looking guy, and smooth as silk."

Elaine put her drink down. Arty saw the look on her face and placed his hands, palms down, on the table in front of him, a subtly defensive piece of body language. Lying flat on the white tablecloth, his hands were narrow as a woman's. "Let's clear the air, Arty. Besides being your major investor, I am Max Glass's daughter, not some JAP with her head up her ass."

"God forbid I should think that Elaine, it's just…"

She cut him off. "And I am not fucking Buddy Graves!"

A squeamish little smile puckered Arty's face. "Jeez, Elaine, I would never go there. C'mon, partner, I'm sorry. Graves is a good fit for us. With your stamp of approval, I don't worry." The waiter delivered the salads. Arty jabbed the grilled salmon with his fork and said, "What about Izzy? Have you told him yet?"

Elaine pushed her salad away and picked up her drink. The question startled her and she felt her blood racing. "No," she said, shaking her head, "but that's who you should be worrying about."

49

Buddy finished his loop and was on a ladder at Eugene Freyerson's house before noon. He painted in quick angry strokes, with the sun baking his back. He fully understood why there was bad blood between him and Brad Mueller, and he had no use for the bastard. But what LT's report implied about Brad and Elaine intensified Buddy's dislike to hatred. In his whole life, Buddy hadn't truly hated more than two people.

When he was done painting for the day, he put the ladder away, cleaned the brushes in turpentine, and sealed and stored the remaining paint. Then he raked all along the house's perimeter, cleaning up paint chips and any other detritus left from the job. Eugene Freyerson came outside, paced slowly around the house, nodding to himself. Then, on some unspoken signal, Buddy followed him into the house. There were two glasses of whiskey on the table. Buddy walked over to Old Sam parked on his dog bed, patted him on the head and sat down.

The old man lifted his glass and said, "Well now, the old house looks twenty years younger. Wish a coat of paint could do that for me."

Buddy smiled, and nodded toward the small, white-handled pistol. "You haven't told me that story yet."

"Right, OK," Freyerson said. "See, when I was a boy growin' up in Mississippi, the world was a different place. It's still a cold hard place, colder an harder for some, but back then…well, bein' an educated man, you know all about Jim Crow. One thing the history books don't tell is the look on a man's face when he's beaten down, lost his pride. My momma died when I was born. She got the poisoning in the blood, died two days later. Daddy raised me by hisself, with some help from his momma. I don't think he ever looked at another woman, that's how heartbroken he was. He was a janitor at the local school, used to clean nights. Sometimes he'd take me along.

"There was this white man, couldn't have been more than twenty years old. He was Daddy's boss. My daddy was a big man, wide at the shoulders, could split a cord a wood in less than an hour. He was about forty, forty-five then. That twenty-year-old white man, skinny little thing with big ears, he'd call my father 'boy' an daddy would answer, call him *Mr.* Skinner. Every time that white man was around, Daddy looked like he'd shrunk, like he *was* a boy. Anyway, I stopped goin' to work with Daddy, think he knew why, an that hurt him, but there was nothin' he could do about it. That's the way it was, would always be far as he was concerned.

"I was fourteen when Daddy got sick with the cancer. In those days, folks just curled up on a bed, covered themselves, an prayed the end would come quick. So Daddy took me into his room an told me that I was a young man an I had to go North, ride the rails up there an find me a job. At the time, I was working at Pelote's drugstore, stockin' shelves. It was terrible seeing Daddy cry like that. He looked so small, like he was goin' back into the womb. We prayed together. Then he gave me this here pistol, told me that I was a black boy in a white man's country an that I might need it where I was going. He showed me how to use it, told me how to catch the freight train, how to ride it, what to watch for. He gave me eighty-six dollars, all the money he had in the world. Then he lay down on his bed an curled up.

"That was the last memory I had of him. I left in the morning, caught the Southern, riding a boxcar with some other boys. Word had it there was plenty of restaurant work on the boardwalk in Atlantic City, New Jersey, so that's where I headed. I like the sound of it. *Boardwalk*. Eugene Freyerson goin' to the Boardwalk. Took me near on a week to get there. One night, just nearing Jersey, I was on this flatbed, the sweetest car to be on in the summer 'cause it was wide-open an' full of breeze. I was dozing off when, all of a sudden, I hear this big thump. I look up an there's the brakeman jumped down from the box, a big bald fella with a handlebar mustache. He comes at me real quick saying, 'Hey, you burr-headed nigger, you're on *my* train. No niggers ride on my train.' I was up, but he was on me with his billy club. He was a big thick man an he caught me on the shoulder, I went down an he kicked me like a piece of trash, all the time sayin' that no burr-headed nigger rides on his train. I looked up, thinkin' I was gonna die that very moment. Then I sailed over the side.

"When I hit the slab track an rolled an rolled, all I was thinkin' of was my daddy. I look up an saw the brakeman standin' on the flatbed as the train went on down the track. Standin' there with his club, feeling good about his-self for knockin' a colored boy off *his* train, never mind he mighta killed me."

Eugene paused and refilled their drinks from the Mason jar.

"Mr. Freyerson, I am so sorry this happened to you," said Buddy.

The old man ignored Buddy's remark and continued. "Well, I was young an wiry at the time, an aside from being bruised an shaken up, I was OK, 'cept for in here," he said, thumping the center of his chest. "That SOB callin' me a nigger—nuh uh, that wasn't gonna fly, not after leaving my daddy an ridin' the rails all the way from Mississippi. So instead of movin' on, I stayed there, out in the weeds, nothin' to eat. I stayed there for a whole damn day, twenty-four hours, knowing that freight train would be comin' on back, prayin' that same brakeman would be aboard. I remember that it started to rain, not a hard rain, just a constant drizzle blown slantwise in the wind. I get a shiver to this day, thinkin' how cold I was.

"When I heard the train off in the distance my heart started poundin' my chest. It took a long time 'fore I saw the headlamp. Then I heard that long moanin' whistle as it crossed the switching gate up yonder. When it finally came into view I crept up near the track, close as I could get without being seen by the engineer. It happened quick. There that brakeman was, wearing a slicker an a big hat. I knew it was him, saw the way he walked, with his billy in his hand. Just as the car came up to me I burst outta the weeds screamin' 'Nobody calls Eugene Freyerson a nigger!' I think he mighta heard me 'cause he seemed to turn just as I aimed the pistol and fired. You couldn't even hear the little gunshot in the wind and noise from the train. I knew that I'd hit him though, cause I saw him swayin' an staggerin.' Then he disappeared."

The old man paused, entranced by the memory. He shook his head, wet his lips with his tongue, and rubbed his face. "It wasn't 'til I got to Atlantic City the next day that I found out. It was in the paper. 'A brakeman named James Braver was shot by an unknown assailant.' Braver's body was discovered near the tracks. He left a wife an two children behind. The investigation is ongoing.' I felt bad about the wife an two children, but to this day I never lost any sleep over the brakeman," Freyerson said, stiffening his back.

For a long moment the old man seemed to forget that Buddy was there. "I had nightmares," he said, "but not about the brakeman, about other things." He looked at Buddy and said, "Well, now you got the goods on me. You're the only one I ever told that story to."

"Why's that, Mr. Freyerson?"

The old man smiled, showing all his teeth. "'Cause you're the only one ever asked. So, what do you think about all that?"

"I think that nobody calls Eugene Freyerson a nigger."

The old man nodded to himself, a quiet self-contained gesture.

As Buddy was stepping through the door to go home, Freyerson took him by the wrist and said, "That fool across the street. He comes over here callin' me Uncle Gene, an runnin' his fool mouth about some damn ownership thing he got goin', as if I give a hoot. But that boy is hopped up on something. He ain't right in the head. I saw what happened that morning, least part of it. Tyrell Walker ain't nothin' but trouble. You keep away from him, you hear?"

"I'm trying," Buddy said.

50

Izzy was finishing up his last meeting in DC before Congress went on recess—breakfast with Josh Seabury, a top-ranking Democrat on the Science, Space, and Technology Committee—when his iPhone vibrated. A message from one of Izzy's more valuable contacts on the Hill, Carson Severich, insider, fixer. The text read: MEET ME OUTSIDE HART BLDG 11:30.

Seabury bit into a cream cheese and lox bialy. "I can't say what will happen, Izzy, these are strange times. But man, you are a set of walking, talking brass balls and I will do everything in my modest power to move this audacious project along."

"Isn't the audacity of hope what got us here?"

Seabury smiled, napkined an errant fleck of cream cheese from his lip. "Well, *yes*, it is, but you bring new meaning to the word, and I say that with admiration, Izzy."

"OK, Congressman, I know you'll be in my corner as we move this project forward."

"Rest assured on that," Seabury said, sealing it with a handshake. "The country needs something of this size to get us back on track."

❦

At 11:30, Izzy's car pulled up to the fortified circle by the Senate Hart building. He got out and walked to a marble sitting area. Carson sat on a bench in a tropical suit, fanning himself with a Panama hat. Izzy sat next to him.

"Hot enough for you?" he asked, without looking at Izzy.

"Nice suit. Planning a trip?" said Izzy.

Carson lit a cigarette. "There's a new demonstration project out of HHS. It's got major backing from the Oval Office."

"OK, why should I be interested?"

"The project is designed to gauge and control hospital-acquired infections, and ward off the possibility of huge class-action law suits."

"Again, why should I care about this?"

"They're attaching it to Medicare fraud, the hidden kicker. The project gets the Feds in the door, looking for infections, and oh-by-the-way, finding other things. They're looking at claims data. Billing patterns tell a story and I've heard that your nursing homes are being red-flagged."

"Who's leading this demo project?"

"A guy named Hickman, Roy Hickman, a PhD. He's the visionary behind it, got this gal, a nurse, heading up the task forces."

"Hickman...never heard of him. What's his story?"

"He's been around, led major stuff for WHO, mostly in Africa. Works for HHS now. He's from the South, old family. He lives in hotels."

"Some motherfucker is gonna be sniffing up my ass and all you give me is that he's a fancy redneck who lives in hotels."

"He's sort of a blank page."

"Our relationship is based on your filling blank pages," Izzy barked.

Carson fanned more quickly. "It's just started. I'll keep on it."

"What about the nurse?"

"All I know is, she's from Long Island. I'll find out more."

"See that you do."

∂∽∾

Izzy got back in the car. "Let's get the hell outta here, Jack. I've got a doctor's appointment back in New York at six."

"Ready to roll," said Jack.

"By the way, how was Seabiscuit?"

"Nice story. Tough little horse. Secretariat woulda beat him running on three legs."

Izzy grunted a little laugh as he closed the partition and speed-dialed Courtney.

∂∽∾

"Ever had your hand up a cow's ass, Ernie?" Izzy said, lying on his side on the examination table of his internist and long-time friend, Ernest Reed.

"This is about as close to that experience as I plan to get," Reed said, palpating Izzy's prostate gland. He eased his hand from beneath the green gown, snapped off his surgical gloves, and gave Izzy a box of sterile wipes. "Get dressed and meet me in my office next door. I'll be there in just a few minutes."

When Reed came into his office, Izzy was in his suit working his cell phone. The doctor sat at his desk, a sleekly modern piece of furniture with a cutting-edge computer system, engineered with touchscreens. "Can't understand why docs resist electronic health records," he said, pulling up Izzy's records. "I couldn't run my practice without it."

"Half the country has its head up its ass, and the other half's stuck in the past," Izzy said.

"Thanks for that upbeat assessment," Reed said, then he cleared his throat. "Izzy, considering your yearly exam occurs about once every four years, could I have your attention for a few minutes."

Izzy pocketed his cell phone.

"You're in pretty good shape, your prostate is small and smooth, PSA well in range, heart has that nice slapping sound we like to hear, your lungs are clear, and remarkably, to me, your liver enzymes are normal, and there's no distension. All your blood levels and values are in range..."

"So I'll live, said Izzy, fixing his tie-knot and adjusting his bulk in the chair.

"Except your cholesterol. It's off the charts. We have to address it, Iz."

"Cholesterol? I haven't eaten a steak in twenty years. I sent a million fucking cows to the slaughterhouse—cows, pigs, sheep—but I don't eat 'em."

"Izzy, Izzy, we've been here before," Reed said raising hand to mouth in the universal sign for boozing.

"How can I have high cholesterol? Christ, I'm practically a fucking Buddhist"

"A fucking Buddhist who drinks like Rasputin. And has a genetic predisposition."

"Ernie, I do not have my first fucking drink until 4:30 in the afternoon. I'll push that up and drop the volume a bit."

"Izzy," Reed said, looking at the computer screen. "You need meds for this. There are a number of statins out there," Reed began, then he saw Izzy from the corner of his eye smiling like a toad and grabbing his crotch. Reed pulled his glasses off, pinched the bridge of his nose, and spun in his chair.

"Look Izzy, I don't want you to die, at least not yet. You're always on. Even your...how should I put this...pleasurable pastimes are work. Why don't you take a vacation, go to an island, no laptop, no iPhone, no drinking, just a chair on a beach for a week."

Izzy looked at Reed and shuddered. "Oy. Listen, you goy hump, you'll be sitting shiva for me before I go to an island and park my fat keister on a fucking beach chair."

"It's your fucking funeral."

Izzy said, dreamily, "Ernie, ever see a beautiful woman enter a room. I'm not talking good looking broad, I mean drop-dead gorgeous. It's like the *weather* changes."

Reed looked at his friend. "And what in the hell does this have to do with your cholesterol?"

"Nothing, I guess."

"You're a nut, Izzy. But while we're on the subject of beautiful women, how's Elaine doing?"

"Hey, she's livin' the high life with Izzy; how bad can she be? Besides, I just got her tits and ass done. That Joel Friedman is a fucking Michelangelo. From the neck down she looks like a thirty-year-old. She's a hot piece of ass."

Reed shook his head. "Jesus Izzy, that's your wife. You're a fucking animal." Standing bolt upright he said, "I can't believe this. I'm a pillar in the New York medical community. I'm around you for 20 minutes and I can't utter a sentence without saying 'fuck!' This is the effect you have on people."

Izzy grinned broadly and stood. At the door, he turned and put his hand on Reed's shoulder. "How long you been sticking your finger up my ass?"

"Is that your way of asking how long we've been friends? A long time. Why do you ask, Iz?"

"Just wondering why you've never invited me to play at your club. You've been my guest lots of times," Izzy said, looking meaningfully at Reed.

The atmosphere cooled. Reed cleared his throat and stepped back so that Izzy's hand dropped from his shoulder. "Damn, Izzy, you've caught me off guard. You have a way of doing that to a man. The only thing I have to say to that is my club is a little oasis, a place I go for escape with a bunch of gentile squares. I guess it's because you're scary—always charging like a wild bull. I really don't know what else to say. I'm sorry."

Izzy pinched Reed's chin. "I was just asking. Don't be a putz. I'll see ya at the tournament next month. It's gonna be a blast."

"It always is," Reed said.

51

Courtney's bare foot eased off the gas pedal as she drove past the gated apartment complex overlooking Manhasset Bay. After a quarter mile, she made a U-turn and passed it, for the fourth time, dreaming that she was already settled into her new duplex. *Garden on the Bay*. The name of the complex itself made her feel glamorous, like she'd made it. It was a long way from Levittown. She liked seeing the uniformed guard in the gate booth; a spit-shined man with a buzz cut and a square jaw. Izzy had told Courtney that the security at the *Garden* was top-notch, lots of city cops moonlighting.

She pulled onto the side of the road and watched the water, a huge undulating band of greenish blue. A white boat, faintly veiled in the slanting light of dusk, crossed the bay toward Connecticut. She wondered who was in the boat. Switching off the ignition, Courtney put the window down. A slight wind had come up, warm and briny. The tide chuckled over the stony beach, talking to her.

Courtney eased back and tried to clear her head of the chaos that had erupted since she'd returned from Scotland. She pulled her yellow legal pad from her briefcase and ran over her notes. Although Izzy sent several e-mails detailing his latest DC trip and laying out the groundwork for the next trip, one that she'd be on, she found a certain retro pleasure in jotting notes on the big pad. She smiled, looking at the word **CLOTHES** scrawled in bold. Tomorrow she'd go on a shopping spree, part of her new expense account. "Everything is a write-off, and yes, clothes do make the woman, although you'd still be a head-turner dressed in a burlap bag," Izzy said, laughing. "Shop till ya drop on the Miracle Mile, doll, then take dinner at my table at Milly's. Don't work too hard, bubbala," he'd told her, his last words before signing off for the day.

When Courtney felt her iPhone vibrate she looked at it and said, "Oh, shit."

"Hi Kate, what's up?"

"Dad can't take much more of this. He's not in good health, you know."

"Maybe he should cut down to two packs a day."

Courtney heard her sister huff and she made a face at the phone.

"C'mon, Courtney. Don't you get how much this hurts Dad?"

"I get that he doesn't get it, got it?" said Courtney, with a silly laugh.

"You are so cold. You have always been so cold."

"Derek cut a hole in the screen and stuck a flower in it. Dad was fine with that. He thinks Derek loves me, but he doesn't care that I'm afraid of that freak. That's *not* how a father is supposed to act."

"But he is."

"Who is, *what?*"

"Derek. He's crazy about you, he loves you."

Courtney shook her head, feigned a scream into the phone. She felt sick and dizzy from thinking about Derek, visualizing him on the lacrosse field with his mean, insistent swagger. "I don't know the meaning of 'quit,'" he once told her, toward the end of their senior year. He was sending her a message. At that moment, she'd begun the mental separation.

Courtney's eyes began to well up, but she shook it off. Kate was talking, but her voice sounded far away.

"Derek has a life, Courtney. He's got friends, lots of them. Ever wonder where your friends are? Where are your girlfriends? You've never really had any. That's normal? Now this thing with an old Jewish guy…It's creepy, Courtney."

"Shut up, please."

"No, and do not hang up on me. Look, I was always jealous of you… your good looks, OK? But I'm not jealous anymore," Kate insisted. "I actually feel *bad* for you, for the choices you've made. I'm happy with *my* life."

"Congratulations."

"You're gonna end up hurt and alone."

"Thanks."

"Do yourself a favor and make it better with Derek while you still can."

"Jesus, Kate! I'm actually afraid of him, and all you and Dad do is tell me to *go* to the thing I'm afraid of."

"He loves you!"

"But I don't love him! I never did."

"You told him you did, you said the words!"

"Girls say a lot of things when they're fucking!"

"I feel sorry for you," Kate said bitterly.

"I know, Kate. But tell me now, as my sister, what exactly did you tell Derek?"

"I said you got a new job working for some investor, that you had traveled to Scotland on *business*," said Kate, then she clicked off.

෧෬

Courtney cried. She let herself cry and it felt good. She was *not* going back the way she'd come. Nor would she apologize to anyone for where she was going. The sun was dipping. She started the car and pulled out onto the road. Glancing in her rearview mirror, she was startled by the twin hard gleam of headlights, like open staring eyes. The car seemed to come out of nowhere, pouncing like a big cat, lying in wait. She saw it, the red Charger and said, "Oh God, please."

Courtney hit the gas pedal, driving wildly along the North Shore's winding, tree-lined roads. When she turned onto Route 25A, the Charger was still following, swerving in and out of the traffic. Courtney surged past slower moving cars. She fumbled with her cell phone, thinking about dialing 911. That's when she swerved, lost control and fishtailed across two lanes. Screaming a dry soundless scream, Courtney jumped when she heard the *whoop whoop* of a patrol car, its red and white lights flashing angrily. Breathing shallowly, she pulled over. She could hear the blood pounding in her ears.

The officer was out of the patrol car instantly, walking in long purposeful strides. He had his hand on his sidearm, calling, "Step out of the car, now!" She opened the door, but a cold fear clogged her heart and she began shaking. When she looked up, the officer was studying her. She was wearing a short yellow summer dress. His eyes moved to her bare feet, brash pink toenails, then up to her blue eyes.

"Miss, please stand up. Have you been drinking?"

Courtney stood. "No, I have not," she said.

"Do you know how fast you were going?"

She shook her head.

He studied her face, saw the zigzag of fear in her eyes. "May I see your license and registration, please," he said more kindly.

Courtney slid into the car, moving woodenly. As she handed the young cop the documents, he looked at her, searching for a reason. "You're lucky you didn't kill yourself, or someone else."

Her lips moved as if she were whispering something to herself.

"Miss Mears."

She looked at him. "I was being followed. I panicked. I am very sorry about this."

He tilted his head. "Someone was chasing you?"

She nodded.

"A stranger?"

She shook her head and made a facial expression that he seemed to understand, like a coded language.

"Problem with a man? Is that it?"

"An old boyfriend, officer."

He nodded and told her to get back in her car. The he went to his patrol car. As he was writing up the ticket, Courtney saw the red Charger driving toward her in the opposite lane. She started to hyperventilate. "*No, no, no*," she whispered. Courtney kept her eyes pinned straight ahead. As his car passed, she saw out of the corner of her eye Derek's head turn, a quick jerking motion like in the *Exorcist*. Then he was gone.

The officer returned and handed Courtney a ticket. He leaned down and said, "I just wrote you up for speeding, 18 miles per hour over the limit."

"Thanks so much."

He smiled. "I know you were scared and I understand why. You need help on this Miss Mears. It can go very bad, very quickly."

He handed her a card, a stalker hotline number.

"Thanks a lot," said Courtney.

He looked at her and swallowed so that his Adam's apple rose visibly in his throat. Courtney had seen the same struggling look on men's faces before. He wasn't wearing a wedding band. "Is there someone you can turn to?" he said, hoping she'd say no, so he could volunteer.

Courtney looked up and said, "Yes, yes there is."

52

Leslie Quigley was in the car at a quarter to seven. Derek came out of the house ten minutes later, adjusting his tie, running a comb through his long tousled brown hair. His mother shook her head and stiffened as he slid behind the wheel of her Ford Crown Victoria. In the strong scent of his mother's perfume, which was actually his father's old aftershave, he smelled the remnants of the old man's cigar smoke, the whiff of a violated grave.

Derek said robotically, "Mass isn't until seven-thirty. It takes ten minutes to drive to St. Pat's." He could feel her eyes on him. He hadn't shaven.

"You expect me to sit in a back pew? I wouldn't hear the homily."

Pulling out of the driveway, Derek said, "Nobody goes to Mass at 7:30 in the morning, Mother. Believe me, there'll be plenty of empty pews."

She harrumphed, muttering about "queer priests ruining the church." When they pulled up to St. Patrick's, the parking lot was half empty. The faithful, making their way across the already warming asphalt, were mostly old women. During the homily, Derek felt his eyes closing, lulled by Father Paul's somnolent monotone, until a sharp elbow to his ribs brought him back.

After the service, a smiling Father Paul stood in the arched doorway, bidding his parishioners good day. Leslie Quigley's man-strong handshake caught the delicate priest off guard; his jaw muscles jumped.

As always, the Quigleys took breakfast across the street at the Blue Dolphin diner. Leslie fingered the silver cross hanging from her necklace. She had severe good looks, her features sculpted from an ancestry of Irish poverty. A jovial, chubby waitress stopped at their booth and took their orders. Pinned to her breast was a name tag that jiggled when she walked. It read "Raylene."

Sipping her black coffee, Leslie Quigley's eyes trailed Raylene's ass as she moved from table to table. "I can't understand how a young woman can let herself go," she said, pursing her lips. "How can she expect to find a man?"

"She's wearing a wedding band," said Derek.

"For how long?"

Christ Jesus, that's an inane question, Derek thought.

Not getting an answer, Leslie tried another conversation gambit. "Where were you all night?"

"Driving. I couldn't sleep, so I drove around."

"That's why you took your mother to church like this?" she said, reaching across the table, stroking his whiskers.

He pulled back and dropped his head to his chest. A short Hispanic busboy with the bold profile of an ancient Aztec, noisily threw dishes from the next table into a gray plastic tub. Derek scowled at him as Raylene delivered their two heavy white porcelain breakfast plates. While Derek tucked into his omelet and hash browns, Leslie began to eat her scrambled eggs slowly, with practiced, dainty manners.

She looked up from her plate. "Archie sometimes would sleep in his clothes on the couch after getting home from the late shift. He was too tired to change, but he always shaved and splashed aftershave on his face."

Derek bit a piece of toast and nodded.

"Your father was a good man. Neat, hard working. But he wasn't a fighter. Archie was a whiz with numbers, even had an opportunity down on Wall Street," she said, stopping to wipe her mouth. She let the napkin drop to her lap. "You weren't chasing around with *her* last night, were you?"

Their eyes clashed for a hard second. Raylene appeared with a Pyrex pot of hot coffee. Leslie Quigley put her hand over her cup. Derek shook his head. The room was filling up. He leaned forward. "No, I wasn't with Courtney last night."

"She's trash. Move on, get a nice girl. One with less wear on her."

Derek's face flashed bright red, a vein in his neck ballooned. "Don't say that, ever," he hissed.

His mother motioned in the air for the check and said, "When you have so much *fun* with a girl before you're married, what's left for the wedding night?"

Taut with anger, Derek exhaled loudly and closed his eyes as if he could not stand one more minute of this, which he couldn't.

The waitress dropped the check and smiled. Leslie Quigley watched her move to the next table and said, "Lose your figure, lose your man. Even if he doesn't leave, he does."

They walked across Main Street toward the church parking lot. Leslie looked up at the glaring sun and made the sign of the cross. "Better watch that temper of yours," she said to her son's back. "You'll end up God knows where."

☙❧

Stepping out of the shower, Latreece looked at Tyrell in a way he did not like. It was if she pitied him. He leveled a pair of black eyes at her and she felt the mood change. It hung in the air like the heat from her shower. Before there was a confrontation she said softly, "I want it to be like it was before all this shit with him next door started."

"Nothin's ever same as it was," he said.

"I worry that you're trying too hard. So hard, you might not see trouble before it's too late."

"Latreece, you forget I was in the mothafuckin' Army," he said rolling his shoulders. "I was paid to see the shit before it hit the fan."

"Baby, this ain't no Afghanistan. There's different rules here."

"Yeah, but I am followin' my own mothafuckin' rules. There ain't no brakes on the car I'm drivin.'"

"See now, that's the kinda shit I'm talkin' about Tyrell," she said, playfully flashing her breasts, trying to get a smile on his face, thinking to herself that he looked as though he'd aged 20 years in the past month.

"But that house next door is ours now," Tyrell said. Lifting his hand like a prophet, he pointed in the air as he pivoted. "An the one across the street and the Spanish people's house over yonder and that brokedown place next to the Pulaski Luncheonette." Then he launched into his now familiar radical rant; it sounded like shattered glass to her ears. Seeing her wince, Tyrell stopped abruptly.

"I gotta go out and take care of some business."

"I got some business you can take care of," she said, trying to sound playful.

Tyrell looked at her, saw water dripping off her pubic hair as she dropped the towel and slipped into her terrycloth robe. "I got to see Uncle Gene, see how that ol' mothafucka made out with the paint job. Then I got some other shit to see about. Be home later," he said.

"When's *later*?"

"Later ain't no time to it."

ڃڃ

Lately, everything he did was tied to a purpose, but the more he explained what that purpose was, the more confused she became. They had come to one understanding, though: since Latreece was paying most of the rent, it was mostly her house. That meant she had access to his office and computer stuff.

She watched Tyrell through the window, crossing Pulaski to the old man's house. When she walked into Tyrell's office, Angela Davis seemed to be staring down at her accusingly from the poster on the wall. "Easy on the drama, girl. That hair…damn!"

Latreece went into the closet and pulled out Tyrell's metal Army locker. This was definitely off limits, but as far as Latreece was concerned, there were no limits anymore. She dreaded seeing what was inside, but felt a strong compulsion to look, to uncover what her man was truly all about. If she understood whatever it was he kept locked up in that box, she might, just might, be able to stop him from spinning out of control.

Latreece held her breath as she looked through a stack of pictures that captured the ruggedness and desolation of the mountains of Afghanistan. Tyrell and his Army buddies standing in a row, their arms flung casually around one another's broad shoulders. These American giants, bristling with weapons and gear, who'd landed in the middle of buttfuck nowhere, surrounded by hunched up little bearded men wrapped in rags. In picture after picture, Tyrell was the only one who never smiled.

As Latreece removed a rubber band holding together a packet of letters, it snapped. "Shit," she said, putting the rubber band in her robe pocket. She began reading the letters, some addressed to his cousin in Brooklyn, but never mailed. In Tyrell's familiar scrawl, each line was a harangue against the Army, the white officers, the loneliness, the horror of seeing Muslims killed by racist pigs…then she came across an official-looking document.

Article 15: The commanding officer in charge may make inquiry into the facts surrounding offenses allegedly committed by Support Systems Specialist Tyrell Walker…may afford the accused a hearing as to such offenses or dispose of such charges by dismissing the charges, imposing punishment under the provisions of Art. 15, UCMJ, or referring the case to a court-martial…

Latreece heard Tashanda's camp bus lumbering up the block. She ran to Tyrell's desk, fished a rubber band out of the drawer and replaced the broken one. Closing the locker, she put it back exactly where she'd found it, and raced downstairs. Just as Latreece opened the front door, she heard one of the kids on the bus calling out: "See ya, *Dummy!*"

As soon as her daughter was inside, Latreece took her by the hand and led her into the living room. Tashanda pulled toward the TV. "Not yet honey, we gotta talk," said Latreece guiding her onto the couch.

"Now listen, your name is *Tashanda*. Don't let nobody call you Dummy."

"Daddy calls me Dummy."

"I tole you that Tyrell ain't your daddy, honey, OK? He's like your daddy but he ain't."

Tashanda made a face, "So where that mothafucka at then?"

Latreece could barely keep from laughing at her innocent damaged progeny. "Look girl, what did I tell you about that word?"

She nodded up and down, then said, "OK, but where he at?"

"Your daddy's in the penitentiary."

"Why?"

"Cause he's a sinner."

"That mean he won't go to heaven."

"Nah, he gonna find God in that place. They all do," Latreece said, hugging her daughter.

Then Latreece held Tashanda with both hands, pushing her back so their eyes were locked. She said, "Did Tyrell ever touch you, I mean where he ain't supposed to?"

Tashanda scrunched her face, shook her head, nodded, then squealed, "He just tole me about the show we doin' an the white mothafucka next door."

"Tashanda, I told you not to...OK what did he tell you?" said an exasperated Latreece.

"He said that white man was the devil!"

"A show, what show?"

Tashanda shrugged and ran to the TV.

53

Tyrell was growing impatient with Eugene Freyerson as he tried to explain, again, about the significance of black solidarity and land ownership. *That fucking dog smells like it died last month,* Tyrell fumed. *Nasty ol' mutt lies there letting loose his gas bombs; it's enough to singe the hair in your nostrils. And this ol' man, shit, he just sits there noddin' his knotty head, pickin' an suckin' at his teeth, askin' me if I can go more than three words without saying "mothafucka." It's a damn useful word, you mothafucka!*

When Tyrell finished his lecture, Eugene said, "Well, seems to make sense. Not that a fella like me with no formal education can actually understand it all."

"It does get a bit complicated," Tyrell said.

"I know the Lord give out the loaves an fishes. Know'd that since I was a little boy."

Tyrell smiled slyly. "Well guess you gettin' ready to meet your maker, with the cancer an all. How you feelin', Uncle Gene?"

The old man narrowed his eyes. "Jus' fine. No one knows when his time is comin.'"

"That might be so, but some of us is closer than the next," Tyrell said. Then he cocked his thumb toward the road. "How'd that white mothafucka do?"

"You see for your own self. Place looks like new."

"How'd you all get on?"

"He's sorta on the quiet side. Put in a good day's work for a white man."

"Sure did spend a lot of time over here for a boy that's on the quiet side."

The old man grimaced. "A busy man like you got time to keep watch on other folks' business?"

Tyrell smiled again, showing the gold cap on his canine tooth. "Well, that's gonna be my house soon. I'm gonna take out a second mortgage, buy the place I'm livin' in now, rent it to some righteous black folk that are Section 8. One by one, I'm gonna pick up houses all up and down Pulaski, organize a community. An that's just the start."

"How you gonna tell the righteous from the *unrighteous*?"

"If they poor an black, they mothafuckin' righteous."

The old man gave a wink and a big slow nod. "You an important man, Mr. *Tyrell.*"

"I'm fixin' to get that way. I got a connection with Spike Lee. He just might make a movie on what I'm doin.'"

With a befuddled look the old man said, "Spike *who?*"

"Lee, Spike Lee, the mothafuckin' director."

The old man scratched the tip of his nose. "Lee. Never heard of him. He a Chinaman?"

Tyrell stood abruptly and waved his hand in the air. *Sheeeiit.* Pushing through the door he called, "Uncle Gene, what's gonna happen to that ol' dog a yours if you die first?"

Eugene shot an irate look at Tyrell's back. Turning to Old Sam, he called him from his dog dreams. The mutt picked up his head, pricked his ears. "I ain't gonna leave you alone in this cruel world, you can count on that old friend."

శ్రీ~⊸

Tyrell pulled up in front of Finnegan's Taproom, his car sliding to the curb. It was early evening in Huntington and the bar crowd was building, milling about. Tyrell watched the white girls, skinny as rakes, talking on phones, laughing, not a care in the world. These rich bitches came from the Bay. You could hear it in their voices, that fuckin' singsong Valley Girl talk. A minute later Russ Dunn stepped out of Finnegan's carrying a brief case. He got into Tyrell's car.

"You know that you're in violation of the VLT," Russ said.

"VL mothafuckin' what?"

"The percentage of visible light transmission. The tint on your windshield and two front windows is illegally dark," Russ said.

Tyrell eased through the traffic circle, moving his mouth in silent agitation. When he was past town and onto Shore Road, he said, "That's some more a your business, huh? You wanna see illegal? Open that mothafuckin' glove box."

When Russ saw a pistol and several huge blunts he slammed the door shut and clutched his briefcase to his chest. The two didn't say a word until Tyrell pulled onto a dirt road that wound uphill through tall pines and spruce trees, with their eerie blue glow. His car came to a rest on a bluff overlooking Lloyd Harbor. Russ shifted uneasily in his seat. "I come here sometimes to think," Tyrell said, reaching over to pull out the gun and a blunt. He laid the pistol on his lap, fired up the blunt. The two men were instantly engulfed in a suffocating cloud of sweetish smoke as Tyrell inhaled and exhaled mightily. He passed the blunt to Russ.

"I really don't do well with marijuana. And, if you don't mind, firearms make me very nervous," Russ said.

Tyrell picked up the pistol. "Guns is supposed to make a man nervous. That's what they're for. Don't do well with marijuana? Shit, you sound like mothafuckin' pickle-dick eating pussy. Take a hit of that shit, so I know I can trust you."

Russ sucked lightly on the blunt, and immediately felt his head go numb, like he'd been injected with Novocaine. "Jesus, wow."

"Go ahead, take another hit." Russ did as he was told. Tyrell took the blunt back and smoked furiously, all the while studying Russ who sat staring slack-jawed at the sun sinking over the bay. The colors of the sky unfolded, fan-like in Russ's head, a revolving electric stage. "Tell me, paradox of my own pathetic genesis, what do you believe?" he mumbled.

"Lemme ask you something," Tyrell said, piercing the haze.

Russ turned a stoned rubbery face, smiled, and blinked.

"That's the same mothafuckin' suit you had on when we first met, same one I saw you in last time. Now you wearin' it today. Tell me that ain't your only suit."

"I have ten suits exactly the same. Two weeks worth of garments."

"Same mothafuckin' suit?"

Russ nodded. "Einstein used to have five of the same suits."

"Einstein...that's fucked up," Tyrell said. Then he lifted and toyed with the pistol. "How come when I Googled this government shit I found out that these so-called enterprise zones is for real, but I couldn't find your name? I don't even know if you're a mothafuckin' lawyer. Any dude can have a business card. Huh, Russ? How do I know?"

For a moment, Russ didn't answer.

"You a bit deaf ain't you?"

Russ opened his briefcase and slid out his laptop. He pulled up a site and turned the screen to Tyrell. It was an article in the *Wall Street Journal*.

Russell Dunn, magna cum laude graduate of Harvard Law, is slated to become the youngest partner in the history of the powerhouse firm, Gray, Longstreet & Heath. Founding partner, Reese Longstreet, noted that Dunn's outstanding litigation skills and his exceptional talent at mergers and acquisitions have positioned him for this unprecedented promotion.

Russ showed Tyrell several similar articles. Then he clicked on a series of spreadsheets he'd created, demonstrating his work in real estate acquisi-

221

tions and development. Tyrell sat back against the door looking at Russ. Finally he said, "That's some impressive shit. But why ain't you with them mothafuckas no more?"

Russ inhaled, fixed his tie knot. "I'd rather not get into that."

Tyrell gave a short phlegmy laugh. He picked the pistol up, brought it close to his face. His eyes were like wet black stones. "You soundin' like a mothafuckin' nattering nabob of negativism."

Russ smiled wanly. "I got tired of the strictures of corporate America. I saw an opportunity with the current administration to do something that means something. Make a difference."

Tyrell leaned forward. "But you ain't got a Website, nothin'. You're invisible."

Russ said, "I'm right here in front of you. See, Tyrell, in my line of community development, I work with organizers like yourself. I work with my contacts in government, with union reps, blood-sucking racist pricks like Cho. I do not need to leave an electronic footprint of what I do."

Tyrell seemed to like the phrase. "Electronic footprint, huh?"

"There are too many people who want to stop this kind of progress among persons of color," Russ said with conviction.

"An you're in this because you wanna *help* persons of color. Is that it Russ?"

Russ said, "No, I'm in it for the money."

"Good answer. Now you talkin' like a man."

"Thanks *bro.*"

Tyrell waved the gun. "None a that bro shit. I ain't your mothafuckin *bro.*"

"OK then, *dude.*"

Tyrell shook his head, wearily. "You a fucked up mothafucka. *Now,* when's this shit with my house goin' down?"

Russ gazed out the window at the fading sun. At a house overlooking the harbor that used to be his. A place where he'd made love to his wife, planned for the future. Disappearing with the light. "I'm meeting with Mr. Graves in a few weeks. You'll be a homeowner then," he said.

"Cool," said Tyrell. "Very fuckin' cool. I'll give ya this much: you was one big-ass lawyer. Betcha never thought you'd end up smokin' dope in a car with a gun-totin' nigga."

Russ turned and looked Tyrell in the eyes. "We're all at the mercy of the past, Tyrell, all of us…ever had a lap dance?"

54

Buddy sat up watching re-runs of a PGA tournament in Montreal and waiting for Dana to call from the hospital. It was a Monday night in mid-August and she'd been working feverishly to meet her end-of-the-month deadline to finish the infection guidelines. He watched Phil Mickelson fuck up his approach shot, hit the ball fat, drop it into the sand. Always that shit-eating grin with Lefty. *Christ, he got fat,* Buddy thought. *Carrying a belly like he's three months pregnant. He wasn't always such a whale; it looked like it happened overnight.* Just like that, Mickelson looked different, his world had changed. *That's how I feel,* Buddy thought morosely. *My whole goddamn world was altered in an instant. A life-changing event came disguised as a little girl in a yellow blouse with tears in her eyes.* His imagination unspooled. *Had she always been there, lurking in the shadows, waiting for the right time to strike?*

Dana never called. Instead, she e-mailed at 11:33. Buddy was drifting off when he heard the computer *ding*, signaling he had mail. He would have preferred hearing her voice so he could better gauge her mood. An e-mail was too flat, making it nearly impossible to get the nuance.

Hi Buddy, I'm staying at the hospital tonight in the nurse's rec room.
Lots of stuff going on. How's your thing progressing? This is so weird…
but I guess in these crazy times lots of couples go through these
changes. We'll get through it. Talk later, xx D.

"Thanks for the two kisses," Buddy said aloud. He thought about responding, but decided against it. He was sleeping on the couch dreaming about playing golf naked when his cell rang. He grabbed the phone.

"Buddy, sorry for calling…calling this late, gotta minute?" It was Elaine. From that slight thick-tongued lisp, Buddy could tell she'd been drinking. "Yes, sure. Hi Elaine."

"Arty's been asking about you."

Buddy waited.

"He wants to know you're on board with our course design project."

Buddy stood up and walked to the window.

"Buddy, are you there?"

"Yes, I'm sorry. Listen Elaine, that rendering I did for you when I was a kid…I mean, are you sure about this whole thing? I don't want you to stick your neck out…"

"Stop," she said. "OK, please Buddy. Most things in my life turned out different from what I thought they'd be, but not this. Arty saw something in your plan. He's got all the computer-aided thingamajigs. What he needs is talent, vision. You bring that to the table in spades and you haven't even started yet. There is so much opportunity here, babe, for both of us. I need you on this, Buddy."

He swallowed hard. He walked back to the couch and sat down. "OK, Elaine. I have been thinking about it. I'll do it. I'm in."

"Thanks Buddy, thank you so much," Elaine gushed like a schoolgirl. "Let's start fleshing out that original draft. You won't regret this, I promise!" She clicked off.

Buddy tried to concentrate on the TV, but he kept looking at the cell phone, as if he were about to hear Dana's voice. Then he got up and walked to the window again and stared out into the dark.

❧

The next morning Buddy was at the course a little later than usual, slightly hung over and distracted. The conversation with Elaine had made everything real for the first time, and he was confused about what he wanted. Seeing other people kiss or hold hands reminded him of the way he and Dana used to be. That was such a short time ago, but he realized that part of his love for Dana was already in the past, and he was watching it fade, like a spectator from another room.

Brad Mueller passed in a golf cart. He looked at Buddy in a curious way and smiled. Buddy had never seen Mueller smile; it was disturbing. The corners of his mouth were turned up, but his eyes, fixed on Buddy, were cold and gray, a feral vengeance behind them. Buddy inhaled sharply and beads of perspiration broke across his forehead.

LT wasn't in the yard and Buddy asked another black caddy known as T-Bone where LT was. "Jus like a white boy. You think we all sleep together? How the fuck I know where that crazy-ass nigga is? He might be dead in a mothafuckin' car, at the bottom of a river, cut up in a bitch's bed, in jail—who the fuck knows? He crazy for pussy and all the trimmings, so where that mothafuckin' nigga is, well, your mothafuckin' guess is good as mine. We might as well be talkin' 'bout where Osama binfuckin' Laden is, far as where that nigga LT is got hisself."

"Thanks T-Bone," said Buddy.

After their conversation last night, Buddy half expected to see Elaine warming up by the first tee in her yellow slacks, the ones he loved. Their physical intimacy was never more than the brushing of an arm, yet he felt like he knew her in bed, felt her hot tongue in his mouth, his fingers brushing through her hair, seeing her sprawled deliciously across the bed. But dreaming of infidelity was as far as he would let it go. What was it Jimmy Carter called it? Lust in his heart? Buddy wondered: *Am I actually going to get in a car with this woman and drive to Arizona?* It seemed impossible.

When the caddy-master Macgregor called, Buddy was surprised to see that Elaine was not in the twosome of women. "Have fun," Macgregor smirked, adding, "All set for the tournament, Mr. Graves?" To which Buddy replied, as he hoisted the bags, "All I gotta do to get ready is get out of bed."

The twosome, Stephanie Solomon and Cari Frankel, were big-time duffers, sending short errant shots in all directions, cursing like sailors and laughing like girls being tickle-tortured. The women were in their 40s; Solomon was recently divorced, Frankel was recently widowed. It could be a pain in the ass looping such dingbats, but Buddy got a kick out of them. They gossiped about everyone in the club; no salacious details were left out.

"So Cari, didja hear about the Silverbergs' getaway in Anguilla, the key party?"

"You mean the Tea Party?"

"Yeah, right, the fucking Tea party. Sarah Palin was there. *Oy*, haven't you ever heard of a key party? They went with a whole group—the Birnbaums, Millers, Fines, Friedmans. You know, *that* crowd. Anyway, before dinner, everyone throws their room key into a bowl, and after dinner the wives pick a key and shack up for the night with whichever husband they drew. No-holds-barred screwing, *anything* goes. They drew keys for five nights running."

"Jesus," Cari marveled. "But what happens if you pick your own key? You go with your husband?"

"No, for Christ sake, what would be the sense in that? You throw the key back in the bowl and draw again. So the first night, Jessica Miller hooks up with Mark Birnbaum. OK, you won't believe this…"

At the ninth, Stephanie and Cari went into the clubhouse for lunch and came back smelling like a winery. Elaine's name came up, something about her new ass and where she's been getting some side action. "Can you blame her? Married to that dog, Izzy," Stephanie said.

"Yeah, but that dog's got *some* bone," said Cari, to the delight of Stephanie. "You little tramp," she trilled. The two women dissolved in laughter.

Then Stephanie turned to Buddy and said in a hushed tone. "Buddy, I'm bushed from the heat. Will you take this shot for me? Elaine says that watching you play is almost better than sex. See how close you can get to the hole. Make me a believer."

55

It was raining when Buddy woke at 5 o'clock on Wednesday morning. He rolled over onto the side of the bed where Dana's warm flesh should have been and thought to himself, *I cannot dwell on this anymore. I need to go forward.*

A storm was building, towering thunderheads marching northeast over the Sound. Each gust of wind brought runnels of rainwater gurgling through the gutters. He pictured the flooded fairways, the pissed-off members bitching about the rain over coffee and cigars. As LT always predicted, their conversation would inevitably turn to pussy and money, the common denominators of life.

Dana was a lover of storms, the wilder the better. She once said they made her horny, to which Buddy had replied, "breathing makes you horny." He remembered her devilish laugh. Suddenly he felt his eyes go moist. He went downstairs, made a pot of coffee and opened his laptop. Dana had already e-mailed him that morning. *"It's crazy around here,"* her note said. *"I'm tying up all the loose ends."*

He hit the "reply" button and tapped on the computer: *Am I one of your loose ends?* Buddy pointed his cursor to the "send" button. For a moment his hand hovered over the mouse. But he thought better of it and deleted the message.

౷ ౷

He retrieved the sketch of the golf course design that Elaine had saved and studied the creased piece of paper. He'd change the par sequence for the front and back to be identical: 4-5-4-3-4-5-4-3-4. The ringing doorbell broke his concentration. Buddy looked up, waited a moment, then heard the bell ring again. Tyrell did not ring the bell, he banged his fist.

It was Russ. He looked like a wet dog. His red hair was matted to his scalp from the rain, showing the bald spot on top of his head. He shifted from foot to foot. Buddy opened the door and Russ ducked inside, his shoes squishing on the hardwood floor.

They sat in front of the television. Buddy flicked on ESPN re-runs with the sound off. Staring at the screen, he asked Russ, "Want some coffee?"

Russ looked up sheepishly. "Wouldn't mind a beer."

Buddy looked at the clock. It was 9:48 in the morning. He got Russ a can of beer.

Russ took a heavy pull on the brew.

"Breakfast of champions, eh?" Buddy said.

Russ's expression fell, Buddy's sarcasm cutting deeply. "I usually don't have my first until...around noon."

"What time zone?"

Russ cleared his throat. "So, I have the paperwork for your quit-claim deed."

"How much do I owe you?"

Russ got up and paced back and forth, the can of beer in his hand.

"Preparing for your summation, *counselor*?"

Russ stopped, drained the beer and put the empty on the table.

Turning toward the door he said, "Thanks for the beer."

Buddy yelled, "Fucking touchhole!"

Russ jerked his head and stormed back into the room, shouting, "Get over it motherfucker!"

Buddy straightened, pointed toward Tyrell's house and exploded. "Get over what, exactly? That some psycho is blackmailing me out of my house? That my wife hasn't been home in days and in two weeks she's taking off for DC with some fucking PhD?"

Russ, shaking as if he'd just been showered with icy water, pointed at the TV.

Rising, Buddy said, "Sure, I'll get over it! Just as soon as you get over your lap dance."

Stabbing his finger at the TV screen Russ yelled, "That, you stupid bastard. That!"

"Don't go there, Russ. I know you inside and out, partner. Don't Freud me. I've reconciled *my* past. I'm free!"

Russ said, "You can be a cold-hearted son of a bitch, you know that? Anybody ever tell you that?"

"No, usually people tell me what a great guy I am, so easy to talk to. What they mean is, so easy to push around!"

Russ's shoulders sagged and his face seemed to collapse. "I miss my wife, Buddy. Christ, I miss her so much I cannot fucking stand it." He was crying and clutching his head in his hands.

"Aw, Jesus, Russ, I'm so sorry. I just lost it there for a minute. I shouldn't have said that. Dude, I'm sorry."

"I know. But you can't know what this is like every damn day."

"I'm sorry, dude," Buddy said, stepping forward so that only a foot separated them.

"I wake up every morning thinking she'll be next to me, that I'll hear the sound of her breathing," he cried. "But she's not breathing anymore and I am." Russ pounded his head with his balled-up fists, his spear of anguish piercing Buddy's heart.

Buddy gripped Russ's forearms, pulling them to his sides. He embraced his friend and kissed him on the forehead. "C'mon counselor, everything'll be OK. Let's have another beer."

↾↿

Eugene Freyerson was brushing Old Sam's teeth when Buddy knocked. "Door's open," he called.

Buddy stepped in. "Mr. Freyerson, it's me, Buddy…"

"I know it's you, son. Think I woulda yelled for a stranger to come marchin' into my house? I recognized the knock. Go on, sit down, have yourself a sup a whiskey."

Buddy sat. He waited a moment, then said, "You brush your dog's teeth?"

The old man raised his eyes. "Course I do. Ever see a dog try and hold a toothbrush?"

The image made Buddy laugh.

"I also swab his ears and eyes with a solution of peroxide and water, clip his nails, brush his coat. You take care a things, they last. Mink oil a pair of shoes, they last. This throwaway society rankles me, but can't help what other folks do."

Buddy nodded. The phrase "throwaway society" made him smile. Coming from Mr. Freyerson it had a special meaning; he knew what it meant to be discarded. "Need a hand, sir, I mean with anything?" Buddy asked. He was still buzzed from his beer session with Russ and didn't want any whiskey.

The old man finished brushing Old Sam's teeth. "There ya go boy, smile for Daddy."

Buddy looked at Old Sam. He swore the dog smiled.

Eugene got up and sat across from Buddy. "I ever tell you about Rusty Miles?" he said.

"No sir, but I'd like to hear about him."

"When I was a little boy, a fella escaped from the prison work farm. He was a red-headed colored man, kind of unusual, so everyone was on the lookout for him." It had stopped raining but the wind had picked up. Eugene veered from his story, and said, "We lived in a tin-roofed house. And when the wind kicked up, the branches of the old oak tree would scratch the roof. They were filled with Spanish moss, and it softened the scratchy. I can't really describe that sound, but it's still in my ears. Anyway, back to my story.

"There was a young white girl who was raped in our town. She insisted that the man who violated her was a colored fella with red hair. So a group of white men, out for blood, set upon the first black man with red hair they found, a fella name a Rusty Miles. In no time that boy was lynched, hanged in the courthouse square. But when that white girl saw his dead body, she started screamin' 'It ain't him, it ain't him!' It turned out that the rapist was that other red-haired colored man, the one who escaped from prison, and he was still out there. That mob, they kilt an innocent man. But the sheriff just joked, 'Well, we made an honest mistake, boys. Who'd a thought there'd be *two* red-headed nigras in the same county?'

"I remember them takin' Rusty Miles away. Me and my daddy was standin' on the corner as the flatbed truck with his body passed. A wind kicked up, liftin' the sheet over him. He looked right at me. Lord, I hoped never to see such a sight again."

Buddy had tipped his chair back, listening raptly, transported by Eugene's stories. His voice was like the wind, and it drove away all the cobwebs from Buddy's head.

Freyerson waved his hand. "I used to feel like I wanted to cut people's heads off, that's how mad I'd get." Buddy nodded. "Ah, no one wants to listen to an old man tell stories about a time people just wanna pretend never happened."

"I do," said Buddy. "I love your stories. Any you got, I'd like to hear."

"Say, you know who Old Sam's named after? Course you don't. It's Sam Langford, Old Sam, the Boston Tar Baby, the Bonecrusher. Toughest man God ever put into a pair a shoes. They all ran from Langford—Dempsey, the rest of the white fighters. I met Old Sam one time. But that's another story for another day."

Buddy was stepping down the driveway when the old man called in a low voice, "Buddy, watch out for that boy next door to you. He ain't right. He's a whole lotta wrong."

"It'll be OK. Don't you worry, Mr. Freyerson."

"But I do worry," Eugene whispered as Buddy walked away.

56

Dana's parents invited her and Buddy for dinner. Over the past weeks Dana had kept them in the loop, sort of, but they kept asking, "what's going on with you two?" She said she'd be there, but Buddy wouldn't. On the way to the Burkes' house in Hicksville, Dana called Bobbi Holmes.

"How's the princess of darkness?" Dana said, smiling.

"Doing what she does best: comforting the afflicted and afflicting the comfortable."

"I better watch out. Working for the government and all, I might get caught in a big DC scandal."

"In your dreams, girl. Besides you're too much of a straight arrow to get in my sights. I'm lovin' this Jerome Brown drama. He's my fuck-stick du jour."

"I confess, I haven't been following your latest jihad."

"Word on the street is that Jerome 'The Color-of-Money' Brown is getting big-time pressure to dump his white squeeze, Mindy Banks. Seems she's not so good for his image."

"She's the one you outed, right?"

"Yeah. God, I love that word. Anyway, how's it going with Roy Hick-man?"

"He's working my ass off. I'm getting ready for a big meeting in DC. Listen, Bobbi, is there anything you can dig up on him? I'd feel more comfortable if I knew something about him other than what's on his CV."

"Sure. He hit on you yet?"

"No, not really. He flirts. It's part of his good ol' boy routine, but I don't see him hitting on me. This is business. Besides, he knows I'm married."

"Right, government guys *never* mix business with pleasure. They're just a bunch of fucking Boy Scouts!"

"Down girl," Dana laughed.

"Hey I love all that shit. It's my bread and butter. So how's Buddy doing? He OK with all these changes?"

"Well, we're just trying to roll with it."

"What the hell does that mean? Roll with Malcolm X next door?"

"I don't even want to think about that. I can't wait to get away from that."

"So if you're not gonna jump in the sack with your new boss, what are you gonna do for sex? I mean, I know you."

"I'll do what you do."

"You mean buy batteries by the pallet?"

"Bobbi, I miss you. Let's get together soon."

"You hitting on me?" Bobbi asked, sounding mock hopeful.

"Yeah, find something on Roy Hickman and I'll come spank you."

Dana's mother, Marie Burke, was slicing through her meatloaf. "Do you understand this Frank," she asked, querulously, "do you understand any of this? I think I might have overcooked the meatloaf. That new convection oven cooks too fast. Frank?"

"You overcooked the meatloaf again, course I understand that," Frank Burke said, sipping his beer. He winked at Dana.

"Oh, Frank," Marie said, laying thick slices of steaming meatloaf on the plates. She turned her attention to Dana, squinting as if suddenly attacked by a migraine. "I don't understand. You're leaving the hospital. The country's going to hell in a hand basket and you're quitting your job. It makes no sense."

"Mom, I'm not quitting my job, I'm taking a year's sabbatical to work for the government."

"Sabbatical? That's what old teachers do," she said, passing the food. She sat and said a quick blessing. Then she huffed, "Frank, please help me here. You're sitting there with your teeth in your mouth."

Frank put his hands on the table. He looked at the meatloaf, then at his wife. "Dana has a great opportunity. She's not quitting the hospital, but if she wants to move to DC for something better, more power to her. Now how much more help you need, hon?"

Dana picked at the meatloaf. "I'm making a lot of money, Mom, OK? Plus I'm making a lot of great connections. So it's a vertical career move."

"Your brother's worried about this, too," she said. "He called last night, ranting about the president, his administration."

Dana narrowed her eyes. "He's turning his sons into goddamn sissies and his wife's ass is getting as big as a Mini Cooper. *That's* what he should be worried about."

Frank laughed, holding up his hand.

Marie ignored the remark and pressed her lips together. "So you're chasing off with this government guy and your husband's chasing off with this Jewish woman, is that it?"

Dana dropped her fork: a loud clink on the plate. "Oh, for God's sake! I'm not chasing off and neither is Buddy. We're pursuing opportunities that are taking us in separate directions for a while. That's what people need to do today, OK? It's not 19-fucking-60."

Marie took a quick inward breath. "Some mouth, young lady."

"A fucking truck driver," Dana said, stabbing her meatloaf.

Frank Burke's chin lowered. "The son I never had," he mouthed.

57

Later that same night, Dana pulled into her driveway and lingered there with the car's windows open, staring at the house. As she got out of her car, she noticed the upstairs light in the house next door flick off, making her uneasy. She hurried to the front door, knowing she would never again feel safe here.

The clock over the TV said half past eleven. The air in the house was heavy, vaguely musty. "Buddy," Dana called. She went into the kitchen and made a club soda with bitters. Buddy walked in barefoot wearing madras shorts and an unbuttoned short-sleeved shirt. Dana noticed the muscles in his stomach. She stepped forward and kissed him on the lips. "The house smells a little funky. You take a shower today?"

He squinted one eye. "Nah, not since last week. Why do you ask?"

"Maybe it's just me," Dana said with a shrug.

"Maybe it's the partying and busloads of hookers I had over. I hosed the place down, but you know, when I get my *thang* going..."

She rolled her eyes, belched ladylike, lifted her glass. "Bitters. You missed my mother's meatloaf."

Buddy snapped his fingers. "Damn. How's big Frank doing?"

"My father can be a headstrong prick..."

"*Really*," Buddy cut in.

Dana continued, "But he's a straight shooter, not an ounce of BS. He's just very confused over all this stuff between us. They both are."

"And you're not?"

"It scares me silly. But this is the hand we've been dealt."

They fell silent, neither knowing what to say. Here they were, getting set to leave their home, each other. For a frozen moment they gazed distractedly at nothing but the space between them. "I wish we could have had children," Dana said softly to break the silence. It was a clumsy thing to say, and she realized it at once. She reached out to Buddy, but before she touched his warm skin, her cell phone rang. Her hand jerked back. Grabbing her phone from her pocket, she checked the caller ID. It was Hickman.

"Sorry, I've gotta..."

"I know, you've got to take that call," Buddy said as she walked into the next room.

Dana returned two minutes later. "Who was that?" Buddy asked.

"Sorry. Dr. Hickman. He had a schedule change he needed to let me know about."

Buddy looked at the clock, held his eyes on it long enough to make a point. "Is that what you call him, *Dr.* Hickman?"

"I call him Roy," she said, walking right up to him, putting her hand over his mouth as he started to speak. "Take me upstairs to bed," she whispered in his ear, biting his lobe. He pulled away, a gentle but decisive motion. "Not tonight. I'm working on something," he said, seeing the hurt in her eyes.

Just past midnight, Mindy Banks was still hammering away, flooding the Internet with tweets and e-blasts, dropping voicemails on her radio and talk show contacts. She checked Jerome's website, made a few mental notes about needed changes. His site was too old school, he needed to jazz it up. She'd mentioned this to him the last time they'd spoken.

"My grandmother could build a website more hip than this," she'd said.

He'd stiffened, his tone frosty.

"Why so fucking touchy, Jerome?"

He paused, then said tetchily, "I'll touch your white ass to the back of this bus, you get that superior club-girl tone with me." As she hung up, she remembered what her Aunt Sylvie used to say: "There's truth in jest."

That was two days ago. He hadn't called to smooth it over.

Mindy had a glass of wine. Then another. Going to the window, she flung it open and smoked a cigarette, looking out at 23rd Street. She smoked and looked around for an ashtray, but there weren't any since she quit smoking last week and threw them away. Stubbing the cigarette out on the sill, she flicked it out the window. Then she picked up her BlackBerry and dialed Jerome.

"You know what time it is?"

"It's not even one, Jerome. What happened to my 24/7 man? I'm still working on getting out the buzz about your next appearance on Bill O'Reilly's show."

"Maybe you should just cool it."

"What's that mean? Is something going on I should know about?"

"With what?"

"With you, with us."

Jerome started to speak but she cut him off. "Let me finish, let me say this. I don't come from the streets but I'm pretty hip to people. Maybe it's nerves about the book tour, the O'Reilly show, whatever, but you're doing a 180 on me Jerome, OK? I can feel it. I mean when we first hooked up, you used to tell me about the house in Barbados you were going to buy, our getaway spot..."

"It's that *bitch* on the Holmes Report. That's what's got me edgy. She won't let up."

"You forgot to say 'white' bitch."

"You said it for me."

"*Wow*, what's going on?"

"Sounds like you sticking up for that bitch, that's all."

"I'm not sticking up for anybody. But why is Bobbi Holmes a bitch? She's just doing her thing, the same as Page Six, Gawker, the Drudge Report. It's a no-holds barred world out there, Jerome. You're a big boy. Thicken your skin. We're getting ink and that's cool, right baby?"

Mindy closed her eyes, felt her body go limp. She was waiting for him to speak, make one of his jokes, make everything alright. She closed her eyes and ran her hand over her face.

"Well, I'm beginning to understand something now," he finally said.

"What? What are you beginning to understand?"

"Don't worry, everything's cool. Let's focus on the important stuff. C'mon it's late, let an old man get his sleep."

"*Is* everything cool? C'mon baby, no more of this. Talk about Barbados, the little house on the beach. Tell me about it, *please*."

She heard him sigh wearily.

"Tomorrow."

Mindy poured herself a glass of wine. She clicked on the TV and sat by the window, smoking cigarettes into the early morning.

58

It was late August. Courtney decided not to tell Izzy about Derek, about the flowers cut into the screen, the incident on the road, none of it. Every night, she stayed in her room with the door locked, waiting to hear her father come home from work at the restaurant. His routine never varied: smoking out on the front walk, popping a can of beer, trudging upstairs to wrestle with his dashed dreams. He was a neat man. The way he systematically stroked with his razor, tightened the hospital corners of the sheets and blankets when he made his bed. Perhaps neatness was all he had left. That, and his meager possessions, which he cared for as though they were great treasures—his father's fake ruby ring, a pair of beat-up cufflinks, an old Army watch with its leather strap and radium dial. He had a strict and unyielding code, an emotional shield against all the many disappointments in his life. Courtney had heard him on the phone talking about her, using the archaic term "kept woman." *He's hanging on for dear life*, she thought. *Maybe he's counting the days until I leave.*

Stepping from the shower, Courtney called her sister on the bedroom phone.

"I need you to talk to Derek, Kate. You're close with him. You've got to get him to stop harassing me."

"I know he's intense," Kate said, "but wasn't that what you liked about him?"

Courtney dragged a comb through her hair.

"Well, Courtney, isn't that what you said?"

"Thanks, *sis*," Courtney said, slamming down the phone.

❧

After working virtually for nearly a week, Courtney met Izzy for lunch at Mirabelle. She got there two minutes late, which for her was like an hour. The waiter poured the Bâtard-Montrachet and took the lunch orders. Izzy lifted his glass, touched Courtney's and said mildly, "I'm glad to be having a break from meetings in Washington. Congress is on recess now. DC's an interesting town."

"That it is," said Courtney. She sipped her wine, took a bite of her buttered baguette. Izzy watched her chew, touch her lip with the napkin. Her hair was slightly disarranged. He wondered if it was a new look, or if she'd been hurried. In any event, she looked wonderful.

"When you interned for the good Senator Winslow…"

"Wrong."

"OK, when you interned for the sleazeball Senator, did you ever meet his wife?"

"Once or twice at a fundraiser. She was one of these prudish Midwestern women—the kind who hate Washington and are in way over their heads. I think they were high school sweethearts and you know how those things go. After a while, when the kids are gone, the bonds of matrimony fray. She hated me and I didn't care for her."

"And she knows he's a player?"

Courtney lifted her eyebrows and smirked. "Who in that town doesn't know?"

The waiter brought two plates of sole meuniere and filled their wine glasses.

Izzy said, "We're on the cusp of making a deal like no other in recent history. But we have a tough road ahead. I've been getting calls from Winslow. He's skittish. All the pols are these days. Anyway, we need this pompous windbag in our corner. We'll have dinner with him in DC right after my club's big tourney and your move into the condo. You'll be making your presentation there."

"OK. And I'm sure you also want me to jog his memory about what a learning experience it was working in his office."

"Yes, that would be correct. We'll meet with Lawrence Saddler, bigtime union guy and Lance Cramer, a ranking member on the Senate Committee on Finance. He has a vested interest in anything done with the Chinese."

Courtney tasted her sole and moaned softly, appreciatively. "You know, Izzy," she said jokingly, "I never worked for those gentlemen."

Izzy leaned forward. "Doll, you've lost weight. Your face looks so drawn. What's up with you?"

Courtney put her fork down. "Nothing. *Really.* I'm just so excited about the project and I can't wait to get into my new place." She squeezed his forearm.

He sat back, eyeing her. "There's something else. My bullshit detector is registering something here. Is it your family, that guy? What's going on?"

"Just family stuff. It'll blow over. Nothing that's going to interfere with business."

৯৵৶

Later that afternoon Derek pulled around to the back of the Commack Motor Inn. Her car was there. The door to Room 108 was open. When he stepped in, the cooled air hit his sweat-damp body, sending a chill up his back. The shades were drawn. "You're late," she called from the bathroom.

Derek pulled his T-shirt over his head, kicked off his sneakers. "Practice ran a bit long. Fucking kids are out of shape," said Derek.

She came out of the bathroom in a black bra and panties. She walked up to him and ran her hand down his chest across the ripple of abdominal muscles. "You're not," she said.

Derek clutched the nape of her neck and forced her to her knees. "Not what?"

"Out of shape," she said, peeling off his gym shorts and boxers with one impatient yank. She teased him for a moment, then stood and pushed him back onto the bed. "You've got to wait," she said.

There was a paperback book on the bed: *Nine Stories* by J. D. Salinger. She opened it. "Ever read 'Pretty Mouth and Green My Eyes?'"

He undid her bra, sliding it off her shoulders. "In high school, I think. It sucked."

"High school or the story?"

He felt her breasts, one at a time. "Both."

He stroked her abdomen, pinching the slight roll of fat on her tummy.

"Hey, I've had two kids," she said, slapping his hand playfully.

He grabbed her crotch, pulling at the panties.

"Easy, lover, this is Victoria's Secret lingerie. So, let's pretend that I'm the girl you've just made love to and the phone rings and it's my husband..."

"Where is good old Bill?"

"I told you, in Philly, at a medical equipment show."

"If Billy boy only knew."

"Anyway, so he calls, you answer. What do you say?"

Derek tore her panties off. He snatched the book from her and tossed it across the room. "I'd say, hey Bill old boy, can't talk right now 'cause your wife's here and I gotta fuck her."

She was breathing hard now. "I hated it when you were away at camp!" Her brow darkened for a moment and she whispered, "Christ, I feel like such a pig doing this. I still love Bill, but dear God, he can be dull as dirt sometimes."

Derek pulled away and looked at her. "No, it's 'God I feel like an absolute *dog!*'"

"Right, that's what Joanie said in 'Pretty Mouth.' So you did read it." She took his hand, tried to pull him to her.

"I like pig better, myself," Derek said.

"Well, either way, I need this."

He took her chin in his hand, and said, "Now tell me, is Courtney fucking that old guy? You know, so tell me."

"I really don't know. I swear!"

"Kate, you little pig," he said, wrestling her over onto her belly. Grabbing a fistful of hair, he leaned to her ear. "She's your sister. You know. Now tell me."

"You're hurting me."

"*Tell me.*"

"If I do, will you still see me after you're with her?" It was a pathetic whine, but Kate was beyond caring.

He pulled her head up, breathing hard into her ear. "Oh, yeah. Now tell me."

"Yes," she whispered, "She's sleeping with him."

She felt his body tighten. Then he flipped her over and fell between her parted legs, moving soundlessly, machine-like.

59

When Dana looked at the clock, it was 3:39 am. She figured Buddy had fallen asleep downstairs. She slid from bed and found him hunched over the drafting board, mumbling to himself; so intent was he on his work that he didn't realize she was in the doorway. She watched for a moment, then stepped to him and touched his shoulder.

"Jesus, Dana," he said, jumping.

"Sorry," she said, bending at the waist, inspecting the rendering. "Wow, it's really coming along."

"Well, let's hope Arty Wagner's impressed," he said, shifting around in his chair, stifling a yawn with his hand.

"Arty Wagner?"

"You know, my new boss," he said. Thumping his forehead with the heel of his hand, he flashed a goofy, pained smiled and said, "Christ, this is still so weird."

"I thought the Jewish lady was the boss."

"Elaine. She's *Elaine*. Like Roy, he's *Roy!*"

She stepped back. "*Stop*, OK? We're just in a tough patch."

"I don't even want to know what you're doing anymore. *That's* how tough it is."

"Let's not get started on that shit. Tell me about this," she said, pointing to the drawing.

Buddy looked away. A truck blew by the house, air brakes exploding the quiet as it shuddered to a stop at the red light on the corner. "God, I hate this place," he said.

Dana touched his shoulder. "Buddy, I want to understand more about what you're doing. It's not too late."

Buddy absorbed what she'd said, "Too late for what?"

"Anything, c'mon," she said sleepily, nodding at the sheet of paper spread before him.

Buddy cleared his throat. "I came up with this design when I was 17. A par 72 course. Long, 7,478 yards, lumpy waves of fescue rough and 328 bunkers that could just as well be played as hazards. This cliffhanging par 3 with an elevated green surrounded by three bunkers is a death sentence for hacks. You can just make out the top of the pin, the green is blind."

"What's a hack?"

"A golfer with a very high handicap."

"What's a handicap?"

"Stop playing dumb," he smiled. "It's a number to calculate a golfer's level of performance under the parameters set by the United States Golf Association. The higher one's handicap, the more strokes that he or she is awarded toward par during a round."

"Sounds complicated."

"It's not really. Golf is a lonely and unforgiving sport. A handicap is a piece of charity to give poor players the ability to compete with good players," he said, reaching up and clicking off the desk lamp. "Got it?" he said.

Dana took his hand and said, "C'mon, let's go to bed."

On the way upstairs they saw the tiny glow from the upstairs bedroom next door. "Doesn't that crazy fuck ever sleep?" said Dana, closing her eyes, gripping Buddy's hand and following him like a blind person.

60

Peering through his window, Tyrell waited until he saw the light in Buddy's bedroom go out, then whispered, "Nighty, night, white boy." He pictured Buddy's face. Not a pretty boy, but the kind of careless good looks that give white men like him access to anything they want. He pictured a fish on a hook flopping about on a boat deck, gasping, those bluest of eyes all panicky, turning dull as Tyrell put his boot on him, yanking the hook out, watching him die, slowly gasping for air. "Maybe it just sags like a heavy load. Or does it explode?" he recited. *Yes, Brother Hughes, I'm listening.*

Tyrell was still angry at Latreece for nagging at him that night. She had come up the stairs, stomping her feet all the way to let him know she meant business. Barging into his office, she started complaining about his drug use, his late-night hours.

"These days, you're high so much I wouldn't recognize you if you was straight."

"Why don't you go back down to the TV and watch those fat white people trying to get skinny!"

"I respect anyone who *tries*," she said, folding her arms across her chest, her jaw set.

They glared at one another.

"Girl, what do you want from me?" Tyrell finally said, weary and irate.

Latreece wiped her eyes, roughly brushing away tears. "I'm trying to build my life, get a better job, raise my kid. I thought we was partners. But lately, I see that my life is goin' in a different direction from yours."

"When did *that* happen?" he asked with a sneer.

"Well, maybe not yet, but it's *gonna* happen," she said, her voice trembling. "Sometimes I feel my chest hurt, like somethin's trying to jump out. There's stroke in my people. Mother, two uncles gone from it before they was forty. Is that what you want for me? Or maybe you got some other big plans!"

That's when he noticed her eyebrows. She'd plucked them into a swooping arch over her eyes. He smiled cruelly, ran a finger over his own brows and said, "What up, girl? You think you look like Beyoncé now?"

Latreece spun around and stormed out, calling from the stairwell, "You gotta make up your mind." Tyrell nodded to himself, not knowing or caring what she meant. He popped three Adderall, washed them down with Diet Coke, and lit up his hash pipe. Leaning back, he closed his eyes. *Waiting for that express train*, he thought. In a launching flash of clarity, he was hurtled away. This speed rush was so much better than just the muffled stupor of straight hash. Jazzed by the Adderall, he felt the zing of the Roadrunner, dusted with immortality.

Tyrell got up to stare out the window down Pulaski Road. The old man across the street puzzled him. *Ol' Uncle Gene's half in the grave, but he acts like he's gonna live forever*, Tyrell thought. *Somethin' has come over him since that white boy painted his house.* Turning to his laptop, Tyrell sent his last e-mail of the night to Jerome Brown: "So begins my not-so-private war with the powers that be."

It was nearly two o'clock in the morning when the phone rang. Jerome looked up from his laptop, to check the caller ID. He figured it would be Mindy, drunk on wine, crying and bleating with that pinched up white face. When he peered at the readout on the phone he was relieved to see it wasn't her, but taken aback by the name that appeared there. His mouth set tight, Jerome cleared his throat and answered the phone. "What's an old man like you doing up at this hour?" he said.

"I was about to ask you the same question," said the man on the other end.

There was a long pause, then they both started talking at once, loud energetic voices in a head-on collision. Then laughter. Then an air of sadness and they were quiet again. A moment passed. Like boxers circling the mat, each waited for the other to strike first. "Earl Caldwell," said Jerome. "Three years nothing, then *bam*, you call me at two in the morning. So, you're not mad at me anymore? Or calling in the middle of the night, maybe you are."

"Never was, my brother. We just had a difference of opinion...well, you know how these things go. Anyway, now that you're famous, thought it'd be a good time to touch base," Caldwell said, in his rumbling radio voice.

"Famous. Yeah, right. How you been? I try to catch your broadcast on Fridays. You're keepin' it real, man."

"You the one keepin' it real. That's some powerful stuff, that *Vanity Fair* piece. I got the galley of your book. You're hittin' it man. I'm proud of you."

"That's why you called at this hour, to say you're proud of me? I don't think so."

246

Caldwell laughed, a deep chesty sound. "Well, I called to catch up *and* invite you on the *Caldwell Chronicle*. Since you're in the big time, I was a bit gun-shy about asking you to come on the radio. TV, O'Reilly. I seen you on that show. Hear you're gonna be on again soon."

"Man, I'm very touched. Sure, I'd love to be on your show. About that O'Reilly stuff, man. I just gotta do a return trip, set the record right, if you know what I mean."

Caldwell paused, then said, "I always expect the worst, and I'm usually right about things. Guess years of being a black reporter in a white industry got me that way. But anyway, you've hit on something that no one is talking about 'cause it scares them to the bone. You're speaking truth to power and that ain't no cliché."

Jerome said, "I appreciate that."

"Your message is important, man, but so's the messenger. You gotta watch who you clientele with 'cause there are certain elements that will tear you down for it. I'm speaking from experience."

"You mean the white girl, huh? You can say it, Earl."

"Looks like I don't have to, my brother."

61

Considering he was working on only four hours of sleep, Jerome felt surprisingly good. He took a long thoughtful jog through Central Park. On the return trip he stopped at the corner of 68th Street and Broadway to pick up coffee and a bagel from the deli. His conversation with Earl Caldwell was still fresh in his mind. Jerome could hear Caldwell's warnings in the thrum of the car tires racing past. The grizzled old reporter had been bloodied in the trenches of the civil rights struggle. In their conversation last night, it was almost as though Caldwell was judging Jerome's emergence into that world—the world that used to be his—and wanting Jerome to take bold but measured steps forward.

His thoughts drifted to Mindy. Things had started getting weird with her right after the first O'Reilly appearance. It was like he was going too fast and she was afraid he'd leave her behind. Jerome had enough insight into man-woman relationships to know it was a constant power struggle and that concession was the highest card in the deck. He just wasn't sure how much of him Mindy wanted and how much he was willing to concede. He smiled to himself. *In some ways, Mindy is just like my ex. Celia wanted more and more power over me. Now she has none, except for trash talking about me to that white bitch Bobbi Holmes.*

Rain began to fall just as Jerome got back to his building. Oscar the doorman made an inane remark about good weather for ducks. He had the clammy, beady-eyed look of an inveterate gambler and he was a talker, always ready to strike up a conversation about things Jerome couldn't care less about, like basketball. Jerome nodded and said a quick hello. But as he strode across the lobby, Oscar said from the side of his mouth, "Someone was asking about you, Professor." Jerome stopped in his tracks, his half eaten bagel falling to the ground.

Oscar quickly bent and picked it up, holding it out stupidly as Jerome cleared his throat and said, "OK, did he leave a note or anything?"

Oscar looked from side to side, then leaned forward. "Just this," he said, handing Jerome an envelope decorated with hand-stamped images, "and it was a she, a white she." Before Jerome could ask anything further, Oscar mustered his best imitation of Sergeant Schultz: "I see nothing, I know nothing."

As Jerome disappeared into the elevator, Oscar nodded to himself and thought of the dirt he could dish to Benny, his afternoon relief guy. Brushing off the half-eaten bagel, he took a bite. "No cream cheese, the cheap prick," Oscar mumbled.

❧ ❧

Buddy and Dana slept in. She heard him stir and whispered, "Aren't you working today?" He said he had a meeting with his new boss. Then he fell back into the deepest sleep he'd had since his troubles began. He dreamed of a golf course by the sea, dotted with snow-white bunkers. Hitting a perfect wedge from a hanging lie, his ball plopped down with backspin onto the green, pulling within six feet of the pin. Elaine was in his dream, standing in the wind waving at him and smiling, her yellow linen slacks bright in the sun. When he woke, Dana was sitting on the bed holding two cups of coffee.

"I was staring at a birdie lie and I three-putted," he said, sitting up and taking his coffee.

"What?"

Buddy shook the sleep from his head. "Just a dream."

"Was I in it?"

He looked at her. The prettiest face without makeup he'd ever seen. He swallowed. "You bet you were."

Dana said, "OK. Now, I want you to go over everything about Russ, the house, your plans, the mental case next door, us. *Everything*, alright? Take your time."

❧ ❧

Jerome sat in his easy chair and closed his eyes. The envelope was ripped open on the desk. He took his time, letting his emotions drop from boil to simmer, until he was in control, breathing normally. He reassessed what he was going to say to her, saving what he thought was important, discarding the rest. It was cleansing, like going through a closet jammed with old, stained, and useless items and tossing them out, wondering why in the world you'd saved them in the first place. Then he picked up the phone and called Mindy's office. Her assistant put him right through.

"You broke a very important rule, today. Why?"

"And good morning to you, Jerome. *Rule?*"

"You came by my building. I thought we were clear on that, especially since I'm doing O'Reilly on September 9th."

"I miss you, OK? I really *miss* you. Christ, Jerome, do I have to spell it out? Besides, all I wanted was for that doorman to give you my note, a romantic little thing I made for you. What a loser that guy is. He looks like a child molester."

"OK, Mindy. Please don't do that again. You know what's at stake here."

"When can I see you?"

"Not now. Soon," he said distractedly. "By the way, I'm doing the Caldwell Chronicle on the radio next week. So, you can get out that buzz too. I spoke to Earl this morning."

"Earl? Caldwell? Help me out here."

"You're in PR and you don't know who Earl Caldwell is? Tell me you're pulling my leg."

"Yes, there *is* a leg I'd like to pull...OK, I give up. Who's Earl Caldwell?"

"He's a legendary black journalist, columnist, and professor. Earl Caldwell was the only reporter present at the assassination of Martin Luther King, and he was a working for the *Times*. He was also in with the Black Panthers. Caldwell refused to disclose information to the FBI and the Nixon Administration about his sources in the Black Panther party."

"Cool, I never knew that."

"The case, United States v. Caldwell, went all the way to the Supreme Court and led to the enactment of shield laws, protecting reporters' sources."

"Wow, never knew that, either. What station is he on?"

"WBAI."

"Oh, *please*. That's the wacky station with Al Lewis. You know, Grandpa in the Munsters."

"Lewis is dead."

"So is that station."

"Do your homework, Mindy. Caldwell is an icon in the black activist community. You're supposed to know this stuff!"

"OK, I'll check him out. Listen, I was invited to be part of a panel discussion at the 92nd Street Y on the ethics of web-based reporting. David Remnick from the *New Yorker* will moderate. Isn't that cool?"

Jerome was listening with one ear, a half-hearted "*uh uh, yeah*" dropped in at appropriate moments.

"So I'll be on a panel with TMZ, the Huffington Post, and guess who else?"

"Ah, Lady Gaga?"

"Bobbi Holmes, *The Holmes Report* herself."

Jerome bolted out of his chair. He felt his hands shake. "You are not going! That bitch will set you up, set me up! Do *not* go."

A long pause.

"Is that another one of your rules?" Mindy asked, her voice tight.

"Yes, and if you break this one, there will be consequences."

"Jerome, it sounds like you're threatening me."

"I am."

62

Later that afternoon Elaine was sitting in Arty Wagner's office in Great Neck. Arty was peering out the picture window at the traffic passing on Route 25A, kvetching about the pastrami sandwich he'd had for lunch. A man named Robert Newquist had recently bought the deli Arty frequented. "How do you figure a guy named Newquist as a deli man? And he wears his hair in a flattop. It doesn't fit. Do you see my point, Elaine?"

Elaine was studying a laptop on the small conference table. "Jesus, it's a hundred-and-three in Scottsdale. How do people play golf in that heat? You'd have to pack my ass in dry ice."

Arty thought about that, picturing her luscious ass, swaddled, the dry ice vapors rising around her sinuously. He shook his head to clear the image.

They were waiting on Buddy. He was running twenty minutes late, and although Elaine had assured Arty that everything "was kosher," her stomach was doing flip-flops. There was that slight frisson of distrust. Could she count on him? After all, he had done it before—put fame and fortune on the back burner so he could chase up and down the coast of South America on a tramp freighter. It made her head hurt just thinking about it.

Arty looked at his watch. "Maybe you should give Buddy a call, no?"

"Don't worry, he'll be here."

Arty began pacing. "I have an appointment with my fourth wife's attorney at five o'clock. I don't need this kid giving me any more stress."

Elaine said firmly, "He's not a *kid*, and maybe you shouldn't marry every broad you stick your tally-whacker into."

Just as Arty turned to her, raising his finger to make a point, Buddy knocked on the doorframe and stepped into the office carrying a portfolio case.

&⤜ ⤛&

Latreece eavesdropped on Tyrell's telephone conversation, putting her ear to his office door. It was obvious Tyrell was talking to the white guy who sold him all those pills. Tyrell's voice was high and strained as he labored to convince the dealer that he would catch up on his back bills in another week. He just needed to get over this little hump. Tyrell was doing a fair imitation of a black guy talking to a white guy in phony Ebonic-speak. He sounded like Chris Rock goofing on a white audience. She knew the dealer just had to be some white dude who was probably eating it up, having this real-life homey begging him for credit. If it was a brother on the other end of the phone, he'd laugh his head off at the jive shit Tyrell was dishing.

Then she heard Tyrell say, "Thanks man, this is a solid I won't forget. Right, I'll meet you behind the sports complex at I'll meet you behind the sports complex at college in twenty five." A pause, then, "True dat! Man, that's crazy, man, that's some crazy, sick shit." More sucking up to the white guy for his damn pills. It made Latreece sick. And it made her think of her days on the street in East New York, doing whatever she had to do to put rock in her pipe. She held on to those memories as a warning. For Latreece, looking back wasn't a mistake. She wanted to hear the footsteps of her past, to remind her how easy it is to get so low. *I'll be damned if I ever go back to that,* she thought grimly.

Hearing Tyrell hang up the phone, Latreece danced away down the stairs on tiptoe.

৯৶৹

Buddy spread his draft on the table, securing the four corners with two ashtrays and two little statues of golfers that he took from the shelf. Arty's eyes swept the paper and he grinned.

Without waiting for Arty or Elaine to speak, Buddy began to explain his concept. "The tee shot on this double dogleg par five is demanding, but it rewards a courageous shot over the left edge of the protruding dune..."

For twenty-five minutes, he spoke, without notes, without stumbling, his words drawing vivid pictures in the air. Arty circled the room, nodding to himself, stopping to peer over Buddy's shoulder, smiling and punching the back of his chair. Elaine barely stirred, seeming to hold her breath. When Buddy finished, he said, "Well, there it is. Needs some fine tuning, but I think it's a helluva course."

Arty rocked back and forth on his heels. Running his hand over the drawing he boomed, "This is one of the prettiest, best laid out courses I've ever seen! Fantastic job. I'm impressed, to say the least."

Buddy nodded, thanked Arty. Elaine beamed at Buddy and winked at him. Under the table, she knocked her knee against his.

Arty leaned over the table. "Golf is essentially a pissing contest. It drives honest men to become cheaters. Hell, it's easy for some shit-weasel to nudge his ball out of the rough, fudge his card. The game drives people fucking nuts. I've always found that the key to happiness on the course is not to give a shit. But I've got a public course mentality. In fact, I hate the fucking game," he said with a belly laugh. "But the customers we're going after are true devotees. Now look, I've got three potentials lined up and I'm going to pitch this to them. I see this as a two-and-a-half-mil deal. We can't compete with Nicklaus or the Shark on exclusive 18-hole courses. And why would we want to? So, this is my angle."

Arty swiveled his computer monitor so Buddy and Elaine could see it. He clicked on a program. "This database has more than three hundred very wealthy people who *live* for golf. And all of them own estates with enough acreage to accommodate a single par three golf hole." Arty ran his finger over the eighth hole on Buddy's drawing, the par 3 he'd talked to Dana about. "This wicked little beauty will be our prototype. A million bucks a pop," Arty said, dreamily. Then he looked at Buddy. "Hope you like to travel."

Arty went to his liquor cabinet, took out a bottle of Springbank 32-year-old single malt. He put the bottle on the table with three crystal tumblers, poured out two fingers in each and said, "This bottle of Scotch cost me seven-hundred-and-fifty bucks. I just thought I'd mention that because the only time I've drunk from it was when I divorced a wife or sealed a deal. And *this* is a fucking deal. Cheers, partners."

After his phone call Tyrell had made some weak excuse to go out. Latreece simply nodded. She sat with Tashanda to help her do her lessons. At the library, Latreece had read up about challenged children and found lessons she thought would be best for her baby. She'd told Tashanda that, from now on, before the TV went on, she had to do her studies. Prizes were part of the new routine, of course, but she was amazed at how Tashanda took to the challenge; it made her proud and weepy-eyed. Giving her daughter a hug, Latreece released her charge, who went skipping to the television and settled in to watch her favorite Sponge Bob show.

Latreece went back upstairs into Tyrell's room, directly to the closet, and gingerly opened his Army locker chest. She bypassed the letters home and went right to the official documents. *Five days before the attack, on 8 July, a platoon from the Second Battalion, 503rd Infantry Regiment, 173rd Airborne Brigade Combat Team established Vehicle Patrol Base (VPB) Kahler and a separate observation post called "OP Top Side" near Wanat. 8 July, 2d Platoon, Chosen Company, departed from Camp Blessing after sunset in a ground assault convoy for the 90 minute long drive to Wanat...The sexual assault complaints included 11 rapes, 13 indecent assaults, and 1 sodomy. Of the 25 allegations, 15 (60 percent) were substantiated, 4 (16 percent) were unsubstantiated, and 6 (24 percent) were unde-termined due to insufficient evidence...System Support Specialist Tyrell Walker...*

Page after page of sexual assaults on young women, bloodless descriptions in dry military jargon, Tyrell's name woven throughout the report. No wonder he always avoided talking about his time in Afghanistan. The sickening phrase "insufficient evidence for court marshal," was repeated over and over. What voice, what chance did those women have? Some were just girls. It was like seeing all the ugly things laid bare in the aftermath of Hurricane Katrina. After the water had receded, root systems of trees were exposed, filled with garbage; bloated bodies of animals lay with their feet sticking up in the air; human corpses floated face down—the horrifying heart of destruction and willful neglect.

Still, she couldn't pull her eyes away from the document. Time's arrow quivered and stilled. The walls of the cramped closet bent inward, and she felt her body go numb. Latreece could barely breathe or move, so filled with dread was she. Who is this man she slept with, made plans with, got caught up in this scheme with? *Who is he?* Then her head snapped up. Tashanda was squealing. "Daddy, Daddy! Daddy's home!"

❦❧

"So, you come home with a slight buzz on and in a very good mood. What gives kiddo?" said Izzy, as Jasmine filled his wine glass and went to fill Elaine's. They were having dinner together, something husband and wives should do occasionally, Izzy had announced without a hint of irony.

"I can't be in a good mood without you getting suspicious?" Elaine replied.

"So, where were you?"

"Like I told you, with Marcy Fortgang. We were talking. We had a drink. Joel is away, and you know how she gets. Now lay off. I don't give *you* the third degree about things."

Izzy smiled. "And if I pick up the phone and call Marcy Fortgang..."

"She'll tell you exactly what I just said."

"Thick as thieves," Izzy said, fixing her with a hard stare.

"Oh, don't be such a drama king," Elaine said airily, taking a sip of wine.

Izzy called Jasmine in. "That's it for tonight Jasmine." The housekeeper started to say something about dinner but Izzy waved his hand in the air. "Mrs. Weinberg is going to do something she hasn't done in twenty years:

serve dinner. But remember, Jasmine, the tournament is coming up on the tenth, so I'll need you basically round the clock."

Jasmine bade them goodnight.

"Is everything set for the tournament?" Elaine asked.

"Yeah, I have a meeting with the steering committee tomorrow night."

"Right, that's where you men steer yourselves into the barroom for a bullshit session over drinks and cigars."

"Exactly. By the way, we're gonna have a house guest for the tournament. A very important associate of mine from China."

"Oh, is he one of those yellow, dog-eating fucks you detest?"

"Yes, but he has a sense of humor, for a Chink at least. And he's got an eye for the ladies, so I need you to fawn over him a bit. You know, be a little flirtatious, show some cleavage, let him dream that in another time and place he might get lucky with you. In other words, just be yourself."

Elaine drained her wine and said, "My God you're a roaring asshole."

Izzy rose and walked around the table. Standing behind Elaine, he bent to her ear. "You've been a naughty girl, but you can't fool Izzy. I'm gonna find out what's up with you."

Elaine put her glass down, and began to protest, but Izzy hushed her, gently pressing his finger across her lips. Whispering into her ear he said, "I think I lost my appetite. Now, Mrs. Weinberg, you're gonna do something else you haven't done in a while," he said seductively.

Elaine tilted her head and smiled slightly, in spite of herself. "Oh, and what's that?"

"Fuck your husband. C'mon, I love seeing the stuff I paid for."

63

As September approached, the nights arrived a little earlier, leaving old dogs and old men feeling the ache of diminishing time. The wind off the Sound picked up at this time of year, scaring up miniature dust devils. For-sale signs lining the road flapped desperately, like castaways waving for all they were worth at a passing plane too high and too far away to see them.

Eugene Freyerson had come to expect a daily visit from Buddy, anticipated it like a cup of good coffee or an afternoon nap. Sometimes their talks would last an hour, sometimes only a few minutes. Buddy would always knock, that polite three-tap tattoo that was as familiar to Eugene as Old Sam's snoring. He'd say, "Hello Mr. Freyerson, I was just wondering if you needed anything today, anything I might help you with."

The old man liked that Buddy said "hello" instead of "hi." He liked the way Buddy patted Old Sam's head, scratched his ears. He liked how Buddy sat, with good posture, always looking him in the eyes when he was telling one of his old timey stories. The old man knew that Buddy was in a spot with that fool next door. But even when Eugene asked him about it, Buddy would deflect the question, make an off-handed remark that cut Tyrell a little slack. He liked that too. In fact, he liked everything about this young man.

When he heard Buddy at the door, Eugene poured out two whiskies. They sat at the kitchen table, sipping their drinks and talking companionably, their comfortable ritual. As Freyerson delved into one of his childhood memories, Buddy would listen so intently it was if he was memorizing it, word for word.

But this evening the old man sensed something was wrong; there was worry on Buddy's face. Out of politeness, he didn't pry, but before he started his story he couldn't hold back. "What's going on, Buddy? Don't tell me nothin' 'cause I didn't get this old being stupid."

Buddy looked at Eugene. He placed his hands on the table, as if for support. "I'm going away in a couple of weeks. I'll be gone for a while."

Freyerson blinked moistly. "You ain't in trouble?"

Buddy said, "No. It's not that kind of going away." He gave a brief rundown of his plans.

Freyerson digested it all. "Sounds like a good opportunity for you. Everything cool with…?" he said, gesturing vaguely. Buddy knew he meant his wife.

"We've got some issues, but we're smoothing it out. Everything's going to be OK."

Buddy told Eugene about Russ Dunn, said he would be staying at his place temporarily. "He's a good man—before noon that is," said Buddy with a sly smile. "So if you need anything, Russ is there."

"I don't need much. A little heat in the winter and a cool sup of water in the summer," said Freyerson. He paused a moment, letting the air settle in the room, before saying, "Did I ever tell you about the time we all snuck into the carnival freak show to see the he-she man and the human torso? An those rednecks that damn near killed us? No? Well my best friend—boy we called Little Earl, on account a his daddy was Big Earl—well, me an him had just finished our chores and we decided, well actually *I* decided 'cause I was always the boss man…"

Jerome Brown was looking at a YouTube video of his first appearance on the Bill O'Reilly show, trying to find some clue into what tactic this big Irish bully would use next week. Jerome was taking a calculated risk. He didn't know if the benefits outweighed the risks of appearing on the show. He could not allow O'Reilly to push him into a verbal corner and make it seem like Jerome was a lightweight fighting a heavyweight. O'Reilly had this annoying and condescending way of declaring himself the victor in any argument, leaving many a guest sputtering and fuming.

Jerome then called Earl Caldwell to confirm his appearance on WBAI.

"Brother Caldwell."

"Is it Dr. Brown or Professor Brown that you prefer? Just want to know for when I introduce you on the show."

"Professor's better, I think. So, do I need to prepare anything?"

"Get out of bed and put your slacks on, that's about it. We're just gonna have a conversation, nothin' for you to worry about. But that's not why you called. You're still chewing on the last thing we spoke about, eh? The white girl?"

"Yeah, she and I had words. I just think she might be getting the wrong idea about things."

Caldwell laughed, a hard bark. "Oh man, you do know how lame that sounds. All the shit you pedaled is now coming back at you. And you're blaming the girl? My guess is she took your words literally, a bit too literal for you and your big plans. Am I getting warm, brother?"

"Yeah, you're warm," Jerome said ruefully. "Anyway, it'll work out." Looking forward to doing your show."

"Likewise. I got two suggestions. One, take care of the situation with the girl, and be careful about it. With all this electronic shit, the web, Twitter, Facebook, revenge can be nasty. And two, don't let that cracker O'Reilly get on the offense. Take it to him, 'cause he's gonna try and make righteous black anger out to be the whining of a people that can't get it going. Make him feel your heat, brother. People are noticing you; don't let 'em down, man. Don't let *yourself* down."

☜☞

Dana spent the afternoon going over the work Roy Hickman had e-mailed her at 3:45 in the morning. *Did that man never sleep?* Along with spreadsheets and PowerPoint slides, there was an e-mail thread detailing the specific points they needed to hit during their DC meeting, set for Monday, September 12th. Her thoughts raced as she scrolled to the bottom and began working her way up. Hickman wanted her to do cross-section analyses of different infections, their prevalence, and the costs of treating each type of infection versus non-treatment, and then crunch the numbers by hypothesizing the effect of the project's infection control protocol. She closed the laptop and called Bobbi Holmes.

"Drink? It's on me and I'll meet you halfway at Reston's, you know, on Bell Boulevard."

"Alright, doll," Bobbi said. "It's good timing. I've got some stuff for you on Hickman. How about seven o'clock?"

Dana left Buddy a hand-written note on the kitchen table.

☜☞

Nestled in a corner booth, Dana surveyed the scene at Reston's, an upscale pub bustling with hard-drinking stockbrokers and lawyers. She and Bobbi sat close and leaned into each other.

"Nice to see you out of hospital scrubs," Bobbi said.

"I'm not used to it yet." "So, what'd you find? Anything interesting?"

"Hickman's family has quite a history," said Bobbi. "Both great-grandfathers were Southern officers in the Civil War, his father was a Georgia shipping magnate who belonged to Augusta National. You know, the golf club?"

Dana nodded. "OK, Southern gentry, got that part."

"That's the snootiest white man's place on the planet. They wouldn't let Bill Gates play there because he didn't have a member sponsor him. That's how old Southern money the Hickmans were."

Dana leaned closer, turning her head slightly. "Were?"

"Yeah, the family empire tanked. What you call a reversal of fortune. It was a long slide down. Bad investments, union troubles, double–digit inflation, and a turn toward the sordid: gambling, loan sharks, some creative bookkeeping. Anyway, Roy's mother died very suddenly under suspicious circumstances, and a year later his father, Conrad Haley Hickman—they called him 'Connie'—walked into the family stable and shot himself."

Dana said, "So, Southern gentry falls from grace, but what about Roy? Just a guy escaping his family's downfall?"

Bobbi sipped her wine and looked over at the bar. "What a congregation of dipshits," she said. "I can predict every banal sentence five minutes before they say it. No wonder I haven't been laid in two years."

Dana jerked her head. "Two years!" then she took Bobbi's wrist. "What about Hickman?"

"Something happened with Roy Hickman, and his family made sure the information was destroyed—or at least redacted. But whatever it was did more damage to the family than losing their fortune."

64

The following night, just minutes after Izzy left for the steering committee meeting, Elaine called her boy toy. Hearing his voice, barely audible above the rock music blaring in the background, she swore to herself it was the last time. Not just with him, but with all of the men she'd used to satisfy that sheltered place where her dark stories were kept. Over the past month, a change had occurred: something slipped away, and it felt good. She thought about Buddy. A brief clean thought, a well-shaped puzzle piece that fit into something larger. All that remained was binding up the loose ends.

This *thing* started when she was seventeen. Then, it was older men, but always the same breed: hard-hearted and low. Years spent on a couch talking to shrinks for two hundred bucks an hour, Elaine had discovered as much as she ever wanted to know about herself. The truth was, she had found an undeniable peace in her sordid and confused liaisons, a peculiar truce that made other parts of her life bearable. But the wreckage of the aftermath was finally piling up too high. And instead of finding a release through these punishing encounters, she felt trapped. *Time to spring the lock*, she thought as she looked in the mirror and slashed on her lipstick.

She was more than a little tipsy; *better not to drive myself tonight*, Elaine thought. She called Jasmine's cell phone and asked her for a lift. Jasmine was already off duty, but she never begrudged doing a favor for Elaine. When Jasmine had first arrived in New York from Barbados, Elaine had taken her under her wing, helped her build a life in a strange land. It was Elaine who convinced Izzy to pay $10,000 to an immigration attorney to help both Jasmine and her daughter become legal. Elaine made sure the housekeeper had a decent place to live, in a safe neighborhood. She always treated Jasmine with respect. For that, and more, Jasmine would be forever grateful.

When Jasmine pulled up in her 10-year-old Subaru she was startled to see her elegant boss standing in the dark in a gown with a shawl over her shoulders. "Mrs. Weinberg, you OK?" she said, as Elaine got into the car.

"I'm OK, you're OK. Just drive honey," Elaine smiled.

"There, park there," Elaine said when they arrived, pointing to the massive oak tree sheltering the Tudor house. "Come back in thirty minutes. I'll be out here, waiting for you."

Elaine saw the look on Jasmine's face. She touched her hand. "I'm fine, thanks. See you in half an hour."

Elaine rang the bell, the key in her hand. A shirtless Brad Mueller yanked opened the door.

࿐

On Thursday morning, September 8th, Jack pulled the limo up to Izzy's house, Starbucks in hand for his boss. They were off to JFK to pick up Secretary Qian; on the way they'd stop in Queens for the translator William Lo.

The Belt Parkway was in its usual snarled state, a slow-motion riot with car horns blaring, refrigerator-sized potholes, drivers red-faced with road rage, and crews of union construction workers, coffee-breaking on the side of the road amid flashing signs, needlessly warning the passing cars to slow down. Izzy shook his head wearily. "Willya just look at this clusterfuck. We're running out of money and we can't move. The whole fucking country's stuck in neutral."

Pulling up to the arrivals area, Jack asked about their pick-up, to which Izzy growled, "You can't miss him. He's five-foot nothing, wears a Howdy Doody haircut, a suit they wouldn't hang on the clearance rack at Wal-Mart, and a set of choppers that make Wink Martindale's look like baby teeth."

When Qian Qichen settled into the limo on the banquette across from Izzy, they spent the requisite time on formalities, queries about the flight, polite small-talk praising the Chinese rail system. Izzy poured Cognacs for himself and the Secretary, apologizing for the ghastly traffic.

It was Qian's first visit to the U. S., and Izzy had Jack take a grand tour of Manhattan. Stopping at Ground Zero, Izzy described the events on 9/11, the aftermath, the effect on the city. He wondered whether he'd said too much, too bluntly, used terms that Lo could not easily interpret, and offended the Secretary.

A moment passed and Qian nodded solemnly. "We too have our barbarians," he said. With his hand he made a slicing motion across his throat. Then, smiling, he laid two fingers across his forearm. Izzy gently lifted the Secretary's hand, moving it up to his elbow.

"You can't be shy with a pregnant cow. You have to go *all* the way in," said Izzy. Lo translated and the Secretary beamed. Izzy was happy.

࿐

By the time they arrived back to Huntington, spirits were high. The conversation had turned to golf, with Izzy explaining the history and structure of the Club's annual tournament, which always fell on the weekend after Labor Day. The Secretary was impressed that he was paired with the club's pro and delighted to be named the tournament's guest of honor.

After a tour of the club, they went to Izzy's house. It was clear that Qian was awestruck by the Weinberg manse. The big, open, generous space appealed to him. It was clearly a reflection of his soon-to-be partner. Izzy was a man of great energy and resilience, Qian believed, but he knew that, like most people of great dreams, this out-sized man was no doubt a plotter, schemer, and perhaps even a liar. Qian also knew that he was losing something, the precious nuance of language, stiffened by translation. *This man Lo, should I trust him?* Qian wondered. *He comes from a respected family in China. Blood, one must trust blood.*

Though still somewhat guarded, the Secretary had come to feel comfortable with Izzy, even to like him. Despite Izzy's crass and cowboyish behavior, he had a rare interior balance, a quality that was essential for the massive undertaking they were planning. But what really appealed to the Secretary was Izzy's face and hands. On them was everything one needed to know about him: the unmistakable imprint of toil and strength.

As the Secretary stood in the marbled foyer, a slim, very pretty woman glided down the staircase, smiling warmly, reaching her hand out. "Secretary Qian, welcome to our home. Please consider it yours. You must be tired from your long trip. Jasmine will show you to your room," Elaine said, as Lo translated.

On the way upstairs, Qian turned once, catching a quick rear view of Elaine. *Gorgeous ass,* he thought to himself, *something our catlike women in China lack.* He always had an eye for natural beauty: birds in flight, distant flower-covered hills, bands of color in the distant sunset. But this man Izzy, he knows the *power* of beauty, female beauty, in particular. He enjoys it, uses it—a man after his own heart. Qian wondered where Izzy was keeping the exquisite Courtney.

That night, the Weinbergs hosted a lavish dinner party in honor of the Secretary. It was a grand affair; Izzy had called in a favor with Daniel Boulud, who agreed to cater. Twenty-two guests ranged around the dining room table, all of whom had been handpicked by Izzy, a cross-section of movers and shakers, unabashed lovers of unfettered capitalism, dripping with the spoils of their money-making conquests. Qian was seated between Lo and Elaine. He was so close to Elaine he could smell her perfume, feel the heat off her skin. It occurred to him after his third drink that, even though he found these rich Americans slightly boorish, they were fun to be around.

"Do you play golf?" he asked Elaine.

"Oh yes, I live for it."

"It is nice to see a woman who knows what she likes," he said, politely as the Tournedos Rossini were being served.

She smiled. "Mr. Lo, how do you translate a smile?"

"My playing partner is the club pro, Mr. Brad Mueller," continued the Secretary. "I'm eager to meet him, to improve my game. Do you play with him?"

Elaine stopped her glass an inch from her lips and said, "On occasion."

As the evening progressed, the party became more animated, fueled by the continuous flow of champagne, wine, and after-dinner drinks. Izzy held court, making sure the Secretary was engaged with the guests. Then Izzy led the party out to the back lawn, to his lighted putting green. More drinks were served. Cigars were smoked and Frank Sinatra's voice filled the air. The Secretary stood at the edge of the green next to Elaine, watching with amusement as Izzy and company began putting for money, littering the ground with tossed hundred-dollar bills.

A small smile touched the corners of the Secretary's mouth. "Do you do this often?" he asked her.

She laughed, a sound so sharp and filled with life, it pierced the night.

65

Jerome Brown was not naturally given to exercise. But hypertension ran in his family, so he tried to stay active to ward off the ill effects of his bad habits—smoking and an abiding fondness for short ribs and Scotch whisky. It didn't stop there, but those vices were reason enough for his daily jogs.

It was Friday morning. He took a long run in the park, heading north toward Harlem, up the path where the infamous Central Park jogger rape had gone down in 1989. The victim was a 28-year-old white investment banker. Five black teenaged boys were tried for and convicted of the vicious rape and beating. But their convictions were vacated when another man claimed to have committed the assault and DNA evidence confirmed his involvement in the rape. *Wilding.* That was the term flogged endlessly in the mainstream white press. It ratcheted up the fear and racial mistrust in the city.

At the time, Earl Caldwell invited Jerome to speak at a rally, decrying the lynch mob mentality. But Jerome wasn't yet tenured, and a fellow professor suggested he rethink the invitation so as not to jeopardize his chances with the centrist-leaning tenure board. In the end, Jerome declined, making a lame excuse. That's when the rift with Caldwell began. It had taken years to heal.

Jerome slowed to a walk. He stopped and stared down the tree-lined path. That poor woman, he thought. But it always boils down to color. If it had been a sister, the story would have been buried on page ten.

Wilding. Animals...Even the liberal Governor Mario Cuomo had called it "the ultimate shriek of alarm."

Jerome threw his head back, eyes closed tight. "I gotta shriek of alarm for you, mothafuckas!" he bellowed. Even though the words were his, their sound startled him. He looked around. A young couple in shiny spandex was coming up from behind. He turned for home, running like a man being chased.

⇜⇝

Back in his apartment, Jerome showered and shaved. He unfolded his body into the easy chair by the window and looked out at Central Park West. He lit a cigarette, promising himself he'd quit smoking after this O'Reilly shit was behind him, after *all* the shit was behind him, he thought, checking his BlackBerry. Five pep-rally messages from Mindy. For her, his appearance on

O'Reilly tonight was a fucking game and she was the cheerleader. *Leave me alone!*

Jerome picked up the document he'd downloaded, a compilation of Tyrell's e-mails, outlining his grand scheme for a black enterprise zone, his manifesto, and the pitch to BET for a reality show, complete with character sketches and an outline of Year One of the series. It was the first time Jerome had actually read this stuff carefully. He yawned, felt sleepy, but in that leaden few moments before closing his eyes and falling away, Jerome realized that Tyrell had indeed captured some zeitgeist moment. Beneath the off-the-charts crazy rants, his message was resonant, not unlike the Tea Party's, Jerome thought ruefully. In fact, the reality show actually sounded as if it would work. But that was just it. You couldn't separate the crazy from the message; they inhabited the same dangerously friable mind.

⮞⮜

Courtney stepped out of the shower and onto the scale. When the needle waggled and stopped, she frowned. Eleven pounds lost since Derek had returned from lacrosse camp and planted the flower in her window screen. She smiled to herself. *Maybe I should go on Oprah, and talk about the "stalker diet."* But a glance in the mirror knocked the humor away; her eyes showed the strain, withdrawn sockets shining like dark wax. Courtney blew dry her hair and went to her room. Her father had stopped coming home on his afternoon break, a ritual he'd maintained since she was a small child. *It's like I have TB, or something. He doesn't want to be near me,* she thought to herself, brushing her hair.

Courtney called the mover to make sure everything was set. Then she checked her e-mails from Izzy. He'd given her reams of work in preparation for DC next week. She couldn't wait to settle in to her new place tomorrow, set up her computer, and get ready for the trip. Taking a deep restorative breath, she called her sister. After a few rings the answering machine clicked on.

"Hi Kate, thanks for offering to help me move, but I've arranged it already. I'll be in this weekend, so give me a buzz on my cell phone. I'd love for you to see the new digs. Sorry about everything, OK? Let's just move on."

⮞⮜

Latreece was in the kitchen finishing up cooking dinner. She could hear Tyrell rapping in the next room. He was waiting for that show, the one Professor Brown was gonna be on. Latreece was already building an invisible wall between herself and Tyrell. Reading about him in the Army, the names of the accused attackers, unpunished, unrepentant—it had all made her shrink back. But she couldn't let on what she was thinking, planning. Not yet.

"For the niggaz who be claiming my hood, an really ain't from my gang, better lay low, I hope he don't be thinking I'm just talkin' an I won't do a thing, really hope so..." Tyrell chanted from the couch.

"You a rapper now too? That revolution a yours got time for another career?" Latreece said, coming into the living room with two heaping plates of dirty rice, pork sausage, and chicken livers.

Tyrell eyed her. "You might think a doin' standup, all the funny shit you been comin' up with."

She made a face, put the plates on the coffee table. Tyrell changed the channel, turned up the volume. He shoveled a forkful of food in his mouth. "Tell Dummy to keep quiet when the show's on. I'll smack the fire outta her she starts up."

"Nobody better be layin' a hand on my baby," Latreece said, stabbing a piece of sausage with her fork.

The green room at Fox News was a windowless, claustrophobic space decorated in airport waiting room chic. Two TVs carried the endless 24/7 news loop. The amenities consisted of an artery-clogging snack buffet and a fridge stocked with bottled water. Jerome Brown, fresh from makeup, was sitting on the couch trying to calm his nerves. Juan Williams had stopped by to chat, telling him how powerful the *Vanity Fair* piece was. After he left, Brown couldn't remember one word he'd said.

A production assistant came in to wire Jerome and escort him onto the studio set. He heard the music, O'Reilly's voice, the Talking Points Memo segment...

"With me now is Professor Jerome Brown, author of the controversial Vanity Fair piece online called *Rage Without End: Why Black and White America Will Always Be at War*, an excerpt from his book of the same name. Well, first off, Professor, I gotta say I read the galleys of the book and it is over-the-top racism..."

"There you go again, Bill!"

"Now that's a Ronald Reagan phrase. I'm *sure* he was one of your heroes."

"Man, do you even know what racism is? You can't, so don't sit there and…"

O'Reilly leaned forward, his eyes glittering. "OK, here we go. Look I'm a simple guy, but justifying the kind of violence, making a parallel between an Islamist suicide bomber and…"

"Bill, do you know what critical thinking is?"

"I know what a threat is, Professor Brown, OK, and this book is a rant, a racist threat that you've perpetrated. And on top of that, what's worse, what's much worse, is that I think you're just gaming the system." Holding up his hands in a time-out position, O'Reilly turned to a monitor showing a screenshot of The Holmes Report and the photo of Mindy and Jerome kissing.

"I'm here to talk about my book! That photo was a setup!"

"But your affair with the white publicist Mindy Banks seems to contradict…"

"What have my relationships—and by the way, I am not involved with that woman…"

"Are you wagging your finger at me and saying 'I have not had sex with that woman?' Are you, Professor? Because that seems absurd to me."

"What have my relationships got to do with my book? There is a cauldron of latent black anger out there, a group of easily radicalized angry black males, and this is enough to scare the [bleep] out of people. Because contrary to the reports, we are not in a post-racial era. We are in an era that's set to explode…"

"OK, you quote Eldridge Cleaver who said that raping white women was a political statement. That's vile, racist misogyny. So my question to you is, are you going to denounce that statement, or are you now saying that your relationship with this white woman…"

"Is it possible for you to stay on point!"

"Denounce that vile statement, in front of America, that's the point Professor Brown!"

"The only thing I'll ever denounce is your Brown Shirt tactics…"

"We're out of time, Professor."

࿓࿔

"My boy bitch-slapped the honky mothafucka," said Tyrell, falling back into the sofa, clicking the TV off.

"Your boy lost his cool," Latreece said. "I think it was a draw." She picked up the dinner plates. "That girl of his, that Mindy whatever? He can come off like he was just gettin' his and bein' all casual. But I saw the look on her face. That girl's got her claws into your boy, and she ain't lettin' go."

66

Friday, the opening day of the tournament, the crowd fairly exploded into Woodcrest Country Club, riding a cavalcade of Mercedes, Jaguars, and Bentleys. It was a carnival atmosphere, with shouts of laughter and the reassuring clink of ice in glasses, clusters of members chatting about summer in the Hamptons, the upcoming season at the Met, and juicy tidbits of gossip still circulating about Jessica Miller and Mark Birnbaum at the Anguilla key party. The first round of golf was followed that evening by the black tie gala with dancing under the stars and a Grucci's fireworks show to cap the night off. Secretary Qian was in fine trim, having shot an 82 on the first 18. With his 8 handicap, he and Brad Mueller would have topped the foursome leader board were it not for Elaine and Izzy, both of whom were shooting well below their games.

Only once that afternoon did Buddy have to coach Elaine, telling her to keep her right elbow in on her irons. "You're swinging like a gate in the wind, Mrs. Weinberg." Izzy was within earshot, so Buddy did not want to get too familiar.

She shot Buddy a grateful look, smiling tightly. The clock was ticking; after the tournament she planned to tell Izzy she was leaving him. The strain showed in her face.

Izzy kept his eye on the Secretary at the post-golf gala. He could tell Qian was having a wonderful time. He liked noise and drinking and gaiety and pretty women, and there was no shortage of any of that. Izzy watched as the Secretary sipped his Scotch, smoking a cigarette European style, and casually flicking his ashes on the floor, all the while regaling a forty-year-old beauty with tall tales. William Lo was by his side, like a ventriloquist's dummy, translating effortlessly.

Brad Mueller had played like a demon, tearing the course up. He was also tearing Elaine up. Every time he got near her, he'd drop a vulgar aside, just loud enough for Buddy to hear. LT, who was carrying for Mueller and the Secretary, grew agitated. *That motherfucka is up to no damn good,* he thought.

On the monster 588-yard par-5 18th hole, Mueller bombed a huge drive. In on two, he drilled a twenty-three-foot putt for an eagle. It was a startling exhibition. The Secretary burst into applause. Mueller looked at Elaine, then directly at Buddy, smiled, and tossed his putter to LT.

On the way back to the clubhouse, LT said, "Listen up, Buddy. That mothafucka Mueller's got it in for you. Watch him tomorrow, OK?"

"Right."

"What the fuck does *right* mean?"

"It means, *right*."

"Man, here I am trying to talk sense...shit, what are you gonna do?"

"Right now, go have a cold beer."

"Buddy. You fucked that boy's daddy up. He ain't never forgive you. You watch that mothafucka, hear me?"

"*Right*," said Buddy.

LT barked, "You know, for a smart mothafucka you are one dumb mothafucka."

Sleep eluded Tyrell on Friday night. Minutes before the O'Reilly show he'd popped two 36mg-tabs of Concerta and a 60mg Adderall; then he smoked two pipes of Thai hash, pacing the backyard. He tried to relax in bed with Latreece, closing his eyes, but it was no good. Tashanda wandered into the room, a barefooted apparition, her teeth and eyes glowing. Tyrell glared at her, but the child seemed to just want to look at her momma, touch her face, and be led back to her own bed.

Early Saturday morning, Latreece awoke lying on her back. Tyrell was snoring softly next to her, having just dozed off after a restless night. She opened her eyes, looked at the ceiling and said, "What do you want?" She seemed to have made up her mind before turning away from Tyrell.

He felt the bed shift and sat up. Latreece's words were stuck in his head. *That girl's got her claws in your boy and she's not lettin' go.* When Latreece talked like that, so full of knowing confidence, he hated her, wanted to slap her face. He went into the bathroom, knocked some things out of the medicine cabinet. The noise was startling. He splashed water on his face, trying to remember when he'd last slept a full night. He suddenly had a craving for a sugar donut, the kind he used to buy on Nostrand Avenue.

Tyrell went to his office, sat in the whispering air conditioning, lifting and flapping his shirt to cool his belly. Opening his laptop, he Googled Mindy Banks. Her website came up, her picture, that self-satisfied smile. Her home page boasted of her commitment to personalized attention and unorthodox methods. She had a long list of influential clients. He clicked the *In The News* button. Mindy Banks was appearing on a panel tonight at eight o'clock: Ethics in Web-based Media, hosted by the *New Yorker*...the 92nd Street Y. Tyrell scowled at the screen, riding a high-flying wave of amphetamine and hate.

67

On Saturday morning, Courtney lay in bed, picturing a kaleidoscope of vacuum-tubed maglev trains zooming at supersonic speed through tunnels under the earth. She stretched luxuriously, smiling to herself, at her new world of dreams, big goddamn dreams. The early morning sun cast a wedge of bright light into the room. She could hear the birds trilling their individual songs. She could feel the trees lifting their branches skyward. Somehow, everything seemed more acute, crisp, new. Everything moving forward was new.

She rolled out of bed and reviewed her mental checklist. All the packing had been done, phone calls to the utility companies had been made. This morning was all about final separation. Her father had already left for work, much earlier than usual for the Saturday lunch crowd. He yelled a quick goodbye moving through the door, as if escaping.

Courtney took her time, moving about the room, touching the things left from her childhood. She remembered the little bracelets she and Kate had, with their names on them. She opened the closet, the pungent scent of cedar. Her father, a bookish man who didn't know which end of the hammer to use, had paneled it himself. He'd been so proud of his handiwork: a moth-free closet for his little girl. Courtney felt a flush of emotion. After she'd dressed and tidied up her old room for a final time, she left a note on the kitchen table: *Dear Dad, I'm sorry for your heartache. But I am happy and looking forward to an exciting career. It might be hard to understand, but please try. I will make you proud of me. I love you. Call me when you feel like talking. Please take care of yourself. Love, Courtney*

ॐ⌁

They had coffee by the first tee watching the sun rise. For the second day of the tournament, Elaine was wearing the yellow linen slacks that Buddy loved to see on her. As LT and Buddy walked toward her, she winked and said, "Look at these two." They were waiting for Brad Mueller. Impatiently, Izzy looked at his watch and said, "There are two goddamn things a man is *never* late for—a date and tee time."

A minute later, Mueller pulled up in a cart. He tossed his coffee onto the ground and stepped out, telling LT to park the cart for him. Izzy looked at Mueller and said, "Awfully decent of you to show up, Mr. Mueller." Before Mueller could respond, Izzy said, "I play some of my best golf with a slight hangover. I feel like I'm gonna kill this course today."

As they prepared to tee off for the final round of the Woodcrest Invitational Tournament, Izzy looked at Secretary Qian and said, "Christ, you look like shit." Lo hesitated, then translated.

"Thank you, so do you," Qian said, grinning. "It was worth it, Izzy. Every minute. Now, let's play golf."

"I'd like to crack that mothafuckin' Mueller across the teeth with an eight-iron," LT said as he and Buddy walked down to the fairway.

"Why?" said Buddy, watching Elaine's tee shot sail into the air, dropping on the fringe of the rough.

"*Why?* Cause that dick-eatin' mothafucka got a nasty mothafuckin' mouth. That's why," said LT.

"Thank you for pointing that out, sir," said Buddy.

"Any mothafuckin' time, Buddy boy," said LT, whistling as Mueller's 295-yard tee shot left him a perfect second shot to the green.

☙❧

Pulling up to the Garden on the Bay condo complex, Courtney took a deep breath, exhaled. The guard at the gate was Robert Caulfield. He was straight-backed and formal, without being stuffy. He addressed her as Ms. Mears. Caulfield verified her ID, her condo number, the security code, the panic button, and ran over a list of people she'd list as preferred guests. *He's like the velvet rope at a hot New York City club*, she thought, driving away.

Courtney put the key into her door, turned it, then she was in. She closed the door, locked it, and leaned against its solid oak feel. You'd need a tank to break it down. She spun around, doing a silly little dance with her eyes closed. Clean lines, hardwood floors, skylights, a loft. She went to the Sound side and flung the big windows open. The salty air rushed in. *Music and laptop,* she thought. *Let's get those essentials up and running while I'm waiting for the movers.*

Half an hour later, the intercom buzzed. It was Robert Caulfield.

"Ms. Mears, Precision Movers are here. OK to let them up?"

"Yes Robert, send them up, and thanks."

☙❧

By the time they were teeing off for the fourth hole it was mid-morning. The drink carts, manned by buxom servers, were flying all over the course. In its second day, the tournament had taken on a more devilish air of drunkenness. The Secretary, puffing on a Cuban cigar nearly as big as his forearm, asked LT to club him for his second shot on the eighth hole. LT said that considering his distance so far, and the wind kicking up, he'd suggest a five-iron. Hearing it, Mueller paced over and said, "Too much club. Hit a seven."

The Secretary kept a perfectly straight right arm, swinging right through impact. There was the *tock* of a perfect strike, but his ball bounced twenty yards short of the green.

"I told the man to hit a five iron," LT muttered to himself.

Mueller stepped forward, jutting his jaw out, "The fuck you say! Huh?"

LT stopped, hands up in a passive gesture. "Nothing important, not a damn thing important."

Glaring, Mueller barked, "You gotta lot of fucking nerve for someone who sleeps in a car!"

A tense moment passed. Watching, Izzy spun a pitching wedge in his hand like a baton twirler. Then LT walked away. Buddy knew that behind his easy-going front, LT was a man of deep pride. So seeing him retreat from Mueller made Buddy feel disgusted, but he decided to leave it alone. He watched Mueller strut down the fairway, like a boxer who had just scored a knockout. He was a nasty little man, phony and harsh, Buddy knew. A guy of limited intelligence, but with an animal's instincts.

The Secretary asked Lo to translate the exchange between Brad Mueller and LT. Lo balked. The Secretary tilted his head, squinted. Lo translated. Qian paused for a moment, looking at Mueller. He whispered something that made Lo smile.

The clash didn't escape Elaine's notice. "This just *too* much fun, Izzy?" she said sarcastically.

Taking a huge draw from his cigar, Izzy smiled and said, "Not yet, but it's gonna be. You can bank on it."

68

R uss was at Finnegan's Taproom when his cell phone rang. He glanced at the Caller ID, then answered in a sonorous, formal voice, "Russell Dunn speaking."

"Where you been?" said Tyrell. "I ain't heard from you in a few weeks."

"Excuse me, to whom am I speaking?"

"Man, it's Tyrell Walker, the one you're doing business with, remember?"

Russ didn't answer. Even though he wasn't finished with his beer, he was already signaling the waitress for another pint.

"What's up? What's all that noise? Where the fuck are you?" said Tyrell.

Russ coughed into his hand. "Actually I'm at a rally, a union rally, helping these union brothers get organized. On the front lines of the struggle," he said, pouring Bass Ale down his throat.

Tyrell listened suspiciously to the background noise. "OK, just make sure you get your ass over here to *my* struggle."

Russ grabbed his fresh pint and pushed through the crowd, making his way outside to the street. Tyrell was yelling into the phone as Russ bummed a cigarette and a light from a young, baby-faced guy outside, smoking with a girl. He listened patiently as Tyrell vented about the project, the old man he called Uncle Gene, about him dying of cancer, with no family to get in the way.

"Last thing I want is for the state to get that house. I've been working on him, telling him about the importance of black ownership, how he can be a part of this…"

"Care," said Russ, draining his pint, stifling a belch.

"Say what?"

Russ then launched into a rambling discourse on the strategy that would enable Tyrell to take ownership of the old man's house in exchange for a guarantee of lifetime care. "It's a win-win for you *and* Mr. Freyerson."

"Win-win, huh?" Tyrell liked the sound of that—winning.

Walking back into Finnegan's, Russ paused. He shifted uneasily, thinking of Tyrell. There was something unhinged about that guy, the way he could just go off on people. Russ lifted the pint glass to his mouth, but it was already drained. He thought for a moment. Better than most, Russ understood that some mistakes couldn't be corrected. He remembered his wife's advice. She'd been on the swim team in high school and college. One night when the two of them were skinny dipping at Robert Moses beach, she took his hand, guiding him in. "On calm nights like this you don't have to be afraid of the ocean," she'd said. "Just be part of it."

Russ raised his hand, signaling for another draft.

☙❧

By the time they reached the back nine, Izzy was getting pissed off. Mueller's play was superb, but he was insulting Elaine every chance he got, and there was that nasty little scene with LT. It was the act of a bully. Izzy gave no quarter and asked for none, as long as the game was between equals. He had killed quarter-of-a-million dollar deals over dinner because the guy across the table acted lousy to the server. Izzy detested bullies. Right now, he was thinking that Brad Mueller's lovely Aryan nose would benefit from a few whacks with a Louisville Slugger.

So on his approach shot to the 13th Izzy bellowed like a speared bull, clutched his lower back, and winced exaggeratedly. As he walked to the 14th, a wicked little 176-yard par 3, Izzy said he was done. The rest of his foursome, Lo, and the caddies, looked at him, waiting.

"I need a drink. My back is shot. Whaddya say we have some sport?" Elaine, reading his mind, gripped his arm and sank her nails deep into the flesh of his bicep. "Isidore, do *not* do this," she hissed in his ear.

Izzy smiled and looked at her innocently, kissing her cheek. "Don't worry, my dear," he said, patting her arm. Then he pulled his iPhone from his pocket and speed-dialed. As he walked away, Elaine could hear him say, "I want every fucking Jew on this course with a set of balls and a wad of cash to get their fat keisters over to the 14th."

Within minutes, golf carts filled with drunken millionaires tweeting each other were streaming in from all directions. Weinberg was up to something and they didn't want to miss out.

Izzy put in a quick call to Courtney. "Everything OK on your end?" he asked.

"Oh yeah, the movers just got here. I'm happy Izzy, very *very* happy," she said.

☙❧

They gathered around the tee. Now it was Izzy's show. The green on the 14th was an elevated tabletop. All you could see was the tip of the flag. It looked like a fluttering emerald, the color of money.

Drink in hand, Izzy said, "There's a common belief in golf that the more frequently you play, the better you'll get. I got a grand right here that's gonna debunk that belief. My caddy, Buddy Graves, plays once a week, or he used to. On the other hand, our pro, Brad Mueller spends his life on this course."

Mueller threw his shoulders back. "Are we playing golf here or what?"

There was pure malice in Izzy's grin. "Oh yeah, we're playing golf, al-right. OK, let's see who gets closest to the hole. My money's on Graves." Izzy pulled a horse-choking wad of bills out of his pocket. He set off a frenzy of bets, men bulling forward, clutching cigars and Scotch-filled bar glasses, thrusting their money into someone's upturned porkpie hat. The Secretary got caught up in the heat. Dizzily, Lo tried to keep up with the action as he reached for his wallet and shouted, "What's happening?"

"You don't have to do this," Elaine whispered, moving past Buddy.

"Yes I do," he said.

෨෴

Courtney had the music pumped up. She sang to herself as the movers, four nice-looking guys in khaki uniforms, worked with quiet efficiency. Each piece of furniture was carried into place with such ease it seemed as though they were transporting things on currents of air. Courtney had a quick sand-wich, then did some work on her laptop in preparation for her trip to DC with Izzy on Monday. She lost track of time. It was a good feeling, a pleasant, dopey high. Dropping her chin into the palm of her hand, Courtney closed her eyes and sighed. It was quiet here, a thick-walled quiet that felt so peace-ful and secure. She looked at the clock, thought about the night ahead. Work, more work. "Yes, yes, yes," she whispered. That's when one of the movers came in carrying the last box.

"Where should I put this?" he said.

Startled, Courtney looked up and saw damp footprints. He was hold-ing the box up high, his face obscured.

"What?" she said, standing. The box dropped to the floor. It was Derek. He was smiling.

"No!" Courtney shouted, bolting for the kitchen.

He was on her, his big hands pinning her arms as she struggled for the panic button under the counter. Suddenly she was airborne, crashing onto the floor. She kicked and tried to squirm away, but he was frenzied, panting, manhandling her into the bedroom. She screamed. Derek slapped her face numb, pressing her onto the bed. "Gave the movers a hundred, told 'em I wanted to surprise my girlfriend," he said, shoving her summer dress above her hips. "Surprise!"

"No, please, please," she said. He slapped her again, so hard, the world around her spun into flashes of light. She felt her mouth go numb, felt panties ripped off, her legs splayed, fighting to close, and torn open. He choked her, kissed her, clashed teeth, reached down and shoved his fingers into her, raking her insides.

"Remember?" he said. "Remember what you told me?"

Then he stopped, pulling his clothes off. She could smell his sweat. "Please," she said again. He spit on her, ripped open the front of her dress, and grabbed her shoulders. Bending down, he bit her breast so hard that she fainted, coming to as he was thrusting into her, saying, "Remember the first time? You said if I ever get some of this it would spoil me for anything else. You were right. Happy now?"

69

Brad Mueller did not want any part of this. It was a pathetic sideshow beneath his dignity as the Club's pro. But he was encircled, trapped and there was no mistaking where this was going.

Izzy flipped a coin and said to Mueller, "Call it." Mueller called heads; it came up tails. Buddy nodded for Mueller to swing away. The bettors hushed as Mueller pulled out his 7-iron. The money was with him, five to one. He took two easy practice swings. Then he addressed the ball, waggled the club head, took a slow easy breath and swung, a controlled backstroke, then *pock*, the ball sailed high and straight, clearing the two bunkers in front of the green. "Sit down," someone called. Then someone else said, "Yeah!"

"That's on," said Bernie Schwartzberg. He had a grand riding on Mueller.

Buddy took an 8-iron from Izzy's bag. "Mizuno Blades. Fancy bag of clubs, Mr. Weinberg," he said.

Schwartzberg, swilling *Veuve Clicquot* directly from the bottle and full of confidence, whispered loudly, "He's under-clubbing. Gonna end up in the beach."

As Buddy approached the tee box, Elaine edged away, taking a series of small backward steps like a deer moving through a thicket. She looked down, biting her lip, a slight tremble in her legs. "Graves doesn't waggle his club head. Never did. Why is that Graves?" Elaine heard Izzy say.

"Life's too short to spend time waggling," Buddy replied. "I just hit."

Buddy stepped up, looked at something in the distance, a cloud moving slowly over the green. He addressed the ball, rocked slightly on his feet, and swung, a picture perfect pendulum, sending the ball high into the air, disappearing in the sunlight before it dropped. So did Mueller's jaw as Schwartzberg lamented, "He's on. Christ I thought he was gonna hit the fucking bunker. An 8-iron, yet. Fuck me."

The crowd was moving down the fairway, one big raucous mob caught up in the drama. The ones who had been there the day Buddy dismantled Brad's father, Mike Mueller, were spouting off, saying that Brad was twice the golfer of Big Mike.

Huffing along, as the drink girls were doing figure eights in the bar carts, the crowd reached the tabletop green. It was bathed in sunlight. Both balls were on, one a good three feet closer to the pin. Schwartzberg was the first across the green, standing over the closer ball. He was squat and chunky-legged, sucking wind from the uphill dash. His wife, Toots, was screaming that he was going to have a coronary. It sounded more as if she were willing it instead of warning against it. Schwartzberg stared at the ball as the green filled with members and their guests. "What'd you hit?" he yelled to Mueller.

"Titleist 1," said Mueller.

Schwartzberg stared down, bending at the waist. He wiped his forehead with his hand and rose slowly. "It's a fucking Callaway Tour. Buddy's ball," he said.

Mueller saw Elaine's face beam. He mouthed, *"Fuck you."*

Izzy bellowed, "Let it roll. Four more holes of match play. Grab your balls and your wallets, fellas."

Moving toward the 15th tee, Izzy split from the crowd to call Courtney and find out how the move had gone. There was a message from Carson Severich, his guy in DC, letting Izzy know that he'd been working overtime to see what he could find out about the big demo project and this nurse, who, he now knew, was Dana Burke, from Long Island Jewish. *Imagine that,* Izzy thought, *here I am trying to drag this country into the next fucking century, the administration's fixating on infections, and this Burke bitch has got a fucking hard on for my nursing homes.*

When he speed-dialed Courtney, he got her voice mail. Not like her. She's always a second ring gal. At the beep he left a message: "Hello Ms. Mears. I trust the move went well. If it didn't, heads will roll. Hope you're packed and prepped for DC. I can think of just two reasons you're not answering the phone. Either you're working so hard you didn't hear it ring or you're in the sack with some young stud. I'll try later."

Brad Mueller had recovered his nerves after the closest-to-hole loss. By the 18th he had a one-stroke lead. The money had compounded, hole after hole. The Secretary had changed horses; his money, a huge wad, was now on Buddy. The crowd had settled into a simmer; there was too much at stake for shouting. Even though Buddy was down a stroke, he'd been chiding Mueller all the way. Slow, easy smart-mouthed banter that brought Mueller to a boil. LT knew Buddy was working Mueller and he could see the effect it was having. As LT handed Buddy his driver, he whispered, "Eagle this bitch. Put your nuts on that motherfucker's tonsils."

Izzy said, "OK, Mueller with a stroke lead. He'll tee off. Place your bets."

The 18th was a monster 574-yard par five with a dog-leg right. To have a chance to be on the green in two, you needed to fade a huge drive over a stand of 80-foot-high poplars. The best golf shot dictated a straight drive, using a three wood, bringing the ball in line for a safe layup, then a wedge to the green. A good wedge shot would set you up for birdie.

Mueller set to tee off. He took a three wood and walked slowly to the tee box. A slight breeze had kicked up, coming straight at the tee. It was dead quiet; even the drink girls had taken an interest. Elaine looked over at Buddy and smiled at him.

Mueller took a practice swing and addressed the ball. He drew back and hit a perfect shot, a line drive that dropped exactly where he wanted. It brought applause. He bent and pulled his tee out. Buddy walked to the box with Izzy's driver.

"He's hitting a driver," said Schwartzberg. "He's got a set, I'll give him that."

Buddy stepped to the tee box and placed his ball. He looked up at the sky, waited. Then he stepped back, took a practice swing and addressed the ball. When his backswing was at the top, he made an all-body, no-arms turn, leaning his body toward the target. He struck the ball, sending it in a high fading arc, clearing the poplars by 30 feet.

"Jesus. That had to be 310 yards," said Elaine. "Jesus."

A thunderous applause broke out. The crowd was moving on a carpet of booze and kinetic energy. Mueller hit a perfect second shot, leaving his ball 60 yards from the pin. He was talking to himself as he walked down the fairway.

Buddy's ball had landed just at the fringe of the fairway. It was a difficult lie to hit solidly. He took a three wood. The consensus was he'd try to get a solid hit, lay up for a chip shot, try and birdie the hole. If Mueller made par, it would force a one-hole playoff.

Buddy addressed the ball. This was the shot of the day. Elaine's eyes were shut tight. She didn't see Buddy hit, but she heard Schwartzberg say, "Holy fuck, he's on! He's on the fucking green. He's putting for eagle!"

Mueller looked sick, taking deep little breaths as he walked alone toward his ball. He took an eight iron and made a pretty little shot, dropping on the green eight feet from the cup. Buddy was four feet from an eagle.

Absolute silence.

Mueller was away. He took his putter and walked to the ball. His face was taut, his breathing shallow now. He stood over the ball. He made a nice even stroke, but the blade of the putter was moving too fast. The ball went straight for the cup, just past the right lip and rolled ten feet past.

You could hear a collective sigh. Mueller approached the ball. He closed his eyes, dropped his head. Then he stood over the ball and putted. The ball hit the rim of the cup, made a half circle and dropped in. "Yeah," he said, fist-pumping the air.

Buddy had a very tough putt. The greens were like glass and his lie was slightly downhill. "This is hard to watch," someone said.

Then Buddy walked to the bunker and grabbed the rake. "What the fuck is he doing?" someone asked.

"Jesus Christ, just like he did to Mueller's father. I don't believe this," said Schwartzberg.

It happened in a slow-motion sequence that left mouths agape. Buddy walked to the ball, planted his feet, looked over at Mueller, and struck the ball with the rake, sending it in a perfectly read arc into the cup. Buddy dropped the rake, snatched the ball from the cup and flipped it to Elaine.

The crowd exploded. Whoops and cheers. They had never seen an act of such ballsy aplomb. LT was smiling, nodding his head, calling out, "You the man, Buddy, you the *man!*"

As they reached the clubhouse, Elaine grabbed Buddy and kissed his forehead. Mueller was watching. He had tears in his eyes. He tried swallowing, but couldn't. He paced over, saying, "You're a fucking caddy, a fucking loser Graves. Even that," he said, motioning at Elaine, "If you do get some of that old shit, just remember. It's my sloppy thirds, fourths, Christ, over and over. That's what you'll get. At least I got paid."

Buddy punched Mueller's face. He shook it off and hit Buddy in the stomach, sending him down. Buddy bounced up, but Mueller was stronger and faster, he punched Buddy at will, bloodying his nose. Buddy went down again. Mueller was berserk. He kicked at Buddy. Elaine was screaming for him to stop. The crowd pressed forward, but Izzy held up his hand. Buddy finally struggled to his feet. Elaine had grabbed an eight iron, flailing impotent strokes at Mueller. He swatted it away, sneering. That's when LT stepped forward.

Mueller!"

Brad turned with his fists up, but LT threw a perfect right that made a loud pop, hitting Mueller's chin. Mueller went down like his bones had turned to dust. He rolled around, pulling himself upright. He sat there, goo-goo eyed, staring into space.

Izzy looked around. The violence had incited a pandemonium. Men were shaking up champagne bottles and spraying the crowd. Three couples rolled on the ground groping each other. One woman was loping in circles as she waved her bra over her head like a rodeo roper. And the Secretary had gone sailing down the lane with two blouseless drink girls in a runaway cart.

Mueller struggled to his feet, screaming at LT. "You are finished! Get your black ass outta here." He was brushing himself off when Izzy said, "Other way around, Mueller. You're the one who's through. I want you out of here by the end of the month."

Mueller glared at Izzy and spluttered, "I have a contract!"

"Which will be taken care of," said Izzy waving him away.

70

It was after eleven o'clock Saturday night and Mindy was flying high. She'd made some great contacts at the 92nd Street Y, exchanged business cards, glad-handed, played it strategically cool. At first she felt out of her depth. After all, the host was David Remnick, editor of the *New Yorker*, fucking Pulitzer Prize winner. But she'd held her own and more. The half-Xanax tab she'd popped an hour before didn't hurt. Neither did the notoriety of being the young white girl swapping spit with the black radical professor, Jerome Brown. His *Vanity Fair* article, the forthcoming book, the O'Reilly slugfest, *The Holmes Report*—Christ, it couldn't get any juicier. Life was good. They were calling her Mindy. All at once, she was *someone*.

Right after the panel discussion, she called Jerome. She wanted to secret him away for a drink, a long-awaited kiss. As Mindy walked down Lexington, she left a message on his phone. "Fuck it, Jerome, I'm going for a drink, by *myself*. Wanted to tell you about my night. It was good for us. I'll call you on the way home—that is, if I don't get picked up first. Only kidding!" she sang gaily into her cell phone. "Kiss, kiss."

As she sat in a Third Avenue bar, sipping a glass of Merlot, Mindy replayed Remnick's opening remarks. It still made her tingle: "Let me introduce Mindy Banks, an upstart publicist, a savvy web thinker who understands how to combine speed, voice, and depth to create and build audiences for her clients. But does she have 'web ethics,' or, for that matter does she give a damn?"

Applause!

Leaving the bar, Mindy wasn't drunk, but close enough to measure her steps as she entered the 86th Street station and carefully descended the steps. She stopped to look at the stone murals lining the walls of the station, thinking dreamily about the nice looking guy who'd hit on her. They'd perched on the stools for a half hour; never once did he say what he did. Considering the self-impressed assholes she was used to, it was refreshing. They'd exchanged numbers. Thinking of Jerome, she felt naughty about it. But it felt nice. In fact it felt fucking great to be Mindy Banks tonight.

She was hungry. Maybe she'd stop for Chinese take-out on the way home; curl up with the TV, catch some *Sex in the City* reruns. She put her hand on her hip, feeling the taut curve. That elliptical machine and Weight Watchers had done the trick. *You're looking hot, girl*, she thought to herself.

She tried calling Jerome, one last try to hook up tonight. The funniest part of the story, the thing she couldn't wait to tell him was *guess who didn't show?* Mindy stepped to the yellow line, leaned over, peered down the dark tunnel. In the distance she heard the train. Jerome's answering machine kicked on. This is Jerome Brown, I am…*"Blah, blah, blah,"* sang Mindy, then at the beep she called out, "Jerome, I forgot to tell you. Bobbi Holmes, the bitch of the East, bailed on the panel. But fuck her, because I miss you and…"

Mindy felt the violent shove, a sudden *thump*. But her mind didn't register what had happened, even as she was tumbling over the edge onto the track. Her knees hit, sending shards of pain through her body. The screech of metal-on-metal, wet, hurt, panic, the light bearing down on her, the face of the engineer frozen in a silent scream. Then a rush, a metallic wave that carried her away, bones clattering into darkness.

The engineer, John Conrad, was three weeks from retirement. He staggered from the train clutching his head. Looking down at the tracks, he could see the arm, a detached piece of ragged flesh. "Oh my God," he heard himself say. He'd seen her face, so young and full of life. She'd stared up at him, shocked, pleading. John Conrad fell to his knees on the platform, sobbing, calling for help. People were running now. A man was yelling for someone to call the police. Conrad heard a woman scream. He heard someone call out to God. Then he got sick on the platform.

Over coffee early on Sunday morning, Buddy was trying to explain to Dana why he had a black eye, a swollen jaw, and scuffed knuckles. He was due at the course in an hour, for what was called "The Round-up." The members and their guests had an outdoor buffet brunch, then played nine holes of raucous golf. No score cards, but plenty of drinking and gambling.

"So, the club's pro attacked you," said Dana. "Is that it?"

"I actually attacked *him*," said Buddy.

"Why? Tell me again."

"Just bad blood between us."

Dana shuddered. "What happened after that?"

"The pro was fired, sort of. Just told he was through."

"But why did *he* get fired? You attacked him."

"It's complicated. Elaine's husband, Izzy Weinberg, is sort of a wild man."

"The woman you're working for? Her husband. This is such a soap opera. Buddy, what does he say about her going off...with you?"

"He doesn't know yet. She's afraid to tell him. You'd understand if you met him."

"When does she plan on telling him?"

Buddy explained that Elaine was going to put a letter in Izzy's bag explaining everything. "He's going to DC on business Monday. She'll leave a message on his cell phone about the note. That's how she needs to do it, or she won't. It's that simple."

Dana walked to the sink and dumped her coffee. "I don't know. I really don't know," she said. "Christ, Buddy. You don't attack people. That's just not you. I'm leaving for DC tomorrow and you have a black eye."

Buddy got up. He moved to her and took her gently by her shoulders. "OK, I've got a black eye. So what?"

She looked at him, tears in her eyes. "Because I'm going tomorrow. I hate to leave you with a black eye."

"You sound silly."

"I know," she said, dropping her head on his chest.

Buddy pulled her into him, moving slowly across the kitchen floor as if slow dancing at a wedding.

71

Still sleeping, Latreece heard church bells and knew it was Sunday, the only day of the week she languished in bed. Church was the one childhood memory Latreece allowed herself to dwell on. Amid the guns and drugs and ruptured veins of the inner city, church had been her respite from the ugly maw of the streets. Latreece's sleep-shrouded thoughts blipped off. She thought she'd been stung. Then she heard a *snap* and felt a sting and came awake all at once, making a sucking noise as she tried to pull herself up. Then *pop*, on her face. She heard herself scream, "Ouch!"

Tyrell's skeletal face loomed over her. His eyes looked like glistening black marbles. He was dangling a rubber band over her face. She tried to wrestle out of bed, but he moved over her, with his knees pressing her down. "You been in my personal shit. Sneaking around, digging into my shit," he said, snapping her face with the rubber band. Latreece shook her head, seemed about to deny it, then stopped, looking up at him wide-eyed with fear.

"Once you broke the rubber band it was over. Your deceit got fucked up. That band was five years old. This is new. Don't you get it? The shit I got comin' down, the plans...you bitch!"

Pop!

Ouch!

She struggled underneath him. He slapped her. She let out a sharp scream, crying, "Please, you're hurting me." He slapped her again, leaned down, snapping his teeth near her nose. She could smell his stale breath, a fog of pot vapor on her face. "It's too late for you to start loving me," he said, placing his hands on her neck as a crushing Adderall headache gripped his brain. Tyrell moaned and closed his eyes, wincing against the pain. For a second he suddenly seemed vulnerable.

"It's not your fault," Latreece said softly, feeling his grip loosen. "You need some sleep baby," she whispered.

"I can't accept that," he rasped hypnotically. "Will you believe me...the war has come home...I thought they were white people in the trees waiting for me."

"You need sleep, that's all," said Latreece. He was all sharp bones against her.

Just then, Tashanda screamed, "Momma! *Momma!*"

Tyrell's eyes popped open, and as his face fell to the left, Latreece used her leverage, throwing her hip upward. Tyrell teetered, off balance. She swung with savage force, the heel of her hand hitting flat on Tyrell's ear, making a loud *whock*. He bellowed in pain. Latreece's adrenalin rush carried her out of bed, sending Tyrell over onto the floor. She stumbled ahead, grabbing Tashanda's hand. They ran down the stairs, sliding to the floor at the bottom. Latreece heard Tyrell behind them screaming, "I gotta tell you. I'm not gone yet!"

Latreece grabbed her cell phone from the counter and dragged her daughter into the bathroom, slamming and locking the door. A second later Tyrell kicked the door, screaming, "Here comes mothafuckin' Johnny!"

It was a heavy door. Latreece steeled herself against the thuds, each one syncopated with her pounding heart. When he tired, she could hear him sucking air. "I got my phone, Tyrell. I don't hear your car go out the driveway, I'm calling the police!" she screamed through the door, hugging Tashanda.

"Quit that now," she said.

Latreece braced for more kicks.

"I will not. All souls are lonely. Here we go," he said, and it was then she realized he was talking to himself.

After a minute she heard him laughing quietly, then a soft sob. Footsteps. The sound of his car pulling out across the gravel. A horn blaring and fading on Pulaski Road.

"It's OK now, baby," she whispered to Tashanda.

᙭᙭

Tyrell pulled off to the side of the road. His hands were still shaking with rage. *What did Latreece not understand?* For a brief second he felt things slipping away. *Trust yourself,* he thought, trying to shut out the doubters, the nattering nabobs of negativity. He rubbed his face and punched his cell phone's speed dial.

On the other end, not bothering to check the caller ID, Jerome Brown answered. He was lying in bed watching the news, manically flicking the channels, hearing the same phrase over and over...*the grisly murder of up-and-coming publicist Mindy Banks, pushed to her death on the subway tracks, has police and her family and friends baffled. So far, the only information the police will release is that an unidentified man in a hooded sweatshirt pushed Ms. Banks into the path of the number six train and ran off. One witness thought the attacker might have been a black man but because of the angle of the hood, couldn't be sure...*

Jerome said, "Yeah," into the receiver. He had a vicious hangover and even the effort of talking made him feel like vomiting. When he heard Tyrell's voice, a harried detonation of barely suppressed shouts, he mumbled, "Oh God," and rolled over.

He held the phone away as Tyrell harangued. When he spun into a hate-filled riff about O'Reilly and the nattering nabobs of negativity, Jerome said, "Tyrell, man, what the fuck are you talking about?"

Tyrell paused, seemed hurt. He explained that he was using Brother Cleaver's term for the white power elite. Jerome felt that sweaty, pre-vomit clamminess, the bile rising in his throat. "Man, who's been playing you? That fucking cracker Spiro T. Agnew said that bullshit line. Nixon's Vice President, man. Cleaver? I gotta go man, I'm sick," Jerome said, sliding from the bed, reeling toward the toilet as the room tilted and spun.

72

On Sunday morning before the final nine-hole drink fest ending the tournament, Izzy took the Secretary to MacArthur Airport in Islip, where Qian and William Lo would catch a private jet to Washington in advance of Izzy. Meetings with prominent Chinese-American businessmen and politicians had been arranged.

Saying goodbye to Elaine, Secretary Qian was uncharacteristically effusive in his praise for the American sense of joy and spirit. Lo confided to Izzy that he'd never seen a Chinese man of this stature show such emotion.

"Well, well, another Izzy Weinberg life-changing moment," Elaine rejoined. Izzy grinned at her, giving her a "you-betcha-kid" wink.

As Jack eased the big limo out of the driveway, Elaine waved to his three passengers and started upstairs to her desk. She'd just do this thing and put it out of her mind. Her stomach turned. She felt faint, sat on the step breathing in and out. She looked at the clock. *Maybe a quick one to take the edge off.* She shook her head no, hauled herself up and climbed the long sweeping staircase.

"Damn," Elaine whispered, starting the letter to Izzy. She hated herself for not having the guts to tell him to his face. But even this, putting her words down on paper was wrenching. She started to cry and then admonished herself. "Do not break down, Elaine. Izzy has always done exactly as he pleases and he never shed a tear. Remember that, girl."

Halfway through, she re-read what she'd written. Then a thought hit her so hard it made her blink and say aloud, "Oh, I haven't even told our daughters. Jesus, Elaine." She ran her hand over the letter and let her tears run freely.

❧❦

Tyrell raced up and down Pulaski Road. He'd called Russ Dunn five times, leaving increasingly threatening messages on each call. Nattering nabobs of negativity! It had sounded so intelligent when he first heard it...But when he'd repeated it to Jerome Brown Tyrell actually heard him chuckle. *Now Brown thinks I'm a fool, a mothafuckin' lightweight*, Tyrell thought. His head hurt and it was getting worse. *That mothafucka Dunn promised I'd be a hom-*

eowner in a month. The American dream. But it's been more than a month, hasn't it? Tyrell couldn't keep his thoughts straight. He blew through the light at the intersection, just missing a delivery van.

He pulled to the side of the road again, panting, and called Russ. To his surprise, Russ answered.

Sipping a beer in bed, Russ listened to Tyrell's blistering tirade about nattering nabobs of negativity. When Tyrell finally took a breath, Russ said, "Tyrell, I may have gotten my terms and those who spoke them mixed up. But if you remember correctly, you were blowing Jamaican grass smoke in my face. I got stoned off my gourd."

Tyrell hesitated, then asked, "Never mind that bullshit, When am I gettin' my house? I got leverage over that mothafucka next door, *real* leverage."

Russ said, "The deal will transpire within a few days. Sorry, I've been consumed with this pesky labor union issue I'm trying to settle."

Tyrell pressed his ear to the phone, trying to catch any background sounds. Then he said, "Who the fuck are you?"

"Pardon?"

"You better not be fuckin' with me, mothafucka, I'm a fuckin' badass, man."

"Now listen, I understand my methods are a little unconventional."

"A *little?*"

"I have a proven record of established multi-million dollar deals, many of which were closed under..."

Tyrell cut him off, "You know how crazy you sound sometimes?"

"What I said?"

"No, just you. I killed a mothafucka in Afghanistan. He had a wife an five kids. I even know his name and what kinda work he did."

"Why are you telling me that?"

"'Cause I just wanted you to know. *Now* what about the other thing, with the old man dying a cancer, his house."

Russ cleared his throat, "Right, well, as I explained earlier, we'll be offering him a great opportunity for a person in his dire position. Lifetime care in exchange for a deed transfer. The person giving the property is called the grantor while the one who is getting the property is called the grantee..."

Tyrell barked, "We nothin'. I'll take care of Uncle Gene. You'll scare that old guy off, crazy-sounding as you are."

Tyrell clicked off. Russ stared at the empty can of beer in his hand and threw it against the wall.

వా∾ు

Tyrell pulled into Eugene Freyerson's driveway and got out. He banged on the door. A minute later the old man answered. "You fixin' to bust the door down?"

Tyrell looked at him through the screen. The old man blinked, scratched his chin.

"Well?" said Tyrell.

"Well what?"

"I got some business we gotta talk about."

Eugene smiled. "You gonna put a new roof on my house?"

They sat at the table. Tyrell refused a drink, said he'd quit drinking alcohol.

"Looks like you quit eatin' too," said the old man. "A woman don't like a man all skin an bones."

"I don't have no problem gettin' bitches. Got 'em crawlin' all over me."

"Bitches," the old man said, glancing at the picture of his wife on the wall. "Mind that nasty mouth."

Tyrell dived into his spiel about lifetime care and security. For a man of your age with cancer, it was a win-win situation, he told Eugene. Then he launched into black property ownership. His mouth dry from the Adderall, Tyrell struggled, making a pasty clicking sound with his tongue. The old man looked at him oddly when he started talking about the black community's responsibility to do this and that, all for the cause of national unity and pan Africanism. Finally, Eugene held up his hand, said, "Whoa."

Tyrell stopped.

"You got two things wrong in all this stuff, this big plan a yours," the old man said.

Tyrell sat back. "Wrong?" he said. "Wrong. Man, this whole day's been wrong. I don't need no more *wrong*."

"Well then I'll apologize 'fore I say it but I ain't got the cancer. I'm gonna live a long time. Heck, my uncle Owen, who everyone said I favored, lived to 109!"

"You don't got cancer? You just don't not have it," Tyrell said, in a pained screech.

The old man stood up, went to the cabinet. "I never did. Buddy showed me the paper."

Tyrell stuttered, "Bu, bu, bud Buddy who?"

301

"The boy crost the street. He was some kinda...I don't know, but he's smart. He tol' me that this stuff I got just make you have to pee," he said, showing Tyrell the paper from the clinic.

Tyrell looked around the room. He stood up and began pacing, mumbling. The old man was laughing trying to pronounce "benign prostatic hyperplasia."

Tyrell finally got out the word, "house."

The old man looked at him. "That's the other thing you got wrong. I don't own this house, Cho do."

"Cho?"

The old man nodded. "Cho."

"Cho!"

"Yes, Cho. The Chinaman from Queens," Eugene fairly shouted. *How thick is this boy?*

"He's a mothafuckin' Korean!"

"OK, an he owns this house. Cho the Korean."

"I don't understand. You mow the mothafuckin' lawn every day. Do all this bullshit work, gardening..."

"Cho might own it, but I live in it," the old man said firmly.

Tyrell couldn't catch his breath. He thought about Buddy, Russ, Cho, Jerome, Latreece. "You dumb old nigger," he screamed. "Dumb...old...Uncle Tom...*nigger*. Old school nigger!"

The old man's eyes narrowed and his heart turned cold. A lifetime of insults borne and rage suppressed just boiled up. He saw his father stoop and scrape in front of that twenty-year-old white boy, felt the kick that sent him flying out of the moving flatbed car. Tyrell was still yelling that word when Eugene reached over and grabbed the small pistol, the same one that killed the brakeman James Braver. "Damn you!"

A loud *pop* and Tyrell staggered back, closing his eyes and raising his hand to fend off the next. Another *pop*, as he grabbed the table on the way down.

Old Sam barked, whined, covered his face with his paws.

Eugene turned to his dog and dropped the pistol thudding to the floor. Tyrell was moaning, kicking his legs. "We're in a spot now, Old Sam. I'm sorry I put you in it too, but *nobody* calls Eugene Freyerson a nigger."

73

The end of the Woodcrest golf tournament on Sunday was an anticlimax to the previous day's wild doings. Members played a little golf and drank, mostly drank. They stole glances at Buddy and shook their heads, in awe of his wasted talent.

But everyone wondered: What the hell had gotten into them yesterday? Izzy Weinberg had set off some kind of mayhem in people who thought of themselves as...well, not like *that*. Somehow, they'd got caught up in his rolling freak-show of a life. It had been thrilling in the moment, but afterwards they asked themselves, mortified, "Did I really do that?" They all knew that Teflon Izzy was immune to such prosaic feelings of regret.

The man had balls. He'd summarily shit-canned Brad Mueller in front of the whole club. He didn't have the authority to do it. But Izzy didn't ask anyone's permission, and they'd all backed off. "He insulted a member of our club," Izzy said afterward. Of course, it was his wife. To top it off, he was seen laughing and shaking hands with the black caddy who'd clocked Mueller.

Izzy Weinberg. What a pisser.

Buddy was thinking about Dana as he drove home from Woodcrest. She was in Washington by now, likely in a cab on the way to her hotel. He was musing about his wife, naked between the sheets in a hotel, when he saw the flashing lights. *Probably a wreck at the intersection, another gory reminder of how much I fucking hate this place.* But as he got closer to his house his chest tightened. An ambulance was pulling away from Mr. Freyerson's, siren and lights going. He watched it round the corner heading toward the hospital. Then he saw the maroon Honda Accord with its dark tinted windows in Eugene's driveway, and four police cars parked helter skelter on the street. People were out on their porches, standing with their arms crossed, talking. Buddy pulled into his driveway and jumped from the car. *Something's very wrong*, he thought as he bounded across the road.

"What happened?" he yelled. A burly Suffolk County cop held up his hand for Buddy to stop. "Mr. Freyerson!" Buddy shouted. The cop looked at him, sizing him up, wondering whether he'd have to deal with this guy in a physical way.

Then the old man came out, a cop on each side. His hands were cuffed behind his back. He was talking to the officers, animated, upset. As they led him to the car, he saw Buddy. Eugene craned his neck forward. Buddy tried to get to him, but the cop blocked him. "Stay right there, sir!"

"Buddy," cried the old man. They were pushing him into the car, but he struggled. "Buddy, they won't let me take Old Sam!"

Buddy choked up.

The cop had his hand on top of the old man's head, but Eugene pushed up, like someone fighting against drowning. "Buddy!"

"I'll take care of him, Mr. Freyerson, don't worry!"

"God bless you, son," were the last words he heard. Then the police cruiser backed out and pulled off down Pulaski Road. Buddy wiped his eyes as he watched the cruiser fade away. A cop was stringing yellow crime-scene tape across the front of the house. Buddy came up the driveway calling, "Officer, officer."

The cop looked at him. "Sir, there's been a man shot. You cannot come up here."

Buddy stopped. He knew it was Tyrell.

"There's a dog inside. He needs help. Can I please just get him," Buddy called.

The cop looked at him, then spoke into the walkie talkie perched on his shoulder. "Sir, an animal control officer is already on the way. He'll remove the dog from the house and bring him to you. You live right over there?" asked the cop, gesturing toward Buddy's house.

"Yes, I do. Thank you. His name is Old Sam. He's paralyzed."

"Yeah, I was wondering why the dog didn't move. He just kept looking at the old guy and crying. Gave me the willies. Sounded just like a baby."

74

Early Monday morning, Izzy kissed Elaine goodbye on the front steps of their home, reaching around and giving her backside a gentle pinch. "This ass is to die for," he said.

"Then die…for it," she said, smiling and waving to Jack.

Her body was shaking, a barely perceptible tremble, as though she was chilled by a damp breeze. "I would," Izzy said solemnly. "You know that, right?" He put his hands on her shoulders, stood back and looked in her eyes.

"Izzy, go make your big deal."

"Wanna come with me?"

She flushed. "No, you know business bores me into a coma."

He kissed her mouth. She pushed him away playfully. "C'mon, you're embarrassing Jack."

"You can't embarrass that Irish hump. He's been around *me* too long!" Izzy walked toward the limo, turning to blow her a kiss.

Izzy had every reason to be happy. Secretary Qian had left for Washington in high spirits to meet with the top drawer Chinese-American operatives, all of whom were in Izzy's corner. Izzy had taken a gamble with Qian, and it paid off. Had he not read this man correctly, it could have ended in disaster. The Chinese don't fuck around with business dealings—they act on millennia of gut instinct and tradition. It's a bit of a minefield for an American. All this weird etiquette: the way you shake hands, the colors of clothes you wear, certain hand gestures, the gifts you give. Of course, Izzy had motored right over dozens of time-honored traditions, but he could get away with it.

When Qian left yesterday, he shook Izzy's hand, placing his left hand on top of Izzy's. "See you in DC, partner."

Izzy's instincts had been fashioned in the snarling pit of cattle ranchers, hustlers, and conmen, guys that trudged through steaming piles of cow shit in thousand-dollar ostrich skin cowboy boots. They'd kick your nuts into your throat for a cross-eyed look. So on the way to pick up Courtney, Izzy's gut said today would be filled with challenges, starting with his wife. He'd known for weeks that something was up with her. Then this morning, she was awake at dawn, fussing over him, checking his bags, flitting around him like a hummingbird. He'd squinted at her, asked if she was OK. She just smiled and said, "Why wouldn't I be?"

Something was going on all right. But for the life of him, he couldn't remember when she'd looked sexier.

The limo pulled up to Courtney's complex. Jack went to get her bags. *Then there's this one*, Izzy thought. *She's got some issue she won't spill.* All Courtney talked about was business, which was good, but when Izzy mentioned their swanky accommodations at the Hay-Adams, she got tongue-tied. Said something about having a female thing going on, she'd have to hold back on any fooling around for a few days. But it was the cagey way she said it that gave him pause, as though she was hiding something. Why? Izzy wanted to get to the bottom of it. He needed to keep things in order—his assets, his business dealings, his women.

Courtney came out chatting lightly with Jack. He opened the door and she slid in, smelling fresh from the shower. They said good morning and as soon as Jack had pulled from the complex and onto the Expressway their laptops were open. Courtney was going over her PowerPoint slides and Izzy was on the phone with a congressman on the Ways and Means Committee who would be meeting Secretary Qian at a luncheon hosted by the Asian-American Government Executives Association. Izzy clicked off and looked up in the air, "What a fucking putz. God give me strength." He turned to Courtney. "So, the new place, are you loving it?"

She nodded. "Uh-huh."

"Well that's not exactly a ringing endorsement. Everything OK there?"

"Sorry, yeah, it's great. I'm just a little preoccupied."

Izzy narrowed his eyes, watching Courtney stare at her computer.

Halfway into the trip Izzy got a call from Elaine. Her voice was shaking as she told him to look in his briefcase pocket, the one inside where he keeps his hip flask. Before he could unearth this mystery she said, "Gotta go, I love you."

Hmm, he thought, as he reached into his case. He pulled out the envelope and began to read. "Jack, pull over please."

"OK if I wait until there's a spot where we won't get killed?"

"No, pull over now."

Jack weaved through traffic, horns blaring as he swung the big car onto the shoulder. Izzy jumped out with his iPhone. Every nerve in his body was firing as he paced angrily, flattening the grass. She answered with an apology. "Sorry?" he said. "Elaine, you are a fucking train wreck. Do *not* do this. Do not run off chasing a dream with that fucking loser caddy. I will *not* allow you to do this."

Izzy's booming voice was lost in the rushing traffic, tractor-trailers blowing by at eighty, two yards from the bellowing mogul.

By the time they reached DC, Izzy had subsumed his wife's flight of fancy to the business at hand. He'd briefed Courtney on it, said it wouldn't last. Elaine would get some of the young goy she'd been dreaming about. But it would end quickly, he'd see to that. Smiling, he said, "Anyway, my wife just left me, temporarily. You have a sad story to top that one?"

"Izzy, I'm so sorry," she said, heartfelt. He shrugged his big shoulders. All in a day's work, he mused. Hey, sometimes it's hard being Izzy Weinberg.

While Jack was checking them in at the hotel, Izzy and Courtney sat in the lounge talking. It was just past one. He suggested they split up. "Why don't you go to the suite, order in some lunch, do a little more prep. I'll be up way before our dinner meeting."

His fixer, Carson Severich, had left him a message with more information on this pissant infection demo project. It was starting to get under Izzy's skin. These small-minded people, fucking around with his empire, right when he was on the verge of a game-changing deal. It was this Dana Burke he wanted to find out more about. According to Carson, she was in Washington now for a scheduled meeting. She was the point person, the attack dog for the project. Her big claim to fame had something to do with bleach. *Christ Jesus*, Izzy thought. *Bleach*.

There was something else: Severich had been hacking into Dana's computer at the hospital. He was able to retrieve a grainy photo of a white man appearing to molest a little black girl. The man's features were too indistinct to identify, but Carson said it was intriguing enough to follow up on. Why would her computer contain that photo and who was the man? "I can probably enhance the picture, but it'll take me a while. In the meantime I'll keep digging," Severich told Izzy as he signed off.

Izzy had Jack drive him to 1350 Pennsylvania Avenue where the Council of the District of Columbia building was located. The meeting Burke would be attending was just about to convene. "Give me about thirty, Jack," said Izzy, lighting a cigar and waiting outside the building. Halfway through his smoke he saw her. She matched Carson's description: nice looking dark-haired gal, clean, serious looking. She was preoccupied with her BlackBerry when Izzy walked up and said hello. Dana looked up, startled. Her eyebrows arched and dropped, and Izzy noticed the near fluorescent glow of her skin. He checked the impulse to reach out and stroke her face. "Izzy Weinberg," he said, extending his hand. "Is there something I can do for you?" she said, somewhat warily.

Izzy smiled. "I hate clichés, but the one about a small world, well it holds true in this case. You worked at Long Island Jewish Hospital, right?"

"Yes, I did."

"So I have friends on the board there. And my wife, Elaine has done a lot of fundraising for the hospital."

Dana could feel her heart pounding. *Izzy Weinberg. His wife is Elaine,* Buddy's *Elaine. Holy shit, if this bastard finds out Buddy is my husband...*Everything suddenly went fuzzy in her head. Weinberg was talking but she could not make out the words. She needed to sit down. Dana looked around, saw a bench, and took long uneasy strides toward it, sitting heavily and trying to catch her breath. He was standing over her, asking if she was alright. A moment passed. She stood abruptly and looked at her watch. "I have to go," she said, walking away quickly, the scent of his cigar trapped in her nostrils.

Izzy had a bite to eat in a small French bistro, made some calls, then he told Jack he was going to walk back to the Hay-Adams. He did some of best thinking walking in cities. It took him a good hour to get back to the hotel. Along the way he'd called and left a message on Elaine's voice mail. He then phoned the concierge and asked that a chilled bottle of Dom with two flutes be brought to his suite. *Maybe sex is out while she settles her female thing, but champagne and a kiss are always in order*, he thought as he rode the elevator up.

The bathroom door was open a crack, so he walked in and said, "Surprise," just as Courtney stepped naked out of the shower. She screamed and grabbed the towel. Izzy could see the bite marks on her breast, her bruised arms. "My God," he said. Courtney staggered past him, tears spilling down her face. "Please Izzy, give me a minute."

He stepped aside, ashen, then quickly turned red. His fists balled. Through clenched teeth he said to her, "Did he do this to you?"

Courtney flung on a cotton robe and wiped her face. He walked toward her. She slumped on the bed and buried her face in her forearms with her hands over her head. "He came over the sea wall from the back of the property. Bribed the movers. He...he..."

The strain of submerging the rape, of holding it together, finally became too much. Her emotions broke over the dam.

Gently, Izzy took Courtney in his arms, holding her close to his chest like a father while she sobbed.

Derek Quigley is a dead man.

75

Tuesday morning, Buddy woke in the quiet of the pre-dawn darkness, rousing himself from a dream filled with the same monsters that had stalked his childhood nightmares. His father walked through the middle of one, shaking his head in disgust. Buddy rolled from bed, washed up, dressed, and soft-footed downstairs with his suitcase and golf clubs, placing them by the door. Then he flicked on the coffee pot. He opened his laptop, checked his e-mail. Two messages from Dana sent late last night. He decided not to open them. Dana still had a claim on a tender, weak part of him. He'd read them on the road.

Buddy drank a cup of coffee, took an envelope from the cabinet and walked to the front door. Although he couldn't distinguish between them, he could hear Russ and Old Sam snoring in the guest room. When he stepped outside there were no cars passing on Pulaski Road and all the houses up and down were dark and dead looking. Mr. Freyerson's place was still cordoned off by yellow police tape. He stood there thinking about that old man in a jail cell, missing his dog. His eyes watered. Wiping them with his forearm, Buddy kicked the ground, and walked across the driveway. "Shit," he said softly.

He stood at the door for a good two minutes before knocking. Three firm taps. After a moment, three more, each tap progressively harder. A light popped on in the upstairs window. A face silhouetted in the backwash of light. Through the small rectangular window in the door he saw her coming down the stairs, clutching her well-worn blue chenille robe. They stared at each other through the glass; her eyes were wide and flashing with anger. She pulled the door open and said sharply, "I am not believin' this. I mean you *got* to be kidding. What are you doin' here?"

"Latreece, sorry about the time, but I need to talk to you."

Maybe it was hearing him say her name, or maybe it was the way he said it. But her eyes softened, just a bit. "And this couldn't wait until a decent time?"

"I'm leaving in a few minutes. I'll be away for a while."

She looked at him, at his black eye. "What happened to you?"

"It's nothing. May I come in?"

"No. Don't even know why I opened the door."

"Please Latreece, just a minute, please," Buddy said.

She narrowed her eyes and stepped back, her hand still on the door. Scowling, she relented and motioned for him to step in. As he stood in the vestibule, Buddy heard Tashanda calling from upstairs. "Momma, where are you? Is that Daddy?"

Latreece, jerked her head and called, "No baby, it's no one, just go on back to sleep. Momma'll be up in a minute."

Latreece motioned for him to follow her into the kitchen. She turned, crossing her arms over her chest. "Well," she said. "Say what you gotta say."

Buddy pulled the envelope from his back pocket and laid it on the kitchen table. "I'm sorry as hell about what happened. This is a little some- thing I…" he said, then his voice choked.

Latreece eyed the envelope. "A little something *what*?"

"Money, a little money." Buddy met her gaze. An ambulance siren wail- ing down Pulaski stirred the quiet. She picked up the envelope and opened it—a few hundred-dollar bills. She dropped it on the table as though it had burned her hand.

"Why are you doing this?"

"I don't know. Just tell Russ if you need anything."

"Say what? *Russ*?"

"You know, Russ, the guy who…"

She said, "*Yeah*, I know. That crazy man who was playin' Tyrell."

"He was trying to help me."

"My man's shot. I got the police here askin' me questions about the old man cross the street. He's in jail, you goin' off somewhere. An now I'm here at five a.m. talkin' to you. So I'll be sure to ask *Russ* if I need any more help."

"He drinks too much but he's got a good heart. He's staying next door with Mr. Freyerson's dog."

Quizzically, Latreece pointed in the direction of Buddy's house. He nodded. Sitting down in a chair she put her elbows on the kitchen table and rested her head in her hands, staring at the wall. He could tell she was reliv- ing the shooting, imagining it in her mind, frame by frame.

Buddy cleared his throat, said, "He's not your man."

"What'd you say?"

"Tyrell's not your man."

Latreece motioned for him to sit. "I'm gonna say something an I want you to listen, then I want you to go. You know nothin' about me, about my man. *Nothin.*' You came here this mornin' to make yourself feel better about whatever's botherin' you inside. An whatever you got goin' on ain't none of my concern. I know you didn't do nothin' to my girl…I think I knew that right off, but I wanted to believe Tyrell so bad. OK, I got drunk on every damn dream he was sellin'. He was goin' to college, makin' a future for me an

Tashanda. Then he got strung out and just went off," she said, snapping her fingers, a loud pop in the quiet room.

"I'm sorry," said Buddy.

She leaned forward, "Don't say that. I'm not finished!"

They both turned. Tashanda was standing in the doorway holding a baby blanket. The little girl stared at Buddy, smiled and said, "The motha-fuckin' devil!"

Latreece got up and rushed her into the living room. Buddy heard her scolding her daughter. Then the TV went on. Latreece came back. She put on a pot of coffee. She sat, fixing her robe, stifling a yawn with her hand. Buddy noticed her long legs looking muscular and soft at the same time.

"I don't tolerate that language. Tyrell told her you was the devil. All white people was the devil to him. Said they don't like a nigger walking around like a man. You feel that way about black folks?"

"I don't feel that way about anyone."

Latreece stared hard at Buddy. For a moment neither one spoke.

"What happened, Latreece? I'm still trying to figure that out. Everything changed in an instant."

Latreece stood and leaned on the table.

"A young black man walkin' down the street in Alabama in 1960 turns his head toward a white girl. Next thing he knows he's in a pickup truck with a bunch of rednecks sayin' 'you're gonna be sorry, nigger.' That young man asked himself the same damn thing: 'What happened here?' Buddy, what happened here happens all over this country every day. *You* sort out the guilty ones. I sure as hell can't."

"Is that what Tyrell said?"

"Yeah, that's what he said. Twistin' up what's right and what's legal. He had me half convinced that them lies he told were the right thing to do. Then he went crazy on me, on you—on himself!"

Latreece placed the two cups of coffee on the table. She went to the fridge and pulled out a carton of milk. "Tashanda! Come get some breakfast." The little girl charged from the TV room, barreling into Latreece, laughing. Latreece swatted her backside playfully, poured a bowl of cereal and told her to go watch TV. Tashanda backed out of the room holding the bowl, milk sloshing on the floor. She giggled and stared big-eyed at Buddy.

Latreece sat down. She sipped her coffee and pointed to the TV room. "Her daddy's in Attica, twenty-five to life. So Tyrell was movin' up for me. I had two abortions before havin' her. I was on the street givin' blow jobs for three dollars to put rock in my pipe," she said. "Nice, huh? I used to see your wife comin' out of the house in her nurse scrubs. She was so together. That's what I wanted. To be her, have her life. I hated her. You could dip her in a bucket of mud and she'd come out lookin' clean an together."

Buddy started to say something, but Latreece waved him off. "You don't need to say nothin.' None of this was your fault, but you got the kind of luck that makes it seem like it was. I wished that old man was a better shot. Wished he'd killed Tyrell. I don't want him back. I want to go on myself. I got plans."

"Don't take him back," Buddy said. "Follow your plans. Live your life."

Latreece shook her head, sighed.

Buddy stood up. "I have to go. You take care of yourself, OK, Latreece?"

"Ain't nobody gonna do it for me," she said, pushing the envelope toward him.

"No," he said. "That's for you. Buy Tashanda some school clothes. It's not much."

Latreece got up and walked Buddy to the door. "Wait right here, just a minute," she said. She ran up the stairs to Tyrell's office and came back down holding his laptop. "You should take this. Throw it in the trash if you want. That's probably where it belongs anyhow."

As Buddy was walking across the driveway she called, "I hope it changes, Buddy."

He turned. "You hope what changes?"

"Your luck," she called, closing the door.

76

When Buddy opened the door Russ called, "Good morning" from the guest room, a raspy sound, friendly as an old pair of slippers. He was sitting up on the bed scratching his chin and moving his bare foot up and down Old Sam's back. The dog looked up when Buddy stepped into the room. "Some pair," Buddy said, smiling.

Russ said, "Yup, two crips."

"You're not a cripple."

"Close enough, anyway. So, you ready for the big adventure?"

"Ready as I'll ever be."

"You're nervous."

"Did you have to say that?"

"That's to be expected, old Bud. There's a fine line between nervous and excited. I'm *excited* for you, man. You deserve this break. If anyone does, it is Mr. Buddy Graves." He stood, telling Old Sam to chill. They went into the kitchen and drank coffee, leaning against the counter.

"Let's go over a few things, Buddy," said Russ. "Just the logistics of the house, the dog, that psycho Tyrell. Just so we're on the same page."

"OK counselor, shoot."

⤜⤛

From a balcony of the Hay-Adams overlooking the White House, Izzy lit a cigar, took a puff, and watched the sky lighten with the sunrise. He blew a smoke ring into the early morning air and tossed the cigar down to the street. For Izzy, a slight hangover fueled his restless creative energy. But as he turned and looked through the French doors at Courtney's shape under the sheets, Izzy's thoughts were not on creating, they were on destroying. He'd given the hotel manager explicit instructions. Showing the manager a picture of Derek that Izzy had downloaded from the Internet he said, "If this man asks about my associate, Courtney Mears, you and your staff are to inform him that she is in a meeting, and then contact me immediately, no matter what time of day or night."

He clicked his iPhone on, launched the Web browser and typed in "Duke Lacrosse. All Americans." There he was, Derek Quigley. *The United*

States Intercollegiate Lacrosse Association (USILA) selected Duke University stand-out attack Derek Quigley to first-team All American. Quigley's special breed of all-out disregard for the body is imitated but rarely achieved by other athletes...

Izzy stared long and hard at Quigley's photo: the jawline, the eyes, so full of the undaunted arrogance that comes with an extraordinary athlete's sense of physical conquest. He'd already read some stories about Quigley in the sports section of *Newsday*. Each story noted Derek's exceptional physicality, the reckless abandon of a player who would not be denied. Looking at Courtney, he felt the heat of his anger rise up his back. Izzy closed the balcony doors so as not to disturb her slumber. Then he hit his phone's contact list and dialed.

"Good morning Gerry."

"Good morning, Izzy. How goes it?"

"I just threw an unsmoked $70 cigar from my hotel balcony."

"And why did you do that, Izzy?"

"I wanted to watch it fall."

"So what's up?"

"Well you know me, and you know I do not let things get personal with many people. The good news is, I'm on the verge of the one of the biggest deals in this country's history. But Elaine has decided to sprout wings, go independent on me. As we speak, she is barreling across the country to begin a golf course design company in the lovely state of Arizona. Sitting next to my sexy wife is a 30-year-old caddy she has the hots for. I could really use Elaine's talents here, with me and my deal, and right now I'm picturing her in a lip-lock on this caddy's Johnson. Ah, young love, right?

"Then there's another issue: I have a new assistant, a Ms. Courtney Mears. She has surpassed all expectations. She brings a vitality and seriousness to my new venture that makes her literally worth her weight in gold. Plus, I am *very* fond of her. And I respect the hell out of her. Unfortunately she had a dalliance in college with a lacrosse player by the name of Derek Quigley who became obsessed with her, and wouldn't take no for an answer. This obsession recently led to an attack. I will not use a certain word defining the attack because it incites in me such a rage, I might have a coronary. I will deal with Elaine. But about Courtney: I need you to deal with Quigley. I'll forward you a dossier on this motherfucker."

"Work is good, keeps me out of trouble."

"Yeah, *right*."

Izzy opened the French doors, feeling exhausted. Courtney was awake, sitting cross-legged on the bed. He sat next to her and gently pushed the tip of her nose. "Morning, bubeleh."

"Morning, meshugeh," said Courtney.

Izzy pulled his head back, "It's meshuge*na*. But do you even know what that means?"

"Sure, *crazy*."

"Well, I am crazy about you," Izzy said, the words out before he realized what he was saying.

Courtney blushed. "Nice to see you smile. I think it went well at dinner last night."

"It went great, don't change the subject."

Courtney nodded, shrugged.

Holding her hands in his mitts, Izzy said pointedly, "Derek Quigley is not going to be bothering you anymore, OK? You've got too much on your plate and I need you. So I don't want you to worry."

"Izzy, you don't know Derek. He does not quit. Please, don't get involved, he's insane. It's my problem."

"Which makes it mine."

She looked away, shook herself, turned. "You were on the phone, just now. Any business I should know about?"

"I was just touching base with an old associate, guy named Gerry."

"Gerry?"

"Gerry Terry."

"Gerry Terry, that's a funny name."

Izzy pushed her nose again and said, "Gerry's a funny guy."

১৯৯৬

Buddy heard Elaine's big Cadillac rolling over the gravel driveway. He could feel sweat dampening his forehead.

"Good luck," Russ said, shaking Buddy's hand. Overcome, he gave Buddy a quick, hard embrace.

"Take care of Russ, Old Sam," Buddy called to the dog, as he pushed the screen door.

Elaine smiled and popped the trunk. It was huge, but nearly full. He stuffed his bag and clubs in. She slid over to the passenger side so Buddy could get into the driver's seat. The back seat was crammed with suitcases and boxes. It looked as though someone running for their life had packed it.

Elaine turned her head from him and said, "Don't look at me until I put my face on. All set?"

Backing out and pulling onto Pulaski Road, Buddy said, "I have $800, a suitcase full of old clothes and a set of golf clubs—my worldly belongings. I inventoried before I left. Don't think I forgot anything."

"You're funny," Elaine said. "You OK?"

"You still sure you know what you're getting into?"

"You bet. You?"

"Nope."

"Nice shiner, Buddy. Jesus, what a scene. I was so glad that caddy, LT, punched Brad's lights out. What a shot!"

"Mueller took me apart."

"But you got him where it counted. My God, you were wonderful."

Buddy touched his black eye.

Elaine grabbed his hand, "Well, it makes you look rugged."

"I'm not much of a fighter. Never was."

"You're a golfer. A stud golfer."

They drove in silence for half an hour. Finally, Elaine finished applying her makeup. She put the bag under her seat and said, "I love a road trip, don't you?"

Buddy looked at her with a sidelong glance.

"I'm nervous as hell," she confessed. Elaine's cell rang. She answered by saying, "Bye Izzy," and shut the phone off.

"Talk to me about golf, Buddy, anything that comes to mind."

Buddy held forth until they got to the New Jersey Turnpike where Elaine asked him to pull over, saying she wanted to drive. Cars and trucks sped by. They switched seats. The sun lay ahead; it seemed to throb. Elaine squinted into the sky. "Just two thousand, three hundred and twenty miles to go," she said brightly. Glancing into the rear-view mirror, Elaine took a last look behind. A tear pearled in the corner of her eye. Buddy touched the wattle of skin beneath her chin.

"Don't be fresh. Here we go," she said, mashing down on the gas pedal. The tires screamed as they gathered speed.

Buddy gently squeezed her shoulder. "Easy girl," he said.

As her car ate up the highway, Elaine said, "*Why?*"

Coming Soon
Book Two
of the
DREAMLAND series

At a roadhouse motel in Texas, Elaine and Buddy have just checked into separate rooms next door to each other. The sexual tension has intensified as they've driven west toward their new Arizona golf course design business.

Meanwhile, a bat-wielding assailant puts Izzy's long-time chauffeur, Jack, into a coma as he stands watch outside Courtney's apartment. There's little doubt that the attacker is Derek Quigley. Izzy's muscle, the enigmatic Gerry Terry, sets a trap for the lacrosse player turned thug.

Meanwhile, Dana, despite being wary of Roy Hickman's secretive past, joins him in DC and launches a dangerous assault on Izzy's nursing home empire, not knowing the power that Izzy can wield.

And back in Huntington, Eugene Fryerson is charged with attempted murder. When Tyrell is released from the hospital, he heads straight for Latreece, and things really start to heat up in Dreamland...